E^{The}mpty Grave

BOOK FIVE

ALSO BY JONATHAN STROUD

LOCKWOOD & CO.
The Screaming Staircase
The Whispering Skull
The Hollow Boy
The Creeping Shadow

THE BARTIMAEUS BOOKS
The Amulet of Samarkand
The Golem's Eye
Ptolemy's Gate
The Ring of Solomon

Buried Fire
The Leap
The Last Siege
Heroes of the Valley

JONATHAN STROUD

The Empty Grave

Lockwood & Co.

BOOK FIVE

DISNEP • HYPERION
LOS ANGELES   NEW YORK

All rights reserved. Published by Disney • Hyperion, an imprint of Disney Book Group. No part of this book may be reproduced or transmitted in any form or by any means, electronic or mechanical, including photocopying, recording, or by any information storage and retrieval system, without written permission from the publisher. For information address Disney • Hyperion, 125 West End Avenue, New York, New York 10023.

First Hardcover Edition, September 2017
First Paperback Edition, September 2018
1 3 5 7 9 10 8 6 4 2
FAC-025438-18215
Printed in the United States of America

This book is set in Electra LT Std/Monotype

Library of Congress Control Number for the Hardcover Edition: 2017029086
ISBN 978-1-4847-9006-9

Visit www.DisneyBooks.com

SUSTAINABLE
FORESTRY
INITIATIVE

Certified Chain of Custody
Promoting Sustainable Forestry

www.sfiprogram.org
SFI-01054

The SFI label applies to the text stock

For my family—
Gina, Isabelle, Arthur, and Louis—
who tell the best ghost stories of all

Contents

I
The Tomb

Chapter 1

Want to hear a ghost story? That's good. I know a few.

How about the one of the sightless blue face, pressed against the cellar window? Or the apparition of the blind man holding a cane made of children's bones? What about the evil swan that followed me home through the lonely, rain-washed park, or the giant disembodied mouth seen opening in the center of a concrete floor? What of the milk jug that poured blood; or the empty bathtub from which choking gurgles sounded after dark? What of the orphan's spinning bed, or the skeleton in the chimney; or the vile spectral pig, all bristles and yellow tusks, glimpsed snuffling through the dirty glass of a shower-room door?

Take your pick. I experienced them all. They represent a typical month's work for Lockwood & Co. during that long and desperate summer. Most of them were written up in our casebook by George on the mornings after the events concerned, in between sips of scalding tea. He did this in his boxer shorts, incidentally, sitting cross-legged on the floor of our living room. It was a sight that was frankly more disturbing than all the hauntings combined.

Our black leather casebook has since been copied and filed away in the National Archives in the new Anthony Lockwood gallery. The good news about *that* is you don't have to negotiate all the crushed potato chips in the pages of the original if you want to know the details of each job. The bad news? Not every case is in there. There's one that was simply too terrible to be written down at all.

You know how it ended. Everyone does. The city was already full of it on that last cruel morning, with the rubble of Fittes House still steaming around the bodies of the lost. But the beginning? No. That's not yet public knowledge. For the hidden story of murder, conspiracy, betrayal—yes, *and* ghosts—you need the account of one who survived it. For that, you have to come to me.

My name is Lucy Joan Carlyle. I talk with the living and the dead, and it sometimes gets so I can't tell the difference anymore.

Here it is, then: the beginning of the end. Here's me, two months ago. I'm dressed in a black jacket, skirt, and leggings, with heavy-duty boots suitable for staving in coffin lids and scrambling out of graves. My rapier's at my belt, a holster of flares and salt-bombs is slung across my chest. There's a spectral handprint on my jacket. My bob's cropped shorter than before, though this doesn't disguise where a few strands of hair have recently turned white. Otherwise, I look the same as ever. Fully equipped for psychic investigation. Doing what I do.

In the outside world, the stars were out. The day's warmth was folded up and done. It was shortly after midnight—the time when spirits wandered and all sensible folk were tucked up safe in bed.

Me? Not so much. I was shuffling around a mausoleum with my bottom in the air.

In my defense, it has to be said that I wasn't the only one doing this. Elsewhere in the small stone chamber, my colleagues Lockwood, George, and Holly were also on hands and knees. We had our heads low, our noses near the flagstones. We swept our candles close to walls and floor. Occasionally we stopped to press fingertips into suspicious nooks and crannies; otherwise we worked in silence. We were looking for the entrance to a grave.

"Do you lot *have* to bend over like that?" a voice asked. "It's making my eyes water."

A thin, red-haired young man was sitting above us on a granite block in the center of the room. Like the rest of our raiding party, he was all in black—in his case, whopping big boots, skinny jeans, and a turtleneck top. *Unlike* the rest of us, he had an enormous pair of bulbous goggles clamped across his face, giving him the look of a startled grasshopper. His name was Quill Kipps. He was readying our tomb-cracking equipment, laying out crowbars and coils of rope on the surface of the stone. He was also keeping watch, blinking at the shadows. His goggles allowed him to spot ghosts, if any were around.

"See anything, Quill?" That was Lockwood, dark hair hanging over his face. He picked with his penknife at a gap between the flagstones.

Kipps lit an oil lamp, tilting the shutters so the light stayed low. "With you in that position, I've seen *plenty*. Particularly when Cubbins comes into view. It's like watching a beluga swimming by."

"I meant ghosts."

"No ghosts yet. Aside from our tame one." He tapped a large glass jar perched alongside him on the block. Green light flared evilly within, and a spectral face of unusual hideousness materialized, moving closer through a vortex of ectoplasm.

"*Tame?*" A disembodied voice that only I could hear spoke in indignation. "*Tame?! Let me out of here and I'll show that scrawny idiot how tame I am!*"

I sat back on my heels, brushing my bangs out of my eyes. "Best not call the skull tame, Kipps," I said. "It doesn't like it."

The face in the jar bared serrated teeth. "*Too right, I don't. Lucy, tell that boggle-eyed fool that if I was out of this prison I'd suck the flesh off his bones and dance a hornpipe with his empty skin. You just tell him that.*"

"Is it offended?" Kipps asked me. "I can see that horrid mouth moving."

"*Tell him!*"

I hesitated. "Don't worry," I said. "It's fine, really. It's cool with it."

"*What? No, I'm not! And what's he doing tapping my glass like I'm some kind of goldfish? I swear, when I get free of this, I'm going to catch Kipps and pull off his—*"

"Lockwood," I said, tuning out the ghost, "are you *sure* there's a trapdoor in here? We haven't got much time."

Anthony Lockwood straightened; he was kneeling in the center of the floor, one hand holding his penknife, the other running distractedly through his hair. As usual, our leader was impeccably dressed. He wore a dark jersey instead of his long coat, and sneakers instead of his normal dress shoes; these were his only concessions to the demands of breaking-and-entering a national monument.

"You're right, Luce." Lockwood's pale, thin face was as relaxed as ever, but his brow had an elegant kink in it that told me he *was* concerned. "It's been ages, and there's still no sniff of it. What do you reckon, George?"

With a scuffling, George Cubbins levered himself up into view from behind the granite block. His black T-shirt was dirty, his glasses were skewed, and his pale hair was spiked and matted with sweat. For the last hour he'd been doing the exact same thing as the rest of us, but somehow he'd contrived to get completely covered in a layer of dust, mouse droppings, and cobwebs that no one else had even seen. Such was George's way. "All the accounts of the burial mention a trapdoor," he said. "We're just not looking hard enough. Particularly Kipps, who isn't looking at all."

"Hey, I'm doing my job," Kipps said. "The question is, have you done yours? We're risking our skins tonight because *you* said there was a way in."

George unwound a cobweb from his glasses. "Of course there is. They lowered her coffin through the floor into the crypt. A silver coffin. Nothing but the best for *her*."

It was noticeable that George didn't care to mention the name of the person whose tomb this was. Noticeable too that even the *thought* of that silver coffin gave me a hollow prickling in my gut. I got the same feeling whenever I glanced at the shelf at the far end of the chamber—and looked at what was sitting there.

It was an iron bust of a woman in late middle age. She had an imperious and austere expression, with hair swept back above a high forehead. The nose was sharp and aquiline, the mouth thin, the eyes astute. It was not a pleasant face, exactly, but strong and hard and watchful, and we knew it very well indeed. It was the same face as the one on our postage stamps and on the covers of our agency manuals, a face that had shadowed us from early childhood and entered all our dreams.

Many remarkable things had been said about Marissa Fittes, the first and greatest psychic investigator of us all. How, together with her partner, Tom Rotwell, she had devised most of the ghost-hunting techniques that operatives like us still used. How she had improvised her first rapier from a snapped-off iron railing; how she'd conversed with ghosts as easily as if they were flesh and blood. How she'd created the first psychic detection agency, and how, when she died, half of London came to watch as her coffin was carried from Westminster Abbey to the Strand, the streets strewn with lavender flowers, and all the agents in the city marching along behind. How the bells in every church had rung as she was interred beneath her mausoleum, which was still maintained by the Fittes Agency as a special shrine.

Remarkable things . . .

The final one was that we didn't believe she was buried there at all.

The Fittes mausoleum, in which we stood, lay at the east end of the Strand in central London. It was a compact, high-ceilinged chamber, roughly oval in shape, built of stone and swathed in shadow. Aside from the big sarcophagus-sized block of granite in the center of the room (which had the single word FITTES carved into the top), the place was empty. There were no windows, and the iron doors that led to the street were closed and tight.

Somewhere beyond those doors stood two sentries. They were only kids, but they had pistols and might have used them had they heard us, so we had to go carefully. On the upside, the place was clean and dry and smelled of fresh lavender, and there weren't any obvious body parts lying underfoot, which instantly made it preferable to most of the other places we'd been that week.

But at the same time, there didn't seem to be anywhere for a trapdoor to hide.

Our lanterns flickered. Blackness hung over our heads like a witch's cloak.

"Well, all we can do is keep calm, keep quiet, and keep looking," Lockwood said. "Unless anyone's got a better suggestion."

"I've got one." Holly Munro had been zealously combing the floor at the far end of the room. Now she got to her feet and joined us, light and silent as a cat. Like the rest of us, she was in stealth mode: she had her long dark hair clipped back in a ponytail, and wore a zip-up top, skirt, and leggings. I could go on about how well the all-black getup suited her, but why bother? With Holly, that was a given. If she'd gone around wearing nothing but a dustbin suspended from her shoulders by a pair of polka-dotted suspenders, she'd have somehow made it look chic.

"I think we need a fresh perspective," she said. "Lucy, can't the skull help at all?"

I shrugged. "I'll try, Hol. But you know what mood it's in."

Over in the jar, the translucent face was still talking animatedly.

I could just see the old brown skull clamped to the base of the glass beneath it.

I let myself tune back in to what it was saying.

"*. . . and eat them. Then I'll freeze his toenails off. That'll fix him.*"

"Oh, you're not *still* going on about Kipps!" I said. "I thought you'd finished ages ago."

The face in the jar blinked at me. "*Weren't you even listening?*"

"No."

"*Typical. I went into all kinds of grim, inventive detail just for you.*"

"Save it. We can't find the entrance. Can you help us out?"

"*Why should I? You won't believe anything I say.*"

"That's not true. It's because we *do* sort of believe you that we're standing here right now."

The skull snorted rudely. "*If you took my word in any conventional sense, you'd be sitting at home with your feet up, rotting your innards with tea and chocolate biscuits. But no. You have to 'double-check' my story.*"

"Are you surprised? You say that Marissa Fittes isn't dead, but actually alive and well and pretending to be her supposed granddaughter, Penelope Fittes. The same Penelope Fittes who is head of the Fittes Agency and probably the most powerful person in London. That's quite a claim to make. You'll forgive us if we need to check it for ourselves."

The face rolled its eyes. "*Piffle. Know what this is an example of? Skullism.*"

"What nonsense are you spouting now?"

"You've heard of racism. You've heard of sexism. Well, this is skull-ism, pure and simple. You're judging me by my outward appearance. You doubt my word solely because I'm a skull, lurking in a jar of slime-green plasm. Admit it!"

I took a deep breath. This was a skull known far and wide for its outrageous whoppers and virtuoso fibbing. To say it sometimes stretched the truth would be like saying George sometimes stretched the seat of his pants when tying his shoelaces. On the flip side, the ghost *had* saved my life more than once and—on certain important matters—hadn't always lied. "That's an interesting point," I said, "and I look forward to discussing it with you later. In the meantime, help me out. We're looking for the entrance to a crypt. Do you see a ring or handle?"

"No."

"Do you see a lever?"

"Nope."

"Do you see a pulley, winch, or any other mechanism for opening a hidden trapdoor?"

"No. Of course not. You're getting desperate now."

I sighed. "Okay. I get the message. So there's no door here."

"Oh, of course there's a door," the ghost said. *"Why didn't you ask me? It's obvious enough from up here."*

I relayed this to the others. Holly and Lockwood acted as one. They vaulted up onto the block beside Kipps. Lockwood grabbed one of the lanterns and held it out in front of him. He and Holly both rotated, scanning the floor, faces locked in concentration. The light washed slowly over the flagstones like water, spilling up against the base of the walls.

"*This is pitiful,*" the skull said. "*I saw it straight off, and I don't have an eyeball to call my own. Well, I'm sorry, but you're not getting any more clues from—*"

"There!" Holly grasped Lockwood's arm. He held the lantern steady. "There!" she said. "See that little flagstone set *inside* the bigger one? The big one *is* the trapdoor. Pull up the small stone and we'll find the ring or handle hidden underneath!"

George and I ran over, bent close to where she pointed. As soon as she said it, I knew that she was right.

"Brilliant, Holly," Lockwood said. "That *must* be it. Tools ready, everyone."

It was at times like this that Lockwood & Co. was at its fluent best. Knives were brought out, and the cement around the smaller stone cut free. We levered it up with crowbars; Lockwood pulled it aside. Sure enough, a hinged bronze ring lay beneath, set into the larger stone. While George, Holly, and I loosened the edges of this stone, Lockwood and Kipps tied ropes around the ring, testing and double-testing the knots, making sure they could take the strain. Lockwood was everywhere at once, softly giving orders, helping with every task. Energy crackled off him, spurring us all on.

"*Isn't anyone going to thank me?*" The skull watched disgustedly from its jar. "*Thought not. Good thing I'm not in the business of holding my breath.*"

Within minutes we were in position. Lockwood and Kipps stood by the first rope; they would lift the stone. On the opposite side, the second rope hung slack. George and I held this—it was our job to support the flagstone once it was lifted, and help lower it quietly back onto the floor. In the center, by the ring, Holly knelt ready with the crowbars.

The room was still. Up on the wall, our lantern light quivered on the iron head of Marissa Fittes. It was as if she were watching us, her eyes glittering with malevolent life.

At moments of maximum tension, Lockwood always made it his business to be the calmest of all. He smiled at us. "Everyone ready?" he asked. "Right—let's go."

He and Kipps pulled. At once, smoothly and without noise, the flagstone moved. It lifted up as if on oiled hinges, and a waft of chill air rose from the crack beneath.

Holly pushed the crowbars under it in case the others faltered, but there was no need. With surprising swiftness, Lockwood and Kipps pulled the flagstone upright. Now it was George and I who had to support its weight. Our rope went taut; we took the strain.

The hinged slab wasn't nearly as heavy as I'd have guessed— perhaps it was some special hollow stone. Slowly we began to lower it on the other side.

"Set it down gently!" Lockwood hissed. "No noise!"

We eased the flagstone down. It met the ground with a sound like a mouse sighing.

Now we had a square hole in the center of the floor.

When Holly shone her flashlight into it, we could see a flight of stone steps leading steeply into blackness. Beyond the steps the light was swallowed utterly.

A damp, dark, earthy smell rose invisibly around us.

"Deep hole," Kipps whispered.

"Anyone see anything?"

"No."

There was a brief silence. Now that we had gained access to the crypt, the enormity of what we were about to do fell over us. It was like the darkness hanging above our heads had suddenly, silently, shifted lower. Marissa's face watched us from the wall.

We all stood there quietly, using our psychic senses. None of us got anything. Our belt thermometers showed a steady fifty-four degrees, and we detected no supernatural chill, no miasma, malaise, or creeping fear. There was no immediate likelihood of an apparition.

"Good," Lockwood said. "Collect your things. We'll proceed as planned. I'll go first. Then George, followed by Holly and Luce, with Quill at the back. We'll turn our flashlights off, but carry candles. I'll have my rapier; the rest of you keep your weapons ready too. Not that we'll need them." He gave us his best grin. "We don't believe she's there."

But a nameless dread had stolen up on us. In part it was the power of the iron face, and of the name inscribed in stone. And it was also the feel of the dank air rising from the hole. It coiled around us, entwining us with unease. We gathered our things slowly. George passed among us, flicking his lighter, igniting our candles. We lined up, hefting rapiers, clearing throats, readying our belts.

Kipps vocalized his thoughts: "Are we *sure* we want to do this?"

"We've gotten this far," Lockwood said. "Of course we do."

I nodded. "We can't wimp out now," I said.

Kipps looked at me. "You're right, Lucy. Maybe I'm being overly cautious. I mean, it's not as if our tip came from an evil talking skull that probably wishes us all dead, is it?"

Everyone glanced over at the open backpack I was carrying. I'd just put the jar inside. The ghost's face had disappeared now; only the skull was showing. Even *I* had to admit that its death-black sockets and leering toothy grin weren't entirely reassuring.

"I know you have a lot of faith in this skull," Kipps went on. "I know it's your best friend and all, but what if it's wrong? What if it's simply mistaken?" He glanced up at the wall. His voice dropped to a whisper. "*She* might be waiting for us, down there."

Another moment and the mood would have shifted irrevocably. Lockwood stepped between us. He spoke with crisp decision. "No one needs to worry. George, remind them."

"Sure." George adjusted his spectacles. "Remember, all the stories say that Marissa Fittes gave orders for her body to be placed in a special coffin. We're talking iron inlays and silver casing. So, if the skull's wrong, and her body *is* there, her spirit won't be able to bother us," he said. "It'll be safely constrained."

"And when we open the coffin?" Kipps asked.

"Oh, that'll only be for a second, and we'll have our defenses in place by then."

"The point is," Lockwood said, "no ghost is going to attack us on the way down. Right, George?"

"Right."

"Good. Very well, then." Lockwood turned to the stair.

"Obviously there might be a few traps," George said.

Lockwood paused with his foot hovering above the top step. "Traps?"

"Not saying there are. Just that there might be some." George pushed his glasses up his nose and gave an encouraging flourish with one hand. "Anyway, Lockwood—the stairs await! Off you go."

Lockwood did a sort of reverse swivel. Now he was facing George. "Hold it," he said. "What traps are these?"

"Yes. I'm quite interested in this, too," Holly said.

We all were. We gathered around George, who did something with his shoulders that was probably meant to be a casual shrug. "Oh, it's just silly rumors," he said. "Frankly, I'm surprised you're interested. Some say Marissa didn't want grave robbers interfering with her tomb, so she took precautions." He paused. "Some say these precautions might be . . . supernatural ones."

"*Now* you tell us," Holly said.

"When was *this* little fact going to be mentioned?" I demanded. "When a Specter put its fingers around my neck?"

George made an impatient gesture. "It's probably nonsense. Besides, it would have been a distraction earlier. It's my job to distinguish between solid fact and rumor."

"No, that's *my* job," Lockwood said. "Your job is to tell me everything so *I* can make the judgment."

There was a heavy pause. "Do you *always* argue like this?" Kipps asked.

Lockwood gave a bland smile. "Usually. I sometimes think incessant bickering is the oil that lubricates our efficient machine."

George looked up. "You reckon?"

"Oh, for heaven's sake, are you going to bait me on *that* as well?"

"I thought you *liked* some bickering! You just said—"

"I don't like anything *that* much! Now, can everyone please shut up?" Lockwood gazed around at us. His dark eyes locked on ours, holding our attention, steadying our collective purpose. "Traps or no traps," he said, "we can handle this. We have two hours to check the tomb, close it up, and be ready to go when the sentries change again. Do we *want* to learn the truth about Penelope Fittes and Marissa? Of course we do! We've worked wonders to get here, and we won't panic now. If we're right, there won't be anything to worry about. If we're wrong, we deal with it, as we always do." He smiled. "But we won't be wrong. We're on the verge of something big here. It's going to be good!"

Kipps adjusted his goggles dolefully. "Since when has anything good happened in a crypt? It's going to be bad by definition."

But Lockwood was already heading down the stairs. Beyond him, light flickered on the iron face. Its thin lips seemed to smile as we descended into the dark.

Chapter 2

O kay, let's just pause for a moment, while we're still at the top of the stairs. Nothing nasty has jumped out at us. No traps have been sprung. We're all alive and well. That makes it a good time to consider just how the five of us (five and a bit, if you include the skull) came to be there at all, descending illegally into the most famous tomb in London.

I don't mean the mechanics of *how* we got inside the mausoleum, though that's a story in itself: the long nights George spent watching the movements of the guards; the weeks Kipps spent shadowing the sergeant with the key; the stealing of the key (this a masterpiece of timing, with Holly distracting the sergeant while Lockwood plucked it from his jacket, took a wax impression, and returned it, all in thirty seconds flat); finally the forging of a replica, thanks to an underworld contact of our disreputable friend Flo

Bones. I don't even mean how we snuck in during the changing of the guards.

I mean why we took the risk at all.

For the answer to *that* we have to go back five months, to a walk that Lockwood and I took through a dark and frozen landscape. This little stroll completely shook up how we operated, and changed the way we saw ourselves.

Why? Because, entirely unexpectedly, we had stepped out of our world and into another place. Where was this place? That's hard to say. Some call it the Other Side; I guess it has other names, too, which people in the old religions and the ghost-cults use. But from what *I* saw, it wasn't a heaven or a hell; just a world very similar to our own, only freezing cold and silent and stretched out under a black sky. The dead walked there, and it was their home—while Lockwood and I were the interlopers. *Ours* was the unnatural presence in their endless night.

We had ventured there by accident, and only just managed to escape, but we discovered there were other living souls who had deliberately chosen to explore that forbidden path. One was no less a person than Mr. Steve Rotwell, grandson of Tom Rotwell, and head of the giant Rotwell Agency. He had been carrying out experiments, sending employees (protected by iron armor) through a gate or portal to the Other Side. His exact purpose we could not tell. When he attempted to silence us, our confrontation ended with Rotwell's death and the destruction of his secret research facility. The repercussions of this were far-reaching. For a start, the Rotwell Agency was taken over by its archrival, the Fittes Agency, headed by the formidable Ms. Penelope Fittes, who swiftly set about establishing herself as the most powerful woman in Britain.

But there were darker consequences, too. Our experiences had indicated that there was a strong connection between the activity of spirits—in particular their keenness to return to our world—and the presence of living persons on the Other Side. It seemed that when the land of the dead was invaded, the dead became active, and much more likely to invade the land of the living. This discovery was of vast importance. For more than fifty years, the Problem— the epidemic of ghosts infesting Britain—had spread and worsened, confounding all attempts to understand or halt it. We held in our hands a clue to the possible cause, and we itched to spread this news.

Only we couldn't. Because we'd been forbidden to do so.

This edict had come from none other than Penelope Fittes herself. She didn't know about the strange journey Lockwood and I had made (we had told nobody but our friends), but she knew something of what we'd discovered at the Rotwell Institute, and she wanted no word of it getting out to the ordinary population. It wasn't a friendly piece of advice either, more a coolly delivered threat. We were under no illusions about what would happen to us if we chose to give up our silence and go our own way.

This, by itself, was outrageous enough: the woman at the heart of the fight against the Problem was telling us not to explore its possible cause. Exactly what her motive might be was unknown, but it was hard to imagine an innocent explanation. Yet there was something else, something more disturbing still; and for that insight we had the ghost in the jar to thank. Long ago, it had spoken with the great Marissa Fittes; now it had seen Penelope, and it had big news for us. According to the skull, Penelope *was* Marissa—they were precisely the same person.

However much we might distrust Penelope Fittes herself, it was clearly not easy to establish the truth of this extraordinary claim. But we *could* check one thing.

We could see whether Marissa was in her grave.

The stairs were steep and narrow. We descended slowly, step by careful step. Lockwood was at the front, then George, with Holly and me following. Kipps brought up the rear. Each of us held a candle raised at eye level, and so our circles of light fused together, making a little radiant worm or caterpillar, inching its way into the earth.

Behind us, the dim gray cone of lantern light seeping through the trapdoor faded from view. To our right was a wall of neat stone blocks, shiny and gleaming with moisture. To the left was an open, unknown space, which our candlelight could not penetrate. Lockwood risked a brief flick of his flashlight, revealing a shocking well of black that made us all flinch toward the right-hand wall. Then, disconcertingly, *this* wall vanished too, and we were descending, with an abyss of darkness on either side.

Your head did weird things in such a place. Your legs shook; you no longer had full control over your muscles. You kept feeling you were about to lurch aside and plunge into oblivion. The problem was compounded by the need for high psychic alert, the fear of something rising toward you out of the dark. Every couple of steps we had to stop and use our Talents, and this straining against the silence made your head spin even more.

It didn't help that the skull in my backpack insisted on doing a running commentary, constantly adding little reminders of the peril we were in.

"*Ooh, this is a nasty bit,*" it said. "*Careful you don't suddenly step sideways and plunge horribly to your death.*" And: "*What's it like, falling in pitch-darkness, I wonder?*" Or simply: "*Crikey, don't trip now!*" And so on, until I threatened to toss it over the edge.

The wall returned, and at that point the steps veered abruptly to the left, going down no less steeply. The green glow at my shoulder flared with sullen light. "*I'm bored,*" the ghost said. "*It's Lockwood's fault. He's such a dawdler.*"

"He's being sensible. He's checking for traps."

"*He's like an old granny crossing the road. I've seen algae move faster.*"

It was true that Lockwood was taking it steadily. Down beyond the heads of the others I could see him, on the fringe of the candlelight, stooping, peering, patiently checking each slab before treading on it, inspecting the wet stones of the wall. That was where he always was—at the forefront of the group, standing between us and the darkness. How poised and graceful he was. His presence gave me courage, even in a place like this. I smiled at him. He couldn't see me, of course. It didn't matter.

"You all right, Lucy?" That was Kipps at my shoulder. "Got gas or something?"

"No. I'm fine."

"Just saw you grimacing there. Tell you what, my goggles are fogging up. Wish we'd get to the bottom of this wretched vault. Lockwood's taking his time."

"He's doing what he has to," I said. We both fell silent. Down we went, with the coils of candle smoke binding us together, and Lockwood calm and tireless at our head. For a while there was nothing but stone and smoke and silence, and the shuffle of our boots in the dark.

"HURRY IT UP!"

That was the skull roaring like a howler monkey in my ear. The sudden psychic outburst made me cry out with fright. I jerked forward, jabbing my candle flame directly into Holly's neck. She cried out too, and barged into George; George stumbled and kneed Lockwood in the backside. Lockwood, who had just been bending over to inspect the step below, lost his balance entirely and tumbled down the stairs, falling head over heels, *bump, bump, bump.* He dropped his rapier, his candle disappeared over the edge. He finished upside down, long legs waving in the air.

Dead silence. Everyone stood frozen, listening for the creak of moving traps, for shifting stones, for the rustling of casket cloths. Personally, all I could hear was the raucous cackling of the skull. Nothing happened. Lockwood got stiffly to his feet. Picking up his rapier, we hurried down to join him.

"I don't know what you're so upset about." This was the skull, a few moments later. We were clustering around the jar, bug-eyed and livid, while the face grinned out in high delight. *"You know me,"* it said. *"I'm excitable. Can I help it if I get caught up in the action?"*

"You endangered us all," I snarled. "If Lockwood had triggered a trap—"

"But he didn't, did he? Let's be positive! We now know those last twelve steps are safe, because Lockwood's bum tested them for us."

Oddly, when I passed on these words of wisdom, they didn't go down well.

"It's gone too far this time," Holly said. "I vote we take it to the furnaces tomorrow."

"Oh, don't be so harsh," Kipps said. "I'm grateful to the skull. That was one of the funniest things I've ever seen. I'll treasure the memory on my deathbed. Anyway, I assume you haven't brought the ghost along for its personality. The best thing is to put it to good use."

There was much sense in Kipps's words, and everyone acknowledged it. I moved to the front of the group, just behind Lockwood, with the skull peering from the top of my backpack.

"*This is great,*" it said. "*The best seat in the house. With luck I can watch Lockwood trip over his own feet again. So, fill me in. What do you want me to do?*"

I took a deep breath. "Scour the rest of the stairs for snares, levers, wires, flip-stones, ghost-traps, and anything else that might threaten us. You see something, you let it rip. Otherwise keep silent. Not another word. Agreed?"

"*Okay.*"

"Then let's g—"

"STOP!" The skull's scream was even louder than before.

I cursed. "What now?"

"*Hey, relax. Just doing my job. There's a trap on the next step, I think you'll find.*"

And sure enough, when I stabbed my flashlight on, I could see a thin wire stretched across the step below us, just at ankle height.

"Trip wire," George breathed.

"Yes, and maybe something more than that." Lockwood indicated where the wire disappeared into a small groove cut into the wall. He lifted his candle; one of the stones above was larger than the rest, and seemed less well embedded, too. "Think this might've dropped on our heads after we'd tripped and fallen?" he asked. "It's possible."

Holly swallowed audibly. "Tell you what, let's not find out."

One after the other we stepped down over the wire. The evident but unknown malice of the trap sent a chill through all of us. Lockwood wiped perspiration from his brow.

"We owe the skull for that, at least," he said. "Let's keep on. It can't be far to go."

We continued down the slowly curving stairs. The skull remained silent. There were no more dangers to be seen. At last our questing candlelight bent and folded against the carved stones of a wide, almost semicircular archway. The stairs stopped just short of the arch, ending at a paved expanse of floor.

No one spoke. We were all on high alert. We used our psychic senses, probing ahead of us into the dark. Nothing was seen or heard. I ran my fingers over the walls, too, in case Touch might pick up something, but the stone was blank. Our thermometers showed a temperature of forty-four degrees: chilly, but not exceptional. It gave no cause for concern.

That didn't mean we were putting our rapiers away. Lockwood and I set down our candles and switched on our flashlights. With weapons at the ready, we walked slowly beneath the arch into a large stone room.

The burial chamber of Marissa Fittes was a high, domed space, with an oval outline that echoed the shape of the mausoleum far above. Our flashlight beams crossed and recrossed it, picking out the same curved walls of closely fitting blocks, the same clean flagged floor. There were no doors, no niches, no alcoves to be seen. But in the middle of the vault . . .

Our beams speared inward to meet at the central point. This was a raised rectangular plinth of smooth gray stone, a few feet high, with bunches of dried lavender propped against it. It had the word FITTES inscribed along the side.

On top of the plinth, glinting coldly in our flashlight beams, was a silver coffin.

The coffin had been covered with a magnificent silver drape, emblazoned with the famous Fittes symbol: a rampant unicorn.

"Don't want to rush to any conclusions," Lockwood murmured, "but I think we might be there."

George too spoke in a whisper; it was not a place for noise. "That's the special coffin in which she supposedly lay in state. Three days in Westminster Abbey, with mourners filing by. Then they brought her here."

"If she *is* here," I said. I was Listening again. No, it was okay. Everything was still.

"That's what we've come to find out." Lockwood walked purposefully across the vault. In the briskness of his movements, he was allaying our unspoken fears. "Won't take five minutes, then we're gone. Do it like we practiced. Chains at the ready."

Time and again, in the peace and comfort of 35 Portland Row, we'd gone through this part of the operation. We'd known it was the crunch point, when fear might make us forget essential things.

So we'd rehearsed on a sofa in our living room, circling it with iron chains, looping their ends carefully, sowing salt and iron filings on the floor, setting up lavender candles at regular distances all the way around. Good protective measures, carried out swiftly and well. In moments we had the plinth surrounded in this manner, sealing in the coffin—and whatever it contained.

We stood ready, just outside the chains.

"All right," Lockwood said. "Now for the coffin. George?"

"As predicted, it's an Edgar and Soames special edition, lead-lined, silver casing, double clasps. Should have a counterweighted hinge, so it opens to the touch." George spoke calmly, but there was sweat running down the side of his face. This was not a normal tomb, and all of us were clammy with nerves. Holly's face had blanched; Kipps looked as if he were trying to chew off his own bottom lip. Even the skull at my shoulder had gone quiet, the green glow dulled almost to nothing.

Lockwood took a deep breath. "Okay, so this is my job." He looked around at us. "Old Marissa started everything—the agencies, the fight against the Problem. That's her legacy, which everyone takes for granted. But we know something else is going on. And part of the answer lies inside."

"Move fast," I told him.

He smiled at me. "Always."

George and Kipps held their candles ready. Holly and I unclipped magnesium flares.

Lockwood stepped over the iron chains and approached the plinth.

The coffin was at waist height. With a delicate touch, as if pulling a blanket off a sleeping child, Lockwood took the unicorn drape and drew it to the foot of the coffin, where he let it fall to the floor. The lid was pristine, shimmering with reflected candlelight. It had two double clasps. Lockwood flicked them open—one, two—each falling against the coffin side with a clink that set my heart juddering.

This was the moment. If the skull's story was true, the coffin would be empty.

Lockwood took hold of the lid and pushed it upward. In the same motion, he jumped back beyond the iron chains.

George was right: the lid must have had some kind of concealed counterweight, because it continued to open, smoothly and sound-lessly, of its own accord. It tipped up and up and over—and came to a gentle halt, hanging back at an angle.

The interior of the coffin was a slot of thick darkness, black to the brim.

Kipps and George lifted their arms. Light from their can-dles scooped out the slot. Now we could see that the interior was upholstered in red silk—

And filled with something. Something long, thin, and covered in white linen.

For a few seconds, no one spoke. Holly and I had our arms raised, flares cupped in our hands. The others were likewise frozen, rigid, breath rasping between bared teeth. We stared at the shrouded shape. It had an awful kind of gravity that held us all transfixed.

"Well, *somebody's* at home," Holly said in a small voice.

Kipps swore under his breath. "So much for that skull's promises."

This was a fair point. I came to life, rapped on the ghost-jar. "Skull!"

"*What?*" Faint green light flared sullenly within the glass. "*This had better be good. I can't hang around. There's too much silver here for me.*"

"Never mind that! Look in the coffin."

A pause followed. "*Oh, well. Could be any old corpse in there. Might be a pile of half-bricks wrapped in sacking. I can tell you one thing: it's not Marissa. Uncover the face and see.*"

The light faded. I told the others what the skull had said. None of us much enjoyed hearing it.

"Suppose we *had* better take a look," I said.

Lockwood nodded slowly. "Right . . . Well, it's easy enough."

The body of that quiet someone in the coffin was not wrapped tightly, but instead concealed by a loose cloth. Whoever pulled it back would have to step inside the chains, reach in close to the shrouded thing.

"Easy enough . . ." Lockwood said again. "It's just a dead body, like any other, and we've all seen plenty of *those*."

He looked at us.

"Oh, very well," he sighed. "*I'll* do it. Stand ready."

Without hesitation he stepped over the iron chains, reached into the coffin, took hold of a corner of the cloth, and, with a fastidious movement, flicked it away. Then he jumped back. We all flinched with him. As Lockwood said, we'd seen enough decomposed bodies to want to be as far away as possible when the dreadful sight was revealed.

And it *was* dreadful. Only not in the way we expected.

It wasn't decomposed at all.

Long gray hair lay thick and lush across an ivory pillow. It cradled a gaunt white face, the skin flowing like wax beneath our candlelight. It was the face of a woman; an aged, wrinkled woman— bony, with a nose curved thin and sharp like the beak of some bird of prey. The lips were closed tight; the eyes, too. It was recognizably the same face as on the iron bust upstairs, only older and frailer. What was awful about it was that it didn't appear to be long dead, but only sleeping. It had been miraculously preserved.

No one spoke. No one moved. At last a blob of hot wax from his candle dripped onto Kipps's hand. His yelp broke the spell.

"Marissa Fittes . . ." George breathed. "It *is* her."

"Close the lid!" Holly cried. "Close it quick, before—!"

She didn't finish the sentence, but we knew what she meant. *Before Marissa Fittes's spirit stirred.* I'd had the same thought. But I also felt a rush of anger that we'd risked so much for nothing. "That wretched skull!" I said.

Quill Kipps cursed. "What fools we are! We've risked everything for this!" He gestured wildly around the tiny vault. "We've got to get out quick. *She* won't be happy we've desecrated her resting place. Come *on*, Lockwood! We've got to get out."

"Yes, yes. . . ." Of all of us, Lockwood had been the least affected by the dead woman in the coffin. He bent forward over the chains, gazing at the pallid face. "She seems relaxed enough so far," he added. "In fact, she's positively chilled. How did they keep her like this, I wonder?"

"Mummified," George said.

"Like the Egyptians? Reckon people still do that?"

"Oh, sure. You just need the right herbs and oils and natron, which is a kind of salt. Dunk her in that, it dries her out, though you mustn't forget to remove the intestines, and pull the brains out through the nose. It's a messy business. Imagine one of Luce's worst head colds—*that's* the amount of gunk you're dealing with. After that, you'd stuff her various cavities with—"

"Right, so mummification is *possible,*" Kipps interrupted. "We get the idea."

George adjusted his spectacles. "A few details never hurt anyone."

"All the same," Lockwood said, "I've never heard of a mummy looking quite like this. . . ." As he spoke, he stepped across the iron chains again.

"Lockwood," I said, "what are you doing?"

"It's like she died yesterday." He reached in, put his fingers to the side of the face.

"Well, don't *touch* her!"

"Ack! *Lockwood!*"

"Ah, yes. . . ." There was a softly noxious peeling sound, as of skin coming away.

Holly put her hand over her mouth; George made a noise like a throttled cat. Kipps clutched my arm.

Lockwood stood back. He had the old woman's face dangling between his fingers.

"Look," he said. "It's just a mask." He smiled at us. "A plastic mask . . . And check this out. . . ." His other hand came up. The gray-white wig hung heavy in his hand, matted and shapeless like something that had been teased out of a bathtub drain. "A mask and wig," he said, laughing. "It's fake. Everything's just fake. . . . Every-one okay?"

To be honest, that might have been stretching it. For a moment, none of us moved. Then our shock and relief spilled over. Kipps began laughing. Holly just stood there, shaking her head, hand still on her mouth. I realized I'd been holding my flare ready all this time. My fingers hurt. I put it back in my belt.

"Lockwood," I said, "that is *so* icky. That is the ickiest thing I've ever seen you do. Which is saying something."

"It's not really icky." Lockwood considered the thing lying in the coffin. "It's just a dummy. Come and see."

We all stepped over to the coffin. Sure enough, shorn of its cov-erings, the head resting on the red silk pillow wasn't human at all. It was made of wax. It had the correct dimensions, with a rough nose shape and shallow indents where the eyes would be, but there were no real features, just the bubbles and pits of yellowish wax, smooth in places, rough in others.

"What a con!" George bent over the coffin, holding his spec-tacles as he stared quizzically at the dummy. He pulled the shroud farther away, uncovering a wax torso, and rough, spindly wax arms crossed over the breast. "Life-sized, and probably the correct weight, so no one guessed when they were carrying it. The mask was there just in case anyone looked in. . . ."

"She's not there," Lockwood said. "This whole mausoleum is built on a lie."

"Unbelievable." Kipps was still laughing softly to himself. He reached into the coffin and struck the waxen chest with his knuckles, making a hollow tapping sound. "A dummy! And we were all so frightened. . . ."

I wanted to laugh, too. It was the sheer release of the tension that had been building up all night. Everyone felt it. Holly got out some chocolate, began offering it around. Thermos flasks of coffee were located. We leaned back against the coffin.

"We've got to go public with this," George said.

Lockwood frowned. "Maybe. It's only half the story, don't forget. Marissa's not here. So where *is* she?"

"The skull's been telling us where," I said.

Tap, tap . . . Behind us, Kipps rapped out a jaunty little rhythm on the wax. "A dummy!" he said. "We can't keep this quiet. We show the mask, tell DEPRAC, get the press down here." He reached out for the chocolate. "Thanks, Holly. Don't mind if I do."

Holly handed out the last piece. "The difficult thing is knowing who to trust," she said. "Half of DEPRAC's in Penelope's pockets."

"Barnes is okay."

"Yeah. *He* is. But how much influence does Barnes have now?"

Tap, tap . . .

"Decisions for tomorrow," Lockwood said. "Thing to do now is get back topside, before the guards change again."

Tap, tap, tappety-tap . . .

"Okay, Quill," I said. "Maybe you can stop that now. It's getting a little irritating."

"I *have* stopped," Kipps said. "I'm eating my chocolate, same as you."

Everyone looked at Kipps, leaning against the plinth beside

us. He held up both his hands in confirmation. The tapping noise continued. We stared at one other. We swallowed our chocolate in unison. Then we looked behind.

Something protruding from under the rumpled shroud was striking the side of the coffin, making the tapping sound. It was a cupped wax hand, twitching and jerking in spasms. As we watched, the trembling extended up the arm, and all at once the whole wax dummy was shaking, as if in protest at the coils of ghost-fog now rising from the grave.

Chapter 3

Ten minutes earlier, it would all have been fine. Even five minutes earlier would have been okay. We were so keyed up when we came into the vault, the first apparition to show its face would have been impaled by five rapiers simultaneously. As for the coffin, anything jumping out when we opened the lid would have been diced and dismembered before it knew what was happening. But the extreme shock—and subsequent anticlimax—of finding the wax mannequin had fatally distracted us. We had allowed ourselves to switch off. This in turn had lured us into committing the three cardinal sins of psychic investigation: we'd stopped using our Talents, we'd stepped beyond the chains, and we'd turned our backs on an open coffin. Even the rawest seven-year-old trainee knows to avoid *those* mistakes. Rookie errors, every one.

So it was that when we saw the mannequin moving and the coils of ghost-fog looping toward us, we were—for a crucial moment—stunned and frozen. It took our brains a split second longer than normal to react.

This delay was enough. We lost control.

So thick was the mist, it was as if the coffin were filling up with white liquid. It pooled around the edge of the body in the shroud, lapping at its contours, swirling and spiraling as if being stirred by unseen hands. And the stiff yellow figure was infected by the movement. It juddered into life. Fingers hooked over the lip of the coffin. There was a cracking sound as the wax broke. The mannequin thrust itself upward into a sitting position.

"Back! Back!"

It was Lockwood's cry. As one, we threw ourselves away from the plinth, away from the coffin. But panic breeds panic; mistakes escalate. Lockwood was fine—he was already twisting as he jumped, whipping a flare from his belt. He landed lightly, the other side of our iron chains, his right arm pulled back and ready to throw. The rest of us? We didn't possess such finesse. We were just tumbling every which way, crashing down on hands and knees. Kipps knocked over a candle. I arched like a cat to avoid the ring of chains, then rolled unglamorously through a mess of salt and iron. Holly and George fared even worse. Both careered straight into the circle, twisting the links violently out of position.

Looped ends came away from each other; the circle was broken.

A cold wind blew outward through the gaps and across the vault.

I finished my roll in a crouch, and spun on my heels, grappling for a flare. As I did so, Lockwood's canister flashed over me. It arced down toward the coffin, where a thin and faceless figure now sat, wrapped in grave-clothes, its smooth, misshapen head slowly turning in our direction.

The flare struck the edge of the coffin lid, just behind the figure.

Everything on the plinth disappeared in a bursting orchid of bright white fire.

I don't know whether or not it was the acoustics of the vault we were in, but the explosion was more than usually loud. Brighter, too. I looked aside. Kipps cried out—he'd been closest to the burst. My ears rang; a ring of heat buffeted me for a second, then expanded past me and away. It was cold again.

I opened my eyes. White-hot iron was fountaining down like a rain of needles, fizzing and bouncing on the flagstones. The coffin interior was a coronet of fire. Fragments of its red silk lining waved and stirred like seaweed, dancing in the center of each flame.

A dark shape stood above the blaze, stiff, bent-backed, enveloped in a burning shroud.

"The chains!" I was scooping for the loose ends, trying to push them together. The others did the same. But the cold draft that blew from the coffin caught the iron links, sent them skittering apart. And the mist was already spilling over the edges of the coffin, pouring silently down in thick white ropes that uncoiled toward us on the floor. It pushed us back as we fumbled for the chains. We couldn't repair the circle without the mist brushing against our skin. It wasn't your usual ghost-fog, which is harmless. This was thicker and too viscous; you couldn't risk it touching you.

"Forget the iron," Lockwood shouted. "Move back! Hit it with your flares!"

The shape in the coffin moved abruptly, awkwardly, as if it

didn't know how to use its limbs. It gave a lurch, toppled forward out of the coffin, and landed headfirst on the floor of the vault in a spreading plume of ghost-fog. A moment later it vanished in a double explosion of magnesium fire. Two flares had struck it. A third (I guessed George's) had missed completely, exploding against the far wall of the room. The noise buffeted us; we were scoured by a sunburst of violent silver light.

"What *was* that thing?" Kipps stumbled around to join us, one ear bleeding, his jersey a ragged colander of magnesium burns.

"A Revenant," Lockwood gasped. "Got to be."

"But the wax—"

"Its bones are hidden in the wax shell. The ghost is able to make the bones move, and that animates the wax." He took a canister from his belt. "Quick! Help me salt the floor."

Nothing moved in the silver flames, but Lockwood and the others threw salt-bombs onto the ground, lacing the stones in front. I didn't help them. I stood motionless, my flare still unused in my hand. Up until this point my psychic senses had been numbed with shock. Now, as the echo of the explosions died away, they'd suddenly kicked in. And I could hear a voice, harsh and hollow as a crow's caw. It was calling out a name.

"*Marissa Fittes . . .*" it said. "*Marissa . . .*"

"Fall back to the stairs," Lockwood said.

We retreated toward the arch, watching the flames. They were dropping swiftly, revealing a prone and broken figure on the floor.

"Maybe we got it," Holly breathed.

"No," I said. The hollow voice was still echoing in my ears.

"I think we did," Kipps said. "Yeah . . . we did. We got it for sure."

The shape lifted its head, began to rise with stiff, appalling deliberation.

"How's it *doing* that?" Kipps cried. "That's not fair! The Greek Fire should have been enough!"

"Maybe the wax protects it," Lockwood said. He gestured for us to keep going; we were almost at the foot of the stairs. "Protects the bones and plasm. But that can't last. As it moves, it has to break the wax. Look—it's already cracking apart."

And sure enough, the smooth contours of the figure were fracturing. A broken line ran around the center of the neck like a flaked and feathered ring. At the shoulder joints, the knees, and where the legs fed into the hips, the surface had disintegrated entirely. As it got to its feet in painful, jerky movements, small shards of wax fell into the coiling ghost-fog. It began to limp toward us across the stones.

"*Marissa* . . ."

The combination of sorrow and fury in the voice made me gasp. A burning wave of dark emotions flooded my head.

"It's calling out," I said. "Calling for Marissa."

We were through the arch, gathered at the foot of the stairs. George brushed magnesium flecks off his glasses. "Really? Think the bones belong to someone who was murdered? Think Marissa killed them, put them here?"

"Don't know. The thing's certainly not happy."

"*I'd* be grumpy if I'd been killed, coated in wax, and buried in a coffin with an old woman's mask strapped to my face," Holly said.

"Interesting . . ." George looked back into the chamber, where the limping, shambling figure seemed to be speeding up. "I wonder who this is. . . ."

Kipps had thrown himself to a halt against the wall. "Yes, fascinating as the identity of the ghost is," he panted, "I'm more concerned about the fact that it's angry, it's right behind us, and we've a booby-trapped staircase still to climb."

"You're right," Lockwood said. "Flashlights on. Single file. Fast as you can, but watch for the traps. Especially you, George." He drew his rapier. "I'll go last."

Kipps and George didn't need telling; they were already scurrying up the stairs. Holly hesitated, then obeyed. Only I held back.

"You too, Luce."

"You're going to do something stupid," I said. "I know you. I can tell."

He brushed hair from his eyes. "That makes two of us, then. What's your crazy plan?"

"The usual. I was hoping to talk to it and calm it down. Yours?"

"Thought I'd slow it by cutting off its legs."

I grinned at him. "We're so similar."

We pressed close together. The mannequin wasn't far away now; and it was certainly getting faster, its joints entirely free of their wax surround. You could see nubs of bone working at the hips and ankles. Toes protruded at the ends of lumpy feet. There was something pathetic about it. It rolled and stumbled like a seasick sailor, colliding with the arch as it passed through.

"Suppose you'd better go first," Lockwood said. "It won't be very calm in a minute, when it's trying to drag itself up the stairs. I'll give you twenty seconds." He flashed me his brightest smile. "No pressure."

"You spoil me." I took a deep breath, and Listened anew to the lonely, empty voice that rattled, echoing, across the crypt. I quelled my fear, opened my mind in psychic welcome. "Who are you?" I asked. "What did Marissa do to you?" Then, when the figure didn't answer or slow its course: "We can help you. What's your name?"

I waited, giving it time to adjust. The dummy was in a pretty bad way. In places the wax surface glistened where it had been partially melted by the fire. Thin droplets ran down the torso, striping it, leaving it pitted and gouged. One side of the head had been smashed in, either by the fall from the coffin or by the flares. You could see a jawbone inside the hole, a few teeth embedded in the wax. Basically, it was a mess. And the ghost inside would be no better off, maddened by its physical prison and by its mysterious resentments. I reached out to it, offering what I could, which was pity and understanding.

"We can help you . . ." I said again.

The broken thing shuffled nearer. The eye hollows were filled with pooling wax.

"We can avenge you. We are enemies of Marissa."

"*Marissa . . .*"

"Last chance, Luce." Lockwood, at my side, held his rapier ready. "I think you're being way too subtle. It doesn't understand. Move away."

"I've got to try. It's so desolate. . . ."

The stiff arms and wax fingers were outstretched, as in an attitude of love.

"Move away, Luce!"

"*Marissa . . .*"

"Just one more sec— Ow!"

Lockwood barged me aside, just as the shape lunged forward. It moved with sudden swiftness; Lockwood had no time to direct his rapier at the legs. His blade struck the center of the torso, plunging in deep, where it was instantly caught fast in stiff, thick wax. The rapier was torn from Lockwood's hands. Cold air burst around us, numbing our senses. Flaking wax fingers grappled for my throat. I cried out, tried to pull free. Then Lockwood was with me, grasping one stiff arm, avoiding the swipe of another, wrenching the fingers loose. He kicked out at the figure, sending it crashing back against the wall, the sword still embedded in its chest. Great gobbets of wax fell away. I caught a flash of ribs and spine.

"Let's go, Luce!" Lockwood grabbed me by the hand and hauled me up the steps. As we ran, he snatched his flashlight from his belt, directed the beam upward. "*That* was no good," he gasped. "You and your ghost-talking. You almost got yourself killed!"

"Well, you were going to cut off its legs! How did that part go?"

"I lost my best rapier was how it went. Aside from that, it was a wild success."

"Maybe we bought ourselves some time." I glanced over my shoulder. "Oh. No. . . . No, we didn't."

Behind us there was a clacking on the stone. The thing was on all fours now, elbows out, throwing itself up the steps like a rabid dog. Wax dropped from it like sloughing skin. Where the bone showed through, you could see the gleam of ectoplasm.

"Doesn't matter," Lockwood said. "It's quick, but we're quicker.

We can still outrun it, as long as there're no hitches up ahead. . . .
Oh, hell," he said. *"Now what?"*

Because our bouncing flashlight beams had picked out Kipps,
Holly, and George, stumbling back down.

"What are you *doing?*" I shouted. "Turn around! It's right
behind us!"

"There's one up ahead, too," Holly cried.

"What? How?"

"George triggered the wire. Stepped right on it. A stone moved—
a ghost came out."

"Another ghost? George!"

"Sorry. I was thinking about something else."

"We're running for our lives up a haunted stairway and you're
thinking about *something else?*" Kipps roared. "How can that be
possible?"

"Where's this new ghost?" Lockwood pushed past the others.
"Come on, we've got to go up. Going back is not an option."

It didn't take long to reach the step with the trip wire. Above it,
a hollow stone hung open in the wall. A faint figure was hovering
above the stairs a few feet farther on. It had the vague form of an old
woman in a knee-length skirt, shirt, and jacket; she had long gray
hair, and an unpleasantly smiling face. Everything about her was
gray, except for her black and glittering eyes.

Lockwood shook his head. "A little old lady? Terrifying. You've
got rapiers, haven't you? Why aren't you using them?"

George gestured at the edge of the steps, at the dark void beyond.
"We tried. . . . The thing raises some kind of wind—nearly blew us
over the side."

Lockwood cursed. "What are we, Bunchurch and Co.? Give me that sword." He snatched the rapier from George's hands and leaped over the trip wire. The ghost's hair came to sudden life, flaring out around its head. Cold air swept down the steps, pitching Lockwood sideways; he scrabbled desperately, and just avoided careering off the edge into the shaft. Battling the gust, he fought his way back toward the wall.

A lazy green light flared at my shoulder. I sensed the skull's presence return. *"So,"* its voice said casually. *"How's it going?"*

"How does it *look* like it's going?" I said. Lockwood was edging toward the ghost, leaning into the spectral wind.

"Let's see . . . I've only been gone five minutes, and you've managed to trigger two ghosts and get sandwiched between them on the edge of an abyss. By any standard, that's poor. I suppose you'll be wanting a clever solution to your problem."

I looked back down the steps. Around the curve of the wall came the glow of other-light, the shadow of a crawling figure with a rapier through its chest.

"Well, if you've got any suggestions . . ." I said lightly.

"Always. But I want an answer. When are you going to let me out of this jar?"

"Now is not the time to discuss this."

"It's the perfect time."

"Never on a case. I told you. We'll talk at home."

"Ah, but you never talk to me at home. You ignore me. I get stuffed into a corner with all the salt and iron and the rest of the equipment. Well, maybe I should ignore you now."

"We'll discuss it, I promise! Tomorrow! Now, about that

advice . . ." The Revenant on the steps was clawing close. The wax on its fingers had fallen away; I could hear the *clack, clack, clack* of bones as it clutched the stone. Above us, Lockwood was swiping at the second ghost, its white shape veering and distorting to avoid his blade.

"It's so simple as to be embarrassing. I hardly like to mention it. The spirit behind us carries its Source with it—you can see the bones. But what about the spirit up ahead? Where's its Source?"

I scowled around me. "Well, how do *I* know where—?" But even as I said this, I saw the hollow stone hanging open above the stairs, the dark recess within. I gripped my flashlight between my teeth. Launching myself close, I clambered up the stones and peered inside. There was a tiny cavity, lined with beaten silver. Sitting in it was a set of dentures, the plastic gums glinting pinkly in the light.

"False teeth? Who has false teeth for a Source?"

"Who cares? Get rid of them."

I was already clutching the horrid things, wincing at their glassy smoothness and icy cold. Without pause I jumped back onto the steps and hurled them out into the void. They fell without a sound. At once the Specter of the old woman was dragged abruptly sideways, distorting around the middle as if a rope were slicing through it. It held firm for only a moment, black eyes blazing—then it was gone, sucked down into the hole, following its Source. Lockwood was left swinging his sword against nothing; the spectral wind died. We were alone on the stairs.

Except for the ghost rearing up on the steps below us. Lockwood's rapier was still wedged into its chest. On the arms and legs, the wax was entirely gone. In our swirl of desperate flashlight beams, the

Visitor was revealed as a mess of jangling bones, held together by strings of plasm. The fingers were bony now—with the wax gone, they would deliver fatal ghost-touch. The head of wax and teeth grinned up at us.

It lunged. George shouted, Kipps screamed. Holly was there— she swiped sideways with her sword. The tip cut into the neck, lopping through it in a swift, clean movement. The head hung in place, then fell against the wall and bounced away down the stairs.

We paused, willing the rest of the body to follow it. Instead, it remained standing. A ghostly head, faint and cobwebby, was super-imposed where the skull had been. It was a man, I thought, with a long, lined face and wild hair.

"It's not *still* coming?" George groaned. "Give me a break!"

But we were already scrambling away from it, up the stairs. George was in front, and I was at the back, the backpack bouncing against my shoulders.

"*Remember!*" the skull's voice said in my ear. "*Tomorrow! You promised!*"

"If I ever see tomorrow . . ."

Up ahead, the trapdoor to the mausoleum showed as a cone of faint gray light. My legs felt like lead; it was all I could do to lift them.

"*Marissa . . .*" Close behind, the hollow voice was calling. "*Marissa . . .*"

"It really *wants to get to you,*" the skull remarked. "*The plasm's breaking free. If you're not careful, it'll leave the bones behind entirely. Better speed up, Lucy.*"

"I'm trying!"

Something snagged at my backpack, sought to pull me back down. I cried out, threw myself forward, barging into Kipps. He was almost on top of Lockwood, who was shoving Holly and George ahead of him. For one awful moment, we were all stumbling, about to fall. Somehow, in a flurry of flapping elbows, we stayed on our feet. We leaped up the final flight, ghostly fingernails clicking on the steps behind.

Up into the mausoleum's dimly lit space. We burst through, one by one; I was the last. I jumped through, turned, saw the white face swimming up at me, out of the dark.

Lockwood and Kipps already held the corners of the hinged flagstone. They were hauling it up. As I rolled aside, they practically threw it shut. It slammed into position. Lanterns flickered. The building sang with the noise.

Lockwood winced. "The guards . . ."

I hurled my backpack away from me. It lay on the floor, steaming. Three jagged claw marks scored the back.

We sat around the edge of the stone, wheezing and gasping like defective barrel organs.

"Made it," Holly breathed.

"Made it," Kipps said. "Thank God."

In its jar, poking out of the top of the backpack, the skull nodded amiably. *"Nice one. Shut that just in time . . ."* It left a significant pause. *"So the inside of that flagstone's lined with iron, is it? Lucky!"*

Right then I could barely speak. "No, no iron . . ."

"Or silver, then?"

"No. . . ."

The skull chuckled. *"Of course—silly idea! Far too expensive. Must be some kind of barrier, though."* It grinned at me. *"Or . . ."*

Or . . . *Oh.* "Lockwood . . ." I said.

I was already shuffling backward. Threads of white-blue ice were spreading from the center of the flagstone. As one, we retreated in all directions, bottoms bouncing, swords scraping on the ground. At the same time—as if we were pulling it on invisible strings—the ghost rose slowly through the stone. It had left its bones on the other side. First we saw the creased and cobwebbed head, the bare teeth gleaming; next the skeletal neck, then a spiraling shroud of ghost-fog. As it came, its other-light spread across the floor, fixing us where we crouched like woodlice exposed by the lifting of a log.

Somewhere near me, Kipps was trying to get his rapier clear of his belt (and failing: he was sitting on it). Lockwood, on his knees, had found a flare from somewhere. What was *I* doing? Continuing to retreat, because it seemed the ghost's attention was fixed entirely on me. So I shuffled ever back, and the ghost rose ever higher, its linen-covered arms held tight at its sides.

"Eep, he's a big one," the skull said. It had a tone of mild scientific interest.

My back bumped up against the cold edge of the vault.

The shape quivered. At once, like a shark shooting forward with a twitch of the tail, it was above me.

The face of dirt and cobwebs lowered to my own. I smelled wax and grave mold, tasted the loneliness of existence underground. One emaciated arm stretched out, spectral fingers cupped toward me.

Someone was shouting, but I paid no attention to it. I Listened to a harsh voice, calling from far away.

"*Marissa Fittes . . .*"

"Yes!" I croaked. "What about her?"

Behind the ghost, Lockwood stepped into view. He had a flare ready in his hand. "Lucy!" he called. "Roll out of the way!"

"Wait."

Still I stared into dirt and cobwebs. . . .

"Lucy! Move!"

"*Marissa . . .*" the ghost said. "*Bring her to me!*"

At once, the figure blinked out of existence, vanishing as if it had never been. A great pressure left the chamber; I jerked forward, my hair swinging back against my face. In the same moment, all the remaining lanterns went out, and we were plunged into solid darkness.

Someone shone a flashlight across the room. Flakes of dust were floating down around me. Cobwebs lay scattered across my knees.

"Lucy?" Lockwood was bending at my side.

"I'm all right."

"What did it do to you?"

"Nothing. Lockwood . . ." I didn't quite know how to put this. "Have we ever had a ghost-client before?"

He stared at me. "Of course not. Why?"

I let my head fall back against the stone. "Because I think we've just been given a job."

II

La Belle Dame
Sans Merci

Chapter 4

Thirty-five Portland Row, the home and headquarters of Lockwood & Co., was a very special place. Whenever the old black front door shut behind me and I saw the welcoming glint of the Aztec crystal skull lantern on the key table, the weight of the world was lifted from me like a conjurer snapping a cloak up into the air. I'd toss my rapier into the pot we used as an umbrella stand, hang my jacket on a peg, and walk up the hall past the shelves with their odd collection of jars and masks and painted gourds. If it was daytime, I'd peep into the living room to see if anyone was resting or working there; by night I'd check the library, which was where we tended to crash after a job. If all was quiet, I'd stroll past the staircase to the kitchen, where the lingering smells of toast (Lockwood) or tea cake (George and Kipps) gave clues to who might be in. Occasionally, if the tin of dried green tea had been opened, or one or two sunflower seeds lay scattered on the countertop, I knew Holly was around and probably working in the office. You couldn't always tell, though; she was the tidiest of us, and rarely left such clues. Most rare of all, an odor of stale kippers and traces of dried river mud kicked off by the back door gave certain proof that Flo Bones had recently stopped by.

The house was our sanctuary, a refuge from ghosts and other, darker things. And the happiest times of all were the breakfasts we enjoyed after a successful case, with the windows open onto the garden, and the sunlight streaming in.

On such an occasion, the morning after our visit to the Fittes mausoleum, Lockwood, George, and I were sitting at the kitchen table. Holly had gone out to Arif's store to fetch further supplies; the surface of the table was littered with open jam jars, eggcups, butter dishes, and toast crumbs, but we still felt hungry. At one end of the table, the ghost-jar was striped by sunlight coming through the blinds. We had our mugs of tea. George, who had eaten well, was sitting in his chair with a hideous wooden mask propped up on his lap. He was using a damp tea towel to wipe the dust off it. Lockwood had a pen and was doodling on a corner of the Thinking Cloth, the tablecloth on which we noted down ideas, while simultaneously glancing at a newspaper leaning against the ghost-jar. In the jar itself, the ghost was dormant; the plasm stirred lazily in the late morning sun, like green water in a deep and weedy pool.

I sat quietly next to Lockwood, enjoying the companionable silence. My muscles ached, my head was cloudy. Lockwood had a scrape on his left temple, and the lenses of George's spectacles were soft with grave dust. Our exertions hung heavy on us. But we had not yet spoken of the night before.

"Lots of news this morning," Lockwood said, indicating the paper.

I opened an eye. "Good?"

"No."

"Bad?"

"Baddish *and* bad. Two things, and neither particularly great for us."

"Let's have the baddish one first," George said. "I prefer my misery to come at me in stages, so I can acclimatize on the way."

Lockwood reached out for his mug of tea. "The baddish one is just the usual. Dullop and Tweed this time. They've agreed on terms with the Fittes Agency. Old Mr. Dullop is retiring, and the company's being absorbed into Fittes, effective immediately."

"What does Tweed have to say about it?" I asked.

"Nothing. He got killed by a Solitary years ago."

I frowned. "Another small agency swallowed up . . ." I looked toward the window, where bright blue sky shone above the houses at the bottom of the garden. "There aren't many of us left."

"Adam Bunchurch is still holding out," George said. He was dabbing at the teeth of the wooden mask. "Did you hear about last week? They made him quite a decent offer to close down, but he went berserk and threw the Fittes guy out on his ear."

"Didn't think he had it in him." Lockwood sat back in the chair and gave a tentative stretch. "Not sure he'll last long with open rebellion like that. Ahh . . . my back is *killing* me this morning. I blame your skull, Lucy."

"It's not *my* skull. I just talk to it. You mentioned some bad news."

"Oh. Yes. Guess what? They've let Winkman out."

George lowered the tea towel in shock, and I opened my eyes wide. "*Julius* Winkman?" I said. "I thought he got ten years."

"He did!" George cried. "For selling illegal psychic relics! And incitement to violence! And desecration of burial sites! He's not been in jail two years! Where's the justice in that?"

This was George all over. True, justice *was* important, but it wasn't what *I* was worrying about. It was our testimony that had put Julius Winkman away. And Winkman was a vindictive man.

"Out early for 'good behavior,' allegedly," Lockwood said. He flicked the paper with a fingertip. "Says here he was met outside the prison by Adelaide, his wife, and Leopold, his darling little son. Then he drove away, swearing to turn over a new leaf and never be a naughty black marketeer again."

"He'll be after us," I said. "He wants us dead."

Lockwood grunted. "Him and all the rest. Maybe he'll lie low."

George turned the mask over dubiously. "Doubt it."

We all fell silent for a time. But it was a clear, bright morning, and our fierce satisfaction from the night before still lingered, burning away our doubts and fears.

"What's that you've drawn, Lockwood?" I asked, eyeing the Thinking Cloth. "Looks like a piece of angry broccoli."

"What? Are you insulting my excellent sketch of a wild-haired ghost?" Lockwood threw down his pen. "I suppose drawing's not my strong suit. I was trying to capture the face of that Revenant. I got a good look at the end, when it broke clear of the bones. Thought George might figure out who it was, if he had a visual aid to help him."

"If he uses *that*, he'll end up doing his research in the grocery store." When I shut my eyes, I could see the ghost's livid form hovering over me. "It was a man in late middle age," I said, "with a very lined, lived-in face. Long gray hair. That's all *I* can remember—it was his words that struck me more. You off to the Archives again, George?"

"In a bit. We've got a client coming in an hour." George set the wooden mask down on the table between the butter dish and the cornflakes. With the dust gone, its bright colors showed through. Exotic feathers plumed from its top like frozen smoke. "What do you think of this baby?" he said. "Polynesian shaman's mask. Got it from Jessica's room." He glanced across at Lockwood. "I opened the last crate yesterday. Hope that's okay."

Lockwood nodded. "Fine. Anything else good so far?"

"Maybe. Some things I want to show you, actually, after our second breakfast."

I was gazing at the shaman's mask, at its beetling brows and ferociously snarling mouth. "Think this has any power?"

"I think there's some psychic energy in it," George said, "but I'm not as sensitive as you. Might be worth taking a look later, Lucy, if you don't mind."

"Sure . . ." Suddenly I couldn't wait any longer; I had to get it off my chest. "Lockwood, George," I said, "what are we going to *do*?"

They both knew what I meant, of course. Our visit to the mausoleum had been weighing on us all morning. It's quite something when being chased up a staircase by a disintegrating Revenant isn't the most memorable thing about a job, but that was certainly the case here. The missing occupant of the tomb preyed on our minds.

"I've been thinking about Marissa," Lockwood said, "and I believe all we can do is go on as before. There's so much we still don't understand, and it would be dangerous to admit to breaking into her tomb without some proper answers. So we keep our noses clean, do ordinary cases, stay out of trouble. Meanwhile, we follow all lines of inquiry. In particular, George continues to research the link between Marissa and the woman we call Penelope."

George nodded. "The Fittes family's been at the heart of the fight against ghosts since the beginning. If we want to find a solution to the Problem, we'll need to sort this puzzle out, too. Regarding our waxy friend from last night, I'll look at some newspapers from Marissa's last years while I'm at the Archives. It's just possible I'll get wind of an associate of hers who disappeared around that time. The ghost definitely knew her, you think, Luce?"

"It knew her," I said, "and it was very annoyed."

"Someone close to her, then. Someone betrayed and murdered."

"To be honest," Lockwood said, picking up his mug again and frowning at the cold tea inside it, "that ghost is just a sideshow. Our priority is to find out what happened to the woman who's supposed to be in that tomb. Who's supposed to have died twenty years ago. Lucy, try to get some sense out of that stupid skull. We're following its lead, after all. I still feel it's the key to all this."

"*Someone mention me?*" A ripple ran through the murky depths of the jar. The ghost's face materialized behind the glass. Never exactly pleasant, today it seemed more than usually repulsive, like a damp corpse that had been stepped on.

I glared at it. "Can't you look less foul for once? You're making the milk go sour."

"*So I'm a bit the worse for wear,*" the skull said. "*I was up all night, wasn't I? As were all of you. You look knackered, Lockwood's black-and-blue, and Cubbins has some vile disease that leaves yellow blotches on his chin.*"

"George has recently been eating egg," I said. "But none of that's important. You and I need to discuss Marissa."

The eyes narrowed. "*Wrong. We need to discuss my freedom. We had a deal.*"

I hesitated. "Not here," I said at last. "Not now. I'll talk to you later."

"*Later? What's that mean? Six weeks? A year? I know your feminine wiles.*"

"Oh, God. In a few minutes."

The face scowled. "*Sure, I've heard that before. Meantime, there'll be some new crisis that distracts you, and I'll still be stuck here, tapping my fingers in this glassy prison.*"

"You don't have fingers," I growled, "and I don't believe time is of much relevance to you, being dead. And anyway, nothing's going to come up to distract me in the next few minutes. So stop complaining!" I looked up. "Hey, Holly."

There had been sounds in the hall. Holly Munro appeared at the door, carrying her cotton shopping bag. She surveyed us briefly, running a hand through her long black hair.

George eyed the bag. "Get the doughnuts, Hol?"

"I got them." Her voice sounded odd. She walked past us, and began to set out the groceries on the sideboard. She moved swiftly, forcefully, clattering everything down. Her face was set, her lips pressed tight together.

"You all right, Holly?" I asked.

"Not really." She crumpled the bag on the counter and took a glass from the drainer. "I ran into Sir Rupert Gale by the store."

At once we all focused on her. Sir Rupert was an associate of Penelope Fittes, a master swordsman and a dangerous man. He was a fixer, someone who got his hands dirty on her behalf, and he was known to put pressure on her opponents. He had crossed paths with us before.

"*Here we go*," the skull said. "*Cue crisis.*"

I shut the lever on top of the jar. "What was he doing there, Hol?"

"He was waiting for me." Holly filled the glass from the tap and took a long drink, as if to wash away an unpleasant taste. "Ugh! He is *so* foul!"

Lockwood was very still in his chair. "Did he threaten you?"

"Not in so many words, but the implication was there. You know what he's like. Stands too close to you, all pink and smiling, with too-strong aftershave. He was just checking that we weren't 'overextending' ourselves—that's what he called it. 'Sticking to safe projects' and 'simple hauntings.' Not investigating Penelope, in other words."

"Oh, we're being *very* good, of course," Lockwood said. "What else did he say?"

"It was all a coded warning. How if we took on anything too 'difficult,' it would end badly for us. 'We wouldn't want anything unpleasant to happen to our favorite little agency.' Gah!" She set the glass down by the sink. "Oh, and he wanted to know where we were last night."

Lockwood and I exchanged glances. "What time last night?"

"After midnight. He says he has information that we weren't in."

"They're spying on us again," I said. "What did you say?"

"I said I didn't know, that I'd already gone home by then," Holly said. "He caught me by surprise, I'm afraid."

"That's all right," Lockwood said easily. "We've got our story ready, remember? We'll say we were in Kentish Town, dealing with a couple of really boring Stone Knockers. George can forge the paperwork."

"Already done," George said. "Holly, you look upset. Crack those doughnuts open."

"Thanks, I'll have an apple."

He shook his head sadly. "You've got to learn that when you're stressed, an apple doesn't cut it. . . . I feel quite shaken myself, come to think of it." His eyes flitted to the sideboard.

"Yes, grab the plates, George," Lockwood said. "We'll all have one."

And we all did, even Holly. George was wise in such matters; a doughnut made the world seem almost right again. Almost, but not entirely. Because the world *wasn't* right. Marissa wasn't in her tomb. Winkman had been freed from prison. And Holly's little encounter wasn't an unusual one at all.

Traditionally, the activities of all psychic detection agencies were overseen by DEPRAC, the Department of Psychic Research and Control, which operated out of Scotland Yard in central London. DEPRAC had the power to punish misbehavior and ensure high professional standards. Sometimes fines were levied and, in rare cases, companies shut down. But generally the department concentrated more on researching the Problem than bothering agents in the field.

Since Penelope Fittes had taken command of the Rotwell Agency, however, things had begun to change. Ms. Fittes now controlled three-quarters of all agency activity in London, and she had at once set about bringing the rest to heel. Fittes personnel began to occupy many senior posts at Scotland Yard. New rules came into force. Henceforth, independent detection agencies, with their limited resources, had to confine their efforts to small-scale hauntings. Not only that, they had to submit to regular DEPRAC inspections to ensure they were acting professionally. Any firm in breach of these rules would be immediately closed down. Allegedly this was for public safety; in reality it was a means of monitoring our actions.

As the smallest agency of all, Lockwood & Co. found itself at the center of official attention. We were subjected to random house calls. We were stopped in the street and asked to show papers to prove what jobs we were on. And we were *followed* as we went about our work. I don't mean there were spies standing outside our doorway all the time. Instead, we were forever looking over our shoulders and finding nothing—until, one day, with grim inevitability, there *would be* a smirking boy trailing us to Baker Street Station, or a man in a hat standing outside Arif's store, brazenly watching as we trooped by. Sometimes several such incidents happened in a week; other times a fortnight would go by with nothing. The casualness was part of the intention. It reminded you that they thought you *almost* worth ignoring.

In all this we sensed the hand of Penelope Fittes. She wanted to keep close tabs on us. Still, it was Lockwood & Co. she was dealing with. We weren't easily cowed.

When the random DEPRAC visits happened, for instance, the scene they found at 35 Portland Row would be as follows: George would be at the sink in the basement trying to scrub ectoplasm out of his jeans. Lockwood would be in his bathrobe, hair ruffled, palely sipping a mug of tea and making notes on the Visitors disposed of the night before. Holly and I might be slowly sorting through a mess of equipment, or stacking Sources ready for transport to the furnaces. In short, it was a picture of weariness and discipline; of a tiny agency functioning successfully, but at full stretch. The representatives would ask to look at our casebook, take copies of our recent invoices, ghost-records, and client reviews, and after enjoying tea and biscuits and a boatload of Lockwood's tousled charm, head on their way.

Once they'd left, we'd shut the door, lock it, and get on with the things we were *really* doing. Outwardly, we kept up a facade of ordinary, small-scale cases. Beyond that, we had an agenda of our own. This double life had its challenges, and each of my colleagues coped with it in their own way.

Holly met it as she did all obstacles, with brisk efficiency that looked a problem in the eye and didn't blink. Whether it was breaking into the Fittes mausoleum, or standing up to interrogation in the street, she always maintained her trademark Munro cool. It was hard to imagine her ever losing this quality, and somehow, despite everything, that made me confident that nothing really dreadful could or would happen in this world. Her unflappable demeanor used to make me seethe, yet now I found it a source of reassurance. Come what may, I knew Holly's hair would swish like gossamer as she walked; her clothes would flow effortlessly around her curves; her skin would glow with that same coffee-colored luster that spoke of close association with mineral water and green bean salads, and contrasted, reprovingly, with my famous burger-and-biscuit complexion. No, Holly would always be the same, and that made me happy.

George's steeliness was of a different sort. To strangers, it might have seemed that he had none. He was too soft, too scruffy, too disheveled. If he'd ever knowingly shared a room with a hairbrush, there was precious little sign of it. His doughy, featureless face lacked signposts to a personality, let alone a strong opinion. Even those enemies who knew of his fame as a researcher saw this quality as something negative. They thought him a passive absorber of information, a shuffler of papers—someone better wedged safely in a study chair than facing supernatural terrors in the field.

In this, as in everything, they were entirely wrong. George's researching prowess, his ability to tramp from library to library, spending endless dusty hours hunting for the smallest clue, was based on ferocious determination and an iron will. If he hunted for something, he found it; if he found something, he clung on like a terrier and shook it until all the relevant facts fell out. He was relentless. He took the mystery behind the epidemic of ghosts as a personal affront, and the more pressure the Fittes Agency exerted to stop us from investigating it, the deeper George dug in. He would *not* be denied.

And then there was Lockwood. Lockwood, most of all.

He was the center around which we revolved—all of us, even Quill Kipps, our former enemy and new associate; even Flo Bones, the terror of the tide line, one of the most outstanding relic-women of the city, at least in terms of smell. Mostly unnoticed among the ghost-filled streets of London, Kipps and Flo both went about quiet errands on our behalf. They did so because Lockwood asked them to, and that was enough.

The secret to his pull, and to his resilience in the face of the Fittes Agency's spying and intimidation, was his combination of enormous energy and otherworldly calm. Few things fazed him; he remained coolly detached, absorbing pressure with a tilted eyebrow and a small, wry smile, before translating it into swift, sure action. Ghosts had always felt the brunt of his forcefulness; now he brought the same qualities to bear on his living enemies. In so doing he galvanized his friends, even as he kept us all at arm's length.

Or perhaps not everyone.

Of all of us, he confided most in me. We'd always been close, but since my return to the company five months earlier, we'd become closer still. We spent more time with each other than ever before. We worked together, we laughed a lot. I felt comfortable in his presence, and he in mine; it was clear to both of us, I think, that we found greater peace and pleasure in each other than in anyone else. That was the good news.

The bad news? I wasn't quite sure *why*.

Our journey through the frozen land of the dead, shielded by a single spirit-cape, had marked us both forever and separated us from our friends. No one else could properly imagine what we'd seen. Memories of it still disturbed our nightly dreams. It had taken weeks for our physical energies to return. My hair was flecked with white; there were gray twists in Lockwood's bangs. In fact, so overwhelming had this journey been that it cast a shadow over everything that came afterward. And it was sometimes hard to know, while standing in that shadow, whether the changes between us had been caused by *this*, or perhaps by other things.

So, the way Lockwood gazed at me, the flashes of vulnerability in his eyes, the looks we shared, quietly, when the others' backs were turned—on what, exactly, was that intimacy based? On us, pure and simple? On who we truly were? Or on the aftershocks of one overwhelming event, on the *experience* we'd shared?

It made a difference.

Don't get me wrong, I'm glad we had it. I just would have liked a bit of clarity, that's all.

It didn't help that, being Lockwood, he never talked about these emotions much. It didn't help that, being me, I never saw an easy way to broach the subject, either. And it certainly didn't help that we were always so busy, dealing with ghosts, with DEPRAC, with the ongoing mystery of the Problem.

And also with clients who came knocking on our doors half an hour before their scheduled appointments, bringing fresh terror into our lives.

Chapter 5

We'd only just finished eating our doughnuts when the bell rang on the path outside. The echoes died away.

Lockwood frowned. "They're hellishly early. Are we ready for them?"

"Cake's on the coffee table," Holly said. "But the living room is a mess, as usual." She got up, made for the door. "George, put the kettle on again, please. Lockwood, Lucy—you've got thirty seconds to make everything presentable."

We were well practiced at this; twenty-eight seconds later, cushions had been plumped, salt-bombs put in cupboards, and the living room window opened to admit the sunny air of early autumn. In the kitchen, George was making appropriate sounds with crockery. Lockwood and I stood waiting by the coffee table as our visitors came in.

They certainly made an immediate impression. The elder of the two was a short, stout person in a startling yellow-checked jacket, not overly new, with leather patches on the elbows. He wore a gray vest, pushed out to bursting by his protuberant belly, and a shiny white shirt, behind the open V of which gray-white chest hairs played and spilled like summer brambles. His cords were a vigorous deep red. His face was also red; it suggested too close an acquaintance with the wine bottle. He had an impressive crop of very curly gray hair, wedged beneath a worn green felt hat; a snub nose; a wide, elastic mouth; and a pair of small, bright eyes that seldom stopped moving and never properly met your gaze.

Beside him was a thin youth of scrawny, malnourished appearance. He wore old jeans and a baggy jersey that emphasized rather than concealed his lack of width. His nose was large and hooked, and beneath a shock of unruly black hair, his skin had an alarming bone-white pallor. His face was utterly expressionless. In contrast to his companion, he stared out straight ahead. He didn't seem to focus on the room at all.

"This is Mr. Lewis Tufnell," Holly said. "Mr. Tufnell and . . ." She looked at the boy.

"And Charley Budd," Mr. Tufnell said. "Come along, Charley."

Mr. Lewis Tufnell loped forward to meet us, with much nodding and winking and touching of his hat; as one in a trance, the boy shuffled at his side. They were an odd-looking pair, but it was only when they were halfway across the room that I noticed what was amiss.

The man was holding the lad on a chain.

As chains went, it was discreet and clean, with lots of neat, bright links, but that wasn't the issue. It was a *chain*. It ended in a loop of rope tied fast around the boy's wrists.

I glanced at Lockwood to see if he had noticed, too. One look told me he had. He wasn't alone. George, coming in with the tea things, had halted, openmouthed. Holly, following the visitors, was gesticulating furiously at us behind their backs.

Our clients reached the coffee table. Without waiting for an invitation, Mr. Tufnell settled himself into the sofa. At first the lad remained standing; by placing a hairy hand on his shoulder and applying pressure, his companion encouraged him to sit. There was a gentle clinking of chains, then silence.

One after the other, we sat, too.

Lockwood cleared his throat; he was still rather taken aback. "Er, good morning," he began. "I'm Anthony Lockwood. Now, Mr. Tufnell—"

"Call me Lew!" the gentleman interrupted, with a flourish of his worn green hat. "Plain Lew Tufnell! That's how I like it. No airs and graces about *me*, I hope. Proprietor of Tufnell's Theater, not to mention Tufnell's Marvels and Tufnell's Traveling Fairground of Astonishment and Delight. More to the point, I'm also a man at his wits' end, for my establishment is cursed by an evil spirit that threatens me with ruin." He gave an extravagant sigh, then noticed Holly's seedcake on the table. "Ooh. Is that little morsel for me? Smashing!"

"Well, we were *kind* of hoping to share it between us," George said.

Lockwood raised his hand. "Before we deal with cake *or* curse," he said, "there's one thing we need to discuss. . . ." He paused significantly, hoping the visitor would get the hint. "Well," he said finally, "we can't help noticing the chain. . . ."

Mr. Tufnell gave a little start as of mild surprise; a weak and liquid smile sloshed across his face. "What, this chain here? *This* chain? Oh, *that's* just for Charley Budd's own safety. Don't go worrying on your own account."

Lockwood frowned. "I'm not. But—"

"He won't hurt *you*, not poor Charley." With his free hand, Mr. Tufnell ruffled the lad's hair. "Only, he isn't so particular about himself, if you take my meaning. See that cake knife there? If I weren't vigilant, he'd be on it in a trice. Bury it in his own heart, he would, and spoil your lovely carpet."

We looked at the carpet, and then at the cake knife, and then at the boy, who sat quietly in a world of his own.

"He'd stab himself?" I said.

"Assuredly."

Holly had perched herself on the arm of George's chair. She said, "Surely, Mr. Tufnell, if he's . . . if he's ill, he should be in the hospital. He needs doctors who—"

"Doctors can't help him, miss." Lew Tufnell shook his gray head sadly. "Doctors? Medics? Pah! I'd like to see *them* try. They'd drug him and truss him up and what have you, and all the while his life would drain away regardless, till in a day or two he was just another corpse what's spirit's gone a-roving. Waste of time, *doctors*. No, Miss. We need *you*. That's why we're here."

There was a silence. In the kitchen we could hear the kettle boiling. "I'm sorry," Lockwood began. "I don't understand, and I'm not sure what we can do to help this boy. Now, if you say there's an evil spirit in your establishment—"

"It was the ghost what done this to Charley," Mr. Tufnell said.

We gazed at the lad again; at his stillness, his passivity, his unseeing eyes.

"Ghost-touched, you mean?" George asked.

"Not touched *physically*," Mr. Tufnell said, "though it was a close one. But his heart's snared. She's pulling his spirit out of him, making him weaker. I give him another night, maybe two, then he'll cross over after her." Just for a moment the man's eyes stopped their furtive wandering; he gazed directly at Lockwood. "If you can destroy her, maybe it'll break the link. Maybe he'll come back. I dunno."

Lockwood crossed his long legs in a resigned, businesslike way. He still wasn't happy about the chain, but he'd come to a decision. "You'd better tell us about it," he said.

I got to my feet. "I think first we should all have some tea."

"And *I* think," George said, springing to my side, "I should bury this cake knife where it belongs."

"That'll be splendid," Mr. Tufnell said. "I love cake. Nothing for Charley Budd, though. He don't eat no more."

I went to the kitchen, did the honors with kettle and teapot. George took care of the seedcake, casting concerned looks at our visitor's healthy midriff as he did so. While he waited, Mr. Tufnell's gaze flitted ceaselessly among us all. I noticed it lingered longest on me and Holly.

"Well," he remarked, as I handed him his cup, "you're a bright little shower, and no mistake. Scrubbed and shiny and pleasing to the eye. I could find jobs for one or two of you in my shows, if this agency gig doesn't work out." He smiled his washy, ingratiating smile, displaying an array of teeth like broken biscuits. "Couple of little dresses, a few sequins, twinkly tassels in appropriate places . . . You'd fit right in."

"That's nice to know," Lockwood said. "George will bear it in mind. Now, how can we help you in our present capacity as professional psychic investigation agents?"

"Tell us about this evil spirit." Holly spoke crisply; she turned a page of her notepad and held her pen ready. "What it is, how it appears—and how it's affected this poor boy."

Mr. Tufnell balanced his plate of seedcake on one worn knee. "It's not just Charley who's been affected. There's been a death, too. The theater and fairground ain't a safe place for young lads no more, thanks to *her*." He took an enormous mouthful and chewed mournfully. "I'll be brief. I'm a busy man; I can't sit around all day munching cake, even if you can. Well, the background's quickly told. You'll have heard of Tufnell's Traveling Fairground, no doubt. Been in the family a hundred years. My old dad now, Frank Tufnell, he used to take it up and down the country, but what with the Problem, travel's not so easy now. So, the last twenty years, we've taken root in Stratford, East London. There's an old theater on the site—the Palace Theater, it's called; been there a couple of hundred years itself, they say—and we use it for magic shows and circus entertainments, as well as housing Tufnell's Marvels. The fair's set up permanently around it. A ten gets you entry for the whole shebang, and for that, my friends, you have a feast of wonderment that never ceases or runs dry. Plus a free hot dog for kids on Sundays. Now *that's* what I call value."

Lockwood had been gazing out the window. "Indeed. You mentioned something about a ghost."

"I did. It walks the theater corridors by night in the guise of a cloaked woman, fair of shape and radiant, yet with an evil heart." Mr. Tufnell heaved a great shuddering sigh. "One of my lads she's done away with," he said, "and Charley Budd won't linger long. Whatever young man she meets never lives to speak of it. They call her . . ." He leaned forward suddenly, his voice descending to unguessed-at depths. "They call her . . . *La Belle Dame Sans Merci.*"

The echoes of his whisper died away, and all at once the chained boy at his side, little white-faced Charley Budd, who had hitherto been as one carved from stone, uttered a long, low moan. There was something so quavering and frightful about the sound that I felt the hairs rise on my arms.

Mr. Tufnell tightened his grip on the chain, but the boy did not stir again.

We sat for a moment in silence.

"La Belle Dame Sans Merci . . ." Holly breathed. "The Beautiful Lady Without Mercy . . . They call the ghost that?"

"They do."

"On account of its deadly feminine allure?"

"No. Because it's her name. We know who the apparition is, see? Didn't I mention it? La Belle Dame Sans Merci. She was an actress, of a kind, at the turn of the last century. Great star in her day, and a wicked and beautiful woman she was. Now it seems she's left the grave and is walking again. Here, take a gander." From an inner pocket of his jacket he drew, much creased and greasy-looking, a large, yellowed, folded piece of paper. He passed it across the table in a covert motion. "For Gawd's sake, don't let Charley Budd see that," he said.

Lockwood took the piece of paper and opened it. I leaned in close. George and Holly left their seats and came around the coffee table to look over our shoulders.

It was a theatrical flyer, printed in black and gold. It showed an illustration of a blond woman posing languorously among rolling clouds of golden smoke. She wore a glamorous outfit that was hard to describe, partly because there was so little of it. It had a faintly Eastern feel. It was all plunging necklines, cunningly positioned slashes, and tightly fitting curves. It looked both impractical and chilly. The woman's long slim arms were festooned with bracelets; she had a tiara on her head and her fair hair billowed behind her, merging into the smoke. Her eyes were half-closed and entirely hidden behind enormous black lashes. She had her head thrown back, and her lips parted in a way that was either enticing or half-witted, or both. Beside her, written in eerie letters in the smoke, were the following words:

LA BELLE DAME SANS MERCI
Mistress of Illusion
in
The Sultan's Revenge

At the bottom of the flyer, the name and address of the Palace Theater were given, along with a date of more than ninety years previously.

Mr. Tufnell had taken the opportunity to help himself to another slice of cake. "La Belle Dame. Legendary beauty, as you can see."

"Yup," said George.

"Looks a bit overripe to me," Holly said. "Don't you think, Lucy?"

"Definitely."

The impresario grunted. "She was a cruel woman in life, they say. Her looks gave her power over all who saw her, and that's the power her ghost has, too."

Lockwood was frowning at the handbill. "And she's the one haunting you. . . . How can you be sure, Mr. Tufnell? How do you *know* it's her?"

"Because La Belle Dame met her gruesome end onstage in that very theater. She was an escapologist, see? People came from all over London to see her perform marvelous illusions in which she narrowly avoided death. Her most famous stunt was that very one you see there: *The Sultan's Revenge.* She was shut in an upright casket like a coffin, which was hung about with chains. Men then impaled it with swords, with her screaming from inside. Of course, it was all fake. Really, she'd dropped through a trapdoor in the base of the box and escaped under the stage. She was ready to pop back up when the swords were withdrawn. Easy. Until the night it all went horribly wrong . . ."

Mr. Tufnell paused and swallowed. He had spoken with passion and dramatic eloquence; also with his mouth full. The gentle rain of cake crumbs that had accompanied his account now stopped pattering on the coffee table. "Some say it was sabotage," he whispered, "the vengeful act of one of her scorned admirers. Others claim the lad in charge of flipping the lever had downed a drink and simply forgotten his cue. Either way, La Belle Dame did not drop through the floor. She was still in the box when the swords were driven in. The shrieks onstage that night were real."

"A nasty way to go," I said. "Nasty for the audience, too."

"To begin with," Mr. Tufnell said, "no one in the theater understood what had happened—they thought the torrent of blood was part of the act. But it just went on and on. . . ." He took a sip of tea. "I hope I'm not distressing you."

Lockwood was eyeing the damp crumbs on the table. "Only a little. Right, fine. That's the story of how she died. Tell us about the ghost."

Our client nodded. "We do an afternoon performance in the theater. No evening event, naturally—everyone's out before the sun goes down. It's an old-school circus variety show: trapeze artists, jugglers, clowns, and acrobats on the stage. Most are adults, but I've got kids who clean up after the show. A couple of them came to me reporting that they'd seen a woman walking in the back of the theater while they were sweeping the stage. Late afternoon, it was. They'd thought she was a customer who'd strayed in somehow, but when they went to find her, she was gone. Few days later, another kid was passing the main dressing room, just before locking up. Out of the corner of her eye she saw someone in a black dress standing there. When she stepped back, the room was empty."

"All a bit ominous," Lockwood said. "What did you do?"

"Nothing. We weren't *in* the building after dark, were we? This was in daylight. I thought we'd be safe enough . . . until what happened to Charley and poor Sid Morrison." Mr. Tufnell sighed with feeling; he took off his hat and ran his hand through his nest of curls.

"What happened to Charley, Mr. Tufnell?"

"It was late afternoon, three days ago," our client said. "The ghost-lamps were just coming on outside. Sarah Parkins, our stage manager, had forgotten her coat; she went back in to get it, and spotted Charley Budd walking down a corridor, all smiling and blank-eyed, like he was in a trance. She saw something with a woman's shape beckoning to him from the end of the passage. Says it was all dark around the shape, though the lights were on everywhere else. He was going straight toward it." Mr. Tufnell looked at us. "Well, Sarah didn't waste any time. She just upped and tackled Charley, brought him crashing to the floor. As she did so, she says, the darkness at the end of the passage kind of flared, then went out, and all the lamps came on again. And Charley was still alive—but in the condition you see here."

"The stage manager was very brave," I said.

"Yes." Mr. Tufnell nodded. "Sarah's a strapping lass like you. Not willowy and pliant like this young lady here." He flashed his broken teeth at Holly.

"Lucy and I can both handle ourselves very well," Holly said.

"So," Lockwood said, "it was a close shave for Charley. And now we get to poor Sid Morrison."

The impresario's shoulders dropped; he studied his hands. "Sid was our magician's apprentice. Late yesterday afternoon he was on the stage, setting up equipment for today's show. One of our girls, name of Tracey, was down in the auditorium, sweeping the floor. All at once she felt cold. She looked up and saw that Sid wasn't alone. There was a woman with him. The woman was sort of facing Tracey, but she couldn't make her out—it was like she stood in shadow, even though the lights of the theater were on. As she watched, the woman glided back into the dark of the wings. She didn't walk or turn, but just sort of flowed backward, Tracey said, and Sid walked after her. Not running, but not hesitating neither. He disappeared between the side curtains."

"Did Tracey call out or try to stop him?" I asked.

"She says she wanted to speak, but for some reason couldn't. As soon as Sid was gone, she found she could move again. She ran to the steps at the side of the stage and headed between the curtains. It ain't pretty, this next bit."

"Oh, *do* go on," Holly said. "Do you *know* how many ghosts we've dealt with? *Please.*"

Mr. Tufnell accepted the reprimand without complaint. His voice was soft, his earlier ebullience gone. "Tracey went into the wings, and there she saw the woman and Sid again. It was like they were embracing—at least, the woman had thin arms around him, and her face was in his neck. The horrible thing is that Sid's a big lad, but it was like he was all limp and boneless, and the woman was holding him up. And sure enough, when she let go—her arms sort of passing *through* his body—he just collapsed on the floor all shapeless, like a pile of dirty rags. He was quite dead, and when Tracey turned him over, he had a terrible smile on his cold, white face."

Lockwood tapped his fingers on his knee. "What about the ghost woman?"

"Vanished before poor Sid hit the floor."

"You've been slow in coming to us, Mr. Tufnell. Too slow. When Charley had his narrow escape—"

"I know." Mr. Tufnell inspected his hands like they had somehow disappointed him. "I know. It's just—if this got out . . . who would come to see us? The show would fold."

"Better that than further deaths," Holly said, scowling.

"What sort of boy *is* Charley?" George asked, after a silence. "When he's himself, I mean."

"Quiet. Not what you'd call *healthy*. Has a lung condition that prevents him from doing full work. Most people wouldn't give him a job. Me, I'm generous. I keep him busy."

"Was Sid sickly too?"

"Not at all. Strapping. Prime of life. He was a prestidigitator."

A silence. Lockwood nodded. "Ah, yes. Was he? Interesting. Good for him."

"You don't know what that means, do you?"

"Not the foggiest clue."

"Means he was a conjurer, clever with his hands. Strictly speaking, Sid was only an apprentice, but he was hot stuff at the close-up work. He'd go among the crowds, making eggs appear out of ladies' ears, ripping up twenty-pound notes and pulling them whole from gents' sleeves. Smooth, quick, plenty of nice patter. Lubricated the crowd, like. *That's* what he was good at—least he *was*, until he fell in love with one of our Russian trapeze artists."

"Why, what was the problem there?"

"She didn't return his feelings. I tried to persuade her to humor him, that it was in the best interests of the company, but she was having none of it. Sid was lovelorn. Spent weeks moping under the window of her caravan. Stopped sleeping. Stopped eating. He was wasting away. His skills suffered, too; he broke the eggs, dropped coins, sent cards spinning every which way. Hopeless. I'd have fired him if he hadn't died."

"Well, he saved you some trouble there, anyway," Lockwood said. He tapped his fingers again. "This Russian trapeze artist— what's her name?"

"Carole Blears."

"She doesn't *sound* very Russian."

"White Russian on her maternal grandmother's side. Or so she says. If she's got thighs that can swing a grown man ten feet through the air, that's good enough for me. Now, this here cake's been a treat, I can tell you. If no one else is going to join me, I'll happily take the last slice." Ignoring a croak of protest from George, Mr. Tufnell did so. He settled back into his seat. "So, can you help me?" he asked. "This ghost's killing Charley here, not to mention giving me ulcers and scaring my customers away."

Lockwood was gazing at the ceiling. "Mr. Tufnell—how long has this trouble been going on?"

"The ghost, or the ulcers?"

"The ghost."

"Two weeks, maybe three."

"I see. And who has actually witnessed the ghost, aside from Charley Budd here, Sid, and the two women you mentioned?"

"Some of the usherettes, Vanessa the makeup artist; I think an ice-cream girl."

"And they all survived?"

"They live with the horror to this day. Vanessa's hair turned white."

"So in other words, La Belle Dame's victims are all male?" Holly asked.

Mr. Tufnell nodded. "Not one of them could resist her charms. In death as in life. You and this lad here would need to beware, Mr. Lockwood."

Lockwood chuckled. "Oh, I think George and I could handle whatever La Belle Dame might throw at us. Wouldn't you say so, George? Very well, Mr. Tufnell, we'll look into this for you. Give us twenty-four hours to research the case. If you think Charley can last that long?"

Our visitor looked at the chained boy, motionless and blank-eyed at his side. "I would hope so, Mr. Lockwood. . . . But for pity's sake, don't delay too long."

I was glad to see our clients go. I disliked one, and pitied the other. In short, their presence disturbed me. I led them to the door.

As I opened it and stood aside to let them pass, Mr. Tufnell bowed to me. In doing so, he let the chain go loose in his hand. At once, Charley Budd pulled sharply to the side, tearing the chain free. He fell against the opposite wall, beside the big chipped plant pot with its umbrellas and rapiers. Hands still bound together, he grasped the hilt of Lockwood's second-best sword and wrenched it up, out of the pot, so that the blade shone in the morning light. Then he thrust it down and inward, seeking to drive the tip deep into his stomach. His arms were too short, the blade too long. It stabbed into the leather of his belt and caught there.

While he struggled to free it, I was on him, grappling for the blade. Mr. Tufnell caught his arm, pulling at the chain. The youth fought back frenziedly, desperately, with frightening strength. We collided with the coatrack, then the entry table. He made no sound. For several silent seconds, we wrestled back and forth, his pale face next to mine, our eyes locked together. Then Mr. Tufnell clouted him hard on the side of the head and I pulled the rapier away.

Like a switch had been flicked, Charley Budd was placid again. His face was calm and expressionless; he allowed himself to be led out of the door and into the sun.

"I'm so sorry," Mr. Tufnell said, turning at the gate. "You see now how finding the ghost really is his only chance? Please do everything you can to help us."

With that he raised his battered felt hat, tugged at the chain, and led the boy away along the road.

Chapter 6

If we had been largely unmoved by Mr. Tufnell—his combination of sleazy theatrical bombast and slippery evasion wasn't wildly attractive—the evident plight of Charley Budd affected us all. According to Lockwood, who knew such things, it was a rare example of psychic enchainment, in which the victim's mind was snared.

"It's like ghost-lock," he said. "But it's not the *body* that's been trapped this time, it's the intelligence. The will to live just seeps away, and the victim is pulled toward death. Tufnell's right—destroying the ghost is probably the only way to sever the connection."

"Poor boy." Holly was tidying up the mess left in the hall. "How awful to want to do that to himself."

"And did you see his blank, expressionless face?" George added. "Eerie."

"His eyes were empty," I said. "When I fought him, there was nothing there."

"Well, it's clearly a formidable spirit that's snared him," Lockwood said, "and there's no way I'm facing it until we're properly prepared. Can you look into the story when you're at the Archives, George? I'll order more equipment for tomorrow; we left half our stuff in the mausoleum."

"Lots to do," George said. "Marissa, the Problem, *and* La Belle Dame Sans Merci. I'd better get going. Before I do, I wanted to show you the stuff I found in your parents' crates, Lockwood. Mind if I quickly do that now?"

We followed him upstairs to the second floor. It was a place where the representatives of DEPRAC, checking on our activities in the basement office, never thought to venture. Which was lucky for us, because it contained a dark and terrible wonderland, filled with things that threatened one's health and sanity, and I'm not just talking about George's bedroom. There was another room that had once belonged to Lockwood's sister, Jessica—the room she'd died in. Here her death-glow still hovered, dramatically but harmlessly, above the stripped bed, and stacks of crates lined the walls, each stamped with faded export permits from foreign lands. And set out on the one clear area of floor, surrounded by a circle of iron chains, were selected items from those crates: items strange, dangerous, and forbidden.

There were masks, fashioned in the shapes of wild animals and monstrous spirits. There were two newly discovered cloaks, one covered in feathers and one in molting fur. There were peculiar constructions of bone, beads, and animal gut, which Lockwood said were Javanese ghost-catchers. And there were pots, sealed with lead and wax. These in particular we treated with extreme caution. It was in the breaking of one of these that Jessica Lockwood had lost her life seven years before.

It was quite a haul. The sign-waving ghost-cultists who paraded through Trafalgar Square most days would have fallen on their knees before the items on display. Fittes researchers would have sold their grandmothers to have seen them. Rich collectors would have fought each other for them tooth and nail, while relic-men would have cut our throats for them while we slept. Inspector Barnes of DEPRAC would simply have arrested us and confiscated the lot. So we took care to ensure that the collection remained secret, known to nobody except us, Kipps, and Flo.

We stood at the door, looking in. George indicated a row of dusty green glass bottles set out inside the chains. "These are what I found yesterday," he said. "Spirit bottles. Places to trap annoying or unwelcome ancestors. The old shaman would pop a Source inside—it was generally a bit of bone—seal it up, and—presto!—the ghost's contained. The interior's lined with iron, of course, to keep them from getting out."

Lockwood nodded. "Same sort of thing as the skull's jar, then?"

"Pretty much," George said, "only these are superior in a way, because you don't get the horrid visuals. You know, I'm beginning to think that *everything* your parents brought back has some kind of psychic significance, Lockwood. Even the stuff hanging up downstairs. They were very good researchers. I think I would have liked them."

"I'm sure you would have."

I was watching Lockwood's face. As always when his family was mentioned, he remained outwardly calm. But his eyes lost focus for a moment; he was staring out at nothing, or perhaps into the past.

Celia and Donald Lockwood had been researchers into the folklore of ghosts, and their specialty had been the beliefs of far-off countries. Not only had they traveled to exotic locales, they had also shipped home many items of interest in giant crates. Some of this material had ended up decorating the walls of 35 Portland Row, but much of it was still in boxes, having arrived in Britain after the Lockwoods' unexpected deaths.

When we had begun unpacking these boxes, we had at once unearthed two marvelous feathered cloaks, or spirit-capes, that had been worn by Indonesian shamans while conversing with their ancestors. Lockwood and I had discovered that the protective properties of these capes were not mere legend. They had shielded us when we walked the icy paths of the Other Side. Without them, we would certainly have died. One of these original capes was lost; the other remained with us, hidden in the storeroom in our basement, next to our supplies of Coke and beans and chips.

"The thing is," George went on, "half these bottles are cracked. We need to be *very* careful with them for obvious reasons." He glanced at Lockwood. "If you want, we could take them to the furnaces. Might be the safest thing to do."

"No . . ." Lockwood said. "They may come in handy. If they're kept inside the chains, they should be safe enough."

"Well, don't sneeze near them," George said. "That's my advice. When you take all these objects together, it's a cluster of spirits we've got right here. Imagine if they all got out."

"Yes, imagine . . ." Lockwood's glance lingered on his sister's death-glow, hovering above the bed as it had for so many years. Then he turned off the light and closed the door.

We didn't have any jobs scheduled for that evening. This was a good thing, as we needed to get ready for the La Belle Dame case the next day. During the afternoon Holly and I completed paperwork for our recent cases. Lockwood rang Mullet's and ordered more rapiers and chains. He seemed quieter and more subdued than usual; I thought our visit to Jessica's room had perhaps affected him. George was off at the Archives and didn't return. At dinnertime I fixed a hurried meal, reheating one of George's old stews from the freezer, and we ate it in the office.

I was tidying up in the kitchen when Lockwood peered around the door. George was still out and Holly had gone home. It was just Lockwood and me at Portland Row.

"I was just stepping out, Lucy. I wondered if you'd like to come along."

"On a case?"

"Of a kind."

"You want to go now?"

"If you're not doing anything important."

I so wasn't. In seconds I'd joined him at the door. "You want me to get my equipment bag?" I said. "I can run downstairs. . . ."

"It's okay. Your rapier should be fine. I'll take my secondhand one."

So it wasn't a tough ghost, then. We set off up Portland Row. "Are we going far?"

"No. Not far."

We walked east a couple of blocks in the gathering dusk, then turned north toward the Marylebone Road. I wondered if we were going to hail a cab at the depot there, but before we reached the intersection, Lockwood halted beside the rusted girdle of iron paneling that surrounded the Marylebone Cemetery.

"Here?" I said. It was a small abandoned cemetery, heavily salted, and well encased in iron.

"Yes."

"I hadn't heard about trouble here."

He smiled slightly. "If you put your boot in the ivy just beside you, you'll find a post you can stand on. Then you can grab hold of the top of the panels and swing yourself up. There's a brick wall behind the iron. Look, I'll show you."

In moments he was standing, crouched and catlike, just beyond the top of the paneling. "Think you can do that? If you reach out, I can help pull you over."

My only reply was a snort. And I may not have been quite as nimble, and my scrambling might have been accompanied by a *tad* more swearing, but I was soon beside him, ten feet above the sidewalk, looking down into the dark green amphitheater of the overgrown cemetery.

We were standing on top of the cemetery's original stone wall, concealed from outside by the iron panels. Away to our right burned the dull lights of the Marylebone Road. Below us, silence and shadow held sway. It was an old-style inner-city graveyard, where space had been at a premium. The headstones were set almost on top of each other, and were largely submerged beneath a thicket of brambles, with the tallest urns and angels cresting the foliage like boats on a turbulent green sea. Fingers of ivy clung to the inside of the boundary wall. Here and there, old yews emerged like melting candles, joined to the thicket below by strings of ivy and trailing vines. The ground was choked. The cemetery had evidently been abandoned for some time.

It was a melancholy patch of ground, not particularly threatening. Equally, it was not an easy place in which to swing a sword. "What kind of Visitor is it?" I asked.

A cool wind was coming along between the houses, and Lockwood's coat fluttered at his back as we stood together on the wall. He didn't seem to have heard me. "Getting down's easy enough," he said softly. "The wall's crumbling here. It's almost like a staircase, as long as you don't slip. Shall we go?"

"Lockwood," I asked, easing myself after him, "how do you know about all this?"

"I've been here before," he said. "And now," he added, as I landed in a strip of grass with waist-high brambles all around, "we take this little path." He pointed to what looked like an animal trail running off between the stones.

I let him lead the way, keeping my head low to avoid the thorns arching above. The track wound among the gravestones and soon opened out into a small cleared space where the foliage had been crushed underfoot and the ivy chopped back with a sword.

Two headstones stood in the center of the space. One of the last rays of sunlight was shining on them. They were made of gray stone: modern, sharp-edged, and unsullied by wind or rain. Neither was ornate, but the one on the left was larger. It was crowned by a carving of a beautiful, sad-faced woman in a hooded cape. On the plinth below, in strong clear letters, was written:

CELIA LOCKWOOD

DONALD LOCKWOOD

KNOWLEDGE SETS US FREE

The second stone was just a simple slab, inscribed with only two words:

JESSICA LOCKWOOD

I opened my mouth to say something, but nothing came out. My heart was too full, my head awhirl. I gazed at the stones.

"I sometimes ask myself what it's all about, Luce," Lockwood said. "Why we do what we do. When we have nights like last night, for instance—why we put ourselves through all that. Or when twerps like Tufnell come bleating and blustering at our door, and we have to sit there humoring him. When I get that kind of thought, I sometimes pop in here."

I looked at him. He stood beside me in the dusk, his face almost hidden behind the raised collar of his coat. I'd often wondered where they were, his family. But I'd never dared ask. And now he was sharing this most private of places with me. Amid my sorrow for him, I felt a kind of joy.

"This is what the Problem means," he went on. "This is the effect it has. Lives lost, loved ones taken before their time. And then we hide our dead behind iron walls and leave them to the thorns and ivy. We lose them twice over, Lucy. Death's not the worst of it. We turn our faces away."

On the far edge of the tiny clearing, an older headstone had toppled almost to the ground. Lockwood went over to it; he sat cross-legged on the stone, with brambles spun close around him. His dark clothes merged with the shadows; his smile floated palely in the half-light. "I usually perch on this," he said. "Belongs to someone named Derek Tompkins-Bond. He doesn't seem to mind me being here. At least, he's never showed up to tell me so." He patted the stone beside him. "Come and join me if you want. But watch out for that rail."

Sure enough, I'd almost tripped on a black metal rod, no higher than my ankle, that ran through the grass at my feet. I knew what it was: an edge used to mark the boundary of a plot. I hadn't noticed it before, but now I saw that the Lockwood headstones were set in their own railed-off family plot. And I noticed too that while Jessica's stone was set in the center of this space, and the parents' stone was to the left, there was an empty area on the right-hand side.

I looked at this bare patch of grass. And when I did so, everything faded out—the beating of my heart, the whispering of the wind as it worked its way through the holes and hollows of the ivy, the sound of distant Night Cabs on the Marylebone Road.

I gazed at it. At the unobtrusive patch of ground. At the empty, waiting grave.

It took me a moment to realize that Lockwood was still talking. "By the time my sister died they'd shut the cemetery for safety reasons," he said. "There was some controversy about putting her here. But when there are family plots, where it's the clear intention that people should be buried together, it's considered proper to honor the wishes of the dead."

We both knew why. Keep the dead happy. Don't give them a reason to come back.

I stepped over the rail, crossed the grass, and sat on the stone beside him.

"It's nice, don't you think," Lockwood said, "burying the family together? Anyway," he added, after a pause, "I don't want to be left out. I come here sometimes too."

I nodded. I was looking at the stamped, sliced foliage, chopped and broken and savagely hacked back. I found my voice at last. "Thanks for bringing me," I said.

"That's all right."

We sat in silence for a time, pressed close together on the stone. At last I was emboldened. "You never told me how it happened."

"My parents?" Lockwood paused for so long I thought he was going to refuse to talk about it, like always. But when he spoke, his voice was soft; it carried no barbs or warning signs. "Funnily enough," he said, "it wasn't far from here."

"What? In Marylebone?"

"On the Euston Road. You know where that underpass is? There."

I stared at him. "You never told me." The underpass was a short, ugly concrete tunnel where the Euston Road ducked underground to avoid intersecting with another important street. Night Cabs drove us through it all the time, Lockwood and me. He'd never given me the slightest inkling. "So it was a car accident?" I said.

He drew one knee up, clasped it with his hands. "Quite a

spectacular one. It was when I was very young. My mother and father were setting off to Manchester to give an important lecture. It was meant to be a summary of all their research trips, all their findings. But they never even reached the train station. In the underpass their cab was struck by a truck, which ignited, along with all the spilled fuel. It took almost an hour for the fire to be put out. It was so hot they had to repave a portion of the road."

"My God, Lockwood . . ." I reached out in the dark and touched his hand.

"It's all right. It was a long time ago. I barely remember them." He gave me a sidelong smile. "It's odd, but what saddens me most sometimes is that their lecture was lost, too. I would have liked to have read it. . . . Anyway, I remember looking down from your attic window that night, seeing armored vehicles blocking Portland Row, with all their lights flashing and agents standing around while the police spoke to Jessica and our nanny downstairs. They were Fittes agents, incidentally. I remember being fascinated by the color of their dark gray jackets."

A long pause. Dusk deepened around us. Leaves merged; our hands stayed together. I didn't say anything.

"So they told Jessica then," Lockwood went on. "But no one told *me* till the following morning—which was completely pointless, as I'd listened to it all from the top of the stairs. Pointless twice over, because I'd known about it hours before anyone, when I saw my parents' Shades watching me in the garden."

I wasn't surprised. He'd told me that once before. They were his first ghosts. "You knew they were dead?"

"Not exactly. Maybe deep down. Turns out I saw them at the

exact time of the accident. . . . Anyway, that's how *that* happened. My sister's story, you already know. And now there's just me." A sudden burst of energy seemed to pass through him, like a shudder or an electric charge. He sprang up, off the stone and away from me. "Well, there's no use talking about it," he said. "We should be getting back."

I drew in a long breath. In the same way that the graveyard was choked with the winding weeds and brambles, my head felt full now, choked with Lockwood's memories. It was no different than the sensations I got when I picked up psychic feedback through the power of Touch. They didn't *feel* like secondhand emotions. It was like I'd been there, like I'd experienced them myself. I got up slowly. "I'm so sorry, Lockwood," I said. "What an awful thing."

"It can't be helped." He frowned into the dark. His mood had altered, become suddenly brittle. He was impatient to be gone.

"I'm glad you brought me. I'm glad you told me everything, too."

He shrugged. "It's nice to share it with you, Luce. Though all it really does is show how arbitrary everything is. A ghost kills my sister. My parents die in an accident. Why did they die and not me? Believe me, I've looked for an answer, and there isn't one. There's no meaning to any of it." His face was shadowed; he turned away from me. "Well, none of us are here for very long. While we're alive, all we can do is keep on fighting. Try to make our contribution count. Speaking of which, we've a haunted theater to deal with tomorrow, and it's getting late. If you're ready, we should go."

"'While we're alive'?" I repeated.

But he was already setting off along the little track. His sword glimmered in the half-light, but his form was rapidly lost in the sur-rounding press of green. His voice called back with its old easy ring. "Are you coming, Luce?"

"Yes, of course I am!" But I was looking at the waiting grave.

Chapter 7

"*So, how's it going with Lockwood? Pretty well?*"

I was the first one down to the kitchen next morning. The ghost-jar had been on the table all the previous day, its lever shut, its plaintive pulsations ignored. I'd been too busy to humor it. Even so, I did feel slightly bad that I'd neglected it all that time. I flicked the lever in the top of the jar, took a mug from the cupboard, and put the kettle on. Slice it however you like, if you're going to have a haunted skull talking to you before breakfast, you need a cup of tea.

"Yeah," I said. "No different from normal."

I'd been thinking about Lockwood, about how he'd confided in me (which was good), and (less good) how the loss of his family drove him on. How he threw himself into the fight against the Problem with an almost hopeless fervor. I was wondering where this was likely to end. I hadn't slept so well.

"It's just I sense developments. I saw the pair of you slinking off alone last night."

"Spying on us again? You should get a different hobby." I tried to look stern, uninterested, and scathing all at once. "Anyway, what do I care? We were on a case."

The face nodded. "Oh, you were on a case?"

"That's right."

"Okay. I buy that." The skull looked placidly at me. "Let's talk about something else."

I hesitated, then cleared my throat. "Um, okay . . . Well—"

"If you're looking for a clean teaspoon, there's one by the sink."

"Thanks."

I opened the fridge to get some milk. As I closed the door, the face in the jar gave a sudden theatrical start that almost made me drop the bottle. The rubbery eyes looked wildly in all directions; the nostrils flared, the mouth contorted in alarm. "Ooh, I smell something burning. . . . Wait, wait, it's your pants! Your pants are on fire, you massive liar! You so weren't on a case!"

"We were too! We went to a graveyard, and—"

"A graveyard?" The ghost chuckled low and long. "Say no more! In my experience, graveyards can be used for lots of activities, not just ghost-hunting." It gave me a slow, atrocious wink.

"I don't know what you're talking about." But I could feel my cheeks flushing.

The evil face grinned knowingly. "There, I knew I was right. And don't try to tell me you were scrapping with ghosts. You didn't take any equipment."

"We had our rapiers!"

"I can tell when there's ectoplasm on a blade and when there isn't. No, you and Lockwood went for a cozy chat, didn't you? And came back with brambles in your hair."

I spoke as lightly as I could. "Well, it was very overgrown."

"I bet it was."

My snort of disdain was fierce enough to keep the skull quiet while I finished making my mug of tea. I threw the spoon in the sink and sat in the half-dark on the far side of the table, keeping clear of the jar's halo of green other-light. I glared intently at it, pondering my next move. How much to give, how much to seek. It was always a subtle and infuriating business, bargaining with a skull.

This main Talent of mine—psychic Listening—had long been considered the most imperfect of an agent's arts. Usually it was just about ominous sound effects: picking up the thud and drag of a body being hauled along a landing, for example, or hearing the scratches of broken fingernails along a cellar wall. Sometimes you got actual *words* spoken by a spirit, too, but these were always repetitive fragments, echoes of memory without true intelligence behind them. Or *almost* always. In her *Memoirs*, Marissa Fittes, the most famous Listener of all, had stated that other, more communicative Visitors *did* exist. She classified them as Type Three spirits, capable of full conversations. But they were very rare. So rare, in fact, that since her death (real or faked), no one else had come across any.

No one except me. I had the skull in the jar.

Though his mortal career was steeped in mystery, and though it refused to even divulge its name to me, one or two facts *were* known about this ghost. In the late nineteenth century, as a youth, he'd helped the occult doctor Edmund Bickerstaff create a bone glass, the first window onto the Other Side. Bickerstaff himself had been killed soon after the creation of the artifact, but the youth had escaped. His later activities were unknown. However, he had clearly come to a bad end, since his next recorded appearance, half a century later, was as a skull dredged up in the Lambeth sewers. The Fittes Agency, recognizing its potency as a Source, had trapped it in the jar, and the ghost had languished there ever since. Marissa Fittes had spoken with it, albeit briefly. After that no one had done so—until I came along.

I stared at the jar across the kitchen table. The spectral face stared back at me.

"We were going to talk about Marissa," I began.

"We were going to talk about my freedom."

I watched the steam rise from my mug, twisting, coiling like liberated ectoplasm. "Oh, you don't want that," I said. "What does freedom even mean? You'd still be tied to your moldy old skull, wouldn't you, even if you *did* escape the jar? Say I let you out. What would you do?"

"I'd flit about. Stretch my plasm. Might strangle Cubbins. Carry out a spot of casual ghost-touch, now and again. Just simple hobbies. It would be a darn sight more enjoyable than sitting here."

I grinned at it. "You make your case so well," I said. "See how I'm itching to break the jar. Even if I could trust you, which I clearly *can't*, you wouldn't want it anyway. Who would you talk to if you didn't have me?"

"I'd talk to you. I'd stick around, help you out from time to time."

"Oh, sure you would. While strangling my friends."

"I'd strangle your enemies, too. I'm not fussy. How's that for a tip-top deal?"

"Absolute rubbish," I said. "Tell you what: You want a deal? I'll make you an official one. You give me more information on Marissa Fittes, information that helps us get to the bottom of this whole mystery—and perhaps sheds light on the causes of the Problem—and I'll figure out some way to set you free. It'll be a way that doesn't involve George's untimely death, or anyone else's, but I'll see what I can do." I took a sip of tea.

The face looked unconvinced. *"No deaths? Doesn't sound like much fun. Anyway, we've gone over this ground before. What more can I possibly tell you?"*

"Ah!" Frustration bubbled up within me. I banged the mug down on the table, sloshing brown splashes onto the Thinking Cloth. "That's the whole point! You never tell me *anything*! Not really. About Marissa, about you and who you really are, about the nature of the Other Side . . . It's all insults, and no facts—that's the way it is with you!"

"When you're a ghost," the skull said blandly, *"you find that facts are overrated. You sort of leave them behind with your mortal body. It's nothing but emotions and desires with us spirits, as I'm sure you've seen. 'I've lost my gold!' 'I want revenge!' 'Bring me Marissa Fittes!' All that old hokum. Know what* my *desire is?"* It flashed a sudden grin at me.

"Something foul, no doubt."

"To live, Lucy. To live. That's why I talk to you. That's why I turned my back on what waits for us on the Other Side."

"So what *does* wait for us there?" I spoke lightly, but my hand gripped my mug a little harder. This was more like it; this was the kind of detail I was after.

As always, I was disappointed. *"How should I know?"*

"Well, you're dead. I should think that helps."

"Ooh, we are snarky today. You've been to the Other Side, too. What did you see?"

I'd seen an awful lot of darkness, and an awful lot of cold. A place that was a terrible and freezing echo of the living world. I'd thought about it often, lying in bed, dreaming the dreams that made me cry out and then lie awake till dawn.

"Hear any celestial trumpets, did you, while you were there?" the skull prompted.

I'd heard nothing. It had been a ferociously silent place.

"I was too busy trying to survive to take a proper survey," I said primly.

"Yeah, well, me too," the ghost said. *"That's my story too for the last one hundred and ten years. And if it wasn't for my cuddly Source here"*—with this it sort of surged back lovingly around the brown skull at the center of the jar, so that for a moment you could glimpse the face as it would have been in life, less rubbery, wrapped neatly around the bones—*"I'd have been a wanderer in the dark world like all the those other dumb idiots. Agh! No thanks! That's not for me. I keep myself turned toward the light, and it isn't easy, I can tell you, particularly when the living insist on asking stupid questions."*

"When you were at Fittes House long ago, what questions did Marissa ask you?" I said. My hopes weren't high, but it seemed like a decent moment to move in.

Dim lights flared in the ghost's eyes. *"It was so many years back. . . . Similar ones to yours, I think. About the Other Side, about the nature of spirits—what we do and why . . . Also, she was very interested in ectoplasm."*

"Ectoplasm? Why?"

"It's fascinating stuff." The face distorted, reversing into itself so that the nose and brow ridges were pointing backward into the jar. *"It listens, it communicates, you can mold it into funny and obscene shapes. How'd you think I spent the last fifty years? Want me to show you some of my favorites? I call this one the 'Happy Farmhand.'"*

"No, thank you. And I certainly don't see why Marissa would be interested in *that*."

"She wasn't, to be fair. Cheeky origami wasn't her thing. But you have to understand: plasm represents the part of you that survives— that passes from one side to the other. You can call it your essence, your life force, whatever you want. It doesn't decay. It doesn't die. It doesn't really change. That's how I know Penelope Fittes is actually Marissa." The face pressed close to the glass. *"Because their essence is exactly the same."*

"Even though they look so different?" It was one of the things that had puzzled us about the skull's claims. Penelope Fittes was glossy and glamorous, a raven-haired woman in her thirties; Marissa, in later years at least, had been a gaunt and shriveled creature, prey to the frailties of age.

"Looks?" the skull said. *"Who cares about that? It's superficial. Outward appearance doesn't interest me at all. Why do you think I hang around with you?"* It chuckled. *"Insult aside, that's just one way in which I'm superior to every one of you, except for Cubbins."*

I blinked. "What? Why? What's George got to do with anything?"

"What a person looks like doesn't bother him much, or hadn't you noticed?"

There was a scrabbling at the door. I turned in my chair to find George himself tottering into the kitchen in the first throes of wakefulness. He switched on the light, scratching industriously at a crevice in his pajamas. "What's that skull saying? Something about me?"

"Never mind. It's not important." I turned the lever on the jar. "You want tea? How did you get on yesterday?"

"At the Archives? Oh, I found plenty. I'll tell you more soon. Can't think straight before I've had my breakfast."

"Nor me." Especially not today. My head was spinning from the ghost's conversation, and it wasn't yet seven in the morning.

Lockwood came down later than usual, long after Holly had arrived and the day's work had begun. He seemed in good spirits; we smiled at each other but didn't refer to our expedition to the cemetery. We turned our attention to the business of the day.

We had agreed to arrive at Mr. Tufnell's establishment at five o'clock that evening, when there was still an hour or two of daylight left, and we could properly look over the Palace Theater and the surrounding fair. Before that happened, Lockwood had a new rapier and other supplies to pick up from Mullet's store on Bond Street. A delivery of fresh iron was expected, too, and Holly and I had a batch of DEPRAC paperwork to get through. We were also keen to try out some new techniques in the rapier practice room. In short, there was plenty to be done, but—as always before a major new case—George's briefing came first. We gathered in the basement office to hear him.

"Just a quick one first about the whole Marissa thing," George said. He had a pile of notebooks that he'd taken from his battered leather case. "As you know, I've been looking into the beginnings of the Problem, and the way in which Fittes and Rotwell started out. Yesterday I had to stop in the Hardimann Research Library to follow up a lead, and it might be something tasty. I'll fill you in when I learn more."

"Isn't the Hardimann out-of-bounds?" Holly asked. As part of DEPRAC's new edicts, certain occult libraries had restrictions on them. Officially this was to prevent the spread of dangerous ghost-cults among the public; we guessed it was also to discourage curious researchers like George.

"Strictly speaking," he said, "I shouldn't go there without a permit, but the curator's a friend of mine. It's not a big deal. Anyway, more about that later. I was mostly in the Archives, looking into the history of the Palace Theater. And I had some success there, too, as you'll see. . . ."

George sat back in his chair; he spread his notebooks out in front of him and unfolded a yellowed theatrical handbill, similar to the one Tufnell had given us. It showed the same blond woman in another chilly-looking pose, this time with the words *The Hangman's Daughter* written alongside. The *D* was formed of an ominous-looking noose.

Lockwood tilted the flyer approvingly. "Aha, so you found out something more about our glamorous ghost, La Belle Dame?"

"Her real name would be a good start," I said.

"We've got it here." Lockwood pointed to a corner of the hand-bill. "See? 'Featuring our sinister star, Marianne de Sèvres.' Classy. She must've come straight from Paris."

"Or not," George scratched his ear. "Turns out Marianne de Sèvres was only her stage name. Her real name was Doris Blower. She was first heard of at an end-of-the-pier show in Eastbourne a hundred years ago. Within five years she was packing the seats at the Palace Theater in Stratford. Tufnell was right: she was a big star of her day, and it was all based on a certain kind of act—one that combined glamour, sensation, and the threat of violent death." He looked at us meaningfully. "That pretty much summed up her offstage life, too."

"Mr. Tufnell said she was a cruel and wicked woman," Holly said, "who wrapped men round her little finger. Or that was the implication."

"It's pretty much accurate," George said. "The popular papers of the day were full of stories about the rich married men who'd fallen for her, and all the wives she'd wronged—they even attacked her in the street. She never stayed with her lovers for long, and discarded them like candy wrappers. It's rumored that more than one man killed himself over her. When she heard about it, La Belle Dame laughed and said it was life imitating art. All her shows involved that kind of story, too."

"Charming woman," I said.

"And now a charming ghost." George consulted his notes. "Well, it's not surprising she's shown up at the Palace Theater, because that was her base for years. She performed many illusions there, all of which were set up as little dramas or playlets. Each one ended with a staged death that was acted out with the utmost precision. The one she actually *died* in, *The Sultan's Revenge*, was a story about a faithless queen who did all sorts of naughty things behind her husband's back. When the king found out, he had her sealed in a massive coffin and run through with fifty swords." George pushed his glasses up his nose. "Guess that's entertainment for you."

Holly gave a snort of disgust. "What a foul story. Who'd want to see that?"

"Lots of people. It was the sensation of the age. Another of her hits was *The Captive Mermaid*. They built a great glass tank onstage, and filled it with water. La Belle Dame went splashing around with a fish tail; she played an innocent mermaid who was caught by a jealous rival and horribly mistreated. At the end she was tied to lots of weights and—"

"Pardoned, I hope," Holly said tartly.

"I'm going to guess *thrown back into the tank to drown*," I said.

"Points go to Lucy there," George said. "Yes, it was a famous illusion. She thrashes around at the bottom of the vat for ages, goes limp, and finally a black curtain is drawn around, concealing her from view. Then—presto!—the mermaid reappears from offstage, alive and kicking. Well, not exactly *kicking*. She's got a tail."

"And people went to that?" Holly folded her arms. "It doesn't even make sense. A mermaid can't drown."

"It was very good show business. It's said that everyone came—the men to adore her, the women to cheer on the hangman, the drowning pool, the executioner's knife." George sat back with an air of finality. "How much more do you want? There was the celebrated routine called *The Hangman's Daughter*, about—"

I held up a hand. "Don't tell me. About a beautiful girl who hanged herself for love?"

"Hey," George said. "Got it in one. You *are* good."

Holly scowled. "Did any of these women in her shows get to live at all?"

"Not so you'd notice. They were mostly drowned, stabbed, poisoned, or thrown from a height. The point is, they all *seemed* to die—then La Belle Dame would spring back onstage, alive and well, and take the wild applause of the crowd." George blinked at us doubtfully. "So I suppose, in a sense, they all lived in the end."

Holly snorted. "Not in my book, they didn't. What an appalling creature."

"And now," Lockwood said, "she's come back as a malignant ghost with vampiric tendencies. We'll have to tread carefully tonight."

"Yes, I've been thinking about that," I said. "I reckon you should let Holly and me tackle this one."

Lockwood gazed at us. "Alone? While George and I twiddle our thumbs at home?"

"Why not?"

"Not a chance. It's far too dangerous."

"I agree with Lucy here," Holly said. "Clearly La Belle Dame has particular power over addled young men. Lucy and I would be far less vulnerable than you."

"Oh, I don't think that's true. George and I have dealt with attractive female ghosts before. . . ." Lockwood chuckled fondly. "Remember the Hoxton Bathhouse, George?"

George took off his glasses and inspected them. "Do I? You bet."

"Besides, there's no mystery about the two victims so far," Lockwood went on. "Both Charley Budd and Sid Morrison displayed classic patterns of psychic vulnerability."

"That's right," George said. "Didn't you notice? According to Tufnell, the kid who died was totally lovelorn, practically starving himself through romantic misery. If a barrel in a dress had rolled past him, he'd have gone scampering after it. As for Charley Budd, he was sickly. It may be that he subconsciously wanted release— that's why he followed the ghost. In other words, neither of the victims was physically or mentally strong."

"I don't get it," Holly said. "You mean the ghost could sense their weaknesses?"

George nodded. "Exactly. We all know Visitors sense anger and sorrow. They're attracted to people who give off strong emotions. Perhaps they're also drawn to weakness and despair. These two were enfeebled in different ways. . . . They both had weak connections to life. Each was clearly vulnerable to some cut-price supernatural glamour."

"Which we aren't," Lockwood added. "End of story. George and I will be fine. Won't we, George?"

"Yep, we're cold-eyed professionals," George said. "Can I have that handbill back, Lucy? I want to stick it in my casebook as a fold-out spread. Thanks, that's fine."

With that the meeting broke up. Lockwood went off to Mullet's;

the rest of us did paperwork. Then Holly and I practiced with our rapiers until we were hot and thirsty and the straw dummies hanging in the basement were full of holes. Motes of straw floated in the air. Outside Portland Row the afternoon drew on. Somewhere in London a chained boy impatiently awaited death. The first stars showed in the sky.

Chapter 8

To get to the Palace Theater, Stratford, in the East End of the city, we had to take the underground trains, which ran until almost nightfall. Shortly before four, George, Holly and I put on our work belts and snapped our rapiers into position. We locked up Portland Row and walked to Baker Street Station, carrying our bags of iron. The ghost-jar, sealed and silent, was in my backpack. Lockwood was still at Mullet's, and would travel separately. We would meet him at the theater door.

It had been a pleasant early autumn day, heavy with warmth that piggybacked on six weeks of hard, hot weather. The streets were still busy, but with that faint electric charge that always builds up as dusk approaches. The people moved ever more quickly, their faces set, intent on getting home before the hours of the dead began. The sun was low now. Slanting rays sliced the houses into triangular slabs of light and shadow.

As we neared the Marylebone Road, we passed a darkened alley. From among the garbage bags piled in its mouth rose a misshapen figure; it lurched toward us, arms out, rags fluttering, carrying with it the smell of waste pipes and carrion.

Holly jumped; I reached automatically for my rapier.

"Hello, Flo," said George.

Although it wasn't instantly apparent to the casual observer, the shape was female and possibly not much older than me. She had a roundish, mud-flecked face from which piercing blue eyes blinked shrewdly. Her hair, lank, dirty, and yellow, was scarcely distinguishable from the ragged edges of her wide straw hat. She wore rubber boots and a long blue puffer jacket that never came off, whatever the weather. What might lie beneath it was the stuff of whispered legend.

This was Ms. Florence Bonnard, aka the notorious relic-woman Flo Bones. Relic-men and -women were professional scavengers, many armed with decent psychic abilities, who loitered around cemeteries, junkyards, and other places on the margins of society, looking for Sources that had been overlooked by normal agents. They then sold these—to ghost-cults, to black market collectors, even to DEPRAC itself; basically to whoever offered the best price. Flo's patch consisted of the murky banks of the Thames, and these she roamed with a sinister burlap bag that contained God-knew-what damp horrors. She liked licorice, George, and Lockwood, in a somewhat unclear order, and just about tolerated me. Along with Kipps, she was an important, if unofficial, associate of Lockwood & Co.

"All right, Cubbins," Flo said. She grinned at George, showing exceptionally bright white teeth, and—as a reluctant afterthought—nodded curtly at Holly and me.

"Haven't seen you at our place for a bit," George said. "Been busy?"

Flo's shrug cracked the dried mud on the shoulders of her coat. "Nah. Not really."

There was a moment of silence, in which it became clear that Flo was focused intently on George, and that George was watching her expectantly. Holly and I looked from one to the other and back again.

"Well, so I got it, then," Flo said. She scrabbled in the shadows of her puffer jacket and brought out an oilcloth package, tied up with grubby string.

"Brilliant. Thanks, Flo." George unzipped his coat and tucked the package inside.

"'S all right." Flo rubbed at the side of her nose. "So you're good, are you, George?"

"Yes, fine . . . What about you, Flo?"

"Fine."

"Great."

"Yeah."

How long this breathtaking dialogue would have continued is uncertain. At that moment there was movement on the sidewalk a little farther on. Flo glanced behind her. "Oh, hell," she spat. "Not *them*." With that she ducked away and was gone into the alley; the sound of running Wellingtons faded in the gloom.

Four men had come out of a side road and were looking in our direction. At a signal from the slimmest, they sauntered over. We drew ourselves up. We knew who they were.

The leader was a young man with short fair hair and a mustache. He wore a greenish tweed suit, and moved with fluid ease. Even at a distance, the eye was drawn to him; close proximity made for warier fascination, as one might regard a wolverine slinking nearer through a wood. There was an aggressive jauntiness in his manner; a certainty of violence—not now, necessarily, but soon. The mark of that hung at his belt. Swords were forbidden to anyone who was not an accredited operative. Sir Rupert Gale was officially with no agency at all, but as Penelope Fittes's feared enforcer, he didn't see the need for rules. He carried a rapier anyway, glinting in the sun.

The three men with him wore the dark gray jackets of the Fittes Agency. They were big, muscled, and impassive. At some point they had traded in their personalities for a simple air of threat.

As always, Sir Rupert was smiling. He had a lot of teeth. The sharp tang of his aftershave enveloped us. "It's Lockwood's charming little helpers," he said, "out on an evening job. But what was that foul creature with you?" He glanced down the alley. "A beggar, I suppose? You didn't *know* it, did you?"

"No," I said. "A beggar, as you say."

"I can still smell its stench. If it was pestering you, you should have kicked it, sent it packing. The only mercy is that it won't survive long out on the streets, the way the Problem's going. One of these mornings we'll find it in the gutter, staring at the sky." He was gauging our reaction, watching us closely with his poacher's gaze. None of us said anything. "So where's your precious Lockwood?" he went on. "I hope *he's* not dead. Don't tell me he's gone the way of his accident-prone family."

All day I'd been thinking of that empty grave in the cemetery, of Lockwood's brief stillness as he sat with me on the stone, of the grief that haunted him worse than any ghost. Rage rose up within me. My hand hovered at my sword hilt. I couldn't trust myself to speak. George was likewise bristling; I could feel insults incubating furiously behind his glittering glasses. But Holly was good in these situations. She remained impeccably polite. Her smooth, unflustered beauty seemed to have been turned up a notch. As she gazed from under half-lowered lids, her cool demeanor subtly radiated boredom and contempt. By contrast, Sir Rupert's expensive tweed suit suddenly appeared loud and shabby; behind his yellow mustache, his face was florid, sweaty, and much too eager.

"He's off tackling a Specter at a theater in Stratford," Holly said. "We're going to meet him now. Thank you so much for taking an interest in our work."

"Hmm, a Specter? You really need four agents for that?" Beneath his mustache, Sir Rupert sucked at his teeth. "Do you have the relevant papers?"

Holly nodded. "Yes." She made no move to get them out.

"Could you show them to me?"

"I could. It would certainly be possible."

Sir Rupert's lips twisted slightly. "Then please do so."

"Or you could just take our word for it, Gale," George said, as Holly slowly opened her bag. "But probably that's a concept you wouldn't know much about."

"You know the new rules, Cubbins." Sir Rupert took the papers and turned them over in gloved hands. "Agents must have their client agreements when out on a job. There've been far too many unregulated agencies running about, endangering the decent people of London. It's been anarchy. Not a week goes by without rapier cuts and salt burns being reported. As for the damage Greek Fire can do . . ."

"Don't look at us," George said. "We haven't burned anyone's house down for ages."

"Once a plump, bespectacled pyromaniac," Sir Rupert said, "always a plump, bespectacled pyromaniac—that's my philosophy. Well, I suppose these seem to be in order." He handed the papers back to Holly. "Good luck with your very dangerous mission. Oh, and one more thing," he added as we moved to go. "You were seen near the Hardimann Library yesterday, Cubbins. Not trying to do a spot of illicit research, were you?"

"Me? No."

"Because you haven't got the relevant permit. Has he, Grieves?"

The officer to his left was particularly large. If you hung a uniform on a section of concrete pipe leaning against an outhouse wall the result would have possessed more intellectual zip. "No, sir."

"Even Grieves knows," Sir Rupert said, "and he scarcely recognizes his own name."

"I did pop in," George said, "while researching this Stratford case we're on tonight, but I was turned away, because—as you rightly said—I don't have the correct permit. Now, though," he went on, "I'm carrying lots of heavy chains, and I'd appreciate getting them to the theater, rather than being held up talking to flea-bitten schemers like you."

There was a slight pause in which the hidden mechanics of the afternoon moved slowly, silently toward disaster. "Schemer?" Sir Rupert Gale said. He stepped closer. "Flea-bitten? Maybe I'm getting deaf in my old age, but—"

"Holly," I said brightly, "wasn't our appointment in Stratford for five p.m. exactly? We should be going."

Holly had the jolly tones of a mother who had just discovered her toddler eating cat food on the floor of a friend's kitchen. "Yes! Quite! Come along, George!"

George seemed reluctant to move.

"Did you want to expand on your statement?" Rupert Gale said.

"I could," George said, "but why expend the energy? We all know what you are. You know it yourself." He took off his spectacles and rubbed them on his sweater. "Behind all the flounce and swagger, your moral shabbiness fascinates and appalls you. You can't take your eyes off it. Which is why you're so crashingly dull. Oh, and I know the DEPRAC rules as well as you, and if you pick fights with accredited agents off on their appointed tasks, Barnes will have your tweedy backside hauled over hot cobblestones to Scotland Yard. So why not go off and hassle someone else?" He held his glasses up toward the sun and tilted them, checking that any conceivable smudge had been removed. "Good. Sometimes I see so clearly, it almost frightens me." He put them back on and bent to his bag. "Lead on, Holly. Stratford, here we come."

We walked away. The skin on the back of my neck prickled as we went; that was probably Sir Rupert's gaze brushing against it. I kept expecting him to call out after us to stop, but the order never came.

None of us spoke for a full two blocks. Holly and I walked casually enough, rapiers swinging, but we moved to either side of George, like warders leading a condemned prisoner to a cell. We crossed a silent square, where fallen leaves lay on the paths. When we were in the open, where no one could spy on us, we stopped.

"What do you think you were *doing*?" Holly hissed. "Do you *want* us to be arrested?"

"Do you *want* us to be beaten senseless?"

George shrugged. "He didn't arrest us. He didn't beat us."

"No thanks to you!" I snarled. "He's only looking for the slightest excuse."

"Right, and we didn't give him one," George said. "What we *did* do was warn him off, which was something that needed to be done. I'm just alerting him that if he messes with us, he won't have it all his own way." He looked at us as if that settled the matter. "Besides, did you hear how he spoke about Flo? That's not right. Listen, we're running late. If we hurry, we can just catch the train."

Tufnell's Traveling Fairground was a short walk east of Stratford Station. Five minutes before we got there, we could hear faint hurdy-gurdy music and smell hot dogs on the wind.

Perhaps, as Mr. Tufnell had asserted, his business *was* doing well. But in the late afternoon, with the shadows lengthening, it didn't radiate prosperity. The Palace Theater itself was a hulking construction, standing alone on the edge of a stretch of waste ground. At one time it must have been impressive; it had a columned front, reminiscent of a Roman temple, with carved figures above the pillars depicting tragic and comic scenes. But the concrete in the columns was cracked and broken, and half the carvings were gone. The main doors were boarded up. Entry to the building appeared to be from the field alongside, where many tents of faded colors had been erected, their canvas snapping in the wind. A makeshift iron fence, in which snack food wrappers fluttered like trapped insects, surrounded the compound. A siren played a cheesy melody; this was the cue for closure of the fair. The last few sad-faced customers, bearing draggled sticks of cotton candy, were shuffling homeward through the rusty gates.

Lockwood was standing just inside the gates, with Quill Kipps beside him.

"Isn't it fabulous?" Kipps said, as we joined them. "I've seen internment camps that look jollier than this."

"Didn't know you were with us on this one, Quill," I said.

"Nor did I. Bumped into Lockwood at Mullet's. He said you might need help, and I didn't have anything particular to do, so . . ."

I nodded, smiling. "Sure."

Circumstances hadn't been kind to Kipps, who had been ostracized by some of his former Fittes colleagues for helping us out once too often. This, combined with his naturally downbeat temperament, meant that a thin vein of resentment still ran through him, like a layer of bitter chocolate in one of George's raspberry cakes. In addition, he had lost his Talents as he crossed into his early twenties. Despite the pair of goggles we'd given him, which allowed him to see ghosts, he knew the deprivations of age. These experiences had mellowed, even humbled him. Which, given that he was still as abrasive as a pair of steel-wool underpants, showed how insufferable he'd once been.

"Isn't it good that Quill was free tonight?" Lockwood said. "It's the more the merrier on this one." As so often at the start of a job, he was in excellent spirits. The hunt was up and his sense of purpose was at its sharpest, keen as the new rapier hanging at his side. The quiet, reflective boy who'd opened up to me the evening before was nowhere to be seen. He radiated energy and anticipation. "Let's get over to the theater," he said. "We'll ask someone to show us around."

We passed striped tents and a carousel, and crossed into the shadow of the building. Posters and banners festooned its massive brick-lined wall, advertising TUFNELL'S MARVELS, TUFNELL'S MAGIC SHOW FOR CHILDREN YOUNG AND OLD, and similar entertainments. A pair of double doors hung open. A sour-faced girl in an usherette's uniform was just in the process of shutting one of them, applying iron bolts and chains.

The girl regarded us. "Show's over for the day. I can give you tickets for tomorrow."

"We're not here to see the show," Lockwood said. "Is Lew Tufnell available, please?"

He'd given her his best smile, which normally had the melting effect of hot water poured on ice. But the girl's expression did not change. "He's up onstage." She hesitated, hands toying with the iron bolt. "It's not a good time. You shouldn't go in."

"I'm sure he's very busy. But he *is* expecting us."

"I'm not talking about him. It's not a good time to be here, this time of day. *She'll* be walking the corridors soon."

"You mean La Belle Dame?" I asked. "Have *you* seen her?"

The girl shivered, glanced over her shoulder. Before she could answer, a familiar voice hailed us from the dark. Mr. Tufnell appeared, checked shirtsleeves rolled up, vest bulging. "Come in, come in!" His face was redder than ever, his gray curls pearled with sweat. He flashed us his weak, dishonest smile. "I'm just helping the stagehands. We're short-staffed now, what with Sid and Charley. Look alive there, Tracey! Don't block the door, girl! Let them by, let them by!"

We filed through into a makeshift foyer smelling of popcorn, cigarettes, and mildew. There was a ticket booth, and a stand selling chocolate bars and cans of drink. The girl had stepped aside to let us pass. She was a slight, pale-skinned thing with reddish hair, perhaps a year older than me, and she looked very tightly wound. I tried to catch her eye, but she didn't look at us and quickly slipped out into the field, leaving the door ajar.

Mr. Tufnell bobbed and bowed and shook Lockwood by the hand. "Honored that you're here! Come along, I'll show you the stage. We're readying it for tomorrow."

He led us along a broad passage, low-ceilinged and dimly lit, with cheap gold tracery decorating the walls. Other passages led off on both sides. One, labeled TUFNELL'S MARVELS, was cordoned off by a frayed gold rope.

"How's poor Charley Budd?" Holly asked as we went.

"Alive," Mr. Tufnell said, "but not, I fear, long for this world. I've got him locked in my caravan. He started screaming this afternoon, disrupting Coco the Clown's toddler party in the main tent. I'm sorry to say it meant more refunds." The impresario gave a mordant sigh. "In fact, I'll need to see to Charley shortly. I'm assuming you won't mind if, once it gets dark, I don't remain inside? I'd like to, of course, but I'd only get in your way." With this, he pushed open an impressive pair of doors lined with scarlet plush, and we walked through into the auditorium.

As a general rule, Lockwood & Co. didn't hang out in theaters much. True, back in the summer we'd once chased a Specter up an alley next to the London Palladium and blasted it to atoms with a flare. As far as I knew, the theater wall still had the outline of a startled gentleman in a top hat smudged across it in soot. This was as close to high culture as we typically got, so I wasn't prepared for what we saw inside.

The auditorium of the Palace Theater was a world away from its dismal exterior. It was a cavern of gold, twinkling with points of light. We stood in the deepest velvet black, down among the stalls. Above and behind us, electric candles shone along curved balconies, ranged with incredible steepness to impossible heights. To the sides, golden candelabras picked out the ranks of individual boxes. Ahead, rising above the central aisle, the stage was white and spotlighted, flanked by bloodred curtains. A few youths were moving here, sweeping the boards, shifting brightly colored cubes and baskets around. They worked in silence, but I could hear their hurried breathing. The acoustics were excellent—even whispered words carried across the vast dark space.

Tufnell led us down the aisle, our boots pattering on the wooden floor. High above, several long ropes hung from the dark, some ending in trapeze bars, others tied to rings fixed into the balconies. I imagined them in motion, with hurtling bodies in temporary flight.

The idea made my palms sweat. It was hard to get over the scale of the place. You couldn't pick out the details of the balconies without squinting. The ceiling was lost in the warm golden haze.

We climbed steep steps at the side of the stage, and walked out into the light.

"This is it, Mr. Lockwood," Tufnell said. "This is where La Belle Dame met her end." He waved his arm at the youths, who had stopped work and were watching him. "All right, you lot can go. Straight outside, no dallying. You know the reason why."

The stagehands trooped away. We dumped our bags in the center of the stage. Arranged at the edges were wooden cubes of varying sizes and colors, with hinged lids and little doors. At the back lay an enormous blue crash pad, knee-high and very broad. Otherwise the surface of the stage was bare, marked by the tape and scuffs of decades.

Lockwood was gazing around him, eyes narrowed, face calm. I knew he was using his Sight now, hunting for death-glows or other signs of psychic disturbance. "What's the crash pad for?" he asked. "And these boxes? Part of the show?"

Tufnell nodded. "We start with the trapeze act. The acrobats do their thing, then swoop down on the mat. The boxes are for the magic show. The props are in there—you know, caged doves, metal hoops, that stuff. Lots of hidden cubbyholes. Our stage manager designed them. She's very good. But you'll be wanting to see where Sid died. It's stage left, in the wings."

"Thank you," Lockwood said. "We'll start there."

The others moved away toward the curtains. I remained in the center of the stage, taking the measure of the place. Once, long ago, the sultan's casket had sat here, pierced by swords, blood pouring out onto the boards. I looked at my feet, and the bland, smooth wood. I gazed into the golden dusk, imagining the packed house, the stunned silence, the first appalling screams. . . .

No time like the present. I could use my Talents here. There was a strange expectancy in the silence of the great, dark auditorium. I crouched, put my fingertips to the floor. I closed my eyes and Listened. . . .

As if I'd opened a sealed door, I was at once surrounded by a strange, papery rustling, the murmur of an audience making itself comfortable in a thousand seats. The noise rose and fell like the breathing of a giant. I waited, but it did not change.

I took my fingers away from the wood. The noise was still there. Muffled underneath it, I could just make out Tufnell's voice as he spoke to Lockwood in the wings. The two sounds did not collide, but ran through each other, being separated by a century of time.

I stood slowly, turning toward the wings. At that moment a chill moved along my spine, as if someone had run a finger down it.

I stopped, and peered out into the wider dark. What with the stage lights and the auditorium's soft haze, it was difficult to make out anything clearly. Nevertheless, my gaze moved toward a seat at the back of the stalls.

Was that a person sitting there?

My eyes hurt with straining. I glanced aside to see if any of the others had noticed anything. But they were out of sight.

"Then Tracey pushed the curtains aside," Tufnell was saying, "and saw Sid here, locked in the ghost's embrace! She ran forward . . ."

I looked out across the stalls again. The seat at the back was empty.

". . . but alas, too late. He lay like a rag doll! La Belle Dame had drained him of his life!"

I pulled my rapier clear of its Velcro clasp.

The murmur in my head grew loud, turned to sudden wild applause. It came from all around me, starting in the stalls, then rippling in a wave across the balconies and boxes. I looked up, scanning the hazy reaches.

At once the sound cut out.

And now: nothing. It was as if the theater held its breath.

When I looked down again, there was an object in the central aisle, directly opposite from me. It stood far back under the shadows of the balcony. Darkness enfolded it, but I could see that it was a sarcophagus or casket, very large and rounded, and shaped rather like a woman. It was upright, and its sides and belly bristled with innumerable humps and spikes. They were the hilts and blades of embedded swords.

Something was slowly extending from the casket. A dark, thin line; a thread of black that ran out along the aisle. Another followed it, and then another. They unspooled into the light, trickling down the gentle slope toward the stage.

I gripped my sword and stepped slowly forward.

The threads glistened and shone darkly under the gold lights. They linked and separated, lacing the ground. Longer and longer they grew; faster and faster they came. There was no end to them. I found myself frozen on the lip of the stage. I couldn't take my eyes off the rivulets of blood that ran between the stalls.

Chapter 9

"She's here!" My shout echoed out across the theater. "Lockwood! She's here!"

With that, I leaped off the stage, out over the pooling blood, my sword flashing under the lights. I landed heavily on a seat in the front row. Then I was up and jumping from backrest to backrest, arms outstretched to keep my balance, chair-hopping my way up across the rows. There was no way I was going to touch the floor. On the aisle to my side, the dark liquid flowed past like there would be no end to it. Ahead, darkness billowed. I could no longer see the casket, but cold beat against my face.

There in the shadows! A woman's form, striding toward me.

With a savage cry, I took a final leap, swinging my rapier around—

"Are you quite mad?" A tall girl came out into the light. She wore jeans, sneakers, and a bright blue hoodie, and there was a smaller girl behind her. That was about all I took in as I changed direction, dropped my sword, and landed inelegantly beside them in the aisle. Which was now entirely empty of blood. Cigarette butts, yes; gum wrappers and popcorn—but the rivulets of red were gone.

I stood up slowly, breathing hard. I recognized the second girl. It was Tracey, the usherette we'd met at the entrance. I didn't know her companion. The aisle behind them was empty as far as the exit. It wasn't that cold now, either. The Visitation was over.

With a clatter of boots, the others joined us, Lockwood at their head. He put a hand on my arm. "Lucy—"

"She was here," I said. "I saw the casket. Did none of you see the blood?"

Kipps picked up my sword and handed it to me, hilt first. "We saw *you*, playing hopscotch on the chairs."

"But La Belle Dame—" I glared at the newcomers. "Were either of you sitting in the back just now?"

Tracey shook her head. The tall girl regarded me coolly. "Not me. I just came in."

"And you saw nothing odd here, in the aisle?"

"Just you."

She was a tall young woman, broad of shoulder and square of chin. Her blond hair was tied back in a rough braid. She was very large and angry and real.

"The ghost was here," I said again. "I acted on it. That's what I do."

"No one's doubting you, Lucy," Lockwood said. He flashed his smile at the two girls. "You're Tracey, aren't you? Nice to see you again. And you . . . ?"

Mr. Tufnell had been slowest to make it from the stage. The effort had left him gasping. "This good lady," he wheezed, "who your friend almost decapitated, is Sarah Parkins, our stage manager. She's the one who saved Charley Budd the other day."

I scowled at her. "Pleased to meet you."

"Charmed." She curled her lip at me. "I came in to tell you, Mr. Tufnell, that Charley Budd's started howling again. He's upsetting everyone. You're going to have to come out, try to soothe him."

The theater owner was dabbing at his curls with a vast lacy hand-kerchief. "Bless me, if I live another night, it'll be a miracle. Yes, yes, I'll be out directly. Mr. Lockwood, I must leave you to your work. Tracey, you stupid girl, I don't know what you're doing back in here hanging on Sarah's skirts. Don't you have chores to do outside?"

The girl had flinched at his words; she spoke sullenly. "I was frightened out there, what with the screaming. Sarah said I could come in—"

"Against my express instructions! Do it again, you'll feel the back of my hand."

"Actually," Lockwood said smoothly, "I'm glad they're both here. I was hoping to ask them some questions. They've each seen La Belle Dame; they're both witnesses to the ghost." He gave the girls the full warmth of his attention. "Is there anything you can tell us about this Visitor? Where you saw it? The way it made you feel? Anything might be useful, no matter how small."

"I gave you the relevant details," Tufnell said. He was looking at his watch.

"Tracey?" Lockwood went on. "You saw it most clearly, I believe. On the stage—and in the wings. You saw it with poor Sid Morrison."

The girl's face was gray and haggard. "Yes."

"The Specter was beautiful, I understand?"

"Not to me." She looked away. "But I think Sid found her so. She was up on the stage there, wrapped in a golden light."

"Perhaps the stage *is* the Source," Holly said. "That's where the woman died."

Sarah Parkins, the stage manager, shook her head. "I don't think it can be. It's not the original stage. The bloodstained boards were ripped out and burned, right after La Belle Dame's death. Same with the actual sultan's casket. You can read all about it in books on theater history."

"Ah, she's a clever girl, our Sarah is," Mr. Tufnell said. "And committed to Tufnell's, despite our troubles. Though I maybe shouldn't mention it, she was fond of poor Sid in particular. I'm much obliged to her for carrying on in such tragic circumstances. Ain't I, Sarah? But now we really should go."

"All right," Lockwood said. "If there's nothing more—"

"It's not the stage you should be looking at," Sarah Parkins said, as they turned to leave. "I saw the ghost in the dressing room corridor. Girls saw it on the balcony, and down in the basement. . . ." She waved her arm up toward the dim, silent reaches of the auditorium. "Be careful. You never know where it might show up next."

No sooner were we alone than we set off on a careful inspection of the haunted building. We immediately discovered that the Palace Theater was a complex and sprawling structure. It had three distinct areas, connected by a variety of stairs and passages; and each gave us some cause for psychic concern.

At the heart of the theater was the auditorium itself, with no fewer than three levels of seating—the stalls on the ground floor; the first-floor balcony, or lower circle; and the steeply inclined upper circle near the roof. We took a number of psychic readings on every floor, and detected traces of supernatural activity: fleeting chills, subtle miasmas, a pervading sense of unease that came and went almost at random.

The second area was the "front of house." This included the lobby on the ground floor, and two other public spaces directly above, from which the circle seats were reached. There were two staircases, each lined with faded plush carpets, muffling all sounds. One of these seemed colder than the other, for no discernible reason. Next to the lobby on the ground floor was a dark, narrow exhibition space containing Tufnell's Marvels, which turned out to be a collection of amusement machines that animated if money was fed into them. We treated this area with extreme caution, as we'd encountered haunted automata before, but despite the presence of several mechanical clowns, which so often cause trouble, the room seemed psychically quiet.

The final area comprised the stage, and the backstage region beyond. There was a cold spot on the stage itself, close to where I'd heard the sound of the audience from long ago. This was eight degrees cooler than the rest of the auditorium. Lockwood ordered an iron circle to be set up near it, and we equipped it with flares and salt-bombs. We also scrutinized the dressing room corridor, and the musty basement beneath the stage, which was filled with racks of costumes and broken scenery. No further cold spots were discovered, but we fixed up circles in both of these locations, too.

After that, it was time for the hunt to begin.

You might think that with a prowling Specter somewhere at hand, Lockwood & Co. would stick together at all costs. Instead, we spread out slowly across the auditorium, keeping each other in sight, but letting our individual Talents take us where they would. It was risky, yes, but splitting up like this was a standard tactic; the kind of thing done when a haunting covered a wide space, and the ghost's ultimate vanishing point wasn't yet known. We were in pursuit of the spirit, but we were also acting as bait. The plan was to lure it out by being just a *little* bit vulnerable. In the long run this was better than sitting twitchily in one random place for hours, hoping the Visitor would simply drop by.

I stayed at ground level, drifting along the central aisle toward the place where I'd seen the bloody casket. Holly was on the stage, Kipps somewhere in the wings. George and Lockwood were on the far side of the stalls. Everyone was near enough, but I felt the need for extra company, no matter how annoying it might be. I opened my backpack, turned the lever at the top of the skull's jar to allow it to communicate, and was instantly engulfed by a tide of resentful psychic chatter that had been bottled up since breakfast.

"*What kind of bosom friendship is this,*" the skull cried, "*where you go merrily shutting me up for hours on end? You never plug Lockwood's mouth with a giant cork, or stick a gym shoe in Holly's gob to keep her quiet. Which is a crying shame, because I'd pay good money to see both those things.*"

"*They* don't keep distracting me with nonsense," I growled. "And *you* need some peaceful thinking time. Have you figured out the mystery of Marissa yet, while you were in there?"

"*No! With all this silver-glass, it's all I can do to eavesdrop on your private conversations right outside my jar.*" The skull's light flared indignantly. "*Hey-ho. Still, I manage. From what I've overheard, I take it we're mid-case?*"

I gave a brief account of events, while checking for psychic traces. It was very quiet; the temperature was a bit low beneath the balcony, but that was probably a draft from the exit door.

The skull listened with close attention. "*So this ghost shows up full strength out of nowhere after almost a century,*" it mused. "*Interesting. Anybody around here with a grudge?*"

"Lots of spirits suddenly become active for no reason," I said.

"*True, true. This Tufnell . . . popular chap, I suppose.*"

I couldn't imagine *anyone* liking Tufnell much. "He wasn't very kind to Tracey."

The face in the jar looked thoughtful. "*Maybe she's out for revenge after years of cruel treatment. She's found the Source somewhere, and is hoping the ghost will catch her boss and squeeze him till his eyes pop out. . . . No? You don't seem convinced.*"

"Funnily enough," I said, "not everyone is as horribly vindictive as you. Now make yourself useful for once. La Belle Dame's out there. Can you sense her?"

The skull stayed more or less silent, but I could feel its surveillance alongside mine.

"*It's a fierce one,*" it said at last. "*I can feel it out there, flitting in the dark. Fierce, but not strong . . . Its weakness angers it. It envies the living their vitality.*"

"If it catches someone, it sucks the life force out them," I said.

"*Makes sense. It's trying to restore itself, fill itself back up. Only it*"

can't, because it's dead and gone and full of holes." The skull chuckled unpleasantly. "I could tell it not to bother. You suck the living dry,
and the goodness just flows right through you and out the other side.
'Course, you get a kind of buzz, I won't say you don't, but it's empty
calories. Ultimately a waste of time."

"You are so disgusting. You killed people that way?"

"Only one or two. Ooh—did you feel that?"

"No. What?"

"She's made her move."

My heart double-thumped against my chest. The glee in the
ghost's voice was palpable. "I don't—"

"Patience. Patience . . . Wait for it. . . . Ah, yes, there you go."

A scream cut through the silence of the auditorium. It came
from somewhere behind the stage. I began to run toward it. Who
was it? Holly? Kipps? Neither was in sight. Far off on the other side
of the stalls, Lockwood was running too, long coat flapping, mirroring my speed. We launched ourselves up onto the stage almost as
one, plunged behind the thick red curtains into the wings. It was
very dark there, the walls black-painted, stage sets propped in corners. Above us, ropes hung like weary snakes from metal gantries.
Holly was staring up into the shadows, sword in hand. When she
turned to look at us, her face was very pale.

"It's all right," she said, as we halted on either side. "It's gone."

"What was it?" I shone my torch up at the ceiling. Nothing but
ropes, cobwebs, floating dust.

Holly bit her lip. "I heard a horrid little laugh above me. When
I looked up . . . I thought it was one of the weights they put on the
ends of ropes to help pull up the scenery. But it was too long, and

thin, and white for that. I aimed my flashlight up and . . . and it was a woman hanging there. Hanging by the neck, and spinning slowly around, her dress all lank and still, her legs as thin and white as candles. . . . I'm afraid I dropped my flashlight. When I looked again, the thing was gone."

"Sounds dreadful," Lockwood said. "It was La Belle Dame, of course. Did you see her face?"

"Do you know what?" Holly said. "I'm *so* glad I didn't. There was too much hair."

George had been slower to arrive than Lockwood and me. His glasses flashed as he looked around. "Seems she's testing our resolve," he said. "What with the bloody casket Lucy saw—"

He never finished. Another scream made us all jump. It was higher and shriller than Holly's, so we knew that it was Kipps. We were still reacting when he burst in through a door at the back of the wings. He skidded to a halt, ripped off his goggles, and pointed back the way he'd come. "There! There!" he cried. "In the tank! Do you see her? The poor drowned girl!"

We all hurried to the door. "There's no tank there, Quill," Lockwood said. "It's just an empty corridor."

Kipps took a deep breath. "I know that. Of course I know that. I heard Holly, and I was running here, when I turned the corner and saw it. A great long tank, with a body in it! Her head was under-water, her arms all limp and dangly, her long hair stretching out like river weeds . . ."

Lockwood nodded impatiently. "There's no need to get poetic. Did she leap out and attack you?"

"No, she didn't, as it happens. But she was very white and

pasty, and also very dead. Believe me, that was bad enough."

"Looks as if you got *The Captive Mermaid*," George said, as we walked back out onstage. Our psychic senses were quiet now. For the present, the ghost was gone. "Holly had *The Hangman's Daughter*, and we know Lucy got *The Sultan's Revenge*. La Belle Dame's going through her full repertoire."

"She's giving us her greatest hits," Lockwood said. "But gruesome as these images are, they're all just an act—or not even that: they're the *echo* of an act. The ghost's messing with our minds. Question is: What's next?"

I glanced out at the dark expanse of seats, then back at Lockwood. "Have you or George seen anything?"

"No."

"You're the only ones who haven't."

He shrugged. "Maybe we're just resistant to these things."

"Well," George said, "none of this has changed the state of play. We still have to locate the Source, find out how the thing's managed to come back."

"It's not just a question of *how*." Lockwood's eyes narrowed as he stared out over the auditorium. "It's a question of *why*. . . . What's the motivation?"

"La Belle Dame's a malevolent spirit," I said. "That'll do for now, surely."

"Yes, only I'm not necessarily thinking about the ghost. . . ." Whatever train of thought Lockwood was following looped him back into the present. "Right, we'll continue making sweeps of the theater. Her Visitations so far have been fleeting. Sooner or later, she'll hang around long enough for us to react. Then we'll deal with her. Any questions?"

No one had any. Chocolate was shared, and drinks taken. We began our rounds again.

Hours passed and bled together. Outside was darkness; inside, the theater's soft gold glow. The ghost appeared to have exhausted its resources with its three separate Visitations. I left the auditorium, and walked the passages and soft, carpeted landings of the Palace Theater. Sometimes, when climbing the long, curved stairs, I had the sensation that I was being followed, but whenever I looked back, I saw nothing but the electric candles flickering in their sconces and the frozen, laughing faces on old posters on the walls.

Periodically I glimpsed some of the others from afar: Lockwood striding purposefully across the stage, Holly taking readings high in the upper circle. At first we stayed near each other, but as the night grew older and nothing happened, we drifted farther apart. I began to relax a little. Even the sporadic phenomena of the early evening had petered out to nothing.

At an unknown point the skull and I found ourselves (for the second or third time) in the room of amusement machines known as Tufnell's Marvels. It was a dark, winding corridor, with brightly colored mechanical toys arrayed in glass cases on either side. Some were simple figures—hinged bears and clowns and grotesque police-men that could move or dance; others were complex little scenes showing real-life tragedies, such as the Great Fire of London, that would come to brief, cog-driven life if you put your money in.

First thing I did, as always, was check the temperature and use my senses. As before, I got nothing. I peered at the exhibits, and as I did so, a memory rose unbidden in my mind. "I used to see these things at the country fairs," I said, "when I was a little kid. My sister Mary gave me the money to make one go once. . . ."

"Didn't know you had a sister," the skull said.

"I've got six." I didn't mention that I hadn't seen any of them for years; that only Mary still wrote to me from the North of England. I tried to ignore the dull pang that accompanied the thought. It made me seek distraction. "Ooh, look at *this*," I said.

At the far end of the room, near the exhibition exit, was a square glass box. In it was the most intricate toy of all. It took the form of a traditional traveler's caravan, with a bow roof, large wooden wheels, and sides gaily painted in red and gold. The model stood on a field of fake grass with dark trees and a full moon behind. There was a window along one side, with net curtains drawn across it. I could just make out the shape of someone hidden inside. Above the caravan was a sign: ONE POUND. YOUR FORTUNE TOLD. There was a slot below, and a silver hatch beside it.

I looked at it. I had a pound.

"Go on," the skull said. *"You know you want to. What harm can it possibly do?"*

"It's just a silly machine."

But I was bored and lonely, and wanted something to happen. I took off the backpack and set it on the floor, with the skull's jar peeping out. Then I took the pound out of my pocket and sent it clinking into the slot.

At once, a light came on inside the caravan, illuminating a

hideous witchlike silhouette, all pointy nose and chin. There was a deranged cackling. With rhythmic jerks, the side of the caravan swung open. Lights disguised as candles hung from the ceiling; these sprang into flickering life, revealing a badly painted crone hunched over a table, a crystal ball clutched between her gnarled hands. As I watched, a milky brightness flared in the ball. The cackling came again. The hands moved across the surface of the crystal. A mechanical cat chased a mechanical mouse around the back of the fortune-teller, and a mechanical crow on her windowsill cawed loudly. The candles flickered; cupboard doors opened and closed, revealing concealed skulls and demons. The light in the ball flared and went out. A tinny bell rang somewhere, and something rattled into the hatch at the front of the cabinet. Cogs whirred and spun. The caravan began to close.

I put my fingers into the hatch. Whether it was a glitch or not, two pieces of paper had emerged instead of one. I took them out and read them in the light coming from the fortune-teller's window.

The first read:

He will go into the dark.

The second:

He will sacrifice his life for you.

I stared at the slips of paper for a moment, then crumpled them abruptly in my hand. What kind of fortune was that? That wasn't a fortune. It was stupid. It was a stupid machine.

"What did it say?" the skull asked. *"Bet it was something terrible."*

"Oh, shut up. Why don't you ever shut up? You're always going on at me."

The skull said nothing. I waited for the inevitable retort. Nothing. Even in my anger and disquiet, this struck me as slightly odd. When I glanced down at the jar, I saw that the ghost's face was indeed animated, the bug-eyes rolling, the mouth moving urgently. Yet I heard nothing. That's when I noticed that the lever at the top of the jar had swung closed, blocking the psychic contact.

I hadn't turned the lever.

A breeze ruffled my skirt against my legs; chill air parted my hair and brushed around the contours of my neck. A soft white glow extended out across the floor, sparkling on the glass of the cabinets like the light of a cold new dawn. It was a gentle light, and the face of the smiling woman standing close behind me was gentle, too. As I turned, I'd been scrabbling for my sword, but one look at that radiant lady was enough to make me recognize how silly and inappropriate such an action was. I let my fingers hesitate on the hilt; hesitate, then fall away.

Chapter 10

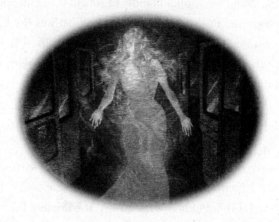

The woman was all fair and shimmery, with a pearlescent wasp-waisted dress that flowed down tight against her legs before spilling out like plunging foam. Her shoulders were bare, her long slim arms as white and sweet as sugar. She did not stand still, but swayed gently from side to side—her arms and body stirring separately, like reed fronds in an underwater current. Her pale hair fell in waves around her neck, cascading over her shoulders, moving, always moving, as if to secret music. And how enticing the face was! I wasn't especially sickly, or a lovelorn boy, so I frankly wasn't La Belle Dame's target audience, but even so I felt the tug of longing as I looked into those fathomless dark eyes.

What was it that made me yearn to walk across? What was it that made me want to give myself to her? It wasn't just that she was exquisite. Sure, you had the gently smiling mouth, the soft full lips, the set-square straightness of that lovely nose. I could take or leave all *that*. You could see similar blandly beautiful young people in any fashion magazine. But she was *flawed*, too. That was the brilliance of it. There was a homeliness to her, something ordinary in the lines of the face that made her seem accessible. It was the flash of Doris Blower behind Marianne de Sèvres. You sensed that deep down she understood what it was to feel imperfect and unspectacular. She understood your need for love.

"Come . . ." a soft voice said. *"Come with me."*

It was as if she spoke directly to my deepest sorrows, those parts of me I guarded from the world. The pang that I'd experienced when I'd thought about my sisters, the anxiety I'd felt when Lockwood had sat beside the empty grave—she could smooth such doubts away. I had an overwhelming urge to share them, let her listen to my fears. I opened my mind to her willingly. I let her sympathy pour in.

"Forget these troubles," the voice said. *"Forget them, and come with me."*

I stood and gazed at the ghost. As if frightened by my scrutiny, it drifted back a little like a startled deer. I felt a plucking in my heart, the need to follow it wherever it might go. I took a stumbling step toward her.

"Well, *she's* a disappointment, no doubt about it."

I blinked, looked around. George had come into the exhibition room from the lobby, and was standing there beside me. He had cobwebs in his hair and a salt-bomb in his hand. He was frowning through his glasses, and a little spear of anger went through me to see him like that—so silly and scruffy and making stupid faces at such an important moment. I didn't want him there. "Meaning what?" I said. My voice sounded odd and thick. "What are you talking about?"

"After all that buildup," he said. "I was hoping for the real deal when we met her. Little bit of glitz, bit of high-end razzle . . . At the very least I was expecting some decent psychic glamour. But not this."

I looked back down to the far end of the corridor, where the ghost swayed and waited, sad and slender as a winter willow, her head tilted to one side.

"She's not good enough for you?" I said.

"Not good enough? She's a sack of pus and bones, Luce. That's below even *my* pay grade."

The woman was gazing at me, her long dark eyelashes beating in time with the rhythm of my heart. Again I felt the tug of longing, again a jarring anger at the vulgarity of George's words. I laughed harshly. "What are you talking about, George? Pus?"

"Well, okay. Technically, it's clear, translucent ichor, manifested into a semi-solidified corporeal state. But when it's all melty and icky and dripping off the bones, I think we can go with pus. The *effect* is much the same."

"Shut up, George."

"Pus, Luce."

I could have punched him. "Just shut *up*."

"No. Look at her, Lucy. *Really* look at her."

And as he said that he stepped forward and clasped my arm, rather harder than I thought necessary. It hurt, in fact, and made me squeak—and with that brief, sharp discomfort, the glamour that had cloaked my brain was momentarily dislodged, like a curtain blown sideways in the wind.

And behind it—what was the shimmering, shining dress? Ectoplasm swirling in a void.

Those lithe arms? Blackened spikes of bone.

That rounded hip? Dark flesh, shriveled and pierced with many holes.

That gentle face? A naked skull.

I blinked. The curtain blew back into position. The wise, sweet woman stood there, beckoning.

I stared at her. Outwardly, I stared at her just as before. But this time, I was willing myself to see reality.

Even so, it was hard. Again the mesmeric swaying of the figure sought to lull my guard; again I felt the pull on my mind and body. But now my focus was on myself, on my own solidity and weight and skepticism, not on the shimmery, undulating thing.

"*Come with me,*" the voice said again. "*Come up onto the stage. . . .*"

I could only croak it out: "No."

It was like snipping a cord with scissors. At once, like a cover falling from a statue, like a cloak being cast aside, the vision fell away, leaving in its place only the grinning, twisted corpse that surged forward. I pulled out my sword and held it before me; the thing at once fell back, mouthing and champing, beckoning me with obscene gestures.

George was at my shoulder. "Want me to pinch you again?"

"No."

"Can do. Arm, leg, buttock, anywhere you fancy. Just name the spot."

"No. It's okay. It's okay now. I see it."

He nodded. "Then perhaps you won't mind if I do this?" He tossed the salt-bomb across the room. It burst at the apparition's feet, showering it with bright green sparks and making it hiss and spit with pain. It drew back, retreating to the shadows of the passage beyond, where it hung for a moment, fizzing, steaming. I could see its pinprick eyes glinting in the dark as it watched me; I felt its malevolence pounding in my head. Then it was gone, and the pull of its glamour with it, leaving me suddenly bereft.

"Wonder where it's off to now," George said. "Why don't you come back into the lobby with me a moment, Luce? We need to regroup, consider what to do."

The lobby was a good place to go. Its chipped gold plasterwork and distinctive popcorn-and-cigarette odor was about as far from spectral enchainment as it was possible to get. George took a chocolate bar from the kiosk and ate it. I leaned back against the ticket counter, water flask in hand, my backpack at my feet. The skull inside was staring at me in mute reproach. I could hardly speak. I was light-headed with self-loathing. Finally: "Thanks, George."

"Sure."

"Next time I do anything like that, don't waste time with words. Just hit me."

"Okay."

"Hit me anywhere. The harder the better." I kicked my heel against the wall. "God!"

George shrugged. "Don't let it get to you. That's what spectral glamour does. Anyone could have been taken in."

"*You* weren't."

"No. Not this time. Frilly ectoplasm isn't my thing." He shrugged. "I hardly think you'd have been fooled for long, Luce. You'd have thrown it off without my help, you know."

"Maybe," I said. "But I was feeling . . . momentarily vulnerable. It was like she sensed it and homed right in." I took a sip of water. "You're obviously much more robust than me."

"Well," George said, "I'm fairly chipper today, that's true. The good news about La Belle Dame is that I don't think it likes being up-front aggressive. What it wants is a passive victim, someone with a psychic wound. As long as we all stay strong, it'll keep its distance. What's not so hot is that it seems to have the run of the place. There's no telling where it'll show up now."

The full shock of my encounter had dwindled, leaving behind a dull agitation—the kind you get when there's something on your mind, and you can't quite think what it is. "Reckon the whole theater is the Source?" I said. "That's possible, isn't it?"

"If so, it's odd that it's never shown itself before now. I suppose new ghosts are always popping up. . . ." George took another chocolate bar thoughtfully. "Doesn't have to be anything suspicious about it."

"The skull reckoned there was foul play afoot. But then, it would."

"Lockwood does, too," George said. "Let's say something has been brought into the theater recently, a Source connected to La

Belle Dame's gory end. It's been hidden somewhere, and that's allowing the ghost to wreak havoc every night. Where would it be . . . ?" Chewing swiftly, he came to a decision. "The most likely places are those old storerooms below the stage. I'm going down to have a look. What about you? Want to come with me?"

I almost said yes. There was something about George that was particularly reassuring that evening. But that agitation I couldn't put my finger on was forcing its way to the forefront of my mind.

"Think I'll check on the others," I said. "Warn them about what happened to me."

"Oh, they'll be all right." George set off toward the auditorium. "We're a resilient bunch. Even Kipps. Though, with those goggles, any ghost would run a mile from him."

Almost before he vanished down the passage. I was moving, too. I was heading for the stairs. I shared George's confidence, of course I did, and yet my heart was pounding hard as I climbed up the carpeted steps to the lower circle floor.

Before George had intervened, the ghost and I had shared a psychic connection. In thrall to her glamour, I'd passively opened my mind to her. Which meant she'd read my thoughts. She knew what I cared about.

She knew *who* I cared about.

I remembered my final glimpse of her eyes, the way they'd glittered at me in the dark.

I realized what she was going to do.

The lower circle lobby was empty, the electric wall lights burning deep and low.

Last time I saw Lockwood, he'd said he was going to patrol the upper regions, the balconies and boxes. He'd be somewhere nearby. . . . But there were so many interconnecting levels, so many stairs and passages . . . I'd start in the upper circle, work my way down.

What it wants is a victim. . . . Someone with a psychic wound . . .

As I reached the next flight of stairs, I saw Holly descending.

"Where's Lockwood?" she said.

I stopped. "What? That's what I was going to ask you."

"Well, did he say where he was going?"

"When?"

"When you were with him just now."

I stared at her. "I haven't been with him. I haven't seen him for ages, Hol."

Something in her face slackened and dropped; she looked at me with wide, dark eyes. "But . . . you were on the lower-circle balcony with him a couple of minutes ago. You *were*." Her voice sounded accusatory, but I read the shock in it, and the sudden fear. "I was *sure* it was you," she said. "The way you beckoned. He was following you toward the door."

"Not me, Holly."

We stared at each other. Then I pulled the rapier from my belt. Holly did likewise. We were already running, slamming open the door to the balcony.

"When was this?" I snapped. "How long ago?"

"Only a minute or two . . . I was up in the highest boxes. I saw you both below. . . ."

"Yeah, only it *wasn't* me, was it? Why did you think it *was*, for heaven's sake? Did it look like me? Face? Clothes?"

"I—I didn't see your face. *Its* face. Or clothes. It was dark-haired, I think. . . . Or maybe that was just the shadow."

I gave a curse. "Geez, Holly."

"There was just something about it. The way it stood or gestured. It was *so* like you."

Well, the thing *had* been an actress, of a sort. We were out on the steep steps of the lower balcony now, and the great soft silence of the auditorium closed around us again. Lights glimmered on the balcony railings below, with the trapeze ropes hanging in the shadows and the dim white stage gleaming across the gulf beyond. We spun around, scanning the sloped seats, looking for Lockwood's reassuring shape. But there was nothing.

"He could have taken one of the other exits," Holly said, pointing. "Gone down different stairs. This place is *such* a maze."

I didn't answer. Black fear rose up in me, like oil welling from the ground.

He will go into the dark. . . .

I clamped my teeth together, forced the panic down. Holly was right. The theater *was* a maze. There was no use just running around hoping to get lucky. Lockwood could be anywhere. *It* could be anywhere.

Or could it? Though the thing had manifested in many random locations around the building, there *was* a pattern when it came to its attempts at psychic enchainment. It had been leading me toward the stage. Charley Budd had been rescued walking toward the stage door, too. . . .

And Sid Morrison, the only one who had actually *been* on the stage?

Much good it had done him. He'd died there.

That was where she wanted us. Why not? It was where *she'd* died, too.

I ran down to the railings, looked down from on high.

At first I saw no one, and when you considered how many of us there were wandering around the theater that night, it made you realize how successful La Belle Dame's diversionary tactics had been. She'd waited patiently until we were all away from the place where the action was. We were scattered, helpless. Holly and me up high; George in the basement; Kipps, heaven knew where. And Lockwood—

There he was now, walking slowly down the aisle. His movements were smooth enough, but there was something placid about them, too unhurried. I thought I saw a wisp of shadow just ahead, moving at the same pace, leading him on.

I called his name. I screamed it. Holly, crashing down beside me, did too. But whereas the acoustics from the stage were so good, here the space just swallowed up the sound. Lockwood didn't turn his head. Perhaps the shadow heard; it seemed to dance more avidly as it led him toward the steps.

"Quick, Luce!" Holly was dragging at my sleeve. She'd made the same deductions I had. "We've got to get down there!"

"Yes—" But even as I said it, I knew we had no time. Too many stairs, too many doors and passages to be negotiated. We had no time. "No, *you* go," I said. "Run as hard as you can."

"But what are you—"

"*Run*, Holly!"

She was gone, leaving only a waft of perfume in her wake. She was too good an agent to argue, though she must have been desperate to interrogate me, find out my plan.

I hardly knew what it was myself.

Or rather, my *conscious* brain didn't. If it *had*, I'd have been crawling, cowering under the nearest seat. But the unconscious bit, that was *way* ahead. It had made the calculations. With Holly sent packing, I turned my attention to the railings on the balcony.

Far below, step by step, Lockwood was climbing onto the stage. His sword was at his belt, his hands hung limp beside his coat. If he was fighting the compulsion, there was no sign of it. How slim he was, how frail he looked from here. Under the lights, the haze of shadow that I knew was still ahead of him was harder than ever to see, but I wasn't bothering about it now. I was clambering onto the rail, beside where the trapeze ropes hung. There were several of them, ends tied to a jutting metal frame. Each rope looped out and downward across the awful space, before extending up toward the distant ceiling.

I seized the frame, steadying myself, refusing to look down at the stalls far below. The nearest rope looked the likeliest; its outward curve was very large. Tufnell had mentioned the way the trapeze artists started the show, so I knew the leap was possible.

That didn't mean it particularly bore thinking about.

Far away, on the hard white stage, Lockwood had reached the center. Something shimmered into existence a short way ahead of him: something in a long white dress with flowing hair. It was radiant and lovely; it cocked its head at him. A slim arm beckoned. I heard a husky voice, whispered on the air.

"Come to me."

And Lockwood moved forward.

Know what? *That* made me mad. How *dare* he go with her? I picked up the rope with my left hand, pulling it toward me. It was heavy, rough, and fibrous. I gripped it, winding it tight around my wrist and arm. Then, with my free hand I slashed at the knot below; the rapier point cut it as easily as a flower stalk, and I had the rope's weight pulling on my arm.

I leaned back, and gave a little jump. Gravity did the rest.

Don't make me tell you what it was like, looping down through the air. *Down* being the key word for that horrific descent. I was basically falling, leaving my stomach somewhere in the region of the balcony, and with the stalls leaping up to receive me. Then I was passing over them at ferocious speed, so close I might have kicked the hats off people sitting there; rushing with my arm nearly pulled out of its socket and my fingers burning on the rope, and my outstretched sword flashing under the lights. And now flying up again, with the stage opening in front of me, and the ghost woman standing, swathed in other-light, and Lockwood walking toward her open arms.

"Come. . . ."

You know me. I love to obey an order. I swung over the stage, passing directly in between them, flashing through a zone of ice-cold air that burned my skin. And the tip of my rapier flashed through something too: namely the neck of that whispering, simpering woman, slicing through it neatly, from side to side. Then I was up and beyond her, flying over the top of the crash pads, which was roughly the point where I thought it advisable to let go.

The next bit, landing painfully on my bottom and doing a

superfast reverse somersault with my ankles around my ears, I'm not going to dwell on. It wasn't gainly and it wasn't soft, but I broke nothing, and it didn't last long. Almost before I'd landed, I was savagely tearing myself upright and leaping back down to the front of the stage, teeth clenched, breathing like a bull.

There was Lockwood, standing where I'd seen him. Arms at his side, relaxed and passive. If he'd noticed me swinging past his nose, it hadn't affected him much, but he was no longer walking toward the shape. My discarded rope was just flashing back the way it had come, and it almost bowled him over. He paid it no heed.

And there, nearby, the headless woman. Or not *exactly* headless—the head was still frowning at me from midair. It was almost in its correct position, but clearly detached from the torso. Its long fair strands of hair coiled around it, slapping against the lacy dress, seeking to bind it back to the stump of the neck.

Even now, she wasn't finished. The lips twisted in a parody of a smile.

"*Come. . . .*"

"You know," I said, "a lot of trouble would be avoided if people like you just lay down and accepted they were dead."

I threw a canister of iron, which shattered against the boards; countless filings went racing beneath the ghost's feet. The nearest particles ignited, surrounding La Belle Dame with a circle of green flames. The figure leaped and jumped in agitation, knocking the head aside. Coils of hair grappled urgently at the bare white shoulders, and with spidery movements resumed hoisting the head toward the body.

Didn't bother me. I had plenty of canisters. I chucked another one, setting more plasm alight. The apparition shivered, lost its focus. Its set smile began to fall away.

Somewhere far off, a door banged. That would be Holly, not far behind.

The woman held out her hands. "*Come. . . .*"

"Oh, get lost."

Maybe I shouldn't have used the magnesium flare, but I'd had enough of the ghost by then. It was too selfish, too needy, too vacuous. I didn't want to share psychic space with it a moment longer. And it had tried to take Lockwood from me. Tufnell could always get himself a new stage. The explosion hit it directly from below— flames went right through its body, blowing the head like a kettle lid high into the air. Half the plasm was vaporized instantly in the blast; the remainder was frail and faint, the merest outline, the ghost of a ghost. I watched as it fled across the stage, diminishing as it went, the head pulled after it on strings of plasm. As it went, the bright dress dwindled, the white limbs shriveled up; the open sword wounds in the body glinted like black stars. It dived toward one of the big wooden cubes, merged into the wood, and vanished.

"Where is it?" Black hair streaming behind her, Holly raced across the burning stage. "Where is it? Where'd it go?"

I didn't look at her. "That yellow box!" I said. "The Source is in there! Find it! Seal it up!" With that, I cast the ghost from my mind. I stood in front of Lockwood, looking up at him. How pale and cold his skin was when I took his hand. His eyes were almost blank; almost, but not quite. I could see his consciousness like a twist of smoke, drifting in the depths.

"Lockwood!" I slapped him hard across the cheek.

Somewhere behind me came a series of violent crashes. That was Holly, getting to work on the box.

"Lockwood . . ." My voice was cracking. "It's me."

"Luce!" That was Holly, too. "I found something! I've got my silver chain net. . . ."

I spoke softly now. "It's me. It's Lucy. . . ."

I like to think it was just coincidence that Holly laid the silver net over the Source right then. I like to think it was the sound of my name that brought him back. Who's going to tell me otherwise? Either way, the twist of smoke rose up and up, and bloomed across the surface of his eyes. Intelligence came with it; intelligence and recognition—and something more than that. He smiled at me.

"Hey, Luce . . ."

I slapped him again, sharply and on both cheeks. Take it from me, that's a hard thing to get right when you're crying.

III

A Body in the Street

Chapter 11

It was afterward said that at the very moment Holly wrapped the silver net around the bloodstained tiara hidden in the box, at that very moment out in Tufnell's caravan on the far side of the field, little Charley Budd stopped howling, sat up, and asked for chicken soup. So the theater people knew instantly that we'd gotten the job done and the ghost was gone. Their subsequent emergence into the auditorium, step by cautious step, was nicely timed, as we were just battling the fire I'd started on the stage. All hands came to help. By dawn, the blaze was out, the theater safe, and the tiara wrapped, ready for destruction in the furnaces. And Sarah Parkins, the stage manager who had built the secret compartment that concealed the Source, and who had promptly admitted to putting it there, was locked in her trailer under the watchful gaze of two of the burliest trapeze artists, awaiting the arrival of the DEPRAC vans.

For Mr. Tufnell, it was a satisfactory end to the affair, though he groaned to high heaven about the magnesium burns in the center of the stage. Sarah Parkins's guilt had likewise dumbfounded him. "To think she should be the cause of all this!" he cried, his face beet red with emotion. "Such betrayal! Such malice! I treated her like a daughter!"

"Actually, it wasn't about you," Lockwood said. Seeming none the worse for his recent psychic enchainment, Lockwood himself had identified the culprit and invited her to confess. He had subsequently spent half an hour talking to her in the caravan. "Sarah told me what happened," he went on. "It was originally about Sid Morrison. You mentioned yourself, Mr. Tufnell, that Sarah had been fond of him, but by your own account he'd fallen head over heels for that Russian trapeze artist with the thighs. Sarah was left rejected, and her heartbreak turned into hatred. She wanted revenge. It so happened that in her work clearing out the prop supplies, she'd discovered a relic of La Belle Dame's last performance—the tiara she'd worn for *The Sultan's Revenge*. All those years it had been kept in an iron box, which must have suppressed the ghost. Without recognizing its psychic significance, Sarah took it out. Subsequent sightings of the Specter—and its particular interest in young men—made her realize its potential. She hid the tiara onstage and awaited developments. It wasn't long before Charley Budd was snared, but Sarah didn't want *him* dead—that's why she saved him. Sid Morrison, a day later, wasn't so lucky."

"Hold on," Holly said. "Why didn't she remove the tiara after Sid's death? Why risk other people's lives?"

Lockwood shook his head. "It's hard to say. Sarah claims she hadn't had the opportunity. Personally, I wonder if her private misery had morphed into a dull hatred for the world in general. Or perhaps she found she simply liked the secret power. . . . But that's a matter for Inspector Barnes, not us. Here he is now. I'll fill him in."

Looking at Lockwood then, as he strode across to meet the DEPRAC contingent, coat swinging behind him, so confident and self-assured, you'd have been hard-pressed to imagine that an hour or two before he'd been a ghost's plaything. His smile was as bright as ever, his energy lit up the stage. A little crowd gathered to listen. Old Inspector Barnes, crumpled and hangdog as usual, hung on his every word. George and Kipps were there, too, standing on the sidelines, luxuriating in everyone's goodwill.

Only Holly and I hung back. In my case this was partly due to exhaustion, partly delayed shock at the drastic action I'd had to take to save Lockwood. I simply didn't feel like joining in. Holly was fine, but she could see the state I was in and wanted to keep me company.

I watched Lockwood through a fog of weariness. From the moment he awakened, he'd seemed his normal self. But I knew what I'd seen when I looked into his spellbound eyes.

They'd been no different to those of Charley Budd. And what had George said about Charley—him and the other victims? *They had weak connections to life.* Enchainment worked on those who, one way or another, were already somehow looking to the next world. The ghost had tried it on me, too. I'd wavered, I'd felt the pull. But Lockwood? He'd fallen for it, big-time. It didn't matter how sprightly he seemed now. For a few short minutes, he'd been back in that overgrown cemetery with his family. He'd been walking toward that empty grave.

An hour later we were standing at the gates to Tufnell's Traveling Fairground, waiting for the Night Cabs to take us home. Kipps had gotten hot teas from a bearded lady who seemed to like him. He, George, and Holly were huddled together, sipping from plastic cups. I stood slightly apart, coat wrapped tight around me, looking south toward the river. You could just see the Thames from here, glinting in broken shards beyond the factory chimneys. It was a cold morning.

Lockwood came to stand beside me. We stood in silence, shoulders touching, watching the gray city grow sharp and definite, hardening into a new day.

"I haven't said a proper thank-you," Lockwood said.

"It's all right."

"I know what you did for me."

My mouth tightened. "Swung down on a bloody trapeze was what I did, Lockwood."

"I know."

"I hate heights."

"I know that."

"I hate trapezes."

"Yes."

"Don't ever make me have to do something so ridiculous and dangerous again."

"Lucy, I won't. I promise." He offered me a sidelong grin. "But listen—you were amazing. Holly told me. Kipps, too—he saw the part from when you landed on the crash pad."

"Oh, he didn't see *that* bit, did he? God."

"You saved my life."

"Yes, I did."

"Thank you."

I wiped my nose with a gloved hand, sniffed at the coldness of the air. "We shouldn't have split up the way we did, Lockwood. And *you* shouldn't have been there at all. I told you and George before we came. You were vulnerable to that thing."

He let out a long, slow breath. "From what George tells me, you were, too."

"I was, it's true. I was thinking about my sisters—and other things like that. It sensed my sadness and took advantage." I looked at him. "What were *you* thinking about when it appeared to you?"

Lockwood pulled his collar up against the chill. He wasn't very good with direct questions like that. "I don't really remember."

"You were so far gone when I got to you. You were completely snared. At the end, even after I chopped the thing's head off, you were still mooning over it."

The DEPRAC vans came through the gates and pulled away, lights flashing, brakes squealing. There was Barnes, following in his car. He waved a lugubrious hand.

Lockwood didn't speak until everything was quiet again. "I know you're worrying about me, Luce," he said. "But you really mustn't. These things happen when you're an agent. You've been snared by ghosts in the past, haven't you? There was the one that made the bloody footprints, and the thing in the tunnels below the Aickmere Brothers store. But it's fine, because I helped you then, and you've helped me now. We're there to help each other. If we do that, we'll get through."

Which was a lovely thing to say, and it made me feel a little warmer. I just had to hope it was true.

Back at Portland Row, normality was resumed, which meant arguments about who paid the taxi fare, three helpings of breakfast each, and George hogging the hot water in the bathroom. Kipps and Holly had gone to their respective homes; midmorning saw George, Lockwood, and me all sleeping late. When I woke up again, sometime after noon, the first thing I saw was the ghost-jar, still protruding from the top of my backpack where I'd slung it on my bedroom chair. It was tilted at an angle, thanks to a fair-sized pile of dirty laundry, and the spectral face inside was staring at me like I'd just shot its grandmother.

Strangely, it was a reassuring sight. I flicked the lever and sat blearily on the end of the bed, tousled and comatose, letting the shrill complaints flow over me.

"*I* didn't shut you off this time," I said, when I could finally get a word in edgeways. "It was the ghost."

"*So? It's still your fault! You can't let any old ghost woman go around fingering my jar. It's your responsibility to look after it. I can't do it, can I? I'm in your care. I call it negligence, pure and simple.*"

"You're not a child. Get over it." I scratched at my hair; the white strands were showing no sign of growing out. Maybe I'd have to dye them. "Skull," I said suddenly, "I'm worried about Lockwood."

The ghost seemed taken aback. "*Lockwood?*"

"Yes."

"*Hey, you know me. I love him like a brother.*" The face adopted an expression of unctuous fake concern. *"What seems to be the problem?"*

I stretched my legs out in front of me, rocking on the edge of the bed. I thought of Lockwood in the cemetery; and of him walking toward the ghost. I also thought of the Fetch beneath the Aickmere Brothers store that had worn his face, almost a year before. It had predicted Lockwood's death and said that he would die for me. Oh, and there was the fortune-telling machine the night before. That hadn't cheered me much, either. I sighed. "I don't understand what's driving him at the moment," I said. "Mostly he seems absolutely fine, but underlying it all . . . I'm not sure what he's really looking for. It might be something that's not . . . that's not that healthy. . . ." I let the effort peter out. It was no good. I couldn't say it.

"Well, thanks for that," the skull said, after waiting to make sure I'd really finished. *"A probing analysis. And about as clear as a bucketful of mud."*

I shook my head, suddenly annoyed with myself. What was I thinking? I couldn't talk to a haunted skull about Lockwood's parents or the graveyard. The idea was absurd. "I know you don't care," I said, "but I just wondered if you'd noticed anything. . . ." I got up, reaching for a towel. "Forget it. It's not important."

"I mean, it's not as if I'm renowned for my empathy, anyway," the ghost said. *"It's a long time since I was alive. I've forgotten what it feels like, having mortal motivations. And of course I hardly know Lockwood at all."*

"It's all right. It's not a problem."

"Aside from his recklessness, his deep-rooted feelings of personal

loss, his mild self-absorption, his obsession with his family, and his obvious death wish, I couldn't tell you anything about him. You and me, we're just as clueless as each other, eh?" the skull added. *"Ah, well."*

I paused with the towel in my hand. "What did you say? Don't be ridiculous. He doesn't have a death wish."

"Fine, you're not comfortable with it. I understand that. We'll let it drop." The skull began humming a light tune. *"Actually, no we won't. It's surely obvious to everyone. He's always had it. It's practically his middle name. And maybe it's more pronounced than ever now, thanks to what happened to you both. Don't forget, you've both been to the Other Side. That'll have had its effect too, you know."* The face grinned at me, eyes narrowing to slits. *"Why do you think La Belle Dame tried her luck with you last night? You're not a boy."*

I hadn't thought of it that way before, but it was true. Of all her potential victims, I'd been the only girl. Still, true or not, somehow the skull's insights always made me angry. "I should have known better than to try and talk to you," I said, bending close to the jar. "Lockwood's got plenty to live for. Plenty."

The face regarded me. *"Has he? What would that be, I wonder? Give it a name."*

With that, the ghost did something to the light inside the ichor, so that it dimmed and went opaque, and I found myself staring at my own distorted face in the side of the jar.

"Care to comment?" the skull said.

I cursed and walked away. "No! I don't need to explain myself to a tatty bit of old bone! And I certainly don't need to second-guess Lockwood's motivations!"

"*You so do,*" the ghost called. "*It's your favorite hobby! And think about it—if you ever actually freed me, you'd never have to talk to me again!*"

Its words bounced off the closing bathroom door.

George and Lockwood were in the library when I went downstairs. Lockwood's long limbs were draped across his favorite armchair as he read the newspaper. George was hunched nearby, inspecting a small sheaf of papers; on the floor at his feet lay a piece of unfolded oilcloth and a length of filthy string. Funny—in all the immediate flurry after our encounter with Sir Rupert, the package Flo Bones had given George had never been mentioned again. He hadn't brought it up, and I'd forgotten to ask him.

I threw myself into a chair. The library being chilly, the fire was lit and blazing.

"More news," Lockwood said, from behind the newspaper.

"Bad or baddish?"

"Baddish, bad, *and* interesting. Sometimes in combination."

"Oh, just tell me what it is."

"Remember the other day, George mentioning old Adam Bunchurch?"

"What, getting all furious with the Fittes Agency for trying to close him down?"

"That's right. Well, he's dead."

"What? Ghost-touch?"

"No. He was attacked last night. Exactly what happened is unclear. He was on his way home from handling a Lurker case in Rotherhithe. Walking alone. Someone lay in wait for him. They beat him up and left him. No one found him until morning. He was taken to the hospital, but died there."

I glanced across at George. "No clue as to who did it, I suppose?"

Lockwood didn't speak for a moment. "Maybe the police will make an arrest. I don't know."

I didn't comment. It didn't seem particularly likely.

"The next thing to tell you is also fairly ominous." Lockwood tossed the paper aside. "We got an official letter this morning from DEPRAC. Tomorrow evening all the heads of the small independent agencies are requested to report to Fittes House, where Penelope Fittes is going to make an announcement. Six p.m." He glanced across at me.

"Closing us all down?"

"It doesn't say."

"Things are certainly happening," George said. He was still engrossed in his papers.

"They are," Lockwood said. "And speaking of which, I've been meaning to tell you both. At the theater this morning Inspector Barnes came up to me and shook me by the hand."

"Doesn't sound like him," I said. "Was he ill?"

Lockwood glanced at his palm and wiped it on his knee. "I do hope not. No, he was thanking us for our sterling efforts. But that's not all. He gave me something, too."

He stretched over and handed me a piece of paper. On it were the words:

17 Alma Terrace, NW1, 8 p.m. tonight

"He wants a meeting?" I said.

Lockwood grinned. "A secret one! Might be a bit more hush-hush if it wasn't scribbled on official DEPRAC notepaper and in Barnes's own spidery handwriting, but there you are."

"So are you going?" I asked.

"I think we all should. What do you think Barnes wants, George?"

"Mm?" There was a gleam behind George's spectacles as he looked up. His eyes were bright, but his mind was focused on something far away. "Oh, he'll be telling us to keep out of trouble, stop poking our noses into things that don't concern us. . . ." He inspected the documents in his hand. "Well, too late for that now."

"Okay, what *are* those, George?" I said. "And how come Flo gave them to you?"

"She's been doing a little bit of research on my behalf, here and there. I'm not always able to gain access to some of the libraries, but Flo knows people who are surprisingly well connected. . . . As for these, they're death certificates." He scratched his nose.

"Does this have to do with your research on Marissa Fittes?" I said. "What have you found?"

George hesitated. "I can't talk about it now. Still thinking. Ask me again tomorrow."

Alma Terrace, the location for our meeting with Inspector Barnes, turned out to be a soot-stained row of narrow houses in northwest London. A few old rusted ghost-lamps lined the northern side, flashing vainly at the coming dusk. We walked between them, from light to dark to light again, looking for number seventeen.

Net curtains hung in many of the ground-floor windows, lit by warm interior light. The blinds weren't yet drawn, and you could sometimes make out hazy images of people moving in the rooms. Already, in their evening domesticity, they were detached from us. The curtains kept agents like us one step removed.

Inspector Montagu Barnes was waiting for us outside the gate of number seventeen. It was a dark part of the street, midway between ghost-lamps; we could see his crumpled form flashing dimly on and off as we approached. The house behind him was not very different from the others, except for the neatness of its tiny garden. It featured grass and gnomes.

"Evening, Inspector," Lockwood said. "Sorry we're late."

"Didn't expect anything else," Barnes said. "In fact, you're only half an hour later than I requested. I'm honored."

There followed the usual awkward interlude while we smiled at him in our young and perky fashion, and he regarded us with middle-aged distaste. There was something slightly odd about him tonight. What was it? Not his general bearing. As ever, his mustache drooped as if shouldering the sorrows of the world. Then I realized I had never previously seen Barnes without either his raincoat or his tie. He had his shirtsleeves rolled below his elbow, and his collar was undone.

"So . . . this is number seventeen." George surveyed the building. "It's a sinister-looking dive. You can bet your boots something awful's happened here."

"Yes. You carrying out an exorcism or something, Mr. Barnes?"

Lockwood asked. "Might be simpler just to knock the old pile down. . . ." He hesitated. "Why are you glaring at us like that?"

"Because this is my home." Barnes gave a heartfelt sigh. "Well, I suppose you'd better all come in."

He held the door open for us. It didn't look so much like a gesture of welcome as a preparation for slamming it hard on George's head. We slipped through as quickly as possible. Before closing the door, the inspector took a good look up and down the street. The ghost-lamps flashed on and off in the quiet dark; no one seemed to be near.

Barnes led us down a narrow hallway and into a cramped dining room, centered on an oval table of dark wood.

"Nice cozy little spot," Lockwood remarked.

"Yes, really lovely brown carpet," George said. "And that row of ceramic ducks on the wall . . . I believe that kind of ornament has become quite hip again, hasn't it?"

"All right, all right," Barnes growled. "You can save your breath. Sit down, make yourselves at home. I assume you'll all be wanting tea." He stomped off to the kitchen.

One by one, we sat around the table. The chairs were upright, uncomfortable, and clearly seldom used. There was a patina of dust on the tabletop. Aside from the ducks, there were photographs on the walls of soft green hills, misty valleys, tumbledown cottages, expanses of air and nature. They reminded me of my childhood, far from London.

A kettle boiled in the distance; spoons clattered; Barnes returned with a heaped tray. To our surprise, chocolate digestive biscuits were included in the offering. The usual ceremonials were completed.

We sat in silence, with our cups and plates, facing the inspector at the head of the table. It was an intimate setting, laced with ambiguity; we might have been about to join in prayers, or play cards for money, or do anything in between. The combination of drab formality and general awkwardness gave it the air of one of those suburban séances where dowdy women tried to summon ghosts.

"I do honestly like these photographs, Mr. Barnes," I said. "I didn't know you enjoyed the countryside."

The inspector regarded me. "What, did you think I'd have pictures of batons or handcuffs on my wall, maybe? I do *have* other interests, you know." He shook his head sourly. "Anyway—yes, I do. But I didn't ask you here to discuss my photos. I wanted to give you a warning."

There was a silence. Lockwood sipped his tea. "A warning, Mr. Barnes?"

"That's what I said." The inspector hesitated for a moment, as if even now he feared to commit himself; then he sat back in his chair decisively. "Everything's changing," he said. "You know that, don't you? DEPRAC, the agencies, how it's all controlled. The big outfits are running the show: the Fittes Agency, the Sunrise Corporation—the people who make a lot of money from the Problem. Independent operations like yours are being squeezed out. I don't need to tell you this. There've been plenty of announcements to that effect this summer."

"There's another one coming tomorrow, I believe," Lockwood said.

"Yes, at Fittes House, and I doubt it'll be any better for you than any of the others. Still, it's a general meeting, so whatever new rules they come up with won't be directed solely at you. However, something's come to my attention that *is*." Barnes's shrewd eyes scanned us each in turn. "I've heard, through the DEPRAC grapevine, that certain prominent people are losing patience with you."

"*Certain prominent people?*" Holly said.

"You mean Penelope Fittes, I suppose?" George asked.

Barnes pressed his lips tight together so that they both vanished under his mustache. "I leave it to your judgment who I'm talking about. It's not necessary for me to say."

"Oh, it is, it is. Go on, say it," George said. "There's no one listening, is there? Unless they're hiding in the teapot."

"Thank you, Mr. Cubbins. You illustrated my point before I could even make it." Barnes eyed us all severely. "It's precisely that sort of irreverent, incautious attitude that's leading you into trouble. Whatever you may think about the new rules we all live by, there's no doubting the fact that we're all being observed far more closely than before. It pays to keep a low profile. And Lockwood and Co. keeps being noticed. That's all I'm saying."

Lockwood smiled. "What can anyone object to? We're not stepping out of line."

"Aren't you?" Barnes said. "If that's the case, why are DEPRAC officers being commandeered to watch your place in Portland Row? Why is that popinjay Sir Rupert Gale so interested in you? Why does Penelope Fittes ask for regular reports on your activities?"

"She does?" Lockwood said. "We're honored."

"No. You're not. You're at risk. You may have heard about Mr.

Bunchurch's little 'accident.' There have been others, too. I don't want to see the same thing happening to you. Whatever it is you're doing, stop it. That's all I'm saying."

"We're not doing anything untoward, Inspector," Lockwood said. "We pay our taxes. We take proper precautions. We leave most of our clients alive." He flashed his brightest smile. "Remember last night at the theater? We do good work."

Barnes nodded grimly. "Bunchurch did good work, too."

"Well, not *very* good work," George put in. "He was actually a bit useless, wasn't he?"

"That's not the point!" The inspector gave a sudden roar. He banged a hairy fist on the tabletop, making his cup jerk in its saucer. A gout of strong dark tea splashed across his plate. "That's not the point! He crossed them, and he's dead!"

We sat there, Barnes breathing hard, the rest of us in shocked silence. Even George looked stunned.

"You've spilled your tea, Inspector." Lockwood handed him a handkerchief.

"Thank you." Barnes mopped the table. His voice was quieter now. "You know I'm not in full control at DEPRAC anymore," he said. "These past couple of years Penelope Fittes has placed a lot of her people in the organization. They're slowly skewing the way we work. Of course, there are still good men and women there, and plenty of them, but we don't have any say in wider operations. I stamp forms, issue orders, go through the motions on a day-to-day level. I can't influence what's going on. But I see things clearly enough. Just as I see that you're lying now. It's in your eyes. It's in the way that Cubbins sits there, all smug and self-important, puffed up like a frog. *I* see it, plain as plain. And if I can, you can be sure other people see it, too."

He finished dabbing with the handkerchief and gave it back to Lockwood.

"Mr. Barnes . . ." Lockwood said hesitantly, "all we've been doing is—just a little research, here and there. We could tell you about it. We'd value your help."

The inspector glared at us from under hairy eyebrows. "I don't want to know about it."

"It's important. Seriously, it is."

"I don't want to know. Mr. Lockwood, you've impressed a lot of people over the years. Personally, I expected you all to be ghost-touched long ago, but your agency has flourished. Impress me again now." Barnes touched the handle of his cup with a stubby finger, rotating it gently on the saucer. "Keep your heads down. Let them forget about you."

We sat in silence around the table in the dark and dusty room.

"Let them forget about you," Barnes repeated. "Even now, it's probably not too late."

Chapter 12

Whether Inspector Barnes's warning left any impression on George was doubtful. The following morning, as I made my way downstairs, his bedroom door hung open. For reasons of hygiene it was never wise to venture inside, but even from the landing the rumpled, unmade bed and strew of papers on the floor told their own tale.

In the kitchen, a scrawled note had been left on the Thinking Cloth:

Need to check something out. Back lunchtime. BE HERE!!

But George was back even before lunch. Holly, Lockwood, and I were in the basement office when a crash from the kitchen sent us scurrying up the iron staircase. George stood at the table. He had swept the fruit bowl off and dumped a great pile of documents in its place. He had a pen between his teeth; with ferocious speed he was swapping papers, selecting maps, spreading the pile around.

"Um, are you ready to chat?" Lockwood ventured.

George made a flapping motion with one hand. "Not yet! Just a couple of things to organize! Give me an hour!"

"Do you . . . do you want a sandwich?" Holly asked.

"No! No time." George was peering at a photocopy of an old newspaper article. He frowned at it, cast it aside. "Oh, but, Lockwood . . ."

"Yes?"

"Can you get Kipps over? He should be here, too. One hour."

"All right. We'll leave you alone till then."

George didn't answer. He was in his own world, buoyed by the thrill of discovery. At such times a physical transformation seemed to come over him. His extra weight fell away; he was swift of movement, light of foot—Lockwood at his most pantherlike and predatory moved with no greater velvet grace. His spectacles shone with light from the garden—in just such a way, one felt, the goggles of a fighter pilot would catch the spark of the sun as his plane performed miracles of flight high above the earth. Even his hair crackled with new energy, swept back from his pale forehead like that of a racing driver negotiating hairpin bends. It was as if the sinewy intelligence that lay concealed behind his doughy frame was suddenly laid bare; its quick workings transferred into the deftness with which he organized his papers, flipped from one file to another, danced around the kitchen table, pausing only occasionally to scribble something on the Thinking Cloth. As Lockwood said later, it was like watching an artist at work; you could have sold tickets for his exhibition on that sunny morning.

Holly went off to hunt down Kipps. While she slipped out, Lockwood and I retreated to the rapier room, where our straw dummies, Floating Joe and Lady Esmeralda, hung on their chains. Lockwood rolled up his sleeves and practiced moves on Esmeralda. I did the same with Floating Joe. As always, the simplicity of this action worked wonders on our moods. The tension between us fell away. Excitement rose; we felt mounting expectation at what George might reveal. Soon we left the dummies swinging and began dueling with each other, grinning as we circled, feinting, dodging, making ornate patterns with our clashing blades.

The hour passed. Hot, sweaty, and in need of tea, Lockwood and I went back upstairs. In the kitchen, the table and most of the other surfaces were invisible beneath a sea of papers. George sat waiting. He looked sweaty, too.

"I'm ready," he said. "Put the kettle on."

Up on the sink, documents lapped at the base of the ghost-jar. The skull rolled its eyes at us. *"Thank goodness you're here. He's been like a plump whirlwind. And there was a most distressing glimpse of pink flesh when he bent down to pick up a paper clip. I'd have feared for my life if I wasn't already dead."*

While we were setting out the tea, Holly returned with Kipps. Every member of our essential team was there. Lockwood shut the door to the hall and drew the blinds at the windows. The light in the room became blue, dim, and conspiratorial. We drew up our chairs. In the jar, the face grew faint and unobtrusive; even the ghost seemed keen to listen. Our mugs were filled, some sandwiches and biscuits handed out. It was time for George to begin.

"First things first," he said. "Take a look at this." With a dramatic flourish, he produced a photograph and set it on the table. "Recognize our friend here?"

It was a black-and-white shot of a middle-aged man in a dark suit, with a raincoat folded over his arm. He was pictured getting out of a car; other people stood around him. But it was his face that transfixed us: it was marked by deep and distinctive lines, and framed by a shock of long gray hair. One side was lost in shadow, and the eyes were almost hidden under shaggy brows. It didn't matter. We had seen that face before.

"The Revenant in Marissa's tomb!" Lockwood said. "The one who chased us up the stairs and spoke to Luce! It's him for sure! Isn't it, Luce?"

"It's him." When I closed my eyes I saw the wild-haired ghost rising through the mausoleum floor. I opened them—and there was this staid and somber gentleman. No doubt about it. They were the same.

"You're a marvel, George," Lockwood said. "So who is he?"

George tried not to look too pleased with himself. "This," he said, "is a certain Dr. Neil Clarke. Not much is known about him, but he was personal physician to Marissa Fittes, and he tended to her in her last illness. It's he who signed her death certificate, and he who confirmed her cause of death in a report to the media." He picked up the documents Flo had found for him and squinted at them through his glasses. "According to Dr. Clarke, Marissa died from 'a wasting disease that affected all the organs of her body, and which had all the aspects of premature old age.' Sounds nasty, but Marissa was cared for up at Fittes House. She didn't go to the hospital, and only Dr. Clarke had access to her." George put down the papers. "I've been hunting around, but after her death he fades from the records and isn't heard of again."

"Not surprising, really," Holly murmured, "since he was lying in her tomb."

Lockwood whistled. "Marissa didn't die. And the person who *knew* that, who'd faked the official records, was silenced immediately afterward."

"No wonder he's so livid," I said. I could still hear an echo of the whispered voice: *Bring her to me.*

George nodded; he set the photograph aside. "That takes care of our friend in the tomb. The next question concerns how Marissa reappears as 'Penelope.' I take it we all agree that this is what happened?"

There was a hoot from the jar. *"You ought to by now!"* the skull cried. *"I've been telling you long enough! Honestly, those digestive biscuits have higher IQs than you."*

"Shut up," I said. "Not you, George. The skull." I glared at the indignant ghost.

"In fact," George said, "I haven't quite gotten to the bottom of Marissa's transformation yet, though I have a terrific lead that I'll tell you about in a moment. What's known is that after the old girl's supposed death, her daughter, Margaret, takes over the agency."

He produced another photograph, this one of a dark-haired young woman. She was officiating at some agency function and didn't seem to be enjoying it. Her face was pale and sad.

"Margaret was head of Fittes for only three years," George said. "She was a quiet, retiring person, by all accounts not well suited to running a big company. Well, she didn't have to do it for long, because she died, too."

Holly frowned. "How did *she* die?"

"It's not known. I can't find any proper death certificate. Then 'Penelope' pops up. On the face of it, she appears to be a real person. I've gotten birth certificates for her; hospital records, all the rest of it. Everything *seems* correct and aboveboard. But it isn't. It can't be, because that doesn't square with what the skull's telling us. If the woman we know is Marissa, masquerading as a younger person somehow, this must all be forged."

"But how *can* it be Marissa?" I said. "How's she made herself look like that?"

George eyed us all over the top of his glasses. We waited. Even Kipps had paused with his mug halfway to his mouth. With careful deliberation, George selected another sheet of paper.

"I found an article in an old Kent newspaper," he said. "It's from sixty years ago, when Marissa and Tom Rotwell were just starting out as a psychic detection team. Back then almost nobody believed in ghosts, crazy as that sounds. They were considered complete eccentrics. The Problem hadn't yet begun to spread. A journalist interviews them, makes lots of cheap jokes at their expense. But listen to this—" He adjusted his spectacles and read the following:

"'Marissa Fittes is a slim, bony girl with short-cropped hair and an attitude of unusual intensity. In clipped, confident tones she tells me of their strange supernatural experiences. "The dead are among us," she says, "and they bring with them wisdom and secrets of the past." She ignores my skepticism and tells me she has already written a monograph on the substance of spirits, which she terms "ectoplasm." "It is the immortal stuff that is inside all of us," she says. "Understanding it will bring great benefits to humanity. Perhaps, if we can exploit its transformative power, it will give us control over life and death." At present, she admits regretfully, her ideas fall on stony ground. Having been unable to find a magazine that would accept her piece, she has had it printed at her own expense.'"

George took a sip of tea. "See? Even then, right back at the beginning of her career, Marissa was interested in gaining control over life and death. I think that, somehow, she's succeeded."

"Sounds like nonsense to me," Kipps said. "The transformative power of ectoplasm? What's that when it's at home?"

Lockwood was frowning. "There's nothing about any of this in her published writings, is there? She doesn't talk about plasm being 'immortal stuff,' as far as I can remember."

"No," George said. "She goes all quiet about that. Which is why I'm particularly keen to track down this missing monograph of hers. It's taken me months to get so much as a sniff of it. But today, I think I cracked it." He gave us a look of triumph. "This morning, in a remote library, I found a reference to something called *Occult Theories*, by Anonymous. It doesn't have Marissa's name attached to it, but it was privately printed in Kent at about the correct time, and I bet it's the one. Only three copies are known to exist. One is in the Black Library at Fittes House; one was bought by our old friends at the Orpheus Society for their private reading library; and one went to the Spiritualist Museum in Greenwich. The first two are obviously inaccessible, but I reckon I could fake my way into the last. In fact, I intend to, later this afternoon. If I can find this paper, it might just help us piece a few mysteries together." George sat back in his chair. "I'll try, anyway."

There was a general buzz of congratulation at this news. The only exception was the skull in the jar, which yawned and blew its cheeks out in cruel mimicry of George, but no one paid any attention. We all took more biscuits.

Lockwood opened a fresh pack of digestives. "This is great," he said. "If we can complete our picture of what Marissa's been up to, we can go back to Barnes—or the newspapers—and make everything public. All we need is concrete proof."

George nodded. "And we also need to connect it to the wider Problem. I think I've cracked that, too." He chuckled. "It's a story of forbidden acts that takes us back more than fifty years."

"Pass me a pillow," Kipps said. "This is going to take hours. I can feel it."

George pushed his glasses up his nose. "Oh, well, if that's the way it is, Kipps, I can certainly keep it short and sweet. Here's my analysis: I think Marissa Fittes and Tom Rotwell are to blame for the Problem. There. That's it. The end." He gathered up his papers and tapped them into a neat pile.

Lockwood grinned. "All right, George. I'm sure Quill didn't mean to sound so wearily contemptuous of all your hard work. *Did* you, Quill?"

"No. It was purely coincidental."

"There. See? Everyone's happy. George, have another raspberry biscuit and fill us in."·

"Okay," George said. "Well, we all know that Fittes and Rotwell started out as two psychic researchers in Kent. I've been through all the local papers. They're first mentioned sixty years back, doing investigations here and there. As we've seen, no one took them seriously. A few years later, that had changed."

"Because of the Problem," Holly said. "It had begun to spread."

George nodded. "Yep, and here's the critical detail. The way you read it in Marissa's *Memoirs*, the Problem was suddenly on the march, and Marissa and Tom were the only ones fighting it. Gradually their methods became accepted. Salt, iron, rapiers . . . the whole range of agency techniques started with them."

"Some famous cases," I said. "The Mud Lane Phantom, the Highgate Terror . . ."

"Precisely. The whole Fittes myth begins here." George sat back in his chair. "But there's another way of reading the data too, and to do this I had to map out all the places where Marissa and Tom were at work. What it shows is that those famous outbreaks—in other words, all the new ghosts that started cropping up—*follow* Marissa and Tom's movements. If the two of them are active in a certain area, new hauntings tend to be reported soon *afterward*. And that can't be a coincidence."

"So you think they were doing things to stir the ghosts up?" Holly said.

"Yep." George regarded us. "And what do we know for sure *really* stirs ghosts up?"

I looked at Lockwood; a shadow had passed over his face. "Visiting the Other Side," I said softly. "You think Marissa and Tom were doing this, all those years ago?"

"Yes, though maybe Marissa found it easier than Tom. I'll tell you why later." George tapped one of the folders on the table. "As Lucy says, everyone knows the cases they investigated. They were a team for four or five years. But then—very suddenly and acrimoniously— they split up. No official word on why. Almost immediately, Marissa starts her own agency. A couple of months later, Tom Rotwell starts one, too. And their companies have been rivals ever since."

"Until now," Lockwood said, "with Penelope in charge of both."

"We met Rotwell's grandson a few months back," George said. "What was he doing? He was making a gate to the Other Side. Remember all the paraphernalia he used? The stolen Sources, the clumsy armor the Creeping Shadow wore . . . It must have been years in the planning. It was big-scale stuff—big, but awkward, too. It smacks of someone who knew what he was about but was doing it the hard way. I think he was trying to copy something that his grandfather and Marissa had once done."

"Visit the Other Side?"

"Right. Rotwell knew the theory, but he was having problems with the technique. On the one hand he was struggling to make a secret gate big enough—we know he created one under the Aickmere Brothers department store a year or so back, and by using it started the Chelsea outbreak. After that, he built one out in the countryside, which immediately caused the ghostly infestation of the local village. Sadly for him, we put an end to both experiments."

"We're annoying that way," Lockwood said, grinning.

"Yes, and the armor his bloke used to protect himself on the Other Side—that was pretty hopeless, too," George said. "Just compare it to the spirit-capes you and Lucy wore. You were far lighter on your feet. And those capes were mostly made of feathers. It's safe to say that Rotwell was playing catch-up, but I'll tell you someone who isn't."

"Marissa?"

"Precisely. She's got some other system, and I think she's been quietly using it for years and years without anybody noticing. She does it somewhere that's nice and private, but also in the middle of things—and the epidemic's been rippling outward from it all this time." George took off his glasses with an air of finality. "No prizes for guessing *where* I think she's doing it. You're going there tonight."

"Fittes House," Lockwood said. "Right by Trafalgar Square, the center of London."

"I would say so."

"But *why*?" Holly cried. "That's what nobody's been able to explain to me! Why take the risks? Why stir up the ghosts? If they know the terrible consequences, why do they keep on doing it?"

"Whatever she's up to," George said, "it's working. She's rich, she's powerful, and sixty years after starting out, she's still here."

I got up to refill the kettle. Standing at the sink, I felt an impulsive desire to check that the garden was empty, that no one was listening to us. I peeped through the blinds at our overgrown lawn, at the houses opposite, at the old apple tree by the wall. I had a sudden image of little Lockwood seeing his dead parents standing beneath it, many years before. There was nothing out there now, just long grass, and a few rotten apples in the shadows of the boughs. The garden was quiet. No one was near.

"A moment ago, George," Lockwood said, when our mugs were full again, "you said that Marissa might have always found it easier to visit the Other Side than Tom Rotwell. Why do you say that?"

"She's a Listener," George said. "One of the two best there are." He looked at me.

I frowned. "What's *that* supposed to mean? I don't go waltzing off to the Other Side."

"No. Though you *have* been there. Thing is, I've been puzzling over what advantage Marissa might have had, and again, the answer's obvious. She talks to spirits. We know what that means: it brings you closer to them. After all, who, out of all of us, is closest to ghosts? Whose conversations with the skull gave us our most important clue?"

Everyone slowly turned their head to look at me—Lockwood, Holly, and Kipps—not accusingly, exactly, but with thoughtful contemplation. It was deeply irritating. Even worse, the face in the jar was winking at me and nuzzling up against the glass in a decidedly overfamiliar way.

"It's like I've always told you, Lucy," the skull said, *"you and me, we're a team. Hell, we're more than that. We're an item. Everybody knows it."*

"We are not," I growled.

"Are so."

"In your dreams." I glared at the others. "Don't ask me what it just said. It's not relevant to anything."

George adjusted his glasses. "Case in point. Marissa talks to ghosts in much the same way as you do. Only maybe in her case it's not just lovers' tiffs. Who knows what secrets they've given her, what mysteries of life and death."

I shook my head. "If so, she was lucky. This skull wouldn't know a mystery of life and death if it walked up and sat on it."

"Hey, I give you plenty of good stuff! You just don't have the wit to understand it."

"Oh, be quiet."

Lockwood had been watching the skull in silence for some

time; now, he stirred. "I'm glad our friend's feeling lively today," he said. "I'd like to ask him something." He regarded the jar. "So, Skull, you've often told us how you talked to Marissa, all those years ago. . . ."

The face rolled its eyes. "*Yes, yes, I chatted with her once. I've said so enough times, haven't I?*"

I passed on the essentials. "It says it did."

Lockwood nodded. "Just to be clear, you both spoke? It was a full conversation?"

"*That's right, bub. Like this one, only more interesting.*"

"Yes, it was a full conversation."

"So how come Marissa didn't keep you?" Lockwood asked.

The face in the jar gave a start. "*What?*"

"It says, 'What?'" I said.

"As in it didn't hear me? Or didn't understand?"

"More like it was peeved. You definitely hit a nerve there, Lockwood."

"*He so did not!*"

I nodded. "The skull's sore about it. Definitely sore."

"*I'm not sore!*" the ghost said. "*Not in the slightest. I simply don't understand the relevance of the question.*"

I relayed this. "Well," Lockwood said, "whenever I read Marissa Fittes's *Memoirs*, I see she makes great play of having spoken with Type Three spirits. She goes on and on about how rare and fascinating it is." He smiled at the ghost. "Which makes me wonder, Skull, why you ended up in a jar in the cellar for fifty years, after this one conversation."

"No need to wonder about that," I said feelingly. "I've long been tempted to do the same with it."

"But you see my point. She knew the ghost's value. It could have told her any number of secrets about the Other Side. Yet she chose to ignore it. Why?"

"Skull?"

"*Search me.*" The face still looked annoyed; the light in the eyes dwindled to a bright green ember. Then, as if from far away, it said, in a small, affectless voice, "*I will say that she didn't seem surprised at my being able to speak. At my robust language, yes. At some of my choicer suggestions about what she could do with herself, also. But at me actually speaking? No. It was old news as far as Marissa was concerned.*"

I repeated all this, as best I could. Lockwood nodded. "Remember that quote George read out just now—what did Marissa say? The dead 'bring with them the secrets of the past'? She'd been chatting to another Type Three."

"*It's possible.*" The skull gave a grunt. "*How it could have been any more fascinating or informative than me, I can't imagine.*"

"Well," George said, "maybe the mysterious little book *Occult Theories* will shed some light on that. I'll let you know tonight, when I get back from the library." He began gathering up his papers. "That's it for now," he said. "I hope you thought it worth waiting for."

"George," Lockwood said, "you've worked wonders. I don't know what we'd do without you."

Chapter 13

Penelope Fittes, director of the great Fittes Agency, was not a publically-minded person. Despite her celebrity, she mostly confined herself to her apartments in Fittes House, the headquarters of the company on the Strand. True, she occasionally emerged for important ceremonies, such as the annual service for fallen agents at the tombs behind Horse Guards Parade. And she was sometimes glimpsed, black hair pinned back, dark glasses on, driving through the capital in her silver Rolls-Royce, on her way to appointments at the Sunrise Corporation or Fairfax Iron. But that was about it. Invitations to meet with her in private were not normally forthcoming. So the summons to Fittes House to hear Penelope speak on agency matters that evening was not one to be ignored, even if you weren't interested in her. And we *were* interested, very deeply.

Even so, only Lockwood and I attended, since Holly had a prior engagement. George was busy at the library. "We'll compare notes tonight," he'd said as he departed. "I'll be back later, hopefully with the book. Meanwhile, you go and see Penelope—or Marissa—or whoever she is. Look her in the eyes, and tell me what you see."

What we saw when we arrived at the great gray building on the Strand were streams of operatives from our fellow agencies arriving in the dusk of early evening. There they all were: the lilac jackets of Grimble, the sky-blue ones of Tamworth, the striped pink blazers of Mellingcamp, and the rest. They congregated by the flower beds, where ranks of lilies had been planted in the shapes of rampant unicorns; they filed slowly through the etched glass doors. Traditionally, herding so many agents together would have been like shoveling a dozen tomcats into a sack and expecting them to cuddle up and keep the peace. Rivalry between companies was deeply ingrained, a function of their independence; in the past, chance encounters in the street often led to arguments and even duels. Tonight, with that independence threatened, the mood was different, wary and subdued. Doors were held open for old enemies; muttered greetings exchanged. Under the watchful gaze of many gray-jacketed Fittes agents, we shuffled through reception and into the conference hall.

As the venue for her announcement, Ms. Fittes had chosen this mighty room, the Hall of Pillars. It was one of the most famous meeting places in London, a grand and gilded space, where marble floors and decorated ceilings showcased the wealth and history of the agency. Nine slender silver-glass pillars stood like birch trees at the center of the hall. Each contained an artifact of historic significance, a powerful psychic Source collected by ghost-hunting pioneers Marissa Fittes and Tom Rotwell during the infancy of the

Problem. By day, electric lamps illuminated the relics for the wonderment of visitors; by night, the trapped spirits swam silently within the pillars. With the light failing outside, they were just beginning to stir.

Lockwood and I took glasses of juice from silent attendants, and meandered to a location on the fringes of the crowd. We studied the room. On a wall at the far end, a banner had been raised. It had the words THE FITTES INITIATIVE written on it in assertive black. Below stood a lectern on a little raised platform; this was covered with a drape emblazoned with a silver unicorn. It was almost identical to the one we'd found lying on Marissa's coffin, in the crypt just up the road.

Soon attendees had arrived from all the independent agencies (even Bunchurch, which in the absence of their leader was represented by two frightened-looking youths). The hall was almost full. The doors were closed, the lamps turned low. Within the glowing pillars, shadowy forms flared and darted like deep-sea fish. Servants entered, bringing canapés on silver trays.

Lockwood took a petite spring roll and munched on it cheerfully. "Forget Tufnell's place, Lucy," he murmured. "Look at this. This is a proper bit of theater, right here."

I couldn't be quite as calm as Lockwood—the announcement we were here for was unlikely to be a nice one—but I knew exactly what he meant. The room was perfect for its purpose, which was to overawe and subdue its guests. The crowd of agents was a vast and colorful array—their jackets resplendent, their rapiers glinting under the light of the chandeliers—and yet compared to the solid, unchanging majesty of the great gold hall, which effortlessly swallowed them all, they seemed somehow tawdry and fleeting, of little consequence. High above our heads, ceiling paintings showed legendary early agents, great martyrs of the Fittes Agency. The pillars were like the treasure houses of a king.

"Better take off your bag, Luce," Lockwood said. "Set it on the floor here, give it a decent view."

Unlike other companies in London, Lockwood & Co. had never bothered with a uniform, and we stood out again tonight. As usual Lockwood was smartly dressed in his suit and coat, while I wore my normal working outfit. I would have preferred to dress up a bit, too, but the large supply bag I carried on my back would have ruined the look. If anyone asked, I was to say I was on my way to a case, which was in fact true. We had two quick jobs in Soho to attend to on our way home.

I shrugged the bag down. The top flap was left subtly loose, leaving a dark but inconspicuous gap beneath.

"*Coo,*" the skull's voice said in my mind. "*Isn't this fancy. They've spruced it up since I was last here. Used to be a couple of beat-up display cases and an old settee. Where's Marissa, then? That's not her. It's a pimply bloke scarfing a sausage roll. I'd have thought even you could see that.*"

"I *know* she's not here yet," I muttered. "We're still waiting. See that lectern? That's where she'll be." I nudged the bag forward with a boot and turned to Lockwood. "The skull's talking nonsense even more than usual," I said. "It's edgy. And so am I."

"No need to be," Lockwood said. "We're among friends."

He nodded his head in the direction of a nonchalant figure in a vile green suit, leaning against the wall near the lectern. Sir Rupert

Gale was idly surveying the crowd of agents; as I watched, he caught my gaze and gave a little wave.

"We ought to run him through and have done with it," I growled.

Lockwood smiled. "Yes, but it would only spoil this nice clean floor." He took a fresh glass of juice from a passing attendant. "Want another drink, Luce?"

"No. I don't know how you can be so relaxed."

"Oh, we have to go with the flow, make the most of being here." Lockwood's body language was as chilled as Sir Rupert's, but his eyes were never still, scanning the boundaries of the room. "Let's move a bit closer to the pillar, shall we? We can lean against it and doze, if Penelope's talk goes on too long."

It was the pillar farthest from the lectern, at the margins of the crowd. It glowed with a pale blue light. On a steel rack inside the glass hung a wicked-looking knife with odd serrations, the very knife with which the Clapham Butcher Boy had worked his horrors fifty years before. If you looked closely and at the correct angle, you could just see the ghost of the Boy himself floating above and around the weapon. He wasn't the most active of the nine trapped spirits in the hall, but he always caused particularly loud shrieks among parties of touring schoolchildren, his eyes having been put out by the mob that had finally run him down.

From somewhere came the bang of a door. The noise of the crowd dropped, became a nervous rustling murmur, soft and dry as fallen leaves.

Sir Rupert was looking toward the side of the room. He gave a nod.

The sound of high-heeled shoes echoed through the hall.

"*Uh-oh,*" the skull's voice said. "*She's coming.*"

At once, Lockwood was at my elbow. "Listen carefully to what she says, Luce. I don't want to miss anything."

"Why, what will you be—?"

But now Penelope Fittes was walking into the hall.

She crossed from a far door, out under the lights, a slim, tall woman with long black hair lying loose around her shoulders. She wore a dark green knee-length dress that molded around her body in a businesslike sort of way. It was glamorous, yes, but functional; she moved with calm precision. I'd been building up the moment so much, to be reminded of her very ordinary human scale surprised me. Then she climbed onto the platform, stepped behind the lectern, gave her flashbulb smile—and spoke.

"Hello, everybody."

Yes, that voice: deep, authoritative, unmistakable. At the sound of it, I was transfixed. There she was: Penelope Fittes, chairperson of the Fittes Agency, associate director of the Rotwell Agency, and de facto head of all psychic investigation operatives in London. For months she had been the focus of our energies, our thoughts and fears, our dreams and plans. Everything extended from her—from her power and her mystery—and everything led back to her, too.

Just by stepping through the door, she had at once become the focal point of the room. She was reflected in a hundred wineglasses, in the curving sides of the nine silver-glass pillars, in a thousand teardrop crystals of the ceiling's chandeliers. Did the ghosts within the pillars turn to watch her as she strode to the curved wood lectern? I wouldn't have been surprised. Certainly the Fittes employees previously standing at the side of the hall were now rigid with attention;

one or two even saluted. My fellow agents did *not* salute, but they were very still. The room had become silent. Only Sir Rupert Gale maintained his louche and tolerant posture, but even he had eyes only for Penelope; his gaze remained locked on her as she took a sip of water, adjusted her paper, and smiled gleamingly at the silent crowd.

"It's very good of you to come along this evening. I know how busy you all are." She was looking at us all, the grizzled old super-visors, the green young agents, sizing us up, taking our measure. "Indeed, that's really why I've brought you here. But before I go on, may I just thank the heads of DEPRAC for inviting me to host this occasion. This hall has seen so many important nights. My grand-mother Marissa often used it to . . ."

Her grandmother Marissa. This was the crux we were fumbling toward. I frowned. Even from a distance Penelope was clearly in radiant shape. She certainly didn't *look* eighty-plus years old.

"Skull," I whispered, "do you see her?"

"It's so difficult from down here. My view's partially blocked. I'm looking through people's legs. And there's one agent there who keeps jiggling around with her particularly enormous—"

"Can you see her or not?"

"Yes. It's her. It's Marissa. Clear as day."

I shook my head in doubt. I turned to Lockwood. "What do you think?"

But I was alone by the pillar. Lockwood was gone.

He did this sort of thing all the time. I shouldn't have been surprised, or particularly worried—but that evening my nerves were brittle. Cursing inwardly, I looked for him at the back of the room, but he was nowhere to be seen.

"I say I know how busy you all are"—Penelope wasn't wasting time; she was already coming to the nub of the matter—"but *busy* isn't really strong enough, is it?" she went on. "*Overworked* would be closer to the truth. We are all struggling to keep afloat in the supernatural flood that threatens to drown our great country." A slender arm was elegantly out-flung. "See these pillars here? These famous pillars, from the earliest days of our battle with the Problem? Nine notorious relics! When my grandmother subdued such ghosts as Long Hugh Hennratty and the Clapham Butcher Boy, she thought she was winning the war. When she compressed the Morden Poltergeist into its silver teapot, she never imagined that two generations later such feats would be a nightly business for so many brave and selfless young people. We might all fill a hundred such pillars, and there would still be no end to the terrors we face. And at what cost!"

Another sip of water; a toss of her long black mane. She had some kind of gold necklace on—laced with diamonds, probably. It sparkled in the spotlight. Everyone waited grimly. We knew what was coming.

"We all remember the difficulties of the Black Winter," Penelope said, "the longest and worst in the history of the Problem. Mortality rates spiked—particularly among operatives in smaller agencies, where resources are so tight." Her dark eyes flashed at the silent crowd. "Think back just for a moment. How many of *your* young heroes perished in those months, trying to make our country a safer place?"

"None of *ours* did," I said, under my breath. "Lockwood and Co. was just fine, thanks." I glanced around; predictably, Lockwood had not returned.

"A new winter is coming," Penelope Fittes went on, "with forecasts suggesting that it will be no better than the one before. Do any of us want to see a whole new line of little tombs behind Horse Guards Parade? Do you want any of *your* employees to lie there? Of course not. And you're quite right. Such mortality rates can't be permitted again. But I am pleased to report that DEPRAC has been giving the matter some thought, and they have come to a decision." Penelope Fittes glanced up at the banner by her side. She waved a gracious hand in its direction. "Yes, they are calling it the 'Fittes Initiative.' Rather than let DEPRAC close you all down, I have agreed that each small agency, for the duration of the winter, will come under the protection of the combined Fittes and Rotwell Group. We will provide extra manpower, money, and resources, and oversee difficult operations for you. The arrangement will start at the end of October and last until March, when it will be reviewed to see . . ."

The crowd emitted a long, soft sigh. They understood what she was really saying. Like it or not, we were coming under her control. It wasn't hard to imagine it becoming a permanent arrangement at winter's end.

A movement at my side caught my attention. Was it Lockwood? No. It came from within the silver-glass pillar. Looking around, I was disconcerted to see the wide, translucent head of the Clapham Butcher Boy pressed right against the glass, jowls wobbling, slack mouth gaping. The thing would have been staring straight at me, if the eyes hadn't been plucked out. I jerked back in consternation.

"*Hey, fish-face, find your own human!*" the skull's voice called. "*You* do *attract them, don't you, Lucy?*" it continued. "*Even behind that thick prison, even dumb and sightless as he is, he knows. He smells someone who's been to the Other Side.*"

I shuddered. "How can it know that?"

"*You carry the taint of it. It can't be shaken off. It's with you always. Lockwood, too. But neither of you are anything compared to Marissa there. She stinks of it.*"

"The Other Side?"

"*She may look good to you, but whatever she's been doing to look so young, it isn't yoga, I can tell you that.*"

"Hey, Lucy." Another movement: not the Butcher Boy this time, but Lockwood—much as before, but with a touch of pink in his cheeks and sweat beading just beside his ear. He still held his glass of juice; he took a sip. "Did I miss anything?"

I glared at him, my anxiety hardening into annoyance. "Only the whole speech." Up at the lectern, Penelope had finished her remarks with a few condescending platitudes. She smiled, waved at no one in particular, and left the stage. *Click, click, click* went her heels as she slipped out of the room. It was all done in dead silence. A few flunkies followed her out; a door closed. She was gone.

Only now did the assembled agents begin to stir. There was a low, indignant muttering, swelling into loud complaint. Then the uproar began.

"Everyone sounds predictably happy," Lockwood said.

"Yeah, it was much as expected." Scowling, I gave a brief summary. "She's turning the screw on us again. She had a nerve bringing up all the dead agents. It has nothing to do with the size of the organization, it's all about the teamwork. Anyway, we're coming under her thumb, like it or not. Where have you been?"

Lockwood smiled at me like he was coming out of a dream. He didn't answer. "What did the skull say?"

"Same as before. Yes, she's Marissa. Outwardly she's different. But her essential nature is identical to when he spoke to her decades ago. And the odor of the Other Side hangs strongly around her."

He nodded absently, as if the information didn't surprise him. He moved back to let a couple of grim-faced Mellingcamp agents past. A wave of guests was making for the doors. A few stayed to mop up the final remnants of food and drink, but most were desperate to be gone. We remained loitering in the shadow of the pillar, where the sightless ghost hovered, staring at us from its pale blue prison. "What's so frustrating," Lockwood said, "is that the answer to everything is so, so close to us right now."

"You've seen something?"

"No. I tried. I didn't find it."

"Then how do you know—?"

He made a gesture of impatience. "Oh, because George is right! This is Fittes House! She keeps it all close, that's how she retains control. She's not stupid like Steve Rotwell, building weird laboratories in fields, doing crazy experiments where anyone could just break in. *This* is where the action is. It always has been. George worked here once, and Kipps did for years. They both said there are big areas that remain out-of-bounds to almost everyone—whole levels in the basements, and Penelope's apartments up top. You've seen the Black Library—that was full of secret stuff, too. But it's the upper floors, where Penelope lives, that *I'd* like to see. That's where we'd find out the truth." He nodded toward a broad inner door. "The elevators are just through there, in the Hall of Fallen Heroes. Five bronze elevators and a single silver one that goes up to her rooms. What I wouldn't give just to pop up for ten minutes." He sighed. "But it's impossible."

I stared at him. "Don't tell me that's what you just tried doing . . . ?"

"It seemed the perfect opportunity." Lockwood grinned at me. "Penelope down here. Everyone busy, all the Fittes crowd gawping at their mistress. I just strolled out. Had to dodge a few people, take a long-winded detour or two. I got to the Hall of Fallen Heroes easily enough. But it was a no-go. There were whopping big guards posted at the elevators. I had to turn around."

"Or you'd have gone up in the silver elevator?"

"Of course."

Anger flared inside me. How far could recklessness stretch before it truly became a death wish? "Lockwood," I said, "you've *got* to be more careful. I can't believe you would do something like that without me. I'd never dream of doing that on my—"

A jovial cry came from across the room. "Lockwood, you old hound! I *thought* I saw you skulking there." Sir Rupert Gale was striding toward us, draining a glass of champagne. "You two still hanging around?" he said. "I'd have thought you couldn't get out fast enough after enduring Penelope's little rant." He gave me a cheery wink. "Were you maybe thinking of scrounging the last few canapés, Miss Carlyle? I could get you both a doggie bag."

"No, thanks," I said. "We were on our way out."

"Yes, perhaps that would be best. We wouldn't want you to be swept out with the trash. That's a very big handbag you're carrying with you, if you don't mind me saying."

"We're off to a couple of cases," I said. "Perhaps you want to see my papers?"

"No, no. We'll take it as read this time." Sir Rupert raised his glass to the bloodstained ghost in the pillar, which was inching around to follow us as we walked past toward the door. "Looks as if *someone* likes you, anyway, Miss Carlyle. Isn't it nice to have a fan?"

"Didn't know you could see ghosts so clearly, Sir Rupert," Lockwood said. "Aren't you a bit old for that?"

An expression of mild annoyance crossed the man's face, as of one caught in some minor indiscretion. "Oh, well," he said. "I'm younger than I look. The doors are just through here. . . ." With ostentatious courtesy, he escorted us back across reception to the entrance. Outside, the fragmenting host of agents was milling around. Some took waiting Night Cabs, others dispersed in little groups into the night. "Where's Cubbins?" Sir Rupert asked suddenly, as we started down the steps. "Not off being naughty in some library again?"

"George will be at home, I should think," Lockwood said easily. "Probably making one of his chicken-and-sweetcorn pies. He's really very domesticated."

Sir Rupert smiled approvingly. "Sounds scrumptious. I must pop round to Portland Row sometime."

"Please do," Lockwood said. "I'd love that."

"Good night, then."

"Good night."

We pattered swiftly down the steps and set off up the Strand.

"One day," Lockwood said, "I'm clearly going to have to kill him. Not now, but sometime soon."

The two Soho jobs turned out to be fairly minor: a Lurker in an apartment above a Chinese restaurant, and a Bone Man in an alley just off Wardour Street. Both were easy to constrain, but it took time to locate the Sources (an antique paper fan and a worn sandstone milepost, respectively) and get them safe and sealed. We didn't get back to Portland Row until shortly before midnight. There was a light showing in the living room window.

"Looks like George is waiting up with his results," Lockwood said. "Told you he wouldn't be able to hold it in."

I smiled. "Let's go and put him out of his misery."

We opened the door. Holly stood in the hall by the coatrack, one hand holding on to the coats as if she needed their support. Her posture was odd, both rigid and subtly off-kilter. She looked at us. She didn't say anything. Her face was taut, stricken.

We stopped at the threshold. It was suddenly a new night, a different one. We had passed from one to the other, and I didn't know where I was.

"Holly?"

"You need to come. There's been an incident."

A deadweight swung from my spine. My legs were water. I knew.

"George?" Lockwood said.

"He was found in the street. He's been attacked. Hurt."

Lockwood's voice didn't sound like his at all. "Is he all right?"

"No, he isn't." The tiny shake of the head made the world tilt under me. "Lockwood," Holly said, "it's bad."

Chapter 14

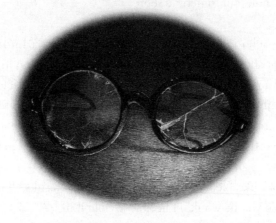

Some months before, Lockwood and I had walked together through a gate made of stockpiled Sources, where ghosts screamed in a perpetual whirlwind and the air was deathly cold. We'd stepped through it and out into another world. This was a place superficially the same as ours, but different; a place where normal rules did not apply. The transition had been instant, sickly, and disorienting, and the effects were almost fatal.

Those experiences were nothing to the dislocation I felt now.

The hall *looked* ordinary, but the colors were wrong, and the objects in the room kept slipping out of position. Holly was both close and very far away. She was talking; her voice boomed in my head like a ship's horn, but it was also too faint to hear.

George.

George.

George.

"Where is he? What happened?" Someone else was speaking. I thought it was Lockwood, but the rush of blood in my ears was like a flood tide carrying me elsewhere. I fought against it, paddled furiously back into the present moment. Like Holly I needed to clutch at something. I jammed my fingers against the wall.

"St. Thomas's Hospital," Holly said. "It was a Night Cab driver who found him. You know that guy Jake we use a lot? He was turning down the end of Nightingale Walk. Just by chance, Lockwood, he was taking a shortcut. If he *hadn't* been, if he hadn't been there, Lockwood, there'd have been no one with George until dawn. And then—"

"So Jake found him," Lockwood interrupted. "I get that. Where was he? What exactly had happened?"

"He was lying on the edge of the sidewalk, half in the gutter, and at first Jake thought"—Holly gulped back tears—"thought he was just a pile of old clothes that someone had *dumped* there, Lockwood. A pile of old clothes! Then he recognized George's jacket. He said he was sure that George was . . . At least, there was so much blood, he couldn't imagine how he could possibly be—"

"Blood?" I said. My hand was clamped over my mouth. "Blood? Oh no. . . ."

"How was he lying?" Lockwood's voice was unfamiliar; he fired the words out, forcing Holly to speak. "Was he faceup, facedown, what?"

Holly wiped her eyes. "He was facedown, I think."

"He'd been beaten?"

"I—I think so—"

"He wasn't conscious?"

"No."

"Did he regain consciousness at any time?"

"No. He was taken to the hospital. Jake called a night-ambulance. Luckily, there was one nearby. He went with them. George is there now."

"Any word on how he is?"

"No."

Lockwood was moving down the hallway. His face was stricken, his jaw clamped tight. He brushed past Holly like she wasn't there. Then he stopped. "How did you hear about it?" he said. "I thought you'd gone home."

"I had. Jake knows where I live; he's driven me home before. He tried here first, then stopped by my place. I came back, waited for you—"

"All right. I'm going to make some calls." Lockwood headed toward the kitchen.

"Lockwood," I said, "shouldn't we—?"

"I'm going to make some calls. Wait here."

He was gone. A moment later, we heard his footsteps clattering down the iron stairs.

Holly and I were left in the hall. We looked at one another, but it wasn't easy to meet each other's gaze. Hugging was better. That way we could be close, while staring out at nothing. There wasn't anything else we could do.

Even now, when so much else has happened, the events of that dreadful night remain mostly a blur to me. Their sequence is unclear. Time did strange things. I have no idea how long I spent anywhere or in what order—in the hospital; in the hall with Holly; later (it must have been later, after our return from a fruitless visit to St. Thomas's, with no word on George's condition) sitting with her under a blanket on the sofa, sleepless and silent, waiting for Lockwood to return. For some reason it's the lights I remember most: the crystal skull lamp in the hall; the tasseled lantern on the living room cabinet; most of all the striplights crossing the ceiling in the hospital waiting room like a row of minus signs, like center markings on a road to nowhere, with the iron ghost-wards dangling beside them, moving in the air-conditioned breeze. Lights, always lights; strong, weak, harsh, or warm, but always indifferent and always on. It was a night without darkness; you couldn't switch off or look away.

How did I *get* to the hospital? How did I get back? I don't remember. Lockwood was there with me, at least at first. I have a snapshot of him in a car, the white glow of the ghost-lamps (those lights again) flashing across his pale, blank face. We didn't talk, not then, nor during the endless waiting. We weren't permitted to see George. We weren't told how he was, or where he was. I have a memory of someone (Lockwood? Me?) kicking a chair across the reception room, but I have no memory of the lead-up to it, nor of the consequences, if there were any. At some point, Inspector Barnes was there, and also Quill Kipps, though neither of them stayed long. Then—somehow—I was back at Portland Row with Holly, a bowl of popcorn wedged between us, and the white dawn showing through the messy crack in the half-drawn curtains.

Night fed into morning and Lockwood did not return. He didn't come back from the hospital all that day. He sent word through

Kipps, who showed up periodically, gallows-eyed and unshaven, with brief accounts of what was going on. What was going on was nothing. Nothing to stop the high, thin noise (too high, too thin to technically be a scream) that rang continuously in my head. George remained unconscious. He had suffered head injuries, and multiple contusions on his back and limbs. Lockwood had been allowed to see him, but only briefly. There was no point in going to the hospital. We would only be turned away.

Holly and I stumbled through what chores we could, focusing on insignificant details in an effort to pummel our existence into some semblance of rightness. I canceled a number of appointments we had for the evening. Holly tried doing some paperwork but quickly gave up. Instead we roamed the house. We sorted salt-bombs and refilled iron canisters. Holly went shopping. She bought a stack of doughnuts and cream buns, but somehow neither of us could bear to look at them. We put them in a cupboard. The day drifted on and on like this, and neither of us could sleep.

Whether through some quirk of empathy or (more likely) an acute sense of self-preservation, the skull in the jar didn't try speaking to me. My head was empty of its psychic interference, which was a relief. In truth, though, it was empty of everything. I was scoured out, waiting.

Toward evening a final message from Lockwood came via Kipps. It bought news that I interpreted as hopeful, in the same way that a drowning man looks favorably on an outstretched twig. For the first time George was showing signs of responsiveness. He hadn't yet woken properly, but there was movement now. Lockwood would remain for a second night.

Even then, it took me a long while to fall asleep. You might have thought that after thirty-six hours without rest, I'd be able to drop off easily. But I was wired into a grid that refused to cut the power. I lay on the bed, staring at nothing, thinking of nothing, and when I *did* doze, I almost as quickly woke again. At some point in the early hours I got up and drove my rapier deep into the bedroom wall.

Eventually, while it was still dark, oblivion must have come, because I was surprised when I opened my eyes and saw sunlight streaming in through my window. The face in the ghost-jar watched me silently. My sword stuck out from a jagged crack in the plaster just beside my chest of drawers. It was almost noon. I was still wearing my clothes.

I washed and dressed mechanically and went downstairs. The house was quiet as a church. It looked very clean and tidy. Yesterday Holly had even dusted the ghost-wards hanging on the staircase and landing walls. As I approached the kitchen I could hear her moving around inside. Little cozy domestic noises, of cutlery and crockery, like messages from a happier time.

"Hey, Holly . . ."

I pushed open the door and saw Lockwood standing at the window. He wore his usual dark pants and white shirt, tie-less, the collar unbuttoned. His sleeves were rolled up, showing his slim arms. His hair had not been combed, and it was not clear to me that he'd slept at all. Certainly he was as pale as I'd ever seen him, and his eyes shone with a strange, unhealthy brightness. But he smiled as he turned and saw me.

"Hi, Lucy."

It was a moment that probably lasted less than a second, but it felt as if we were standing there for a lifetime. A lifetime of me wait-ing for Lockwood, waiting for him to say the necessary words.

I spoke fractionally first. "Is he—?"

"George is fine," Lockwood said. "He's alive." He had his long thin fingers resting on a chair back; he stared at them as if they belonged to someone else. Then he left the chair and walked around the table and put his arms about me and pulled me to him. Time did weird stuff again. We stood like that for I don't know how long. I would've been happy for it to go on longer.

"So he's fine?" I asked once we'd drawn apart. "Really?"

Lockwood sighed. "Well, no—not really. He's got several types of concussion, but we all know how thick his skull is." He smiled at me. "But he'll live. He's conscious, so you needn't worry."

"He's woken up? He's really talked to you and everything?"

"Yes. He's a bit sleepy. But at least he's home now."

"*Home*? What? He's here?"

"Not so loud. He's upstairs. In my bed, as a matter of fact."

"Not his room?" I paused. "Actually, no. I can see that wouldn't work."

"No, he'd just get sepsis. It's fine like this. I'll sleep on the couch."

"Sure. Lockwood—I'm *so* pleased you're both back."

"Me, too. Do you want tea? Silly question. I'll get you some."

"So tell me what happened," I said. "When did he wake? Were you with him? What did he say?"

"He didn't say much—*hasn't* said much. He's too weak as yet. The doctor didn't really want him to leave the hospital, but this morning he had to concede that George was out of danger, so . . ."

Lockwood stared into space, holding a spoon. "Where do we keep the tea bags now?"

"On the shelf, where they always are. Have you had any sleep?"

"Not much. I'm not quite ready yet. . . . What was I doing?"

"You were making tea. Look, I'll do it. Where *is* Holly? She's not yet been in?" Holly had gone home the previous evening, searching for elusive rest, like me.

"Not yet, I don't think." Lockwood hesitated. "How is she?"

"Oh, like the rest of us, I expect." I glanced back at him as I stirred the tea. "While you were gone, I was thinking . . . You were very hard on her, you know—when she first told us about George, back in the hall."

Lockwood took his mug in silence. Then he said, "I wanted every detail. I wanted to see that image of George as if I was there myself."

"It's not your fault, Lockwood."

"No? Barnes thinks it is."

I remembered the inspector, a brown and furrowed presence beneath his raincoat, passing me in a hospital corridor. It was a disconnected image, leading nowhere. There were no details. "How *was* Barnes when you spoke to him?"

"Civil."

"What did he say?"

Lockwood sighed. "He didn't *need* to say anything—his face was eloquent enough. He couldn't talk openly, anyway—he had several police officers with him. And there was George's doctor, too." Lockwood shook his head. "I didn't trust him. Barnes says he's worked for both the Fittes and Rotwell companies. He might be okay, but . . . Anyway, I'm not having George out of our sight from now on. That's why I brought him home."

I looked toward the ceiling. "He's out of our sight right now, if it comes to that."

He shook his head again. "Not exactly. He's got company."

"Who? Not Holly. Not Kipps, surely. Or is Kipps here?"

"Flo."

"*What*? *Flo*? She's in the sick room?" I stared at him. "Is that sanitary?"

"She was very insistent."

"How did she even find out about it?"

"I don't know. She showed up an hour ago and barged upstairs. She brought some black things in a pot." Lockwood rubbed the back of his neck. "I hope they were grapes, but with Flo you just can't tell."

I drank my tea, letting its warmth run through me. As so often, the feeling brought me back to the essentials. The moment became simpler, my needs clearer.

"Lockwood," I said, "I want to see George. I want to see him now."

The bedroom door was slightly ajar, and we were able to push it open without a sound. In the ordinary way Lockwood's room was the opposite of George's, being clean and tidy and sparsely furnished. Not that I went in it much, but I'd always linked it with sunlight and smooth white sheets and the smell of lavender. The sight of Flo Bones squatting in the armchair like a death-cap mushroom blew such associations into sweet oblivion. She lifted her straw hat up a notch and made stern shushing gestures. The air smelled antiseptic and also somehow stale and muddy, courtesy of Flo; the curtains were partly drawn. The bed was dim, the covers rumpled. It was hard to see its occupant at all.

We stole across the carpet. Flo's puffer jacket rasped as she pulled herself free of the chair.

"Don't disturb him!" she hissed. "He needs his rest!"

"I know he does," Lockwood whispered. "How is he, Flo? Has he woken?"

"He's been muttering all kinds of stuff. He asked for water. I gave him some."

"I suppose that's all right, if you've washed your hands. Come to think of it, while we're at it, you could always take your boots off as well."

"Take it from me, Locky, my socks would mark your carpet worse." Though Flo spoke with her usual gusto, she kept her voice low, and I saw her watching me closely as I moved past her to the bed. It was a rare experience for her to linger any length of time in our dry, roofed world. She preferred living under stars and bridges, with water lapping at her Wellingtons, in an isolated and amphibious life. None of that applied now. She was here in our moment of crisis. She was here for George.

The thing that struck me first was how small he looked, how low and sad the bump was under the sheets. You might almost have missed him, your eye drawn instead to the piled pillows or the bedspread half on the floor. But no, there were the distinctive glasses set carefully on the bedside table, with a diagonal crack running neatly through one lens. And there, wedged between the pillows—the sight of it made me catch my breath—was a roundish object, both dark and light. The light part was bandages, with a few sad wisps of sandy hair protruding. The dark part was bruises. There wasn't much in between.

"Oh, *George*," I said.

The shape stirred feebly, making me jump; it gave a groan and said something unintelligible. An arm emerged and flopped down upon the sheet.

"*Now* look what you've done, you silly mare!" Flo hissed. "You've only gone and woken him up!"

But Lockwood and I were already by the bed, bending close beside him.

"George!"

"Hey, George. It's me, Lucy."

George tried to speak. It shocked and horrified me how feeble his whisper was. More even than the sight of that battered face or the shrunken body in the bed, that whisper was an atrocious thing. He tried again: husky, urgent, impossible to hear. We craned our heads nearer. George hadn't opened his swollen eyes. His hand clutched blindly, seized Lockwood's arm.

This time the words came out. "They took it," he whispered.

"What?"

"Marissa's book. I had it, but . . ." The words trailed away.

Lockwood's expression frightened me, but his voice was light and airy. "Oh, don't worry about *that*," he said. He patted George's hand. "All that matters is that you're here at Portland Row. Luce's here, and me, and you know you've got good old Flo here beside you, too. . . ."

George's hand fell back. "Yes . . . yes, that's good."

"Yes. So the important thing is that you need to sleep now, George."

The bandaged head erupted from the pillow. We both jerked back. "No! I *had* it! Marissa's book! The evidence, Lockwood . . . !" He subsided in a fit of feeble coughing.

Flo bustled forward. "Right. You're exciting him. Time's up."

"No, it isn't, Flo. Who was it, George? Who did this to you? Did you see them?"

"No. But . . ."

"But what, George? Was it Sir Rupert Gale?"

It took a long while for him to answer. I began to think he'd drifted off. The whisper was barely audible. "I smelled him. His aftershave. As I hit the ground . . ." The voice trailed off. "I'm sorry. . . ."

"Nothing to be sorry about, George. Just rest up." Lockwood patted the limp hand; he stood up slowly, straight-backed, looking at nothing. "We're going now, Flo," he said. "You'll call us if you need anything?"

She nodded; she was already at the bedside, doing things with blankets. Given that she normally slept on riverbanks and muddy shingle, I was quite impressed. George had sunk back between the pillows. Once again he was just a small, low mound in the center of the bed.

We exited the bedroom and softly shut the door.

"I'll kill them," I said. "Lockwood, I swear I'm going to kill them."

He said nothing; he was very still, standing in the shadows of the landing. I kicked out at the banister, hurting my foot in the process. I had to move. I had to strike at *something*. The fury I felt was otherwise too great.

"Sir Rupert Gale and those big bloody henchmen of his! I'm going to take my sword and go out and find them, and make them pay."

"You're not going to do that, Lucy."

"I am. I'm going to kill them."

"You're not."

"Why?"

"Because you'd only muck it up somehow. Also because it's not our style. We're going to do something better. And we're going to do it as a team."

I stopped trying to destroy his house and looked at him. A shaft of light was coming through the landing window; in its brightness Lockwood looked insubstantial, like he was some figure on stained glass. "Our enemies think we're weak," he went on. "Truth is, I've been holding back until now." He smiled at me, his eyes as hard as flint. "Well, all that ends today. We'll strike them where they least expect it. We'll strike them, Lucy, and we'll take them down."

Chapter 15

ockwood's vow sounded good, especially spoken in that shaft of sunlight and all, but I couldn't help noticing that he wasn't spelling out any details. In fact, he was utterly vague. This didn't bother me particularly, because I knew he'd think of something. I just guessed it would take him a while to figure out a plan.

In this I was quite wrong. Lockwood not only *had* a plan, it was already well under way. I discovered afterward that he had been devising his response to the attack on George almost from the moment it happened. During his long vigil in the hospital, his initial shock had hardened into furious intent. He'd had plenty of time to explore his options, make decisions, and set his strategy in motion. But I only began to realize this when Quill Kipps showed up later that afternoon with a bulging plastic bag in his hand.

"Here you are, Lockwood," he said, pouring the contents out onto the kitchen table. "Four black ski masks, four sets of thin black gloves. Got them from a seedy little shop in Whitechapel. I completely cleaned them out of sinister protective clothing. There's going to be a lot of disappointed criminals in the East End till they get their next delivery."

"Excellent." Lockwood was inspecting a ski mask. "I see they've got mouth holes and everything, so we can speak to each other easily. That's always useful. Great work, Quill. How's the surveillance been going?"

"Nicely." Kipps tapped his backpack. "I've got photos, too."

"Superb. Will it be feasible?"

"At the worst, we might have to rough up a few seniors."

"I think we can cope with that."

Holly and I had been following this exchange like it was a tennis match, heads turning in bafflement from Quill to Lockwood and back again. Now Holly raised a hand. "There'll be some roughing up going on right now," she said, "if you don't start filling us in. No *ifs* or *buts*, please. Tell us what's going on."

Lockwood grinned. "Certainly. We're going to complete George's research for him. Who's up for a spot of burglary?"

A fly on the wall, lured perhaps by the prospect of one of Holly's cakes, wouldn't at first have noticed anything unusual about our meeting in the living room that afternoon. So many missions had been planned there—why was this so different? But it was. There weren't any cakes, for starters—it would have seemed wrong to eat anything, with George lying stricken just upstairs. No cake, no tea, and no George. And we weren't discussing ghosts, either. We spoke in hushed tones, our faces pale and grim.

Kipps got the proceedings going. He took out a packet of grainy black-and-white photographs and spread them across the table. They mostly showed an elegant black door, with whitewashed pillars on either side. A succession of elderly, well-dressed men and women were coming out of it. One in particular caught my eye.

"I *know* him," I said, pointing to a snapshot of a man with white hair. He had a big, bulging forehead and a slight stoop; his long black coat was decidedly old-fashioned.

Lockwood nodded. "Yes. The secretary of the Orpheus Society. This is their front door."

The Orpheus Society was a very exclusive club in central London. Prominent industrialists and businesspeople formed its membership. Its official purpose was to research aspects of the Problem, but we happened to know that this research took a decidedly practical turn. The goggles that Kipps wore, which allowed him to see ghosts despite his advanced age of twenty-two, were an Orpheus Society creation. And Penelope Fittes—or Marissa, as I was forcing myself to think of her—was closely associated with their underhand activities. We had visited their headquarters once, and found a plush and ornate town house, festooned with oil paintings, marble statues, and quiet closed doors.

"I don't need to remind any of you," Lockwood went on, "that when George was attacked, he'd gotten a copy of *Occult Theories*, this important lost book written by Marissa. Rupert Gale took it from him. As far as we know, there are only two other copies in existence. One, in the Black Library of Fittes House, is too well guarded for us to reach. But the other's here at the Orpheus Society, and that's the one I intend to steal tonight. We needn't be embarrassed doing this, because these Orpheus people are definitely in on the whole Marissa thing. Remember that old secretary talking to us when we visited? He said that their main concern was winning a battle—not just against ghosts, but *against death itself.* Which is pretty much what we think Marissa is trying to do."

"She founded the society in the first place," I said.

"Exactly." Lockwood looked at each of us in turn. "Everyone up for this?"

"Of course," Holly said. "Why do you even ask?"

Kipps shuffled forward on his chair. "Okay, so I've been survey-ing the society HQ for the last two days," he said, "watching who goes in and out, seeing what the security procedures are. It's always locked up at eleven p.m. sharp. After that there's no chance of get-ting in by the first floor windows—they put up iron ghost-grilles after dark. A second snag is that the building's never empty. They seem to stay mainly on the lower floor, but activity goes on there for most of the night."

"What kind of activity?" I asked.

"No idea. Could be meetings, weird occult experiments, or maybe they just doze in front of the fire. The members are mostly ancient. You can see that from these photos I took of them leaving in the mornings."

We inspected the pictures. "They're a bit fuzzy," Holly said.

"If George was here," I remarked, "we'd have floor plans of the building, a full list of accredited members, and an annotated history of the organization."

Kipps stared at me. "Everyone's a critic. Know how I got these?

I was dressed as a workman, painting the railings on the house opposite." He shook his head ruefully. "I tell you, it's a devil of a job whipping a camera out of your pocket and pointing it at people without them noticing."

"You did fine," Lockwood said. "Hey, I recognize some of the others. Those are the old twins who run the Sunrise Corporation, aren't they? The society has some very prominent members. How many are usually in the building overnight?"

"At a guess, four or five. The secretary always is. He seems to live there."

Lockwood tapped his fingertips together. "Well, it's not ideal territory for a burglar. Still, they're just a bunch of old codgers. If any of them *do* disturb us, we knock them down, tie them up, and get on with the operation. It's not the most refined of plans, but frankly I'm not in the mood for anything more sophisticated. Questions?"

Holly raised her hand. "It's just I'm not quite sure how we're getting in."

"Oh, don't bother about that. Kipps has scoped it out. Any other questions?"

"What about George?" I said. "Are we happy to leave him with Flo?"

Lockwood nodded. "She's being very attentive. I think he'll be okay."

At that moment a raucous and indescribable sound came from upstairs. I've never heard the noise of a hyena being ritually disemboweled, but chances are this was less attractive. We drew apart in shock.

"I think that's Flo laughing," Lockwood whispered. "She must be trying to cheer George up. Dear God, what a day."

The district of St. James's, where the Orpheus Society had its headquarters, was well defended against the wakeful dead. By night, ranks of ghost-lamps winked and shone along every street, while runnels of water flowed beside the sidewalks, and braziers of lavender burned before the broad black doors. From the rooftop where we stood, catching our breath after the climb, we could see the purple embers glittering far below us, and smell the lavender on the air. Somewhere far off, a siren howled. Lockwood was standing on a roof crest, staring out toward the west. A gentle wind swept his hair back, set the ends of his coat flapping. His hand rested on his rapier hilt. He looked pensive, as if he were gazing into the future and finding something sad. It made my heart hurt to see him.

"He is such a poser," a voice said disgustedly from my backpack. *"He's just doing that for effect. There's no real reason for him to be up there. Bet we're not even going in that direction."*

"We are," I said. "These roofs run all the way to the Orpheus Society building. He's just checking to make sure the route's clear."

The skull snorted. *"Of course it's clear! That's the whole point of being up here, isn't it? Might get a few roosting pigeons, maybe step on a dead cat. Other than that, it's an easy stroll—if we could all stop looking lost and noble and just get on with it."*

Our route *had* been easy, up until that point. We had walked to St. James's, almost to the very street where the Orpheus Society was based, then detoured under Kipps's direction to a town house in the road beyond that was being renovated. Its frontage was covered with scaffolding. Ladders took us to the uppermost floor, and a quick scramble got us onto the roof. We were in a landscape of moon-lit tiles and shadowed gutters, a world of crests and troughs that stretched to the horizon like a frozen sea.

Lockwood beckoned to us; he skittered down the roof on the far side, and reappeared by a chimney further on. Hoisting up our back-packs, we followed in silence, boots slipping and sliding, trying to ignore the fearful drop into the street below. There were no pigeons, no dead cats; after a few minutes we came to a place where a twist of blue fabric had been tied around a chimney pot, and a length of rope, end noosed securely about the stack itself, lay in a neat coil. Kipps had prepared our way the night before.

"Here we are," Lockwood said. "We're above the Orpheus build-ing now." He checked his penknife was fastened to his work belt, and took his ski mask out of his pocket. "It's time. Masks on."

Kipps was fiddling with his goggles. "Do you think these should be worn on top of my mask, or underneath it?"

"On top, for sure," Holly said. "Otherwise you'll look more than usually deformed."

"That's what I thought. Need anything else, Lockwood?"

"No." Lockwood's face was hidden beneath the mask. He tossed the end of the rope out into space. Now he took its length in his hands and began walking backward toward the edge. "Keep your eye on the rope," he said. "I'll tug it when it's safe to come down."

He reached the lip of the tiles, and eased himself out over the void. For an instant he hung there, leaning back, his boots planted on the very edge. Then he went on lowering himself, hand over hand. In a few seconds he was out of sight.

We crouched like gargoyles on the roof, faceless, hunched beneath our backpacks, swords glinting in the starlight. Wind blew the tips of Holly's hair where it showed from under her mask. From somewhere came a tiny tinkling of broken glass. We waited; we watched the rope. We didn't move.

"Bet he's fallen off," the skull said. *"Bet that tinkling was him hitting a greenhouse far below."*

The rope twitched violently, once and then again. I was nearest. As always where heights were concerned, it was a case of not thinking too much. Following Lockwood's example, I took the rope and lowered myself out and down. I tried to ignore the drag of my backpack as it hung between my shoulder blades; also, the surrounding empty space.

I focused only on my boots—always seeing them planted safely, first on slate tiles, then on black guttering, then rough, dark brickwork, down and down and down.

Presently I saw white wood beneath my boots, and the glass of a raised sash window. There was a glow of a lantern; Lockwood was below me, signaling. Obeying his gestures, I walked down the side of the window frame until I reached the opening. His arms caught me, drew me inside.

He grinned at me in the dark. "Enjoying yourself, Luce?" He tugged the rope again. "I had to break a corner of the pane, but I don't think anyone heard."

His lantern was turned to its lowest setting; even so, I could make out the details of the room in which I stood. It contained an oval table with four chairs, and a sideboard with bottles of water and stacks of glasses. A cup of pens sat on the table, next to a small clock. The wall was covered in dark paper, and decorated with framed photographs of Orpheus members from down the years. There was a strong smell of furniture polish and lavender. Automatically, I used my Talents too, though I scarcely expected any psychic disturbance. There was none. It was a private meeting room; I'd seen similar ones in countless offices across London.

I turned back to the window to help Lockwood bring the others in. In moments, first Holly and then Kipps were dangling outside the casement. Nothing went wrong; soon we stood together in the little room, listening to the ticking of the clock.

Lockwood took another rope from his bag and tied it to a leg of the table. "If we have to leave in a hurry," he said, "we throw this out and go *down*. No messing around trying to climb. But this room is our exit. Okay? If we're separated, head back here."

"So where to now?" I said. "The reading room's on the first floor, isn't it?"

"Yes, but that may not be where George's book is. We'll search systematically. Above all, keep it quiet. If we can do this without disturbance, so much the better."

Leaving the lantern burning at the window, we crossed the room, our flashlights sweeping the walls. Lockwood slowly opened the door; beyond was a wide, dark corridor running along the spine of the building. It was dark, but lights glowed at the far end, where it opened onto a staircase. Thick red carpets muffled our footfalls. From somewhere came the ticking of another clock; otherwise there was no sound in the house.

"Skull," I whispered. "Sense anything?"

"Just the flutter of your hearts, the taste of your fear. Is that what you meant?"

"I was thinking more of supernatural activity. . . . Let me know."

Most of the rooms leading off the corridor had their doors open, and we quickly established that these were other meeting rooms, bathrooms, even a little bedroom. All were nicely furnished, but otherwise unexceptional. But there was one door which Holly tried that was of far more interest. As she swung her flashlight around the dark interior, she gave a stifled cry and sprang back, ripping her rapier free.

In seconds, the rest of us were at her side.

"It's all right," she whispered. "It's just, for one horrible moment, I thought it was filled with *people.*"

Lockwood pushed the door open; and, despite Holly's assurances, I couldn't help giving an involuntary start. Our collective flashlight beams lit up what looked like a row of hooded figures standing in line. The Bloody Monks of Ashford, one of our earliest cases, had lined up in a pretty similar way, and they'd shone with the same eerie silver light, except for the bloody bits, obviously. But these weren't ghosts. Even as your skin was crawling, and your legs begging you to run, your brain was picking out the very ordinary clothes rack, the row of coat hangers on which the set of robes were hung. Elsewhere were boxes, stacked neatly, each bearing the imprint of a Grecian harp, which was the Orpheus Society's symbol.

The house was quiet, and it was too interesting a room to bypass, though there were clearly no books in it. I went to the rack and ran my fingers over the silver robes. To my surprise, they weren't made of cloth or silk, but had countless tiny scales, light as gossamer and neatly sewn together. They flowed like water through my hands.

"These cloaks, Lockwood," I said. "Remind you of anything?"

He nodded. "Our spirit-capes were feathery, but otherwise they might almost be the same. Look at the way the silver flakes are held to the mesh." I couldn't see him frowning, but I heard the perplexity in his voice. "They are *so* similar. . . ."

"And look," Kipps said. "More goggles like mine."

He'd opened one of the boxes; inside was a curious helmet, soft and shapeless and also made of silvery scales, with a pair of heavy goggles fixed to it.

"*That's* not so unexpected," I said. "We stole yours from a member of the society in the first place. . . . Lockwood—they wear these things on the Other Side. . . ."

"These idiots are doing the same thing Rotwell did," Lockwood said. "Meddling with things that shouldn't concern them. Well, we haven't come here for this. We don't really have time to spare."

Even so, we lingered. Other boxes contained silver gauntlets to wear on the hands, and mesh boots to protect the feet. Most of the boxes had names scribbled on them, presumably their owners'; some were familiar ones, including heads of industry. Our eyes flashed at each other from within the ski masks. There was triumph in our looks, but also fear. Our finds had deep significance. Way *too* deep. We could feel an abyss opening beneath our feet. If we stumbled, we had a long way to fall.

We left the room and moved soundlessly to the end of the corridor. There was a stairwell there, lit by golden chandeliers. The steps were carpeted in red, and dark portraits of austere, bearded men glowered at us from inside heavy frames. It was the kind of stairwell where you could look over from the top to see the hallway, three stories down. We did so; lamps flickered on the landings below, but otherwise everything was still. Not silent, though. The noise of clocks was louder here. We could hear them ticking deep in the belly of the house. It was a place that seemed very conscious of time.

"We try the next floor, then," Lockwood whispered. "Everyone okay?"

Three nods; four shadows stealing down the steps, pressing close to the wall. We'd traveled light for this raid, keeping our swords and explosive weapons, but dispensing with heavy stuff like iron canisters and chains. The carpet absorbed all sound. Tiptoeing around the curve of the stairwell, we saw the second floor landing before us. It was much the same as the one above. A plaster bust of a heavy-featured woman sat on a plinth, eyeing us with displeasure. There were ferns in plant pots. Beyond was a corridor, and yet more doors.

Somewhere in the bowels of the house a door opened, releasing smatterings of distant conversation. Just as quickly, the noise cut off and everything was quiet again. We stood frozen on the stairs. Nothing further could be heard. At last Lockwood gave the signal and we padded down onto the landing.

A quick glance showed us that the corridor was just as dimly lit and elegantly furnished as its counterpart above. No one was there. Lockwood moved to the nearest door, listened, and eased it open. He gave a soft exclamation. "We may not have to look much further," he whispered. "This is some kind of library."

In seconds we were inside, with the door closed behind us. Holly lit a lantern, and by its light we saw that Lockwood's optimism was justified. It was a broad, rectangular chamber, running along the street side of the building. Two tall windows looked out at the town houses opposite. Each wall, painted a dark maroon, was inset with white wooden bookcases; between them hung old maps and paintings. Heavy reading tables were dotted around, along with leather armchairs, each with its own standard lamp. A bust of a dour-looking man in goggles sat on one table. A vast and beautiful globe, made of countless pieces of colored inlaid wood, hung in a silver frame.

"Got to be in here somewhere," Lockwood said, spinning the globe gently. "So, it's a book called *Occult Theories* that we're after. Let's get looking."

Holly set the lantern on the table. We spread out, scanning the shelves.

It turned out that most of the books had been bound in black leather, with the Orpheus harp imprinted on the front. They also had the name of the author embossed on the spine and had been arranged alphabetically, but since the author of *Occult Theories* was officially anonymous, that didn't help much. Time passed; occasionally I went to the door and listened, but everything seemed still.

At last Holly sprang up from a shelf near the window, with a thin volume in her hand. "Got it!" she called. "*Occult Theories*! This is it for sure."

We gathered around her. "Yes, that's it," Lockwood said. "Well done, Hol. George will be pleased."

"He'd have *loved* this room," I said. "So many weird books. Look at this one: *Dark London, an Interim Cartography*. What do you think *that* means?"

"I don't know, but—"

"Did you hear something?" Holly asked.

We looked at her. "Hear what?"

"Don't know. A clang somewhere."

I was closest to the door. I stole over, opened it, and looked out into the corridor. As before, the lights were low, the carpet soft and gleaming. I listened intently, but could hear nothing aside from the *tick, tick, tick*ing of the clocks.

"Skull?" I said.

"*No psychic disturbance. Everything's quiet. Remarkably quiet.*"

"Good."

"*One might almost say* ominously *quiet. . . .*"

I came back in and shut the door. "We should get out while we can."

Lockwood nodded. "We'll study the book at home. Come on."

We picked up our bags, silently scouring the room in case we'd left anything. Holly adjusted the globe so that it was in the same position as before. "Best to leave no traces," she said, smiling. We gathered at the door.

Except for Lockwood. He was staring at the bookshelf next to him. All at once he darted over and pulled something out. It was a thin pamphlet, bound in black leather.

"More stuff about Marissa?" I said.

"No. . . ." He held up the spine to show us. The word LOCKWOOD was embossed on it in gold leaf. "It's by my parents," Lockwood said. "Remember last year, when we met the secretary of the society? He *said* my parents had once given a lecture here. This must be a transcript of it." He flipped the pamphlet open to the first page.

There was a vibration in my backpack. *"I hear noises,"* the skull said.

"Noises? Where?"

"Somewhere deep. But coming upward through the house."

"Lockwood—we've got to go."

"Yes, of course . . ." Lockwood's voice trailed away. He stared at the pamphlet in his hand.

"Lockwood?" I said. "Are you all right?"

He didn't answer; he didn't hear me. It was like a switch had been thrown. His eyes were round and haunted. Something had altered in his face. His mouth hung open.

Kipps was listening at the door. "Got no time for this! We've got trouble."

Now I could hear it, too: strange thuds and clattering approaching up the stairs.

"Flashlights off!" I ran over to Lockwood and pulled at his arm. *"Lockwood,"* I snapped. "Come *on.*"

"It's their final lecture," he said. "The one they were about to give when they died."

"Well, that's *great,*" I said. "You wanted this, didn't you? So take it and let's go!"

"But the date—"

We were out of time. A great bang sounded in the corridor outside, making us all flinch back. There was an unholy screech, a scream of metal. The door blew open, and a hideous, deformed figure thrust itself inside.

Chapter 16

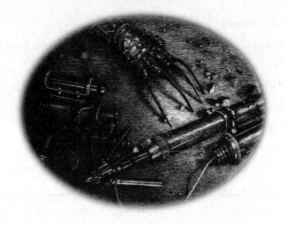

It was a nightmarish vision: gray, shiny, and impossibly large. So tall was the creature, it had to duck to get through the door. The eyes were bulbous, the legs insectlike, long and oddly jointed. The arms ended in enormous claws. It was silhouetted in the light of the corridor beyond. As it entered, it slashed at Kipps with its right hand, shearing through his jacket as he threw himself aside. Its left hand sought Holly, but she had dropped to the carpet, and only a few strands of her hair, trailing from the back of her ski mask, were sliced away as the claws swiped past.

Lockwood and I stood directly in front of the shape as it stretched to its full height. Pistons hissed, metal squealed. Flashlight beams wheeled behind it, but the thing itself was dark. Our brains were trying to process what we were seeing. Not a ghost—too solid, too much iron for that. Monstrous, yes—but not a monster. At the heart of it, surely, was a man.

"What is it, Terence?" a shrill voice called. "What's in there?"

"Thieves!" the thing shouted. "Burglars!"

I knew the voice; and my guess was immediately confirmed, for at that moment Lockwood stabbed his flashlight on and shone it directly at the shape. The blaze revealed the secretary of the Orpheus Society, long white hair pluming out around a giant pair of goggles, a loose-fitting chain mail suit hanging over his dark coat. His feet and shins were encased in the top of a pair of pneumatic iron stilt-legs that adjusted, hissing, as he moved. His hands wore metal gauntlets, their fingers ending in foot-long stiletto claws. He cried out as the flashlight beam blinded him, raising one arm before his face.

"Thieves!" he cried again. "Thieves in the research library!"

"Then get out of the way, you old fool!" another voice cried. "Let us at them!"

A hiss and a spring; with surprising agility, the secretary bounded aside. Clustering at the door behind him came four other misshapen forms, each one a gray-haired man or woman in old-fashioned evening dress, goggles strapped to faces, silver armor clinking. The two women carried peculiar firearms—black, snub-nosed, with coils of rubber hosing connecting them to chrome bottles fixed to the top of the devices. One of the men had a weapon that looked like a harpoon gun. His companion carried a boxlike device strapped to his back. A long piece of brass tubing protruded from it, looped over his shoulder and ended in a gaping funnel. All these items looked roughly made, with patches of soldering holding them together. Roughly made—but clearly functioning.

The four lined up inside the door, with the secretary towering beside them. Holly had scuttled into the far corner of the library, beyond the globe; Kipps, one side of his jacket around his knees, had retreated to the other. I drew my rapier. I glanced at Lockwood, but his face was hidden, his emotions inscrutable. He tucked the pamphlet inside his coat, and let his hands drop by his side.

For a moment nobody moved. One of the weapons gave a barking hum, like a vacuum cleaner revving. Otherwise the room was silent.

"Who are you?" one of the woman said. She was very short and squarish, and the cut of her green tweed dress and jacket under her silver chain mail made her squarer still. She was one of those academic-looking ladies whose long gray hair would have been a lot more flattering if it had been cut and properly styled. But you wouldn't have pointed this out to her, since her gun was bigger than her head. "Speak up!" she snapped. "Tell us your names."

There was no way we were going to answer *that*.

"Agents!" the man with the harpoon gun spat. "Children! Look at their swords."

The secretary shifted position on his stilts; pistons hissed, steel claws clashed. "Give yourselves up!" he said. "Throw down your swords! If you do, we'll let you live." There was something in the way he phrased the words that made it instantly clear he intended us to die. But we could have guessed that anyhow. The Orpheus Society had its secrets to protect. They wouldn't casually let us go.

"I'm losing patience," Harpoon Man said. He was quite bald, his skin leathery and lined. I thought perhaps he'd appeared in one of Kipps's photos, but I couldn't be sure. From memory, most of the members looked like him. His male colleague, who by contrast possessed a wild beard that looked like an explosion in a lint factory, hefted his brass shoulder-funnel menacingly, taking especial aim at me.

The secretary raised a gauntleted hand. "Not in here, Geoffrey," he murmured. "The books . . ." He glared at us, flexing his metal claws. "Last chance!" he cried. "Do you have anything to say?"

There was a pause. "Yes," Lockwood said. "Actually, I do."

His voice surprised me. First, because I'd assumed we'd all remain silent—the secretary had, after all, met us before, and might recognize us from our words alone; secondly, because of the way he said it: quietly, yet with cold assurance, without fear, without haste, communicating utter unconcern. Whereas Kipps and Holly were as calm as cornered rats; whereas I teetered on toe-tips, desperate to dodge the inevitable attack, with sweat soaking into my mask, Lockwood looked as if he were waiting for a bus. He hadn't drawn his rapier; he'd made no move for any weapon. A few feet away, gun barrels tilted toward him, the harpoon point swiveled, some unseen mechanism fizzed and hummed. Lockwood just stood there.

He said, "You have a choice before you. You can either turn around, leave this room, and go back downstairs, or not. Which do you want to do?"

The second woman, tiny, dark, and wrinkled as a currant, cocked her head in puzzlement. "Sorry—is he talking to us?"

"Giving *us* an ultimatum?" Harpoon Man took a firmer grip on the handle of his gun.

"You're elderly," Lockwood said, "and perhaps a little slow. If it isn't clear enough, I can put it another way for you. Get your shriveled backsides out of here sharpish while you can, or face the consequences. It's pretty simple. Up to you."

The tiny woman's body shook with emotion inside her silver armor; she gave a hoot of rage. Again the bearded man—Geoffrey—seemed inclined to do something hasty with the shoulder-funnel. Harpoon Man and the tweedy woman both took impulsive steps toward us, too, but were blocked by the stooping figure of the secretary.

"No," he said, swinging a leg forward. "Let me."

"Take his head off, Terence," the wrinkled woman said.

Few non-spectral situations are as fearsome as being cornered by a deranged senior on stilts, with his ten steak-knife fingers clawing in your direction. Fearsome, yet also faintly ridiculous; and Lockwood's air of calm defiance had successfully communicated itself to all of us. It had allowed us to take stock, and realize that something the secretary had said had given us an advantage.

While in this room, the Orpheus members were unwilling to use their heavy weaponry for fear of damaging their library.

We had no such qualms.

We all reached for our belts. Lockwood moved the quickest—too quick for the eye to follow. The first the secretary knew about it was when the magnesium flare struck him full in the chest, exploding against his chain mail and sending him toppling backward behind a waterfall of cascading silver light. With frantic contortions and desperate footwork, he contrived to remain standing, but my own flare, arriving instants later, propelled him sideways to tip over the back of an armchair. As his legs thrashed at the ceiling, Kipps's and

Holly's flares burst against the four figures at the doorway, sandwiching them violently together and causing the man with the harpoon gun to pull his trigger, so that his missile shot between Lockwood and me and straight out through the window behind us. It shattered the glass, letting the night air in.

After that, things got messy.

Really, it was a pity for the members of the society that they were still blocking the way out—otherwise we might have been inclined to leave them. It was a pity too that in their rage they forgot their sensible intention of safeguarding their research library, and began to fire their weapons. It had bad consequences for them.

The gray-haired woman with the tweed jacket raised her gun, and a jag of bright blue electricity suddenly connected its nozzle with the wall beside my head. One moment it wasn't there, the next it was. It cut across the room like a scribble drawn by a giant child. I felt its force, smelled the burning wallpaper. Sparks fizzed against my jacket and stung my cheeks. She turned the gun, scything the light toward me. I threw myself over the table beside the plaster bust and rolled away behind an armchair. Behind me something exploded; fragments of the bust cascaded to the floor.

I peered around the chair. Both women were now firing their guns; the blue flashes cast everything else into semidarkness. There was movement everywhere, the shimmer of rapiers, the rush of bodies. Another flare burst; in its light, I saw the secretary getting to his feet. His face was a Venn diagram of black and silver scorch marks. His hair smoldered; one strand of it was on fire.

At my shoulder, the skull gave a long, low chuckle. *"These old geezers are completely mad! I've got to say I like them."*

A masked figure—Kipps, I guessed—moved past, sword drawn, to be at once confronted by the bearded Geoffrey. His funneled apparatus was connected to a concertinaed bladder, like a bellows or accordion, strapped under one arm. He jabbed this with his elbow; with a *pop!*, a glass vial shot from the end of the funnel, missed Kipps by inches, and shattered on the wall behind. Colorless liquid dripped down; a familiar fragrance filled the air.

"Is that the best you can do?" Kipps called. "Lavender water? Pathetic!"

"*I have to agree,*" the skull said. "*That's the wimpiest weapon I've ever seen.*"

I grasped the neck of Kipps's jersey, pulled him sharply down behind the chair. The watery substance was eating into the wallpaper, making it bubble and foam; small bits of plaster dropped in wet gobbets to the floor.

"Possibly a bit of acid in there, too," I said.

"*Nice!*" the skull said. "*They're totally insane!*"

Kipps and I took hold of the armchair, driving it forward, sending it forcefully into Geoffrey. He gasped in pain. The funnel popped; a vial of acid ricocheted off the ceiling and burst nearby. Elsewhere in the room, someone screamed. I had time to hope it wasn't Holly. And now here came the tiny wrinkled woman, firing her gun indiscriminately. A bolt of blue stabbed straight through the chair and out the other side, and my hands tingled with an electrical charge. I let go of the chair. Running low, I rushed the woman, striking her around the waist, bringing us both to the floor. Her grip on the gun was loosened; I sent it flying from her hand.

Shadows moved nearby. I looked up; there was Harpoon Man,

struggling to load another dart into his weapon. There too was the secretary, vertical at last and bearing down on me. And there was Lockwood, who stood directly in his path, in the center of the smoking floor. He had his rapier in his hand. The secretary gave a cry; he slashed downward with his claws, finger-knives raking at Lockwood's head. Lockwood moved balletically aside; his rapier struck them away. He kicked the closest stilt-leg, sending the secretary skittering away to collide with the other man.

Beneath me, the tiny woman was wriggling frantically, snarling and spitting.

"Criminals!" she shrieked.

"Maybe," I said, punching her in the jaw, "but at least we're not lunatics, like you."

And so it was that the members of the Orpheus Society discovered a curious thing. It was understandable that they were a little grouchy; what with that, and their superior firepower, they'd probably assumed they would win the day. But crazed as they were, they couldn't match the ferocity that now erupted from all four of us. I'd never punched an old lady before; I didn't have any problem doing so now.

In a way, they were unlucky, for our reaction didn't really have a lot to do with them. It had been building in us for days, ever since George had gotten hurt. Our anger needed an outlet, and here were some senior citizens in armor trying to kill us. That pretty much fit the bill.

During the next few minutes, we notched up many firsts. There was Lockwood, slicing off the secretary's metal fingers, from first one gauntlet, then the other. There was Kipps, grappling with Geoffrey, pulling at his beard and upending him. As the man sought to rise, Kipps stuck his rapier straight into the motor of his opponent's funnel-gun, so that it exploded in a ball of pulsing light. And there was Holly, dodging the savage blows of the tweedy woman; leaping across to the giant wooden globe and shoving it over, so that it pinned the woman to the floor.

Me, I'd gotten up, retrieved the discarded electrical gun, and switched on the dial. The tiny woman in silver armor had likewise struggled to her feet. She rushed at me, shrieking. I flicked the trigger, sending out a jolt of electric current that blew her straight through the nearest wall in a shower of bricks and plaster.

Geoffrey lay unconscious beneath the smoking, twisted coils of his brass funnel. Harpoon Man, however, had readied his gun again. He leveled it at Kipps. Holly screamed a warning. Kipps ducked; the bolt shot over his head. I hit the man with another blast from the electrical gun that sent him back into a chair and the chair back into a bookcase. It toppled over, burying him.

The skull uttered whoops of glee. *"This is great. You're just as bad as them! Worse, in fact. They don't know what's hit them!"*

And the tide of the battle *was* turning. The tweedy woman had wriggled out from under the globe. She fled for the door. So, too, did the secretary, hissing and clanking on his stilts, swinging his clawless metal hands. They arrived at the door at the same time, and fought with each other to be the first one through. Lockwood and I walked after them, he with his rapier, me holding the gun. Out into the corridor we went, toward the landing, stepping over the dust and debris and scattered bricks; also the unconscious body of the tiny woman, which was lodged half in and half out of the wall.

The fugitives reached the landing, at the head of the stairs. As the woman turned to go down, I caught her with a bolt of electricity that sent her through the banisters and out over the stairwell to land on a chandelier. There she swung, senseless and dangling, in a mess of crystal shards and smoking tweed.

Here too the secretary made his final stand. Perhaps with his stilts he couldn't easily descend the stairs; perhaps his desperation had turned to defiance at the last. Either way, he turned and held his ground, as Lockwood approached, calm and remorseless, rapier at the ready.

"You'll die for this!" the old man cried. "She'll make you pay!"

He swung out blindly with an arm. Lockwood moved to the side and sliced with his sword. He chopped neatly through the right stilt-leg. The secretary toppled over the ruined banisters and kept going, out and down. He missed the chandelier; anyway, it was already taken. A moment later there was a heavy impact on the stairs below.

Silence in the house of the Orpheus Society. The gun in my hand was emitting a gentle hum. I switched it off, let it fall to the floor. The chandelier and its occupant swung steadily around and around.

"Oh, is that it?" the skull said. "I was enjoying that. Bit of senseless violence does wonders for morale. You should break in somewhere every night. There are heaps of old people's homes in London. Let's choose another one tomorrow."

Kipps and Holly picked their way among the debris in the corridor to join me on the landing. Lockwood had gone downstairs to check on the crumpled body of the secretary. A power pack on the man's back was spurting out intermittent bright blue sparks.

I looked down through the shattered banisters. "Is he dead?"

"No."

"Don't think any of them are," Kipps said.

Below me, Lockwood stood up slowly. He nudged a limp hand aside with his boot and stepped past the secretary without another glance. He ascended the stairs, pale-faced, dusty, torn of coat, rapier in hand. Only on reaching the landing did he reattach it to his belt.

"Can we go now, please?" Holly asked in a small voice.

Lockwood nodded. "Definitely. But first we need to pay another visit to that storeroom upstairs."

It was shortly after two a.m. when we arrived back at Portland Row. It was silent in the house; nothing could be heard from George or Flo.

Lockwood held a heavy bag, containing certain items we'd taken from the storeroom. He lowered it onto the kitchen table, then pulled off his ski mask. There was blood on his face. He scratched at his flop of hair. "Check the front, Hol," he said. "See if anyone's watching the house. Masks off, everyone. Gloves, too. We'll need to get rid of these."

We threw the masks and gloves down by the door. Kipps took off his ruined jacket and chucked it on the pile. Holly came back from the living room.

"Can't see anyone out there," she said.

Lockwood nodded. "Good enough."

We stood in semidarkness. The smell of smoke rose from our tattered clothes. Our faces and hands were bruised and bloodied, our expressions blank. The same thought was going through all our minds.

"So . . . think they recognized us?" Kipps said at last.

We all looked at Lockwood. He was very pale and there was a cut on one of his cheeks.

"Probably not," he said. "But I'm afraid that they—or Fittes, or Sir Rupert Gale—will put two and two together very quickly indeed. They'll know it was us for sure. And they'll have to act on it. Which makes it only a matter of time before—"

"Before what?" I asked.

Lockwood smiled at me. "Before the end. But it's not going to happen tonight. Which means we should get some sleep. That's the first rule of any agency—rest when you can."

All very true, but I didn't sleep well or long. I was awake at dawn and walking around the quiet house. I thought Lockwood would be sleeping on the couch in the living room, but the door was open, the room empty.

I looked into the library. The curtains were drawn back and light was coming in, pale white and cold. There was a smell of woodsmoke, but the fire had burned out and the air was chilly. Lockwood sat in his favorite chair, his reading light shining over his shoulder. It made a small, harsh circle of brightness on his lap. The other pamphlet we'd stolen from the Orpheus Society lay face-down between his hands. He had his eyes half open, and was staring toward the window.

I sat beside him on the arm of the chair, and switched off the light. "Not been to bed?" I asked.

He shook his head. "I've been reading my parents' last lecture."

I waited. If he wanted to tell me, he would.

"'Ghost Lore among the Tribes of New Guinea and West Sumatra,'" he said. "'A presentation given to the members of the Orpheus Society by Celia and Donald Lockwood.' That's what it says on the frontispiece, Lucy. Word for word. Spells it out nice and clear. It was their calling card, if you like. They'd wanted to join the society. That nice man, the secretary of the society, even complimented me on their talk when we went there last year."

I had a vision of that white-haired thing on stilts, the screaming face, the slashing claws. "You know, maybe it's best they never joined," I said. "Not sure they would have fit in."

Lockwood picked up the book gently. "I should apologize to you," he said. "To you, Hol, and Quill, for what happened back there, just before those idiots attacked us. I'm sorry. I let you down."

"Not at all," I said. "You were—"

"I was frozen," Lockwood said. "I went into shutdown mode. I'm your leader, and that's not right. But I had an excuse," he added, "because I was very surprised by something. No, *surprised* isn't the word. I suddenly *understood* a whole lot of things. They came in a rush, and rather overwhelmed me. And—well, I can show you what it was." He opened the little book, turned the yellowed pages. "It's two things together, really," he said. "Most of this lecture is exactly what its title suggests. It gives an account of how the people of those places deal with ancestral spirits. There's lots about how the bones of the dead are stored in special spirit houses set away from the village, so they're kept out of trouble. And how the shamans or witch doctors dress up in spirit-capes, like the ones we've got upstairs, and go to the houses to consult the ancestors. That's not so new. They talked about that in other papers, as you know. But then my mother and father home in on what they think is *going on* in those spirit houses. . . ."

He had found the extract he wanted; he already knew the piece by heart. He smoothed out the page and, holding it up to catch the frail light of morning, gave it to me to read:

So the wise men truly converse with the ancestors: that is one point on which they all insist. But there is another point, too, even more incredible to the modern ear. When they enter the spirit houses, so the wise men believe, they are no longer in the mortal world at all, but have passed through to another realm altogether. This is the realm of the ancestors, the land of death, where they can meet with ghosts on level terms. "How can this be?" we asked them. "How can your mortal bodies withstand the terrible conditions there (for it is not a pleasant place), and would not the proximity of the dead be fatal to you?" "All this would indeed be true," came the reply, "were it not for the stout protection afforded by our cloaks and masks. The precious materials of the cloaks shield our bodies and keep the ancestors from touching us. The bone masks (formed from the remains of shamans of the past) allow us to see the spirits with clear eyes."

To our mind, these fragile items look scarcely capable of any of this, but the wise men are confident in their power. Yet even so, speaking with the ancestors is not to be taken lightly. The elders regard it as a most dangerous venture to be undertaken only in times of crisis, for the dead are roused to great excitement by their arrival, often following them back into the living world. This is why the spirit houses are built away from the villages, usually across streams.

"You see what they're stumbling toward, Lucy?" Lockwood said. "They're recording the exact same thing that's going on here—the living traveling to the land of the dead. They've spotted *everything*: the way the dead get stirred up, the importance of having lots of Sources piled together to create a gate through, the need for bodily protection on the Other Side. It's all there."

I nodded slowly. "The bit about the bone masks is interesting," I said. "You think they operate like the goggles Kipps has?"

"I hadn't thought of that. Yes, maybe. Though I bet the goggles are copying the masks, in just the same way that those silver capes we nicked are close copies of the original spirit-capes. My poor parents go on to describe the feathered capes in great detail—the way they're made, the types of silver mesh holding them together . . . This was a gift for the Orpheus gang, Luce. Whatever techniques they were using beforehand won't have held a candle to these. They've been taking a leaf out of my parents' book ever since."

"They've been using their findings?"

"I'm sure of it. And I'm sure of something else, too. They may have been delighted to hear all about the clever techniques used by the shamans, but they wouldn't have been at all pleased about another remark in the lecture." Lockwood flipped forward a couple of pages, to near the end of the little book. "Read this," he said. His voice sounded odd.

From what we have seen and heard firsthand, both in the New Guinean hill country and the forests of West Sumatra, we are convinced of the truth of the wise men's accounts in the matter of their ancestors. More than that, we feel that they have much to teach us about our own problem with our ancestors, much closer to home. We all know that the epidemic of Visitors that Britain endures is mysterious and worsening, without apparent solution. Yet could it be that the prime cause of this crisis is somewhere near us, right under our noses? Are we, somehow, disturbing these spirits? Could there be a gate, such as we have described, with mortal traffic going through it? The idea seems absurd, and yet surely it satisfies the evidence. We feel this theory must be explored. Indeed, we devoutly believe that our researches, made at the other ends of the earth, have the potential to unlock great mysteries near at hand.

"Of course, we *know* there were spirit gates near at hand," Lockwood said. "And we know precisely who's been going through them. My mother and father didn't have a clue. Can you imagine them in that cursed building, giving this talk, with the clocks ticking and those horrible Orpheus people quietly watching them?" He shuddered. "It was the wider picture, the stuff about the Other Side, that interested my mum and dad. The parallels between cultures. They thought, quite reasonably, that these ideas might inspire a bit of public interest at home in Britain. In fact, they planned to give that same lecture to a public audience in Manchester a few days later. The thing they *didn't* know, being all excited and eager, and wanting to give their special friends at the society a little preview of their theories, was that they were signing their own death warrants."

His tired eyes looked up at me; our gazes locked.

"The accident," I said.

"Given what they were up to, the Orpheus Society would have been very disinclined to have my parents' lecture heard by the world," he said. "Which brings me to the second thing I realized. The front page of the pamphlet gives the date of the lecture. It's just two days before my mother and father were due to travel up to Manchester. In other words," Lockwood went on, "it's two days before their car was hit in a freak accident and they were killed in a ball of flame. Two days before they, this lecture, and their inconvenient theories were lost to the world forever." He tossed the pamphlet on the floor.

"It wasn't an accident," I said.

"They were murdered, Lucy. Yes."

"And you think that Marissa and the Orpheus Society—"

He held my gaze. "I don't *think* that, Lucy. I know."

IV

The Siege of
Portland Row

Whatever the drawbacks of Flo Bones's nursing techniques—and judging by the state of Lockwood's bedroom when we next looked in, these included a total lack of interest in cleanliness, air quality, and the orderly disposal of bloodied bandages—it could not be denied that they produced results. George was sitting up in bed that morning, wedged among pillows and living room cushions, with Lockwood's best bathrobe draped over his shoulders and a tray of cakes lying at an angle on his lap. His face was horribly discolored, with the bluish-purple flush of a soft plum, and there was a white compress taped over his left eye. Somehow he had contrived to balance his broken spectacles on his swollen nose. He looked like an elderly owl that had recently fallen out with a woodpecker. But his one good eye was open and sparkling with intelligence, and that was enough to have me grinning like an idiot as I sat on the bed beside him.

"Look at you!" I said. "You're alive and awake, and sitting up and everything!"

"Not so loud." George's voice was stronger, but as raspy as a piece of sandpaper scouring an ashtray. "You'll wake poor Flo. She's wiped out." He nodded over to the corner of the room where a still shape in a puffer jacket lay curled up in the center of a nest of tumbled clothes. Flo's knees were drawn up, her head rested on her hands. She had removed her hat, and her matted straw-blond hair radiated around her like a deformed starfish. Her eyes were closed. She was breathing long and deeply.

Lockwood blinked. "Wait! Are those my sweaters? And my best shirts tucked under her muddy boots? You've emptied out the contents of my drawers!"

"She needed something cozy to lie down on," George said. "You wouldn't deny her that, surely."

"There are two spare bedspreads in the linen closet!"

"Oh, yeah. Didn't think of them. Anyway, keep it down. She's been nursing me all night. In all honesty, I feel quite caked out. . . ." With painful movements, George set his tray aside. His good eye inspected our cuts and bruises. "What's all this, then? You trying to steal my thunder here?"

"We've been out," Lockwood said, "getting something for you." He placed the copy of *Occult Theories* on the bedspread. "Hope it's worth it."

The lower half of George's purpled face parted in a crooked grin. "Christmas has come early! Thank you. . . ." He patted the pamphlet weakly. "Which was it, Fittes or Orpheus?"

"Orpheus," Lockwood said. "Speaking of which, if you're no

longer almost dying, you might want to start reading pronto. We may not have much time."

Our raid on the Orpheus Society was a turning point. We knew this without discussing it. First the attack on George, and now our retaliatory expedition—lines had been crossed by both sides, and there was no possibility of returning to the watchful truce of a few days previously. Consequences were inevitable; the question was in what form they would come. Personally, I expected a rapid payback. It wouldn't have surprised me if Marissa Fittes and a crack DEPRAC team had shown up before lunchtime to lead us away in chains.

But nothing like that happened. The day was quiet—or at least it *would* have been, if Lockwood hadn't taken the opportunity to leap into action.

Despite his lack of sleep, the events of the night had galvanized him; he radiated a strange, mercurial energy that would not let him rest—and all of us were caught up in its wake. Sooner or later, our enemies would respond: in the meantime, we had to make preparations, and to that end Lockwood steered our efforts. He was everywhere, his eyes bright, his voice calm and measured, issuing orders and making plans. Kipps, who had crashed overnight on our library floor (having rejected our offer of George's room), was sent into central London with a shopping list as long as his arm, Holly was dispatched to Mullet's, and Flo Bones, once she had finally awoken, was likewise pried from George's bedside and given a job to do.

"I need your ear out there, Flo," Lockwood said, "I need to hear what's being talked about among the relic-men. Any rumors, anything strange that's been heard or seen, particularly if it involves Sir

Rupert Gale or any of the Fittes gang. News travels fast in the criminal underworld, and you've got the best antennae of anyone I know."

From the expression on her face, I expected a trademark Flo diatribe at this point, but she just went quiet, nodded, and slipped away into the garden. When Lockwood really wanted something, it was very hard for anyone to say no.

After that, Lockwood himself departed, leaving me to keep an eye on George. He wouldn't say where he was going, and I watched him stride off down Portland Row with a queasy sensation in my stomach. Since making the shocking discovery about his parents, Lockwood had seemed curiously upbeat, even elated at the turn of events. It was the same brittle defiance that I'd seen in the cemetery, only now sharpened with new purpose. Our enemies were in plain sight, and the deaths of his parents weren't quite as meaningless as he'd believed. I understood why that might please him. Still, given the forces now ranged against us, and the unlikeliness of getting help from Barnes, DEPRAC, or anyone else, I could only be fearful of where it would end.

I peeped into his bedroom. George had dropped off to sleep again. He hadn't yet read the book. I opened the window to fumigate the place, and brought in fresh lavender. Even so, Flo's presence lingered. I went away and left him.

For much of the morning, 35 Portland Row was quiet. Toward lunchtime the house shook with the approach of a large delivery van, inching its way along the street. Quill Kipps sat beside the driver. They had come from a builder's supply yard; under Kipps's direction, men began unloading sections of particleboard, tools, ropes, and other materials, and dumped them in the hall. Before they could pull away, a Mullet's van showed up, with Holly in the cab. It brought fresh quantities of iron, salt, and magnesium flares, and there was a great kerfuffle in the street as the vehicles struggled to pass each other.

I took possession of the deliveries and shut the door on the shouting men and honking horns. Holly and I organized the agency supplies, Kipps the wood and tools. By early afternoon, when Lockwood returned home from his mysterious expedition, we had it all laid out in piles. He inspected everything like a military leader, and nodded at us, well pleased.

"This is perfect," he said. "Nice work, everyone. Now we just need to get the defenses in position. We'll have some sandwiches first, though."

We gathered around the kitchen table. "It's so strange," I said. "I was sure we'd have been arrested by now."

Lockwood shook his head. "No. They won't arrest us. They know we'd kick up a fuss and raise a *lot* of awkward questions. I'm afraid their reaction is likely to be a lot more final."

"Kill us, you mean," Kipps said. He had been unwrapping a shiny new hacksaw. Now he placed it on the table, and took his plate of sandwiches.

"That'll be their preferred option," Lockwood said. "From their point of view, we already know too much. But they can't easily bump us off, either. It's one thing to beat up George in the street. It's quite another to dispose of all of us. That will take a major effort—and would be very risky, because they know we'll be expecting it. Also, it won't happen in public, for obvious reasons. Even Fittes can't blatantly authorize murder. That means it'll be done quietly, when no one's around. And that's why I'm expecting an attack here at Portland Row, probably after dark."

There was a silence while everyone digested this. "Tonight?" I said.

"We can only hope not. We won't be ready. Give us another day and I'll be a lot more confident that we can protect ourselves. Tonight, we'll just have to keep watch and trust in luck. Still, we can get a lot done before then. Let's eat up and get back to work."

Defending 35 Portland Row wasn't impossible, but there were definite points of weakness to overcome. On the ground floor, the front gave little cause for worry. The old black door was thick and sturdy, and adorned with so many locks and chains you would have needed a bazooka to blow it down. The library and living room windows were fairly safe, too, as both overlooked the basement yard, and so weren't easily accessible. It was the kitchen at the back, with its steps leading down to the garden, that worried us. This was where the particleboard came in. That afternoon Kipps and Lockwood hammered homemade barricades to the inside of the windows and across the glass pane of the door. Lockwood also went out and spent quite a bit of time constructing something on the garden steps. "I've been inspired by our visit to Marissa's tomb," he said. "Might be best to avoid using this entrance for a few days." He didn't explain further.

The basement had long been our main point of concern. Again, the front of the house was theoretically less vulnerable. It was true that our office windows opened directly onto the sunken yard below our front door. Steep steps led down here from the gate and, though lots of dead plants in big pots filled the space, intruders could easily reach the windows. However, after a burglary years before, we had added iron bars to these, and it was hard to see how they could be bypassed. This meant we focused all our attention on the back.

At the rear of the office, past the rapier practice room, the storeroom, and the laundry room, you came to the back door. It was made of glass, and opened straight onto the grass of the garden. Of all parts of the house, this door was the weakest point. Kipps put a series of wooden boards across the opening, but we doubted they'd survive a sustained attack. Toward evening, extra defenses were added by Lockwood and Kipps, who spent a lot of time messing with the floorboards just inside the door.

Nightfall came. Holly and I stockpiled weapons and watched the street. Neighbors moved around inside their houses. Arif closed up his store. Portland Row was silent. Our enemies made no move. Toward midnight, George woke up and asked for sandwiches and a bedside light. He began reading the book. The rest of us took turns on sentry duty, two hours at a time, while the others slept.

My turn came. At two a.m., I sat by the living room windowsill, watching the street. I had the ghost-jar by my side. It was late and I was tired. I needed the company.

"There's a spirit standing on the garden path opposite," I said. "I just caught the moonbeams going through it. So very faint. Man in a bowler hat. Very still and peaceful, like he's thinking about something."

Tonight the face in the jar shone pale and silvery, mirroring the moon above the rooftops. *"Oh, him,"* it said. *"Yes, he's thinking about something, all right. In about twenty minutes he'll move toward the house and disappear. At about three-forty a.m. he'll reappear, just briefly, with a dirty big bundle over his shoulder. I reckon it's his dead wife wrapped in a rug, but you only get a flash of a pair of fluffy slippers as he sets off up the road, so I've never satisfied my mind on that."*

I stared across the street. "This happens every night? I've never seen it before."

"Yeah, it's funny how often one doesn't see things that are right under your nose," the skull said. *"So . . . what shall we talk about? I know! Lockwood. He's in his element now, isn't he? Enemies closing in. Endgame afoot. Nice for him! He's chirpy."*

"Nonsense. He's worried sick, like the rest of us."

"Is he? Then he hides it well. If it was me, I'd say he's more than content with the way it's going. Suits the trajectory he's been on ever since his parents croaked. Oh, you can pout all you want, but you know it's true. Going out in a pointless blaze of glory is just how he'd like it: saves him the hassle of doing the boring, complex stuff—you know, like going on living." The face grinned knowingly at me.

As usual, the fact that the skull was precisely echoing my own thoughts gave an edge to my irritation. "That is *such* a lie," I said.

"Isn't."

"It so is."

"Yes, it's our intellectual debates I'm going to miss when you're dead," the skull remarked. *"Hey . . . unless they stuff your skull in with mine in an extra-special double jar! Then we could bicker happily for all eternity. How about it?"*

But I was still angry with the ghost; all day, Lockwood's cheerfulness had propelled us onward in our work, and all day I'd been worrying about him for exactly the reasons the skull described. I scowled. "You're disgusting."

"*So sue me. Or let me out of this jar. I won't bother you again.*"

"Not a chance."

The face retreated sullenly into the depths of the greenish murk. "*There. You're as selfish as Lockwood. He uses you to get what he wants, and you use me.*"

I snorted. "That's not true. Any of it."

"*Of course it is. You couldn't blow your nose without me to guide you. You're desperate for me to stick around. You're happy to take advantage of my raw intelligence and charm, and at the same time you're too frightened of me to even let me out of this cruel prison. Come on, try to deny it.*"

I couldn't deny it. I said nothing.

"*If you trusted me,*" the skull said, "*you'd break my jar right now. And look—there's a hammer right beside us!*" A pile of Kipps's tools lay on the windowsill; we were in the middle of fixing barricades here, too. "*One quick swing, and I'm out! But you won't, will you? Because after all I've done, you still don't trust me, and you're scared.*"

"Well," I said slowly, "maybe I am. But I think *you're* scared, too."

"*Me?*" The ghost pulled a series of faces, each one more eye-poppingly incredulous than the last. "*Baloney! How do you make that out?*"

"What are you *doing* here, Skull?" I said. "What keeps you tied to this dirty old piece of bone? I'll tell you what *I* think. I think you're frightened of letting go. You're frightened of doing what you *ought* to do, which is give up this world and finally go on into the next. You're always boasting about how you're different from other ghosts, how it's all about your conscious desire for life and blah, blah, blah, but I think your fear of death is the real emotion here. Or else why not do it? Why not head off? I bet you *could*. I bet you could break the connection."

The face had grown pale and nebulous as I spoke, and I couldn't read its expression. *"Join the lost souls drifting on the Other Side?"* it said softly. *"But I'm not like them."*

"Oh, but you *are*," I said. "I've seen you there, don't forget." When Lockwood and I had walked in that dark and freezing place, I'd caught a glimpse of the ghost in its full bodily form. Far from being a grotesque face, crammed in a jar, it was revealed as a pale, sardonic-looking youth, thin and spiky-haired. He'd still been tied to the spot where his skull sat in our world, but otherwise he was no different from the other gray inhabitants of the Other Side. "You *could* break the connection," I said again. "You don't have to be stuck here."

"Yeah, well." The skull sounded just as grumpy as I felt. *"The circumstances for* that *certainly haven't happened yet. I'll let you know when they do."*

I shrugged. "Fine. And *I'll* let you know when I decide to let you out."

"If you could see your way to doing it before *your brutal death, I'd appreciate it. Which means sometime tomorrow."*

"I'm not *going* to die."

"That's what I said, too."

Despite such dark predictions, the night passed without incident. No one attacked us in our beds, and the only disturbance was

George calling for cheese on toast at five in the morning. Dawn came at last, and we met again for breakfast. The kettle had only just boiled when a furious knocking sounded on the kitchen door and Flo Bones appeared, looming like a haunted scarecrow at the window. She bore ominous tidings and a rather crumpled box of chocolates for George.

"Excuse the brown stains on the cardboard," she said, brushing at the side of the box. "Just a bit of river mud. I didn't pass an open drain or I would have washed them off on the way here. Well, I see you've all been busy. What's that trip wire thing halfway up the steps?"

Lockwood shut the door behind her. "Sorry, Flo. It's a deadly mantrap. I should have told you."

Flo reached under her hat and scratched at her scalp. "Good thinking, and it seems like you might be needing a few more of them and all." She broke off, and regarded us levelly.

"Why?" Holly said. "What have you heard?"

She shook her head. "I don't know as I should say, seeing as how it'll give you all the willies. And it ain't confirmed, neither. Just a bit o' hearsay what's washed along the Thames and been gathered in her sack by old Flo. But the word is—" She glanced over her shoulder, made a lucky sign, and lowered her voice. "Word is that Sir Rupert Gale's been in deep discussions with Julius Winkman, and *your* names have been mentioned."

So much had been happening these past few days that I had completely forgotten about the black marketeer and his recent release from prison. It took me a moment to understand the implications.

Lockwood was way ahead of me. "Ah, *that's* it, is it?" he breathed.

"Of course . . . They're old acquaintances. Gale used to buy black market Sources from the Winkmans. Sorry, Flo—I interrupted. Do go on."

While he was speaking, Flo had helped herself to Lockwood's mug of tea. "Yeah, Julius Winkman," she said. "Since his release, he's been lying low. There's been word sent out that he don't want to see no relics or stolen goods or any of that stuff. 'Course," Flo went on, rolling her eyes, "that don't mean nothing, as it's his missus, Adelaide, and that young smear of cow-cake Leopold, who take possession of all the hush-hush items these days. So officially, old Winkman is all aboveboard now. But they say that Gale went to see him, and since then Julius has been out recruiting some of his old associates, fellows who ain't so particular about the kind of work they do. Head-crackers, bone-breakers, knife-men, and stranglers— *that* sort of tidy gentleman. Rounding them up, routing them out of the inns and wharf-side stews, getting them tooled and ready for a dicey and unspecified job." Her blue eyes gazed at us from the shadows of her hat. "Unspecified . . . but concerning *you*."

"*That's* why they've taken so long to get going," Lockwood said. "Fittes and Gale are getting the Winkman family to take us out. Marissa keeps her hands clean and shuts us up, while Julius gets the revenge he's been seeking ever since we got him arrested after Kensal Green that time. Hey, presto, everyone's happy."

"Except us," Holly said. "We'll be dead."

No one had much to say to that. "Maybe it's better this way," I said at last. "Maybe it's better that it's not going to be other agents coming after us. They won't be trained, like us, will they? They won't have swords."

"No," Kipps said, "just guns and knives. Hooray."

"We're going to be trapped in here," Holly whispered. "What if our barricades don't work? What if they get in? There'll be nowhere to run."

We gazed at one another. My hands felt cold; a worm of dread coiled tightly in my stomach. By the looks of it Quill and Holly were experiencing much the same thing. Not Lockwood, though. His eyes glittered; a small smile played at the corners of his mouth. On seeing that smile, the worm in my stomach coiled a whole lot tighter.

"Maybe there *is* somewhere we might go," Lockwood said. "Somewhere Winkman's men would never follow." His smile broadened. He gave a little laugh. "You're going to think I'm mad."

We waited. "Anything would be better than getting chopped into pieces by a group of smelly relic-men," Kipps said. "No offense intended there, Flo—you're a girl. Come on, Lockwood—what's the plan?"

Even then, he was slow to answer. He was weighing his thoughts, judging how best to present them to us. Finally he said, "I was just thinking that we could use Jessica's room."

Everyone looked at him blankly. "What, lock ourselves in there, you mean?" I said. "I suppose the door *is* strengthened with iron, because of the death-glow, and we've got a heck of a lot of psychic objects up there we could— Oh." My brain made the required leap, and my mouth fell open. "Surely you're not suggesting— No. No way."

"We've got the objects," Lockwood said. "We've got the chains. We've got the spirit-capes." He turned his beaming smile on Holly and Kipps. The truth had just dawned on them; they too suddenly understood what he was saying. "We can make ourselves an emergency exit," he went on. "If all else fails, we *can* escape. Of course we can. Why not? We've got all the materials we need to create a gate to the Other Side."

Utter silence greeted the statement. Even Flo seemed speechless. We stood there, staring at him in our little kitchen in Portland Row.

"Is this a private wake, or can anyone join in?"

The voice came from the hallway door. Everyone turned: there stood George. He was in his pajamas, and very gray about the face—gray, at least, where the purple bruises weren't blossoming. The bandage on his head had come off, and you could see where the hair was still matted with congealed blood. His sleeves were too short, and there were bruises on his arms. He stood awkwardly, limbs shaking, clasping the doorframe for support. But he was standing, for the first time in days.

"Look at me," he said. "Upright again! Things can't be so bad, surely." He gave us a mottled smile. "Hey, and there's the proof of it! Are *all* those chocolates for me?"

Chapter 18

Dubious as Flo's gift undoubtedly was (my theory was that she'd found the box floating down the Thames and had dried the chocolates out individually on riverside stones before repacking them), it was good to see George taking an interest in it. It helped sustain him during the long argument that followed his arrival.

No one could fault Lockwood's ingenuity, or the audacity of his plan. But the dangers involved with it seemed almost more terrifying than the ones we already faced, and it took all his charm and forcefulness to persuade us even to discuss it. The idea of a making a spirit gate in our own house gave everyone pause.

It had long been known that a single psychic object, or Source, such as the skull in the jar, provided a small hole through which a ghost could pass from the Other Side. The idea of a spirit gate, as made by the shamans in their spirit houses, and as created in secret by the Rotwell Agency and (we guessed) by Marissa Fittes as well, was essentially an extension of this principle. If a great number of Sources were placed in a single location, their powers combined to rip a much larger hole between the worlds. If it was big enough—and if you had sufficient protection, in the form of a spirit-cape—it was possible to pass through and back again. But the assembled ghosts that thronged the gate itself had to be kept in check by vast amounts of iron, and the Other Side itself was perilous, as Lockwood and I knew full well.

"There's the freezing cold, for starters," I said. "And the physical effort it takes to cross over, even *with* the capes. Would you willingly put yourself through that again?"

"If it was a question of survival," Lockwood said, "of course I would."

"Plus there's the threat from the ghosts at the gate. I know Rotwell ringed them with lots of chains . . . but what if they broke out here?"

"They wouldn't break out. We'd build the circle carefully."

"Forget the ones at the *gate*!" Holly cried. "What about the dead on the Other Side itself? The place is packed with them!"

Kipps gave a hoot of agreement. "Right! We get enough trouble from a few stray spirits over here! Stepping across is like stamping on a hornet's nest. From what you and Lucy experienced, they get drawn to the presence of the living. You only just escaped them."

Lockwood shook his head. "That was only because Lucy and I were wandering about the countryside. If we went through here, we'd just be in another version of thirty-five Portland Row. We wouldn't leave it. We'd just stay put."

"Have we even got enough Sources to do this?" I asked.

"Think about the energy already coming from the death-glow over my sister's bed," Lockwood said. "I bet that would do half the job on its own. And we've got a whole cluster of psychic objects in Jessica's room already, plus the things hanging all over the house." He looked through the open door into the hall, where the shelves of pots and gourds could just be seen. "My parents collected them for us," he murmured. "They're there to be used. And I believe my sister would want us to use her room, too. She'd want to help us escape."

There was another silence. We didn't know quite how to respond to that.

"What about George, here?" Kipps persisted. "He's practically dead already. How would he survive going through?"

"We wouldn't be over there for very long. Besides, think about those old folks at the Orpheus Society. They clearly do it all the time, and it hasn't killed them yet."

"*They* had a lot of extra equipment," I put in. "Those weird weapons, for a start. You can bet they're all designed to keep spirits at bay."

"And those crazy mechanical stilts," Kipps said. "We haven't got any of them."

"Who needs mechanical stilts?" Lockwood rolled his eyes. "Or those stupid weapons? We'd only be popping over for a few minutes! Take it from me, one look at the gate and Winkman's men would run a mile. And it *is* possible to build one—don't you think so, George?"

George had been busily working his way through the second layer of chocolates, listening intently but keeping his own counsel, with Flo sitting at his side. Whether it was his quiet air, or his poor bruised face that did it, he carried a certain authority. We all looked at him as he toyed with a walnut whip and placed it carefully back in the box. "We can certainly *try* making one," he said. "We can make the circle, put the Sources in it, do all that before sundown. I don't see what we've got to lose." He adjusted his broken spectacles. "Personally, I'd love to do it. I'd love a chance to glimpse the Other Side."

"That's the spirit," Lockwood said. "Well done, George."

"There's also the incentive of staying alive," George went on haltingly, "so that we can bring Marissa and her friends to justice. It may interest you to know," he said, "that overnight I've read *Occult Theories*, that little book you so kindly brought back from the Orpheus Society. It wasn't a wasted journey, you'll be pleased to hear. I'll tell you why, if someone puts the kettle on."

Someone did. Flo offered around the remaining chocolates. Everyone politely refused.

"The book's definitely by Marissa," George said. "No question about it. I recognize her style from the *Memoirs* and other writings. But it's a strange piece of work. She must have written it when she was very young, because there's nothing about her being an agent, or psychic detection, or anything *practical*. It's all much more airy-fairy than that, full of weird theories about life and death. The thing that really jumps out is her obsession with the stuff that spirits are made of. She thinks ghosts are proof that this substance is immortal. The body falls away, and the spirit continues on."

"We're back to ectoplasm, then," Holly said.

"Yes," George said, "though she calls it by other fancy names, too: 'the soul,' 'eternal essence,' stuff like that. And she doesn't see it as dangerous, like it is when a ghost touches you over here. She thinks that on the Other Side it gets much purer. She reckons that if you could get hold of it somehow, if you could capture it and absorb it, it would rejuvenate your body and make it young again."

"Which is exactly what's happened!" I said. "The woman we call Penelope *is* really Marissa—only young again! That would explain what the skull's been telling us."

"*Absorb* it?" Kipps echoed. "How would that work? What, does she bathe in it or something? Does she eat it? What?"

George shook his head. "In the book, she waffles on about an 'elixir of youth,' but I don't think she really knew at that point. It's all theory. Clearly she's got it figured out now, though. She and her pals must use a spirit gate to go over to the Other Side and collect the plasm. But there's one other thing I noticed. . . . I had to scribble the passage down, it was so good. It's stuffed down the back pocket of my pajama bottoms, if you could just reach it for me, Lockwood. My arms are too stiff."

"Must I? Oh, God, all right—there you go."

"Thanks." George took the crumpled piece of paper. "Remember how we were guessing that Marissa had a pet Type Three of her own to help her? Well, she does. Listen to this quote. It's a beauty:

'Such matters are beyond the wit of man or woman, and we must turn to the spirits themselves to help us. One such, fair of form and wise of countenance, comes regularly to me. I have spoken with him since I was a child. Dear Ezekiel is learned in matters of life and death, he understands buried secrets and the minds of mortals. With his help, we can transcend our baser natures, and make ourselves pure.'" George put the paper down with an air of finality. "Couldn't be much clearer, could it? She's had a spirit advisor, all along."

"This Ezekiel sounds a tad more informative than your tatty old skull, Luce," Lockwood commented. "Thanks, George." He sat back and considered us, his team and his associates, all sitting silently around the table. "Well, here's the situation as I see it," he said at last. "If we could get into the inner regions of Fittes House, we'd no doubt find ample proof of everything George has discovered. We'd find evidence of Marissa's crimes. We'd find the gate she's using to get to the Other Side, too. But we can't get in. The place is too well guarded. Barnes might do it, but there's no way he'd risk a confrontation with Marissa. I went to ask him yesterday, and he again said no." Lockwood shook his head. "The upshot is: we're on our own right now, with Winkman and his men likely to pay us a visit very soon. So I suppose I should say at this point that anyone who wants to leave is free to go. Me, I'm staying at Portland Row. It's my home, and I'm not abandoning it for anyone. But you—"

"Shut up, Lockwood," Holly said. "None of us are turning tail at this point."

Kipps grunted. "No matter how crazy your plans."

Lockwood's grin was wide, infectious. "All right," he said. "In that case, the question I'd ask you is a very simple one." He looked at us. "What are we prepared to do to win?"

An hour later, Holly, and I were sitting with Lockwood outside his sister's bedroom. The door was wide open, and cold emanations from the death-glow above the bed pulsed across the landing. We had emptied the final shipping crate and, amid a sea of scattered wood shavings, were unwrapping the objects it contained. There were wooden masks, carved sticks, brightly colored pottery jars sealed with wax, and opaque glass bottles. Anything that had the remotest psychic potential we piled in one corner; the rest we cast aside. It was the same procedure we'd used when emptying the other crates, only now carried out in double-quick time.

The skull in the jar was with us, too. It was still in a bad mood after our argument the night before. So was I, for that matter. Everything was pretty much as usual, then.

"*Don't tell me,*" it said. "*Another crisis. Or is sitting knee-deep in haunted objects the latest craze for all idiot agents? What are you going to do, play Hot Potato now? 'When the music stops, the Source explodes and a ghost will eat your face.' I can't really see it catching on.*"

"If you could try to be helpful for a moment," I growled, "we're separating out all the strongest Sources. Some we're sure of, but others we're not." I pointed to our "of interest" pile. "What do you think of these?"

The ghost sniffed dubiously. "*Some are psychically dangerous,*" it said, "*but you've got a lot of junk there, too. Particularly that pierced gourd Holly Munro is putting her head in—but that's an issue of hygiene more than anything.*"

"That pointy one? I thought it was a shaman's mask."

"*It's worn in tribal rituals, yeah. But those guys didn't put it on their faces, I'll tell you that.*"

"Er, Holly . . ."

Her voice was muffled from inside the gourd. "What?"

"Oh, nothing. I like the mask! You look good. Keep it on!" I turned back to the skull. "Exact function aside, you're saying it's useless?"

"*There's no trapped spirit in there. Those sealed pots, though—*" they're *more interesting. They've got the whiff of the grave about them. And that dream catcher with the bamboo handle, too . . .*" The face in the jar grinned evilly. "*Why not break them all and see what's inside?*"

"Not until we're ready." I looked into Jessica's room, at the black plasm burn that had eaten away the center of the abandoned bed. That had been caused by a ghost unleashed at the wrong moment. Lockwood had his back to the bed; he was calmly unwrapping another bundle from the crate. He still radiated the implacable determination that carried everyone along with it, the fierce serenity that he'd had all day.

The morning went on. We emptied out the crate and cleared the mess away. A great pile of Sources lay in the abandoned bedroom. Holly and I began to go around the house, taking the ornaments off the walls, stripping the shelves of all the psychic curios brought back by Celia and Donald Lockwood so long ago. All this was taken to the landing. Without the decorations, the hall and living room had that odd, cold, slightly echoing quality you usually get in a haunted, empty house. It was dark, too: Kipps had been working on the barricades, and most of the windows were covered. Thirty-five Portland Row no longer looked itself. It made us all feel sad.

Toward lunchtime, Flo Bones left us. She had offered to stay and help, but it was clear that she found it uncomfortable remaining so long with a roof over her head. I guessed the possibility of an impending attack might have influenced her, too. Before her departure, however, Lockwood took her to the library. They spoke for a long time, alone. Then Flo slipped away, leaving only a few dirty footprints to remember her by.

Midday passed; the sun reached its zenith and began to decline toward the west. Shadows slowly lengthened in Portland Row.

We began to build the iron circle that would surround our spirit gate. George was in charge of this. An easy chair had been brought up from the library and positioned on the landing. From here, surrounded by crumb-strewn plates, he supervised our efforts as we brought great coils of iron chains up from the basement. The Mullet's van had delivered most of these the previous day; now we wound them over each other to form a single iron barrier—a hoop or circle of enormous thickness—that went right around the outside of the old bed and sealed its death-glow within.

It wasn't pleasant work, exactly. The bedroom was a difficult place to spend time in. Cold energy pulsed from the death-glow, freezing your skin and setting your teeth on edge. But it had to be done. We cleared everything inessential out of the room to make space for the circle. Lockwood emptied out the chest of drawers at the back, throwing its contents—old photographs, boxes of forgotten jewelry—into plastic bags and taking them away. Meanwhile, under George's blackened but watchful eye, Kipps started constructing the trickiest part of the gate: the single chain that would provide our entry path, cutting across the circle from our world to the next.

"We need two metal posts," George said, "hammered into the floor on either side of the circle. Then we suspend a thick iron chain between them so that it runs right over the top of the bed. It mustn't touch the bed, or the death-glow. It's got to be hanging in midair, so that we can hold on to it. The iron in the chain will keep the spirits at bay, give us a safe route when we go through the gate."

"*If* we go through," Kipps said. "I'm devoutly hoping we won't have to. Uh-oh—" He broke off as Lockwood and I arrived on the landing. "I don't like the look of *these*."

We were carrying the spirit-capes. We had our original feathered cloak, as beautiful and iridescent as ever, which had already proved itself on the Other Side. We had a second feathered one, too, this of resplendent pink and orange plumage, and a third cape, covered with patchy fur. All these came from Lockwood's parents' crates. From the storeroom of the Orpheus Society, we had two modern silver capes as well.

"I'm going to allocate cloaks now," Lockwood said. "There may not be time later. Lucy, I want you to have our faithful old spirit-cape. Kipps, you take this other feathered one. Holly, this one with the furs is about your size. George and I will wear the Orpheus outfits. We stole enough Orpheus gloves to go around, too. Let's check that they fit. Everyone try them on."

I already knew the feel of my spirit-cape—its warmth and lightness, the soft protection of its plumage—and I had it on in no time. The others were more hesitant. George was stiff and needed help getting his on. He and Lockwood both shimmered with silver; their scaly cloaks had a smooth, reptilian feel. Meanwhile, Kipps's eyes boggled at the multicolored splendor of his feathered ensemble, while Holly cringed at the texture of her pelts.

In its jar the skull cackled long and loud. *"This is like feeding time at the world's worst zoo,"* it said. *"I feel like throwing you all some sardines."*

"Just how many dead animals am I wearing here?" Holly muttered. "I look like a fur trapper. This is awful."

"And *I* look like a stuffed parrot," Kipps said. "Trust you to give me this."

"I think you look adorable, Quill," George said. "Very colorful. Those pink feathers in particular are lovely. And see how long it is. That'll give you ultimate protection on the Other Side."

"You make it sound like a deodorant. If any of my friends see this . . ."

"*Friends*, Kipps?" George gave him a slow and painful wink.

Kipps snorted. "Yeah, well, if I had any before, I certainly won't now." He removed the cloak and went off grimly to hammer a post into the floor.

It was late afternoon. Half of Portland Row was in deep blue shadow. You could taste the onset of evening. Lockwood sent Kipps upstairs to the undefended window of my attic so he could watch the road.

In Jessica's room, everything was in place: the iron circle, the guide-chain running between the posts. It was time to put the Sources in the circle and create the gate. Lockwood and I did this, swiftly and alone. Each object had to be opened—wax seals cut, pouches slit, wooden surfaces pierced—to allow the escape of the spirit within. Anything that contained a Source was broken in this way, and placed inside the ring of iron. It was still daylight, so the work was theoretically safe. Even so, we didn't dawdle. Jars, bottles, masks, and dream catchers—everything was opened and put in.

As we worked, it was possible to feel a slow buildup of psychic pressure in the bedroom. There was already plenty from the death-glow, hanging like a faint oval above the bed, not far from where the guide-chain ran; but now, steadily, an accompanying buzz or hum began to join it, the psychic vibrations from the bones and other haunted fragments littering the floor. The air within the circle began to grow thick and strange; Lockwood and I moved ever faster, watching the window and the dying of the light.

"Think this'll be enough?" With a small hammer, I knocked a hole in one of the final clay pots, revealing a couple of knuckle bones. My fingers tingled as I touched them. I threw them quickly into the circle.

Lockwood's face was set; he snapped the wax seal off the end of a bamboo stick and poured several yellowed teeth beyond the chain. "Can't you feel it? It's not even dark yet, and the light in the circle's becoming hazy. It was the same with the Rotwell gate, remember? You couldn't see the far end of the cross-chain. Give it a couple of hours and there'll be a way through—if we need to take it."

"Lockwood," I said, "do you think we will?"

He only looked at me. We finished our work and left the bedroom. We could feel the throb and pulse of the widening gate even as we went downstairs.

For some reason that none of us expressed but all agreed on, we felt the need for a good supper that evening at Portland Row. Ignoring the boarded-up windows, ignoring the piles of weapons lying around; above all, ignoring the psychic thrum from the room upstairs, we went about the business quietly together, everyone pitching in. Holly made a salad; Lockwood cooked bacon, egg, and sausages; Kipps and I cut the bread and set the table. We ate it quickly, taking turns to go to my attic room to watch the street. Then we washed up (again, it was somehow important to do so), and put everything away. The sun was almost down. We wandered about the house, each lost in his or her own thoughts. We'd done all that we could do.

I unbolted the kitchen door and, avoiding the trip wire that Lockwood had placed on the steps, went down into the garden. I'd been inside all day; I badly needed to be out. As always, it was a mess. We never had time to mow the lawn, so the grass was nearly knee-high. There were apples on the tree that needed to be picked; windfalls were already littering the soil below. I stood looking at the houses beyond the garden wall, where other people lived their separate lives.

"Getting some air, Luce?"

I turned, and it was Lockwood. He hopped down the steps and came toward me across the grass, dark and thin and lit to shining by the dying sun. It was like he was going to ignite. Quite unexpectedly, the sight made me want to cry. All my fears for him, and for all of us, suddenly hit me as if from nowhere.

"Hi," I said. "Yes, just getting some air."

He considered me, his eyes soft and serious. "You're upset."

"It's been a long day. . . ." I brushed my hair out of my face, looked away from him, and cursed softly. "Who am I kidding? I'm frightened, Lockwood. It's like you said the other night. This might be the end."

"No. It'll be all right. It *will* be all right, Lucy. You have to trust me."

"I do. Sort of."

He grinned. "That's nice to hear."

"I trust your Talent and your leadership," I said. "It's the way you seem to be *enjoying* this that I can't quite understand."

He came to stand beside me. The sunlight was still on him. Right then, he was close to the idea I'd always had of him; the picture I saw in my mind's eye when drawing near to sleep. If the skull had been there to see us, he'd no doubt have snorted long and loud. But the skull wasn't there.

Lockwood said, "It's not that I'm enjoying it, Luce. But I can see the *rightness* of everything that's happening now, and that's different. You remember in the cemetery, I told you how arbitrary everything was? How nothing had any meaning? I don't feel that anymore. Yes, my parents died. I now know *why*, and we have a chance to avenge them. My sister died, too. Her death-glow may help save our lives tonight. More than that, we're getting close to a solution to the Problem. You know we are. When we get there, all this will be over and we won't have to do it anymore. It'll be all right, Lucy." He touched my arm. "You'll see."

"I hope that's the case," I said.

"Well, anyway, I didn't come out to tell you that." Lockwood rummaged in his coat pocket and produced a small square box, very squashed and battered. "I came to show you this. I found it in the chest of drawers in Jessica's room. Don't worry, it's not a Source or anything."

"If it was," I said, "we'd have chucked it in that circle." I took it from him and opened the creased lid. As I did so, something inside flared in the last light of the sun. It was a dazzling blue, so clear and pure that it made me gasp. The inside of the box was lined with tissue paper. Curled up in it was a golden necklace, and its pendant was a shimmering blue stone, smooth and oval and darkly translucent. It was supremely lovely. I held it up between my fingers and gazed at the heart of the stone. It was like looking into deep, fresh, clean water.

"What is it, Lockwood?" I asked. "I don't think I've ever seen anything so beautiful."

"It's a sapphire. My father got the gem out East somewhere, and he had this necklace made for my mother. It was her favorite piece of jewelry. That's what my sister told me once, anyway. I'd forgotten all about it until today."

"So your mum didn't have it on her when she—?"

"I don't think she wore it in the ordinary way. It was too special to her. My dad gave it to her soon after they met. It was a symbol of his undying devotion."

I let the sapphire catch the light once more, then lowered it back into the box. I handed it back to him.

"It couldn't be anything else," I said.

"No, exactly. Anyway, Luce . . ." Lockwood cleared his throat. "I was going to ask if you—"

A shrill whistle came from the top of the kitchen steps. We looked up to see Kipps peering out at us. "Hope I'm not disturbing you," he said. "Just thought you'd like to know that the Winkmans have arrived."

Chapter 19

Quill was right. There was activity near Arif's store. Just before it closed, two men had come out of the shop. They migrated to opposite sides of Portland Row and sat on walls there in the deepening dusk. Thickset and silent, they smoked occasional cigarettes; otherwise, they were as one with the bricks and the concrete. Occasionally they glanced along the road, toward number thirty-five. They sat there while the ghost-lamps came on, and the rest of our neighbors retired behind their defenses. Curtains were drawn, the street grew empty. But the red glow of the watchers' cigarettes remained.

They were there to make sure no one was leaving the building. Well, we certainly weren't planning to leave *that* way.

Lockwood held his final briefing in the living room. As in the rest of the house, the walls were bare and marked by stains where his parents' artifacts had hung for so long. One lantern was on, but the room was oddly dark. The boards across the windows blocked out the streetlights. Lockwood stood there with his back to us. As we filed in, he turned and smiled. It was his old grin.

"You all know what's going to happen tonight," he said. "At some point between now and dawn, some unpleasant people are going to try to get inside this building. Well, we're not going to allow that. This is thirty-five Portland Row. We've always been safe here."

George stiffly raised a hand. "Except when that Fairfax assassin broke in one time," he said.

"Oh, yes. True."

"And that time when Annie Ward's ghost was unleashed here," I added.

"And the various times the skull's caused us grief," Holly put in.

George nodded. "Let's face it, it's always been a death trap, hasn't it?"

Lockwood clenched his teeth. "Yeah, but it's *my* bloody death trap, and they're not getting in. So—there are five of us to defend the place. As we know, there are only two really vulnerable points: the rear basement, and the kitchen. George is injured, so he'll remain upstairs with the stash of weapons on the landing. That's where the rest of us will retreat to if things go wrong. Jessica's room is our last resort. Luce and Holly, I want you both stationed in the kitchen. Quill and I will be in the basement. Listen out. If any of us are in trouble, we whistle, and the others help if they can." He smiled at us. "Let's get to our stations, then. Good luck, everyone."

There was one last chore to carry out before taking up my position. The skull in the jar had made so many loud attempts to speak to me over the course of the afternoon that I'd closed the lever just to get some peace. I didn't know whether it wanted to pass on insults or over-perceptive observations, but I had time for neither. While Holly went into the kitchen, I took the jar into the hall and turned the lever.

"Well?"

"*At last! Right. Now's the time. I see a hammer at your belt. One quick swing, and I'll be free. Promise I won't kill Cubbins.*"

"That's good of you. The answer's no."

"*He's half-dead already; to be honest, it's beneath me. Kipps, though . . . Now, he's a different story. No one would miss him.*"

"I'm not letting you out. We've discussed this."

The face regarded me balefully. "*Pity. You're the only person who might have done it, and in a few hours you'll be dead. I'll be stuck in here for decades more.*"

"That's not my concern. Now, if you've finished, I need to get to my post."

"*How very noble. Your leader must be extremely proud.*" The eyes narrowed, the green haze frothed against the glass. "*You realize that I could help you in the fight, don't you? I'd kill all Winkman's men with ghost-touch. Might save dear Lockwood's life . . .*"

The fact that a little bit of me was tempted made me angrier still. "Forget it. It's not going to happen."

"*Well, obviously it won't if you keep me in here. Poor old Anthony. What was on those slips of paper you got from the fortune-telling machine? I never did quite see. . . .*"

I picked up the jar and made for the kitchen. "You'll never know. Now shut up."

"Tell you what," the skull said. *"Put me right there on the table. A stray bullet might shatter my jar. Or better still, your tumbling corpse might squash it. Here's hoping."*

"Argh! Will you *shut up?*" My head was full to bursting and I couldn't stand the sight or sound of that skull an instant longer. I opened one of the kitchen cupboards, thrust the jar inside, turned the lever, and slammed the door on the livid, goggling face. Then I cast it from my mind and went to check my weapons.

Time passed. In the kitchen, Holly and I sat on the floor, our backs against the cabinets, rapiers and ammunition close at hand. We had set a lantern beneath the table, and its dull red light shone within a little forest of chair legs, like an ogre's fire seen far away. The outside door was boarded up and further secured with bars and chains. The countertops were empty; the windows hidden behind Quill's defenses. We'd bored a couple of spy-holes in the planks, and every now and then got up to look through them at the garden. You could just see the apple tree, the garden wall, the shapes and lights of other houses. The night was still. The fridge emitted its usual hum. Faint psychic sounds also came from the cupboards by the door, where I'd stowed the ghost-jar. It was probably still complaining.

"Faucet's dripping," Holly said, after a time. "We must get that fixed one day."

"It's a nuisance. I don't know why Lockwood doesn't take care of it."

"Next week. We'll get a plumber in next week, Lucy. That's what we'll do."

"Sounds a good plan to me, Hol."

Holly had her head back against a cabinet, her eyes looking up at the ceiling. Her hair hung loose about her shoulders, and her legs were stretched out in front of her, with her hands resting in her lap. She was as cool and composed as ever, but there was something artless in the posture that made me think of a very little girl.

"You all right?" I said.

"Yes, of course."

"You think we'll be okay? You think we'll get through this?"

Holly smiled and looked at me. "What do *you* think?"

"We're always fine."

Without waiting for her response I got up, leaned over the sink, and peered through the nearest spy-hole. You had to press your eye really close to the wood to see out; even then, it took a while to focus. Branches moved in the apple tree at the far end of the garden. I watched them. Just the wind.

"All clear," I said.

"They may not be here for hours yet." Holly came to stand beside me.

"Hol," I said, "when you first came to the agency, I'm sorry I wasn't very . . . friendly. I know I could have been nicer to you."

"Oh, don't worry about that. We've talked about it before." She pushed her hair back from her face. "I'm sure I was an utter pain as well. Anyway, it must have been odd, having me show up."

"It was a bit, but—"

"But you needn't have worried." She smiled at me. "Funnily enough, Lockwood isn't actually my type."

In my embarrassment, I'm not sure quite what my expression was right then, though I doubt the eerie red glow in the room made it massively attractive. It was sufficient to make Holly laugh. She moved to look through another spy-hole at the far end of the window, which gave a different angle on the garden. "Don't look so shocked, Lucy," she said. "I know how you feel about him. But, if anything, I had my eye on someone else."

"Good God, you don't mean George?"

Holly laughed again; her eyes sparkled as she glanced at me sidelong. "You must know there are other possibilities in this world." The smile faded, her body tensed. "Hold it—we've got company out there."

I jammed my face against the nearest spy-hole. Yes—something stirring in the garden. Swift forms, soft lumps of darkness breaking free of the night, slipping over the garden wall. They flowed up toward the house, past the apple tree, spreading outward left and right.

I stamped a warning on the kitchen floor. At the same moment someone—Lockwood, I guessed—called out sharply from downstairs. Holly and I moved away from the windows, closer to the table. We stood side by side, facing opposite directions. Our swords were out. We gripped each other's hands.

It was very silent.

Silence . . . That was the worst of it. You hardly dared to breathe. I stared at the garden door. We had the internal doors propped open, so you could see another lantern flickering down the hall; that was the only movement—the tiny wisp of reddish light. In the whole of

35 Portland Row there was not a sound. Holly's hand was damp in mine.

A little scuffle on the garden steps. Holly made a small noise in her throat.

From downstairs came the crash of broken glass.

I glanced at Holly to see if she had heard it—

And there was a terrific *bang*. The room shook; I saw bright white light shine for an instant at the edges of the boards hammered into the garden door. The light of the magnesium explosion faded. Lockwood's trip wire had done its job. There was a thump on the wall as something collided with it, and the sound of a man howling.

Holly was grasping my hand hard. "Lucy . . . !"

I scowled at the wall. "No, Hol. No, it's good. Maybe it'll put them off."

It didn't. Glass broke behind us; beyond the boards, the kitchen window smashed.

"Guard the door, Holly," I said.

I moved to the window and stabbed my rapier out through the nearest spy-hole. I was rewarded by a gasp of pain and then a crunch of broken shrubbery as someone dropped from the window into the bushes below.

From downstairs came a frantic whistling—Lockwood's alarm signal. Holly and I looked at each other across the kitchen.

"You go," she said. "I'll hold on here."

"I won't be long. . . ." I was already careering down the spiral staircase, boots clattering, feeling the temperature drop with every step. I reached the bottom. My skin tingled; my teeth ached with sudden cold. Strips of greenish fog lapped against my boots.

Ghost-fog . . .

From the arch on the left, from the rear of the house, I heard the ringing of steel, psychic concussions, and a screaming voice that didn't come from a living throat. I plunged through, saw Lockwood and Kipps retreating from a massive, faintly glowing form. Its outline was rounded, knobbly, and ill-defined. There was a broad, low-slung node that might have been a head, the suggestion of sloped shoulders, gristly protrusions instead of arms—and nothing else. The rest was a shapeless, glowing mass. It hung just above the floor, palpitating slightly, drifting toward us. As Lockwood struck through it with his rapier, the plasm parted around the wound and just as swiftly reformed.

"Hi, Luce." Lockwood glanced back at me with frankly unnecessary calm. "Thanks for coming down. You see we've got a Limbless. They busted a hole in the door, threw its Source in. It rolled away somewhere in the laundry room. Can you find it? Quill and I have our hands full."

"Could blast it with a flare," I said. I was already moving to the side, looking for an opportunity to dart past the apparition. Never get near a Limbless, lest it suck you in.

"We will if necessary, but I don't like the idea of all that plasm flying around in such an enclosed space. Take a look, will you? Just don't tread on the floorboards by the door."

I darted forward, ducking through a wall of cold, out into the laundry area at the back of the basement. Fragments of broken wood lay scattered about, and our barricade was already partly dismantled. Beyond it, dark forms worked feverishly to break their way inside.

I threw a flare to dissuade them, and by its silvery light scrabbled on the floor among the wood and debris and the odd sock and pair of leggings left there from our washing. I couldn't see anything that looked like a Source. White smoke plumed above me. The barricade was smoldering with white tongues of fire, and someone with an ax was attacking it in a frenzy.

"How's it going, Luce?" Lockwood's call wasn't quite as nonchalant now. From the Limbless came a horrid gurgling sigh; from Kipps, a cry of fear.

I didn't answer. I had my flashlight on, gripped between my teeth. I'd opened a pouch in my belt, held my fingers ready to grasp one of the silver nets that lay folded within. Where *was* that stupid Source? The ax was making short work of the door. I knelt close to the floor tiles, craning my neck to look down the side of the washing machine, among the lint and buttons. . . .

There! A roughly circular fragment of bone—a piece of neck vertebra, most likely, wedged almost beneath the machine. As I reached for it, the last remnants of the barricade splintered. Magnesium smoke swirled, and a short but powerful-looking man clambered through. It had been a while since I'd last seen Julius Winkman. He'd worn a new blue suit for his sentencing, and I'd been high up in the courtroom gallery. Today he wore black and carried a length of metal piping, and I was lying on the floor with my arm under a washing machine. Times change. We recognized each other, even so.

Jail hadn't made him any less muscular. His arms were still knotted like ship ropes, his chest and neck as massive as those of a horse. His lips drew back in a grimace as he saw me. He stepped into the room and put his weight on one of the loose floorboards Lockwood and Kipps had rigged up. His boot went down, the board swung up; it slammed into his face, sending him crashing backward into the men behind him.

At the same moment I pulled the piece of bone out from the crevice and rolled it up in the cool, loose folds of the silver net. Across the room, the giant floating shape crumpled in on itself like a punctured balloon. My ears popped; the Limbless was gone.

Roars of fury sounded in the garden. Someone somewhere fired a gun; I felt an impact on the wall behind me. I left the swaddled Source lying, got to my feet unsteadily. Hands grasped me; Lockwood was pulling me back across the room. "No use waiting," he said, "the door's broken, Luce. They're in. Quill's gone upstairs to help Holly. You come with me."

We ran through another arch into the rapier room. The air was filled with smoke, with flecks of dwindling ghost-fog, with sparks of burning magnesium. The still shapes of Esmeralda and Floating Joe hung on their chains. A thin wire extended from Esmeralda's left leg and trailed away behind a pile of salt sacks in the furthest corner.

Lockwood grasped the wire. He pulled me down behind the sacks.

We waited.

Noises beyond the arch. A man with a long knife stole into sight.

Despite his bulk, he moved silently through the swirling smoke. He glanced up the iron stairs, then looked into the rapier room. *This* made him stop abruptly. He had seen the dummies' misshapen forms hanging on their chains in the soft darkness. They must have been an unnerving sight. A flashlight beam winked on and off; it picked out their straw hands, their painted faces. Just dummies . . . The man returned the flashlight to his belt and inched into the room, knife at the ready. Softly, softly, he padded across the space, making for the doorway to the storeroom, which was near the pile of sacks where we were hiding. As he reached the middle of the room, Lockwood yanked on the wire, causing Esmeralda to swing abruptly toward him like a floating ghost. With a stifled curse, the man reacted; his knife stabbed straight into the center of her stuffed straw stomach, where it burst one of the magnesium flares we had hidden there. Searing white flames erupted from the dummy's torso in a spreading ring, ripping her apart, engulfing the man right next to her. He toppled to the floor in a cloud of burning straw, then rose again, screaming, his hair awash with pale magnesium flames. Frantically beating at his head, he turned, collided briefly with the wall, then careered away toward the office.

We got up from behind the sacks. In the midst of the swirling silver-gray smoke, the dummy's head hung swinging from the chain. Her body was gone.

"Good old Esmeralda," Lockwood said. "Fell in action. We should get upstairs."

Up the iron staircase, around and around. A bullet cracked against the metal tread beneath my feet, sending out a brief, bright spark. We burst into the kitchen. Holly and Kipps were standing side by side across the fragments of the fallen garden door. Two men in black clothes were attempting to get in. They had clubs, which they were swiping frantically left and right. Kipps and Holly swung their rapiers in furious, complex arcs, driving the men back, slicing gouges in the bludgeons, holding the line.

A familiar face appeared in the dark behind the men. I caught a flash of pink cheeks, of blue and bulging eyes. "Out of the way, you idiots," Sir Rupert Gale said. "*I'll* deal with them."

At once Lockwood was there beside Kipps and Holly. "Fall back," he shouted. "Get upstairs." Footsteps sounded behind us on the iron staircase. I took my final flare and lobbed it at the doorway, sending Sir Rupert leaping back into the garden. Even as the explosion sounded, we were already out in the hall and swinging around to climb the stairs.

On the landing, I could feel the pulsations of the gate beyond the bedroom door. George sat calmly in his chair. He had been fixing up makeshift spears, using broom and mop handles and some knives from the kitchen. He nodded at us as we piled up alongside him. "Sounds a bit warm down there."

"It is." One side of Lockwood's coat was black and steaming, presumably from his fight with the Limbless. His pale face was ablaze with energy. "You all right, George?" he asked. "Weapons ready?"

"Yes."

"Carpet ready?"

"Yes."

"Good. Sir Rupert Gale's here."

George nodded. "Knew he'd want to get in on the act."

There were loud thuds; boots on stairs; shouted commands echoing in the depths of the house. Then, rising above it all, a cry of rage in the kitchen.

Holly jumped. "What's that?"

George rose slowly from his chair. "Looks like Sir Rupert just found the little cartoon of him I drew on the kitchen table. Well, when I say *little*, I mean *filling the entire Thinking Cloth*. It's amazing how perfectly that cloth accommodates a picture of a man bending over. I only just found space for my accompanying message."

"Which was . . . ?" Lockwood was readying one of the spears at the top of the stairs.

He told us.

"Gosh," Holly said. "I'm not surprised he's a bit cross."

"What's particularly good," George said, "is that Winkman's men will have seen it, too. That," he added, "is what is known as psychological warfare. It'll destabilize Sir Rupert, make him mad and reckless."

"That's good, is it?"

A red face materialized at the bottom of the staircase. Lockwood hurled the spear; the face jerked back at the last instant and the point embedded itself in the floor.

"Yup," said George. "Watch out, here they come again."

One of Winkman's men had peeped out fleetingly at the bottom of the staircase, then darted across into the library. A moment later the barrel of a gun appeared around the corner. Three shots were fired. We ducked back as plaster fell from holes in the ceiling above our heads. At the same moment, a swift, athletic shape took the opportunity to bound halfway up the stairs. A familiar voice came calling. "Oh, Lockwood . . ." it said. "Where are you?"

Lockwood spoke quickly. "I'm going to buy us some time. The rest of you get into Jessica's room, put on the cloaks. You too, Lucy." Even without looking, he knew that I would disobey him. He drew his sword, stepped over to the top of the stairs.

They opened the bedroom door behind me; at once a psychic tumult beat against my mind. I heard the shrieks of ghosts inside the circle. For an instant I remembered the skull, shut in a cupboard down in the kitchen. I shook the thought away. The others were slipping into the room, Kipps supporting the slowly moving George. But I hung back, watching as Sir Rupert Gale clambered into view. Aside from a peppering of magnesium salt, he had entirely evaded my flare downstairs. He wore his usual green tweed suit and a cerise shirt; his face was eager and smiling.

Lockwood waited at the top, his hair down over his eyes, his rapier ready. He was trying to look relaxed, but I could see that he was breathing hard.

"Anthony John Lockwood!" Sir Rupert said. "Do you realize you've managed to put Winkman *and* four of his men out of action so far? Shockingly unfriendly, I call it. Where's your hospitality?"

Lockwood wiped his lick of hair aside. "Come up," he said, "and I'll give you a little more."

Sir Rupert chuckled. "You know," he said, "for months I've been wondering where this encounter would take place. I must say I had high hopes. On some castle battlements, perhaps. Or in a palace garden . . ." As he spoke, he jumped forward. He ducked under Lockwood's first blow, and met the second with an easy twist of his rapier. "But this mean little staircase?" he said. "In this cramped and dreary squat? It's a trifle disappointing."

Lockwood cocked his head to one side. He struck out again, parried, guarded his legs against repeated side-cuts and low jabs. "Are you insulting my house?"

Sir Rupert's eyes twinkled. "Well . . . the dreadful sofas, those ethnic cushions, that ineradicable smell of toast . . . It's all so frightfully homely. It's just I'd hoped for a more glamorous location, that's all."

He moved up another step. Lockwood edged back from the lip of the stairs. Their arms were moving too fast to see now; the swords blurred and moved, melding in the air. The clash of blades became a continuous burr, a wall of sound. A thin red line appeared on Sir Rupert's cheek; one of Lockwood's hands was suddenly bleeding.

"I'm sorry to hear that Portland Row disappoints you," Lockwood said. He flashed his gaze toward me, where I stood at the door to the room. I gave a signal to show him that the others were ready, to urge him to come on. "And you're right about the furniture," he added. "It *is* shabby. Sadly, the floor coverings aren't much better."

He sprang to the side, bent down, and pulled sharply on the carpet at the top of the stairs. George had loosened it earlier, so that nothing held it tight to the steps. The whole thing came free, wrenched upward in a tight diagonal. Sir Rupert's boots were pulled from under him; he was thrown backward. With a cry he vanished down the stairs, over and over, rolling head over heels. There was a complicated series of bumps as he disappeared from view.

A moment later Lockwood was ushering me through the door

into the bedroom. We slammed it shut and thrust the bolts home. The cold power of the gate behind us thrummed against our skin. Ghosts screamed out our names.

Lockwood turned to look at us all. He brushed his hair back with his wounded hand, leaving a trace of blood on his face. "Well," he said, smiling, "that settles it. Now we've *got* to go through."

Chapter 20

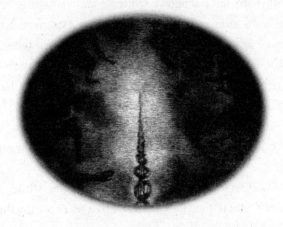

It would be nice to say that locking ourselves behind a good strong door gave us a brief sense of respite, but that wasn't really true. Yes, a house full of murderers was bad. Sadly, being shut in a small room with a spirit gate didn't have much to recommend it, either.

The good news was that our construction of the gate had worked. Everything had gone according to plan. Our superstrong iron circle had held firm, and was fully withstanding the spectral energies now raging inside it. With the coming of darkness, as Lockwood had predicted, the ghosts had emerged from their Sources. Unable to escape the circle, they whirled furiously around and around, radiating hideous cold and psychic dread. My body shrank from the force of it. My head rang with their cries.

There were so many spirits trapped there, so many squeezed into such a tight space, that it was impossible to make them out clearly. The column of air above the circle was thick with their movement; with faint shadows writhing and plunging, figures of billowing black smoke flowing in and out of existence; screaming faces pressed against the invisible barrier that penned them in. The light in the column was hazy and faint. You couldn't see the bed clearly or the objects on the floor; you couldn't see the far side of the room. As for the chain we'd suspended across the circle between the posts, ice shimmered on its links as it disappeared into the haze. The ghosts kept clear of it, loathing its iron. That chain was our way through.

Lockwood seized his silver cloak from the floor, while I took up the cape of feathers that had already survived two trips through a gate just like this. The others were waiting for us, dressed and ready. Kipps wore his bird-of-paradise cape and his trusty goggles; George, his cloak of silver scales. Holly was doing up the belt on her animal-pelt combo. They all had silver gloves from the Orpheus Society, too. It was the same menagerie as before, but now that we were about to use them, the humor in those outfits was gone. The deathly pull of the spirit gate hung over us all. Our faces were stiff with fear.

Behind me, someone tried the handle of the door. A bullet was fired into the wood, but the iron layer on our side prevented it from penetrating.

"Don't forget your gloves, Lucy," Lockwood said. He put his on.

"How are you feeling, George?" I asked. "Up for this?"

He nodded, gave me a weak smile.

"Right," Lockwood said. "Everyone listen. Gale being here has changed things slightly. He might not be as frightened of this circle as Winkman's men will be. . . . But I don't see that we have any choice. If we stay in here, we'll be cut to pieces. Go through, and we'll survive."

Behind us, the ghosts howled. Something struck against the door: wood splintered, iron cracked.

Lockwood scowled. "The ax again. We need to get moving. This was my idea, so I need to go through first. Then George. Holly, can you go after George, make sure he's okay? Then Quill. Lucy, that means you're last—if that's all right with you?"

"Of course it is," I said.

The ax didn't hang around for us; it chopped at the door.

"Remember what Lucy and I told you," Lockwood went on. "Keep firm hold of the chain and walk straight across. The chain and your cloaks will keep the ghosts at bay. They'll rage and shout, but they won't touch you. You can just ignore them."

"Fat chance of that," Kipps said. He was staring at the circle from under his feathery hood.

"When we get to the Other Side," Lockwood said, "it'll be like this room, only different. Darker. Quiet. No enemies. We'll be safe." He smiled, took hold of the chain. "It's just a few yards away. I'll see you there."

Something decisive happened to the door. You could hear the wood being ripped apart, the iron strips screaming as hands tore at them. Suddenly it was obvious we wouldn't have enough time. Lockwood hesitated, looked back in doubt.

Holly stepped forward. "No, you need to guard our backs, Lockwood. Let me go first. George—you follow me."

She held out her hand for George; limping, he joined her at the chain. Lockwood stepped back, nodding his gratitude. He drew his sword and faced the door.

I gave George a thumbs-up. "Cheer up," I said. "You've been dying to do this!" To be fair, it wasn't the best choice of words. "See you in a minute," I added heartily. He looked numb with terror; he didn't answer me.

George and Holly set off along the iron chain, going steadily, hand over hand. Two small cloaked figures, edging closer and closer to the iron circle, to where the chain entered the haze of ghostly light and disappeared.

A particularly loud crash came from the door. It was in pieces now. Two or three men were struggling to pull them clear. You could see the panic on their faces, their hesitation as they saw the gate. But Sir Rupert was there, too. Face bloodied, teeth bared, he drove them on. I pulled my rapier from my belt, went to stand with Lockwood, side by side.

The screams of the ghosts grew suddenly loud. I looked back toward the gate. Holly and George were gone. The chain swung in little rhythmic movements, crisp and definite, like someone was still progressing along it, somewhere inside the circle. The shapes trapped in the column of hazy light whirled in a frenzy of eagerness and—I hoped—disappointment. As I watched, the chain stopped moving. It slowed, hung still.

"It's worked!" I said. "They're through. Quill, you're up next."

Kipps nodded, which sent the long feathers of his hood bobbing madly. He looked like a drab and mournful chicken about to walk a gangplank into a cooking pot. He grasped the chain and shuffled hesitantly toward the circle.

Something scrabbled at the hole in the broken door. Sir Rupert Gale launched himself through. He landed awkwardly, avoided my twirling blow, and struck me aside with a lash of the fist. I fell into Lockwood, catching him off-balance. As we stumbled together, Sir Rupert drew back his sword to get a quick thrust in.

Something flashed past me like a vengeful chicken, striking left and right with a rapier. Sir Rupert was driven back against the door. He seemed stunned; it was all he could do to parry the blows. Maybe it was Kipps's sheer weirdness that contributed to his shock— the bulging goggles, the bird-of-paradise feathers jerking above his head, the pink plumage swinging wildly with every sword-swipe. You couldn't blame him. Kipps was enough to put anybody off.

Sir Rupert's skills remained. He began to exert himself. Kipps's momentum slowed, he backed away. . . . But now Lockwood and I were beside him. For an instant it was three against one, the air alive with clinking metal. Someone slashed with a knife at Lockwood through the broken door. He dodged, spun around, and struck at Sir Rupert's head. Sir Rupert ducked under Lockwood's blow and thrust at Kipps's midriff beneath his cloak. Kipps cried out in pain. I cut down with my sword, slicing into Sir Rupert's wrist. He swore and jumped back, holding his arm.

That was our cue to get out of there. Kipps, Lockwood, and I leaped away and across the room. We grabbed the guide-chain and bundled ourselves along it, Kipps first, then me, then Lockwood. We plunged forward, almost falling over each other, through the blast of cold, toward the swirling column of spectral air. We went so fast we outstripped fear; without pause, without thought, we stepped over the iron barrier and entered the psychic chaos of the gate.

We were right on top of the exposed Sources, and their occupants were very near. Unholy voices screamed and whispered in my ears, using languages I didn't understand. Pulsing figures stood on either side, keeping clear of the iron chain that stretched away before us, over the bed and into dimness. They watched us, clustering as closely as they dared.

Ice crusted on the links of the iron chain; freezing air beat against my face. Ahead of me, Kipps was stumbling, slowing. This made sense; it was his first time. "Ignore it all!" I shouted. "Keep walking! Follow the chain, and don't let go!"

We reached the bed. It was covered in ice, which cracked as we clambered over it. Not just the ice—the mattress itself was cracking, solid and frozen. Crawling things with broken backs skittered under it on hands and knees, like sharks glimpsed through the glass bottom of a boat. When we jumped down on the far side, they darted clear of our swirling cloaks and rose behind us, calling out our names.

We paid no heed. Another couple of steps and we were out over the loop of iron chains again and into absolute silence on the far side of the room.

How *quiet* it was suddenly, and how cold.

Not only had the psychic hubbub stilled, but you couldn't hear anything else, either—not the shouting of Sir Rupert or Winkman's men, or the smashing of the door. The air was dead and motionless, lit by a soft gray half-light that made everything seem flat and dull.

We were still in the bedroom, but it being a bedroom on the Other Side, things were different here. The wall, which was very close to us, was cracked and pockmarked. Frost glittered at our feet. Out of the window we could see a jet-black sky.

"Move away from the chain," Lockwood said. His voice sounded small and hollow in the strange, dead air. Kipps and I backed away. The post beside us was caked with ice. The suspended chain hung still, stretching back into the haze of the circle. Ghosts still swirled there, but now they made no sound. Lockwood and I stood with our swords ready, looking back the way we had come.

We watched the gate. No one came through.

"Thank God," I breathed. "I thought he'd follow us."

"It would have killed him without a cape," Lockwood said. "But I wouldn't have put it past him trying."

We moved slowly, carefully around the edge of the circle to the opposite side of the room. Holly and George were waiting for us there, two huddled, hooded shapes, their breath pluming white and fast. Beyond them, the door to the landing was a black, bare opening filled with mist. No one stood there. No Sir Rupert, none of Winkman's men. We were in another version of 35 Portland Row, and here we were alone.

"What happened?" George said. His whisper echoed through the emptiness. "You took *forever*. I thought they'd got you."

"No, we're good," Lockwood said. "We've made it. Well done, everyone." He lowered his rapier, expelled a long breath of bright, white frost. "You all right, George? How are you feeling?"

"Bruised, battered, scared out of my wits, and, since we're now on the Other Side, also technically dead. Apart from that, tip-top."

"Excellent. Good to hear. What about you, Quill?"

Kipps's face was pale beneath his goggles and the feathery cape, but his voice was strong enough. "Fine."

"I thought Gale caught you there at the end."

"He did. It's okay. There's a bit of pain, but it's not a problem. I feel fine."

"Good."

"Was it your side?" Holly asked. "You want me to look at it?"

Kipps gestured at his voluminous robes. "Under all this non-sense? I don't think you'd ever find it." He shook his head. "Thanks, Holly. It's a scratch. No big deal."

"It's best to keep ourselves well wrapped up anyway," Lockwood said. "Feel how cold it is? The power of the capes is strong, but it doesn't extend far, and if you take them off, you're done for."

"So," I said. I glanced over at the opening to the black landing, the wreaths of mist hanging over the stairs. "What now? How long do you think we have to wait here?"

"Not long, I hope," Holly said.

"I don't know. . . ." Lockwood frowned in the shadows of his hood. "Sir Rupert showing up has put a wrench in the works. He knows Marissa well; if he knows what a spirit gate is too, he'll under-stand what we've done, and he'll take steps to stymie us. He may well hang around. Mind you, if I were him, I'd—" He broke off. "No, I'd better not say."

"You'd do what?" George asked.

There was a brief, dull thud behind us from the far side of the circle. The ghosts trapped within it whirled soundlessly in consternation.

Lockwood stared at us. He bit his lip. He walked slowly back around to the far side of the spirit gate. The rest of us trailed after him. We all saw the iron guide-chain hanging limply from the metal post. It no longer cut straight through the circle at chest height, but meandered uselessly on the floor.

"I'd cut the chain," Lockwood said. "Cut it so we can't get back through."

We gazed at the broken chain and then at him.

"What, so we're *stuck* here now?" Kipps demanded. "Stuck on the Other Side? When was *this* part of your master plan?"

Lockwood shook his head. "Don't raise your voice like that. Don't get angry. They sense emotion. We don't know what might be listening."

"Oh, something might be listening to us now?" Kipps gave a quiet whoop of rage. "Great! That makes it even better! You said we'd be safe here! You said we'd be okay! Now we're trapped in the land of the dead, with hordes of ravenous ghosts just waiting to swoop down on us, *and* we're wearing stupid costumes to boot! Congratulations! It's a terrific plan, Lockwood, one of your very best! You said—"

"I know what I said. I'm sorry. I didn't know they'd cut the chain."

"You might have thought about that possibility before bringing us here to die!"

Lockwood cursed. "Well, if *anyone else* ever did a bit of thinking besides me—"

"Shut up," I said. "Shut up, both of you. This is no time to argue. We need to stick together and think clearly. There *must* be something we can do."

We stood in silence in the little bedroom. As I remembered from buildings I'd seen on my last visit to the Other Side, this place had approximately the same geometry as the bedroom in our home, but it was subtly skewed. The walls looked soft, as if they were about to melt. Seams of ice glistened in cracks in the floor and shone on the surface of our cloaks. The strange flat brightness lit our hunched forms and stricken faces with its cold, indifferent glare.

No one said anything for a time, then Holly stirred. "We *do* have another option," she said. "How feasible it is, I don't know."

"It's got to be better than Lockwood's last appalling plan," Kipps said.

Holly smiled faintly. "I don't know about that. Anyway, here it is. We can't get back through this gate, correct? So there's no point staying here. The only other chance we have is to locate *another* gate, and go back through that. Well, we *do* know that there's another such gate in London, and we're pretty sure where it is."

She looked around at us, her face as calm and unflustered as if she were giving us our weekly schedule of cases, back in the other 35 Portland Row. Lockwood whistled slowly. George let out a noise like a pricked balloon.

"Fittes House . . ." I said. "We have to go *there*."

Kipps groaned. "I take back what I said. Your plan is as bad as Lockwood's. Worse even."

But a small smile was broadening on Lockwood's face. "Holly," he said, "you're a genius. . . . You're right. That's it. That's what we have to do." His voice crackled with excitement. "Don't you see? The layout on the Other Side is pretty much the same as the world we know. So we simply stroll out through that door there. We go downstairs and leave the house and exit into the *other* Portland Row. It'll be there, of course, a dark version of the one we live in. Then we set off across London—the *other* London, I should say. We go to Fittes House. We locate the gate that must be there. Then we step through it, back into the real world!" He chuckled. "And this is the real beauty of it: by doing that, we can catch dear Marissa entirely unawares. We bypass all her defenses, and catch her red-handed! We can get the proof we need to end all this. In so doing, we'll have turned desperate defense into triumphant surprise attack." Lockwood's eyes gleamed in the depths of his hood. "It's a brilliant strategy, Holly. Well done."

She nodded. "Thanks, though personally all I really want to do is just get out alive."

Kipps rubbed the back of his neck. "Hold it. From what you and Lucy saw last time, this 'other London' isn't going to be uninhabited." He swallowed. "It's not some crummy village, with a few dead yokels to worry about. It's going to be *packed*. . . . And what about George? How's he going to cope with this? And how long will our cloaks—"

"I'll be all right," George said abruptly. "I'll have to be. What alternative is there?"

"Lucy? What do you think?"

I was thinking a lot of things, but mostly I was trying to suppress the panic I felt at being trapped on the Other Side. It was the kind of panic that threatened to make you stupid, freeze you rigid where you stood. It was informed by memories of the terrors

I'd experienced on my last visit, and also by a horrid sense that the room we were in was getting smaller. I felt suddenly convinced that if we didn't start moving, I would never find my way to the open air.

"I think Holly's right," I said. "We've got to try to find the other gate. Marissa would be a bonus, of course. But right now . . . please, we've got to *go*."

Like the bedroom, the landing was an echo of ours in the living world. All its warm, soft details and imperfections had been stripped away. It was blank, empty, glimmering with ice. The walls were bare, its decorations gone; the floor had cracks running through it—thin, curved cracks like veins. Mist filled the stairwell. Silence pummeled our ears.

There was no carpet on the steps; the treads were wooden. Our boots tapped hollowly as we slowly filed downstairs.

We neared the bottom. All at once the mists swirled, and a faint dark shape rushed past us along the hall. It was large, hulking—the figure of a burly man. In utter silence, it moved from the direction of the kitchen toward the front of the house. For a moment it was silhouetted at the threshold, then it sped onward out of view.

Lockwood, who was in the lead, had stopped in shock at the sight. He looked back at me, eyes wide beneath his hood. "Who was that?" he whispered.

I had no answer. Lockwood sped up; we came down into the entrance hall and hurried along it to where the front door gaped open under the blank black sky.

A thin mist hung over Portland Row and the street was white with frost. The dull, hard half-light shone over everything. There were no ghost-lamps on; the lamps themselves had disappeared, and the iron gates and railings that ran beside the sidewalks were gone, too. The houses were gray slabs.

The hulking figure was just visible, racing away down the center of the street. It did not look back. The mists swallowed it; stillness returned.

"Who *was* that?" Lockwood said again. "Who else is in our house?"

A thought occurred to me. I knew someone who *was*. I looked back into the darkness of the hall.

"Wait for me here," I said.

I turned and walked back into the house. The wall beneath the staircase was riven with cracks, some so big you could stick a finger into them. The kitchen door was partly frozen, ice melding it to the floor, and I pushed my way in with difficulty. The room inside was very dark, but I could see that there was no table there, and none of our cupboards or cabinets. Out of the corner of my eye, I could sense their outlines, but they vanished if you looked at them.

As I had expected, a thin and rangy youth with spiky hair stood at the side of the room. It was the precise location where I'd left the ghost-jar. The skull's spirit was gray and faint, but fully formed—a scrawny-looking boy, a little older than me. He had a rather gaunt face with very large, dark eyes that were watching me impassively.

"Ah," the youth said, "*I wondered if you'd think of me. You got through the gate, then.*"

"Yes," I said. "We got through."

"*How nice for you.*"

Both his shape and his voice were faint, perhaps the fault of the silver-glass jar that imprisoned him on the living side. It was the first time I'd ever really *looked* at him, at the spirit that he truly was. He wore a white shirt and gray trousers that were slightly too short for his bony legs. His feet were bare. He'd still been young when he died.

"They've closed the gate behind us," I said.

One of the youth's eyebrows lifted in sardonic amusement. *"Have they? What a shame. How does it feel to be trapped somewhere unpleasant? Bet you wish someone could set you free."*

I looked down at my belt, where the hammer I'd been using to break the Sources still hung. I said, "We're going to try to get across London. Find Marissa's gate. I just came to tell you."

"How very kind of you." The youth's lip curled. *"So, walking across Dark London, eh? Good luck with that. Mind you, even if they hadn't shut your gate, it would be best to avoid this house for a while."*

"Why, what's happening?"

"In simple terms, they're trashing the place. Sir Rupert Gale is using some very salty language. Even I've learned a few new words. He's got his work cut out trying to keep control, though—most of Winkman's men don't have a clue about what you just did, and they're freaked out. There's talk of witchcraft and devils." The youth rolled his eyes, and for an instant he looked like the face in the jar. *"Honestly, the average medieval serf would have more wit than them. Anyway, you'll be pleased to know that most of that crowd are injured, too—stabbed, bashed, and otherwise blown up by all your flares. They haven't got an eyebrow among them."*

"Good," I said grimly.

"*Oh, and Winkman just died.*"

"What?" I sucked in the ice cold air. "*What? How?*"

"*As far as I can make out, you walloped him with a floorboard. When he fell back, he collided with one of his lackeys' knives. Well, if you go running around carrying sharp objects, what can you expect?*" The youth gave a callous grin, and again I recognized the ghost I knew so well. "*They brought him up to the kitchen, but he passed across just now. I'm surprised you didn't bump into him.*"

I thought of the bulky, stumbling shape fleeing down the hallway and off into the dark. I raised my glove to my face. There was a coating of ice on the palm; I lowered it again hurriedly. When I moved my feet, I had to break little bonds of ice that fixed my boots to the floor. Panic enveloped me again. I felt that the walls were warping in, closing off my exit. "I've got to go," I said. "But I'll come back. When we all get home—"

"*I won't be here,*" the youth said. The dark eyes regarded me. "*They've just opened the cupboard and found me. Gale's taking me away now. Good-bye.*"

"What? Where to?" I felt a sudden stab of pain. "No, no, they can't do that. . . ."

The gray face flickered and broke apart, as if the connection was being disrupted. "*Of course they can. It's your fault, Lucy. I asked you to let me go, and now it's too late.*"

A great misery rose up in me, a welling loneliness that caught me by surprise. "Skull, I'm so sorry . . . I *would* have done it. . . ."

The shape faded; for a moment, the voice lingered. "*Too late for both of us. I'm trapped, and you're dead. . . .*"

I stared at the blank space where the youth had been. "But . . . I'm not dead. . . ."

"You might as well be, Lucy. You're on the Other Side. . . ."

Stumbling back up the hallway, I had to twist my body past big extrusions of ice that had pushed through the cracks in the wall. But the front door was open, and the others were waiting for me under the black sky. Ice was shimmering on their cloaks. It was utterly silent, except for the rasp of my breathing and the crunch of my boots on the path. In subdued tones I told them about my conversation with the skull, and his news of Winkman.

"Well," Lockwood said, "I've got to say his death isn't going to weigh too heavily on my conscience." He looked off down the road.

"It's good news that he's not hanging around your basement like some victims of violent deaths do," Kipps said. "Otherwise you'd find his ghost glaring over your shoulder every time you went downstairs to wash your undies. You'd be on an endless repeat cycle."

"But where do you think he was *going*?" Holly said.

No one answered. We gazed into the still and silent mists.

"Well, we haven't got time to stand around wondering," I said in a decisive voice. "We have somewhere we need to get to. Who knows the quickest way to the Strand?"

Chapter 21

Our journey across that dark and frozen London had the remorseless, terrible logic of a dream from which it was impossible to wake. It began in mists and silence and ended in a rush of terror, but wrongness and dread hung over it at every step. We walked in places where living feet should never tread; we witnessed things that living eyes should never see. And in so doing, all normal rules were turned upside down. For they were not our streets to walk in. It was not *our* London. We trespassed in the city of the dead, and all our skills and Talents counted for nothing.

The first road we walked down was Portland Row. But it *wasn't* Portland Row, not with that ferocious, never-ending silence, and the frost on the road, and the roofs and chimney pots merging with that dull black starless sky. The houses were familiar—but the dead light that shone over everything and came from nowhere (there was no moon) rendered them flat and lifeless, as if drawn on giant slabs of cardboard.

There was something false about those buildings. You felt that if you knocked on them with your fist, whole walls would tumble down. The doors were either absent or ajar. They were gaping holes torn in the fabric of the street. None of the windows had curtains; they were stark and blank and staring. It made you believe things were watching you from inside the empty rooms.

But to begin with, we saw nobody at all.

We walked down the center of the road. A faint set of marks stretched ahead of us in the frost—the wandering footprints of a solitary man. We followed them as far as the empty shell of Arif's store, where the wide shopwindows hung blank and open, with mist swirling deep inside the carcass of the building. Here the footprints veered away along a side street and were lost to sight. We did not follow them. If it *had* been Winkman we'd seen, he had taken his own way.

"We should go left here," George whispered. Blooms of ice crusted the lenses of his glasses. His voice didn't carry well in the thin air. "That's the shortest route."

"Good." Like mine, Lockwood's face was pinched with cold. "We need to be as quick as we can. The capes are strong, but I don't know how long they'll last."

We walked on. The air was bitter—a dry, dead absence that sucked the life from your lungs and the motion from your blood. It clung to the surface of our cloaks, coating them with ice that creaked and cracked gently as we moved. But it could not penetrate. We existed in fragile bubbles of warmth that sustained us as we hurried on. Even so, the silence bore into our skulls, and the countless watchful windows on every side filled us with a slowly mounting fear.

There were no ghost-lamps in that city. No railings, no cars— nothing of iron—and no running water. The drains and gutters were empty, the runnels dry. Street nameplates were gone, and the signs above the storefronts carried no legible words. The route we took was familiar to us, but the overarching stillness made it alien. During my previous visit to the Other Side, I'd been in the open countryside. Here, in central London, the utter silence had even more of a transformative effect. It turned the rows of houses into cliff faces, the streets into a dark labyrinth of canyons and ravines.

Passing the mouth of one such canyon, we saw a figure walking along it in the distance. It had a broad-brimmed hat and was limping very slowly in our direction. We hurried onward, clambering over a pile of rubble from a partially collapsed building that spread out across the street. There was a junction just beyond, and here Lockwood led us abruptly down an alley, away from the main road.

"What are you doing?" Kipps hissed. The ice on the tips of his feathers made them bend like mad antennae above his face. "This isn't the quickest way."

"I didn't like the look of that thing in the side road," Lockwood said. "Also, there were more of them in the mist up ahead—didn't you see? Two grown-ups and a little child. We've got to avoid contact at all costs. We can double back farther on."

But this was easier said than done. For every street that was empty, there was another with something wandering in the mists. Dark shapes stood at the upstairs windows of hollow houses, staring up toward the sky. Tiny figures sat in frozen sandboxes at the edge of city parks. Lines of adults waited on sidewalks, perhaps queuing for buses that would never come. Men in suits and ties meandered past each other; women walked with hands out, pushing nonexistent strollers. All were silent, gray, and drifting—the colors of their clothes faded, their faces bleached as white as bone. *Lost souls*, the skull had called them, and I knew that it was right. They *were* lost, mindlessly repeating actions that no longer had a meaning.

From all these inhabitants of the dark city we turned away and fled, and were soon worn out from all our twists and turns and switches of direction. Even in our cloaks, the remorseless cold and tension ate away at our energies. Lockwood himself grew slower. George, already weak before stepping through the spirit gate, was suffering. I took his arm, helped him along the road.

"I don't like the trail we're leaving, Luce," he whispered after a time.

"You mean our footprints?" In places the ground was laced with the faint imprints of naked feet, crossing to and fro. Our heavy boot-marks stood out amongst them, trodden deep into the frost.

"Yeah, them—*and* the vapor trail," George said. And it was true. Our icy cloaks were flickering with silent silver flames as the unnatural cold attacked their surface; from this, a thin gray smoke was rising, floating behind us as we walked. "Think they could sense that—smell it, maybe?"

I nodded. "I think so."

"Well, we've got our weapons," Kipps said. Of all of us, he seemed to be holding up the best. At each crossroad he was at the vanguard, going ahead, scouting the way. "I've still got a flare. And with these rapiers . . ."

I shook my head. My limbs were heavy, my breath rasped at the back of my throat. "I don't know, Quill. The rules are different now. When Lockwood and I were here before, we tried a flare—it didn't work. I don't know that even a sword would hold them off for long. Take it from me, if they notice us, all we can do is run."

We had progressed by now into an area that in *our* London was near to the great thoroughfare of Oxford Street. The buildings were larger; mist hung low between them like the waters of a white lagoon. Giant cracks ran across the fabric of the storefronts and hotels; some fissures extended into the streets, causing slabs of frozen asphalt to sheer up like shark fins through the mist. Here there was more activity among the dead: they seemed to move faster, with greater purpose or agitation. Several times we had to duck into an abandoned doorway as gray figures drifted past. But if they noticed our footprints or our trailing smoke, they showed no sign; something else had a stronger pull.

What this was, we discovered farther on. We came to an open square, a place where black and leafless trees stood on a patch of frosted ground, fringed by tall office buildings. Here in the distance, a large number of the dead had congregated. They had their backs to us, and the mist was thick around them, but we could see men and women and children, dressed in a variety of styles. They weren't still, but shuffling and moving around with every appearance of disquiet, and the focus of their attention was something that hung in front of them, dark but also shimmering.

Desperate as we were to keep moving—we were barely halfway to Fittes House, and our strength was already failing—we could not help but stop and stare at what we saw.

If you asked me afterward, I would have said it was a door, though it was unlike any door that I had ever seen. It hung in mid-air, floating a short way above the ground, right in the center of that little square. It was a slab of blackness, without definite shape. Seen from one angle, it was almost oval; from another, as thin as paper. Either way, the edges sort of blurred and faded, as if they were spun out of the air. You could see nothing in the middle of the door but a kind of glimmering, like stars. Fearful as we were, we were transfixed by it. We stayed there, loitering at the edge of the square, entranced by the strangeness of the scene.

"Is it a Source?" Kipps whispered. "A way back to our world?" He ran a tongue over frozen lips. "I feel it calling to me. . . ."

"It's not a Source," Holly said. "It's something else."

Lockwood gave a sigh that was almost one of longing. "I think it's a way of moving onward. Look—they want to. But they can't."

Indeed, it was clear that the dead were making a great effort to get closer to the doorway in the air, but were kept at bay by something that had been erected all around it. This was an ugly-looking fence, silver and shiny and obviously man-made. It looked a bit like one of the silver nets we kept in our belts, only it was much bigger, and supported by poles. The net seemed largely formed of little barbs, on which white flecks hung, twitching and fluttering. As we watched, one of the dead men in the square, impelled by an irresistible compulsion, broke free of the crowd and threw himself against the fence. There was a soft sound, a flash of light; the figure fell back, writhing. New white fronds hung twitching from the net and the crowd stirred in agitation.

"Marissa's work," George croaked. "We wondered how she got her plasm. Now we know."

"They're trapped here," I said. "Poor things. They're blocked and can't get out. . . ."

I felt a swelling of pity for the hapless figures, and with this came a sudden urge to get closer to the glimmering doorway. I knew it would have been fatal to do so—in moments I would have been surrounded by the dead—but I found myself stepping slowly forward. Quill and Holly did the same.

"Wait!" With a great effort of will, Lockwood had turned his head aside. He gave a croak of dismay. "Look behind us," he cried.

The urgency in his voice broke the spell. We turned. Some way off down the street we'd come from, a figure in a broad-brimmed hat was limping slowly through the mists. He was close enough for us to see his white face, the long white fingers poking out beneath his sleeves.

"That *can't* be the same bloke we saw before," Kipps said. "That was ages ago. He *can't* be following us."

"I'm not going to hang around and ask him," Lockwood gasped. "Come on!"

Forcing ourselves into action, we hurried off again, and soon the square, its contents, and the limping figure were left behind. Onward we went, as fast as we could; onward through the city of the dead, the smoke from our capes curling persistently behind us. Now we entered the neighborhood of Soho, where the roads were narrower and the buildings pressed close on either side. Once, far off, we saw another doorway in the air; it too had a silver fence and a company of dead around it. I was glad that our route lay in a different direction. I didn't want to repeat the tug I'd felt when I looked into the strange glimmering void. It was the tug you get on a crumbling cliff edge, when you're tempted to step close, lean over, and look down.

Kipps took the lead again, bustling ahead, his boots sending up tiny clouds of frost. His energy remained high, but the rest of us were flagging.

"You're in good shape, Quill," I whispered, when we caught up with him.

Kipps nodded. "I feel okay. Must be the effect of this coat or something."

"How's the side? Not giving you any trouble?"

He gave a shrug; he was staring up the next street, eyes bright, eager to be gone. "It *did* hurt a bit at first, but it's calmed down now. Don't notice it at all."

At that moment, George stumbled and almost fell. He was the weakest of us, but I too could feel my strength seeping out of me under that black sky. There was no prospect of struggling on. Lockwood gave the order for a short rest.

We took shelter inside the shell of some kind of shop, where the empty front window gave us a good view up and down the road. Everyone slumped to the floor, gasping, wheezing. Our heads were lowered, our legs drawn up beneath our smoking cloaks.

Lockwood came to sit beside me. "You all right, Lucy?"

We stared at each other from under our ice-bound hoods.

"I'm feeling it now," I said. "It's getting hard."

His lips had a dusting of frost; his voice was halting. "We're doing very well. We're almost at Trafalgar Square. The Strand's just beyond."

"I don't know that we're going to make it, Lockwood."

"We'll make it."

I wanted to believe him. But the cold and the weariness were taking their toll. A great weight lay on my heart. I just shook my head. "I don't know. . . ."

"Lucy," Lockwood said. "Look at me."

I did so. His eyes were as warm and dark as ever. He said, "I'll tell you something to cheer you up. I'll tell you a story. You remember I told you once how Kipps and I first fell foul of one another? At the DEPRAC fencing competition when I was young? I beat Kipps and went on to the final, where I lost to someone with a far better grasp of swordplay than me." He looked at me. "Remember I told you that?"

"Yeah, I remember," I said dully. "Though you never told me who it was who beat you."

"I'll tell you now: Flo."

"What?" The sheer surprise cut through the numbness in my brain. When I jerked my head up, bits of ice fell off my hood. "*What?* You're kidding."

"Flo," Lockwood said again. "She was very good."

"Wait," I said. "We're talking the same Flo Bones here? Wellington boots, puffer coat, parts of whose anatomy on which the sun has never shone? *That* Flo Bones? No! Don't you dare raise that frozen eyebrow at me!"

"Well, you just seem to know more about her than I do, that's all," Lockwood said, smiling gently. "Anyway, none of that was the case back then. Not a welly to be seen. I think I could have beaten a girl in wellies, Luce. Come on."

"Forget the wellies! I want an explanation. I've known Flo for years, and you've never told me about this!"

"Well, she was a different person then. She wasn't really Flo Bones, that's the point. She was Florence Bonnard of the Sinclair and Soanes Agency. A young agent, very promising indeed." He shook his head at the memory. "She could swing a mean rapier, that's for sure. She gave me a good thrashing."

I tried to reconcile the two images in my head—the Flo I knew, who squatted under storm drains, poking the mud with sticks—and this other one. No good. The difference was too great. "I've never even heard of Sinclair and Soanes," I said.

"That's because it doesn't exist now. It was a tiny agency. A two-person band, really, run by Susan Sinclair and Harry Soanes. Flo Bonnard was their apprentice. One night, the three of them got surprised by two Limbless in a chapel on Dulwich Heath. Both Sinclair and Soanes were killed instantly and very horribly. Flo grabbed an iron cross off the altar and wedged herself behind it in a corner of the room. She spent the night there, beside the bodies of her companions, fending off repeated attacks by the Visitors. You know what Limbless are like. A quick glance at them gives anyone the creeps. A whole night of it, alone . . . Well," Lockwood said, "Flo survived. But it changed her."

"For sure it did," I said. "It made her cracked in the head."

"That's not true, and you know it." Lockwood levered himself up with difficulty and looked out into the mists. "Anyway, I helped her out, in the early months. I tried getting her another job, but it was clear she'd been broken by the ordeal; she wasn't going to be an agent again. After a while, she drifted into relic-collecting. Sad, in a way, but also *not* sad, Lucy. She's a survivor. She's our friend. That's Flo's story. . . ."

I didn't speak for a moment. "Why are you telling me this?"

"To cheer you up, as I said. And to remind you: we're survivors, too. George, Quill, Holly—we've got to go. Just a few minutes' walk now. This is the final push."

We came out of the empty shop into the street; and as we did so, saw a limping person in a broad-brimmed hat come out of a side road and turn toward us.

Holly's voice was hoarse and high. "What do we do?"

"Just keep walking," Lockwood said. "Take the next turn."

The mists in front of us swirled and parted. At the intersection up ahead, a small group of the dead were standing. There were men there, women, children. They blocked the road.

Lockwood cursed. "Quick! In here." He darted toward the wall on our left, where there was an alley, a slot between buildings. We followed him in, plowed down it. Bricks brushed against my cape on either side. I was afraid it would be ripped, as my first spirit-cape had once been; I drew my shoulders in. The alley became narrower, until I felt as if I would be pressed to nothing. All at once it turned sharply to the right and opened into a tiny yard.

High brick walls towered over us on three sides. In one of them, at head height, was a rectangular opening—a door that in our world was perhaps reached by iron stairs. There were no other doors, and no routes through.

"Drat," Lockwood panted. "Dead end."

"What do we do?" Kipps wasn't breathing hard. "There's a door up there. We might find a way through that building."

"I'd rather not. Who knows what's in there? Maybe that guy didn't spot us. When he's gone, we can take another way."

There was a silence. "Hands up who thinks he didn't see us," Kipps said.

No one raised their hands. We stood in the yard, with black brick walls around us. By and by we heard faint sounds coming from the gap, as of limping feet scuffing along hard ground.

"Door," Kipps said. "It's our only chance. I'll give you a leg up."

"Yes—" Lockwood was already beside him at the wall, clasping his hands ready. "Quick, Hol. You too, Luce."

Neither Holly nor I had to be told twice. I took a little run-up—or as close to a run as I could manage with my deadened limbs—stepped onto Kipps's hands, and was propelled upward onto the ledge. Lockwood launched Holly up beside me. We slipped and struggled, and got in each other's way, but in moments stood in the open doorway. George, heavier and stiffer, was harder work; Kipps and Lockwood had to combine forces to hoist him up to the ledge, where Holly and I bundled him through the door. Lockwood moved back a few paces and vaulted up using Kipps's hands. Then Lockwood, Holly, and I reached out, grabbed Kipps, and dragged him up the wall.

We were just pulling him alongside us when the dead man with the broad-brimmed hat shuffled into the yard.

"Can he get up here?" I said.

We stood in the doorway looking down at the man. He stood looking up at us with dark, unblinking eyes.

He started to walk toward our wall.

"Tell you what," Kipps said. "Let's assume he can. Come on—these old Soho tenements are a maze. They all interconnect with each other. We can cut through here and out into another street quick as anything. Follow me."

He drew his sword, briefly surveyed the passage ahead of us, then plunged along it, deep into the building. We hesitated. If the dark hall back at 35 Portland Row had been unpleasant to walk down, this was even worse. The proportions of the corridor felt wrong, and ice glistened in fissures by the ceiling. There was a sour taint on the air.

Fingertips scrabbled at the wall behind us.

You know, that passage looked just fine. We stumbled after Kipps as fast as we could go.

My memory of what followed is jumbled and fragmentary. We went down corridors, up staircases, into rooms that led nowhere, doubling back the way we'd come, always expecting to meet up with what pursued us. We went through endless doors, some ordinary, others thick with ice and twisted into odd dimensions. All were open—no doors were locked in this dark, cold world. You could go anywhere, but no place was better than another, and we could not find a way out of the building. Sometimes we passed windows, but either they were too high, or too narrow, or so caked with frost that we couldn't see out of them to know if it was safe to jump. There was nothing but the scrape of our boots on the wooden floors, and our breaths like broken pistons, and the flap and flutter of Kipps's feathers just ahead. And somewhere behind, the slow feet following.

Kipps was right: those old houses *were* a maze. We passed through attics, where faint outlines of dollhouses and rocking horses merged with spreading shadows; through rooms where beds seemed half sunken into the tilted floors; through kitchens, where dark objects hung dead and heavy from ceiling hooks; up rattling staircases that grew wide then thin with every twist or turn; and once, out onto a high parapet that ran between buildings, with the white street far below and ice shards tumbling soundlessly beneath our skidding boots. That street unnerved us, and not because of the drop; a host of gray figures stood in it, looking up as we ran like rats into the house beyond.

And now there began to be noises from neighboring rooms, as if other things were keeping pace with us beyond the walls. Kipps was cursing now, moving ever faster, shying away from open corridors, squeezing through cracks, dropping through chutes of ice and rubble; Holly and I came after, ushering the stumbling George, and all the while Lockwood brought up the rear, rapier out, steadily retreating, staring back the way we had come.

And then we arrived at a flight of steps with a long corridor below, and saw at the end of that corridor an arch that gave us a glimpse of open air.

Down the steps, clattering, wheezing, particles of ice falling from our capes.

Kipps halted. "Wait! There's movement out there!"

"Don't stop!" That was Lockwood at the back. "We've got at least four of them close behind!"

There was nothing else we could do, and all our strength was gone. We stumbled along the passage, hearing bare feet slapping on the stairs. Holly and I were pulling George bodily after us; Kipps was cursing. We fell out through the archway into the half-light—and came to a shuddering stop.

The way was blocked. The chase was over.

We were in a street on the edge of Trafalgar Square, and it was thronged with London's dead.

Chapter 22

I t was me who saved us. I was the quickest this time. On either side of the doorway were spreading piles of ice and stones that had fallen from the wall above. Grabbing Kipps's and George's arms, I pulled them with me, over and down behind the nearest pile of rubble. A moment later, Holly and Lockwood were doing the same on the opposite side. We ducked our heads low.

"Don't say anything," Kipps hissed. "Don't move."

As all-time unnecessary suggestions went, it was way up there. Breathing wasn't high on our agenda, let alone movement. My heartbeat was a bass drum in my ears. I was pressing so hard against the stones I thought I'd probably push right through.

Pale shapes came rushing out of the doorway with horrid leaps and bounds. One was the limping man with the broad-brimmed hat. They plunged past our hiding place and continued on into the road.

Now, mindless as the wandering dead most probably were, driven only by mute compulsions, they really should have seen us behind those piles of rock. We weren't hidden very well. For starters, our cloaks still smoked like chimneys, and Kipps's icy crest-feathers poked like crazy periscopes above the topmost boulder. But the shapes that had pursued us took not the slightest notice of us any longer. Nor did the great group of spirits turn aside from where they jostled in the street. There was something else they wanted even more.

A small company of silver-clad men and women were progressing slowly up the road from Trafalgar Square. There were six in total, and we knew at once that they were living. They were far more solid than the milling forms around them, and moved with focused, purposeful movements. Metallic clinks and clattering drifted toward us on the freezing air. They were the first such sounds we had heard in hours; the effect was almost shocking.

All six wore light helmets, and goggles similar to the ones Kipps used. They didn't have cloaks, but long tunics hanging loosely over pants. These outfits seemed to be made of the same material as the capes we'd taken from the Orpheus Society. Their backs were burdened with ice, and flickered with silent, chilly flames.

Two of the company, trudging at the center of the group, had clusters of small glass cylinders hanging over their shoulders. The other four (women, I thought) wore silver stilt-legs, similar to the ones worn by the Orpheus secretary. Their job was to protect the men on foot; they carried long defensive poles with silver tips, which they used to keep the dead at bay.

Altogether, maybe twenty or thirty gray forms swarmed around the little company. They sniffed at the smoke trail, twitching and reaching out for the living with their long pale frozen hands. The proximity of the dead did not disturb the group. The women on stilts waded waist-high through the throng, who rippled back as they sought to evade the painful touch of silver. Occasionally, the stilt-walkers threshed among the figures with their poles, stirring them up as a cook might a stew. There was the smell of burning. All the while, the two men with the cylinders continued marching along the road toward the square. They seemed resigned to the tumult, even slightly bored.

I looked at the cylinders. Under the coating of ice, you could see that some of them shone with a vibrant light. I thought of the silver fences we'd seen, with the bright white flecks of plasm hanging on them. And I knew that this was a team that collected the plasm from such places, then carried it back to the woman at Fittes House. Suddenly, beneath my weariness and desperation, beneath the awful numbing cold, a great anger flared inside me—a desire to see justice done.

When the dreadful group had disappeared, we emerged from our hiding places and went on, slowly, stiffly, going in the opposite direction. No one felt the need to speak about it. Everyone understood what we had seen.

Mists filled Trafalgar Square, and the column rose through them like the launch trail of a rocket, stark and straight and gray against the pitch-black sky. We kept as close to the perimeter as we could; once we had to duck inside the shell of a blackened, frost-blown church as something else on silver legs passed by. Otherwise, we were undisturbed. Soon we came to the great black canyon of the Strand, with cliff-buildings towering above us. It was a scene of desolation, of swirling mists and shadow—and there were the steps of Fittes House rising on the right-hand side.

We knew it was the place. The frost on the steps had been worn away by the passage of many feet, and a silver net hung suspended in the open doorway to keep the wandering dead at bay. It hung there like a portcullis, like a row of jagged teeth. We watched from the shadows of the building opposite. There was no sign of any silver-clad workers. Everything was still.

"Got to risk it," Lockwood croaked. "We can't wait any longer."

"I think my cloak is giving out," George said. "Let's just— Wait, what's that?"

A golden light was advancing far off along the center of the Strand, shining on the mists, illuminating the buildings as it came. It swelled and grew. At its heart were two figures, approaching side by side. We pressed back against the wall and watched. The first was a woman, tall and beautiful. She wore a silver cloak that went down to her feet; it swished and swirled about her and turned the mist to golden froth. Her long hair was pulled back almost out of sight beneath her hood, but the graceful lines of the face were clear enough. It was the woman known in our London as Penelope Fittes—but *we* knew her real name.

Beside her was something that wasn't human at all. It had the vague shape of a man, tall and slim and glowing with a blazing light. It did not walk, but drifted forward in midair. You could see two golden eyes, and above its head was a coronet of pure white fire. Other than that it was too radiant to look upon. It was the source of the beautiful glow that spun around the woman and lit up the street. We watched them ascend the steps and pass through into Fittes House. The nimbus of light flared around the door and was swallowed by it. Darkness fell again.

For a long while, none of us moved. Then we looked at one another.

"Marissa . . ." Holly said. "And with her . . ."

Lockwood nodded. "I think we just saw Ezekiel."

It was a strange thing, entering that other version of Fittes House. What a contrast it was to the one we knew. In our world, the entrance foyer was abuzz with business at all hours, ranks of cool receptionists attending to queues of prospective clients; visitors reading magazines on comfy sofas; a small statue of Marissa Fittes blandly watching over all. Here, the foyer was a black and empty room, like a cavern in a coal mine, with a low-slung roof and wet ice on the floor. A few cracked cylinders and plastic oil jugs lay abandoned in the shadows.

A row of glimmering oil lanterns led us deep into the building, marking a safe route through. It was a necessary measure: in certain places the floor had fallen away completely, or the ceiling had collapsed under the weight of ice. The walls bowed inward; floors slanted. I began to experience the same claustrophobia I'd felt at 35 Portland Row.

Moving slowly, rapiers out in case of danger, we followed the lights, and soon came to the Hall of Pillars—or its dark and dismal counterpart. Here, disconcertingly, the nine trapped spirits stood, faint and flickering, just as the skull had done in Portland Row. They watched us avidly as we passed, rotating to keep visual pace with us. Pinpricks of light burned in their hollow eyes. Long Hugh Hennratty, the highwayman whose ghost had been one of the first captured by Marissa and Tom Rotwell, grinned lopsidedly above his broken neck. The Clapham Butcher Boy made urgent motions to us with his spectral knife. Fortunately the silver-glass pillars on the other side held firm.

The spirits could not speak, but that didn't stop them calling out to us, hooting and crying like owls. As a Listener, I'm used to such stuff, though it was strange to hear it in the silence of the Other Side. It disturbed the others more than me. To their surprise, they found they could hear it, too.

We left the room in haste, and so came to the Hall of Fallen Heroes, where elevator shafts accessed other floors. In our world, lavender fires burned perpetually here beside the shrine to fallen agents. Here the room was a black void; the six shafts nothing but gaping holes, plugged with mist. The lanterns led us past them, and presently we came to a staircase going down.

"The gate must be in the basement," Lockwood said. He mustered a frozen smile. "This is the last push, everyone. Stay strong. We're almost there."

Down we went, flight after flight; and the stairs led us steeply into the earth. We went very slowly now, past openings to unknown levels, and still we saw nothing. Twice, George nearly fell; his legs were giving out, and Kipps and Lockwood had to grapple him under the arms and pull him onward. Holly and I supported each other, too. In this manner, fumbling, disheveled, and almost dead, we came at last to the deepest basement beneath Fittes House. It was all we could do to go on now, for our stamina was at an end.

The lanterns led through a dark and empty chamber toward an arch, and here I finally heard what I'd been straining for all this time: the psychic thrum and tumult of a nearby gate.

Lockwood sensed it as well. He made a noise that in better times might have been a cry of triumph. We roused ourselves and hobbled forward.

"And what time do you call this?" said a voice.

We stopped in our tracks. As one, we raised our hoods a little and stiffly looked around.

"If I'd have known you'd be this long, I'd have put my curlers in," the thin youth said. He was standing on the far side of the dark and icy room. His spiky hair gleamed with other-light; otherwise he was as faint and flickering and supercilious as ever.

"Skull!" A wave of something washed through me. Relief? Pleasure at seeing something familiar in this dreadful place? Whatever it was, it made me warm. "I'm so happy to see you," I said, hobbling toward him. "How did you get here?"

"Well, I'm not actually here, am I?" the ghost said. *"I'm still in my precious jar, sitting in a brightly lit laboratory storeroom below Fittes House, surrounded by cylinders of stolen essence, and with one or two rather fainthearted scientists pottering about. In fact . . . hold on . . . yes, I've just scared one of them half to death by showing him the Happy Farmhand. And all while talking to you. Isn't that clever?"* The youth grinned. *"I rather think it is."*

"But how did you—?"

"Lucy." Lockwood shuffled alongside me, the others close behind. They were peering at the youth in bafflement. For a moment, I couldn't understand their confusion, then I realized what it was: they could *hear* him.

"This is the skull," I said.

Lockwood's mouth was open. "The skull's . . . spirit? He . . . he looks different."

The youth scowled. *"Yeah? You look just the same. I was banking on frostbite taking a few of your fingers, or even your nose. Here's hoping something else has dropped off that I don't know about. If not, I'll be sorely disappointed."*

Lockwood stared. "Does he always talk like this?"

"No. Usually he's worse. See what I have to put up with?"

"Oh, she likes it," the youth said. *"She can't get enough of it. I cheer her up no end."*

"Cheer me up now," I said, "and tell me briefly how you're here—and what's on the other side of the gate. We're going to come across now . . . if we can."

"Shouldn't be a problem," the ghost said. *"The lab technicians have just gone for a coffee break. I think they were getting tired of all my faces. And the last Other Side shift won't be back for another hour. Well, I say it's not a problem. That's assuming you've got enough energy to survive the crossing."* It cast its eyes over us. *"Let's see— hangdog, lackluster, clearly dead on your feet. George in particular looks like he'd fall to pieces if you took off that cape."*

George drew himself up. "Hey, nothing's falling off me. Just a bit stiff, that's all."

"Yeah, sure. In ideal shape for a finale."

"Don't lump *me* in with these lightweights," Kipps said.

"*And Kipps* . . ." The scrawny youth stared at him. "*How are you feeling, then?*"

Kipps blinked. "Me? Great. Why?"

"*No reason.*" The ghost's image flickered out, then returned to cast contemplative eyes around the empty room. "*I'll keep it short,*" it said. "*Sir Rupert Gale brought me to Fittes House to be 'assessed' or 'processed' or chucked in the furnaces, whatever they want to do. He brought me down here, and I've been sitting in this lab ever since, watching a steady stream of madmen put on silly suits and go back and forth to the Other Side. Marissa herself came past just now. She took off her cape and caught an elevator up top. She was in a hurry. Didn't stop to say hello.*"

"Marissa came by?" Lockwood asked. "Was she alone?"

"*Hey, Lucy asks the questions around here,*" the youth said. "*You can't just horn in and take over like you're the leader or something. Where's your respect?*"

I cleared my throat. "Please, Skull, was Marissa on her own?"

"*There—see? That's how it's done.*" The ghost smiled broadly at Lockwood. "*Yes, Lucy, she was on her lonesome. Why?*"

"It doesn't matter," I said. "We've got to follow her." A thought occurred to me. "What time is it now, in the living world? Is it morning yet?" I had a sudden desperate yearning to see the sun.

"*Nope. Clock on the wall says just past midnight. Hours yet till dawn.*"

Lockwood spoke through cracked lips. "Wait! *That* can't be true! Winkman and Gale raided Portland Row just after midnight. It's *got* to be later than that."

"*It is. Twenty-four hours later. I was brought here early morning,*" *and a whole long day's gone by.*" The youth grinned maliciously at us, and in that grin the face in the jar was clearly visible. "*I said you'd been a while.*"

Our faces had sagged. "Impossible," Holly whispered. "We'd have known. . . ."

"*That's the thing about being dead,*" the ghost said. "*You lose all track of time.*"

There was no further delay; no one wanted to stay a moment more. The others shuffled toward the arch. Only I hung back.

"Thanks, Skull," I said. "I'm glad I found you." I hesitated. "Listen, seeing you with a face and body and everything, it seems a bit weird to still be calling you 'Skull.' Can't you tell me your name?"

"*Nah, forgotten it.*" The youth shrugged; the dark eyes glittered. "*Besides, shared names come with trust.*"

I looked at him. "Yeah. Well, whatever. I'll pick you up when I get through."

"*If you want. Oh, one other thing,*" the skull added as I turned away. "*Kipps.*"

"What about him?"

"*Anything happen to him recently?*"

"No."

"*Sure about that, are you?*"

Before I could answer, I heard Holly calling me. Limping as fast as I could across the room, I went in through the arch—and saw the gate.

Actually, calling it a *gate* doesn't really do it justice. It was more than that. It was a bridge, a checkpoint, a highway for the living to pass through. George had been right. Lockwood's parents had been right. For years, hidden here, in this basement below Fittes House in the heart of London, there *had* been a permanent route between our world and the Other Side.

It was a large chamber lit by lanterns, and in the center was a pit. The pit was circular in shape and very broad, and it had a low wall built right around it. This wall, about the height of my knee, was made of solid iron. Thus, at a stroke, the Fittes Agency had dispensed with the hassle and impermanence of iron chains. Although the precise *contents* of the pit could not be seen, I knew it was stuffed with Sources—the familiar column of hazy light rose above it, packed with trapped and rushing forms.

To cross the pit, the designers hadn't bothered with small-time stuff like hanging chains. Instead, an iron walkway or bridge—thin, but very solid—led up across the wall and spanned the center of the pit, before disappearing into the swirling haze. I couldn't see to the far side, but I knew that if we passed along it, we would be back in the living world.

The others were waiting for me at the start of the bridge. I could scarcely recognize them beneath their crusted, steaming capes. Forget the spirits whirling in the pit beyond. We were five shapeless demons, made monstrous by our journey.

"There's just a chance someone will be in the room on the other side," Lockwood said. With stiff, hesitant movements, he drew his sword. "I'll go first. Holly, I want you to help George across. Kipps— you come behind George, with Lucy at the end. It's the same deal as before. Heads down, ignore the ghosts. No one hang back for anything."

He didn't have the energy for more, but turned and stepped onto the iron walkway. You could see him flinch as he approached the psychic maelstrom, but he didn't stop. The haze closed around him, and he could no longer be seen.

Holly followed him onto the bridge; she stood to wait for George.

As George climbed onto the walkway, he tripped and fell. Kipps reached out an arm to catch him. In doing so, his coat of icy feathers swung aside, and I saw his tattered jersey below, with the tear in its side where Sir Rupert Gale's rapier had cut through. The fabric hung open, and I caught a single awful glimpse of the gaping wound beneath.

The coat fell back into place. Kipps steadied George, helped him stand upright. Holly held out her hand to him; she and George moved forward. They shuffled up the walkway, shoulders bent, heads bowed, their cloaks humped and frozen like tortoise shells beneath their burdens of smoking ice. On either side, spirits moaned and chattered; pale arms reached out for them but broke asunder as they neared the strips of iron. Soon Holly and George had passed over the center of the pit and were gone.

Kipps began to follow them.

"Quill," I said. "Hold on."

He looked back at me. "What? Come on! This is what we've been waiting for! We can find Marissa, bring her down!" His eyes were sparkling; he was grinning with the thrill of the chase. I'd never seen him so alive.

"Wait." My voice was thick. "Don't go through."

He scowled. For a second it was the old Kipps, back again. "Why not? Don't be stupid, Lucy."

It wasn't easy to talk, and not just because of the cold. "Why do you think you're starting to feel so good here?" I said. "So . . . at home?"

He stared at me. "What? What nonsense are you talking about?"

"It's just . . . just . . . Quill, that injury you got . . ."

He gave his little barking laugh. "When you say *at home*, Lucy, it's almost like you're saying—" Through the icy goggles his eyes held mine, and then he understood. The light slowly went out of them, like a flower closing. His face was a pale mask. Then he lifted up his cape and, ignoring the steaming, cracking ice that fell from the feathers, looked underneath it at his shadowed side. He didn't move for a while. He let the feathers drop back into position. He nodded once, very slowly, as if to himself. He didn't look at me.

"Well," he said. "That's a mess."

"Oh, Quill . . ."

"Typical. And I was feeling so chipper."

I swallowed down my panic. I was alone with him, and I didn't know what to say or do. "Listen," I said, "maybe you'd better stay here."

He *did* look at me then. "What, on my own? See you all go through without me? Leave me standing here like an idiot in the dark? I don't think so."

"But Quill, that wound— On the other side—"

Kipps didn't speak for a moment. "I know," he said. "Maybe. But if it happens, it's got to be done right, in the proper place. Anyway, I'm not staying here. Especially in this stupid outfit. Now—we need to go through."

Still I hesitated. "Quill," I said, "you were brilliant just now."

"Yeah."

"Without you—"

He grinned at me. "You and Tony and the others would never have made it, would you? Glad I made a contribution."

"Oh, God," I said.

"It's okay. Take my hand, Lucy, and let's go."

He was correct, of course. Whatever happened, it had to be done right. There was nothing else to say. Slowly, I took his hand. We walked together across the iron bridge. The ghosts did their usual. We ignored them. We passed through the psychic vortex, the breach between worlds. Bright neon light shone ahead of us, and I could feel life pouring back into my body. I think Quill felt it, too; his grip tightened on mine, flared suddenly warm and strong. It didn't last. We crossed the iron wall and left the gate, back into our world. We were in the proper place. Before we had left the walkway, Kipps was already falling.

V

Fittes House

Chapter 23

Don't ask me for a careful, reasoned account of what happened after that. I can't give you one. My excuse is that when you step back out through a gate (I've done this since, and know it to be so), you're *always* sick, confused, and ill. You don't see straight; every sense is shrieking with the sudden onslaught of light and sound, with the feel of warm air on your skin and in your lungs; your body goes into a kind of temporary shutdown and muscular collapse. This is particularly marked when you've been on the Other Side for a long time, as we had, and it's not a condition that makes it easy to follow what's going on.

Panic's similar. Sudden, unexpected panic all the more so. So it's hard to piece together the fragments I've retained: Lockwood dragging Kipps and me bodily clear of the circle; blood on the floor; Lockwood bent over Kipps; George holding his hand; *everyone* bent over him, with his cloak of feathers being stripped away; *more* blood—there was such a lot of it; white cloths being brought from somewhere; Holly holding them to his side in an effort to stanch the wound. All this while Lockwood kept talking to Kipps, joking, smiling, pouring out encouraging words. Kipps lay very still. He was white-faced; his hair shone with melting ice. There were faint rings around his eyes where the goggles had been.

"Lucy, George," Holly said, "I want fresh towels and bandages. There must be some in here."

I stood, shakily, and surveyed the room in which we found ourselves. It was a clean and orderly place. Okay, sure, it had a massive ghostly maelstrom at its heart, but all that whirring chaos was nicely contained within the iron circle. Once across the bridge, as we were now, you found a brightly lit and whitewashed room with all the sterile neatness of an operating theater. Racks of goggles and silver suits hung along the walls, each one named and numbered; there were trolleys and wheeled plastic bins with a few discarded suits; a pair of stilts, propped in a corner like the legs of an idling drunkard; even a few safety notices by the doors.

It wasn't so neat and tidy when George and I had finished with it. We stumbled around, wrenching open cupboards, pulling out drawers. George found a cabinet of medical supplies; he dragged it across the room. I went through an arch into a tiled washroom, where ranks of shower cubicles showed where the workers scrubbed up after a hard shift beyond the gate. There were plenty of towels here; I brought a load back and placed some under Kipps's head, while Holly did the best she could with bandages and wadding. She was still wearing her cape of animal fur. The ice in it had melted; it looked forlorn and matted. A puddle of brownish water lay around her. I took towels and did my best to wipe it up.

At last, Holly's frantic efforts slowed and stopped. She knelt back, bloodied hands flopping in her lap. Kipps's eyes were closed. He didn't move.

Lockwood had stopped speaking to him. His head dropped; he sat back in exhausted silence. George and I slumped to the floor. We stared at each other across the body, four pathetic visitations of feathers and fur and snot and melted ice. Our eyes were puffy and red, our faces purpled where the circulation was returning beneath the frozen skin. The grip of the Other Side was lessening with every second, but an icy numbness clung to my heart. I looked at Kipps lying there on the floor.

"I'm so sorry," I said at last. "I . . . I saw him get hurt. I should have known it was bad. But . . . but with so much going on . . . I never thought to look."

No one said anything.

"He was so brave over there. He was so strong, so full of life. . . ." I sniffed loudly. "*Too* strong. It was only at the very end that I realized he was dying."

Kipps opened an eye. "What do you mean, *dying?* I bloody well hope not."

"Quill!" I jerked back in shock. Lockwood and the others sat up, openmouthed.

"Who says I'm dying? Did you see the amount of sheer effort it took me to escape the land of the dead? I'm not going back in now!"

"*Quill!*" In my surprise and joy I leaned down and gave him an awkward hug.

"Ow!" he cried. "Careful! I've got a hole right through me. And watch with those feathers. I'm sure I'm allergic to them." We were all around him now, talking at once, our misery falling away like ice chunks off our thawing capes. "If Cubbins kisses me," Kipps said, "I swear I *will* pass back over to the Other Side. . . . What I really need right now is a drink of water."

That was quickly given to him. Kipps tried to sit up, but the pain was too much. A reddish stain was showing through the thick layers of bandages and dressing that Holly had applied.

She shook her head. "We've got to get you to a hospital, Quill," she said. "Being on the Other Side somehow stopped the blood loss, but now that we're back out here, it's started flowing freely again. It's like you were just stabbed five minutes ago. There's no time to lose." She got up, cast her furry cloak aside, and stood there, arms folded. "Lockwood, what's the plan?"

Kipps gave a hollow groan. "Not *another* of his plans! Please, just kill me now."

Lockwood had also risen. He removed his silver cape, and now stood ready with his hand on his sword hilt. He was smiling down at Quill, and suddenly a great happiness rose in me, a fierce confidence that everything would be well. Yes, we were injured and weary, and deep underground in the forbidden basement of Fittes House, with any number of dangers between us and escape. But we had walked through the Other Side together, and emerged alive. During that terrible journey, my emotions had been suspended—there'd been no time or energy to think of them. Now, suddenly, everything was unleashed. I was full of love and gratitude to Lockwood and to all my friends—between us, we'd come through.

"It's pretty simple, Quill," Lockwood said easily. "We're going to find our way out of this place and get you to a doctor. Much as I want to find that silver elevator and go confront Marissa, we can't until that's done. You're our priority now. We'll take you up to the ground floor and out that way. And if anyone tries to stop us"—he tapped his rapier grimly—"we'll remind them politely who we are. The main question is how we're going to move you. You're in bad shape."

"I can walk," Kipps grunted. "Set me on my feet, I'll be all right."

"You can't even sit up. Besides, you'll just bleed over everything. We need transport."

George scratched his nose. "We could pop him in one of those wheelie bins."

"I'm *not* going in a bin."

"What about that trolley?" I said. "It's got wheels, too. We can get him upstairs in that."

Lockwood grinned. "You might just have something there, Lucy."

We helped Kipps to his feet. He was too weak to stand alone, and the wound was bleeding profusely. Lockwood took off his own coat and with his rapier cut off a long, thin strip of fabric, which he fixed around Kipps's waist, holding the dressings tightly in position. Then we laid him on the trolley. It wasn't a bad fit, though his legs stuck out of the end.

"This is so humiliating," Kipps groaned. "It's like you're serving me up as a dessert course. Ooh! Ah! Careful going over those bumps!"

We pushed him out through an arch in the far wall. The arch was identical to the one by which we'd entered on the Other Side. Beyond—instead of the desolate cavern we'd walked through—there was a large, well-lit laboratory. Like the room with the gate, it was pristine, filled with scrubbed lab tables, technicians' chairs, centrifuges, scales, humming generators, and any amount of sinister experimental equipment I couldn't put a name to. A great number of glass cylinders, the same as the ones we'd seen being carried on the Other Side, were arranged in plastic racks. Some were empty. In others, drifts of that bright and shining substance floated dreamily. The place had a chemical smell. Rows of striplights lit everything and made my eyes hurt. Actually, *everything* in my body was hurting me right then, but I didn't care. Inwardly, my heart was singing. We had survived the Other Side. We would be all right.

At the far end of the room were three elevators, one silver, the others bronze. Lockwood and Holly pushed Kipps's trolley toward them, while I made a detour across the room. The ghost-jar was sitting in precisely the location I'd expected, in the equivalent position to where the skull's spirit had stood on the Other Side. Inside the glass, I caught the face doing something improbable with its tongue and nostrils. When it saw me shambling over, it flinched and raised its eyebrows in simulated horror.

"*You look dreadful,*" it said. "*Like something the cat dragged in. Comes to something when I'm the better looking of the duo.*"

I picked up the jar. "I'm sorry," I said.

"*Sorry for what? Your appearance? Your character? Wait, I bet it's your smell. Twenty-four hours of terror, violence, chases, and being for all intents and purposes dead plays havoc with the armpits. Don't let*"

Lockwood step downwind of you tonight, that's all I'm saying."

"No. I'm sorry for abandoning you," I said. "I shouldn't have left you at Portland Row."

The face raised an eyebrow, and I caught a flash of the dark-eyed youth in the expression, then the plasm subsided back into its normal grotesque position. *"Yeah, well, I've got to admit it's worked out all right. You couldn't have brought me here yourselves. Ooh, I see Kipps died, then. Pity."*

We had reached the others at the elevators. Lockwood and Holly were standing by the trolley, on which Kipps lolled irritably. George had stopped at a rack of large metallic objects and was inspecting them closely.

"Kipps is actually still alive," I said. "See, he's moving."

"Are you sure? That could be gas escaping. Corpses do that, you know."

"Is the ghost talking about me again?" Kipps mumbled. "What's it saying?"

"Nothing important. What have you got there, George?"

It was unquestionably the case that Quill had functioned better than the rest of us on the Other Side. Perhaps because of his wound, perhaps because he truly *was* much closer to death than any of the rest of us, he had coped unusually well. By contrast, George had been nearly finished off by the night journey; but now his energies were fast returning. Bruised and battered as he was, he shared my elation at our return to the mortal world. There was now a glint behind his cracked spectacles that I hadn't seen for some time. He indicated the rack behind him.

"I've found a row of guns," he said cheerily. "They've got the

Sunrise Corporation logo, and they seem remarkably similar to those electrical jobs you were telling me about, the ones the Orpheus bunch had. And look at these babies. . . ." He patted some large egg-shaped metal objects. "These look like industrial-strength flares to me—the kind Fittes sometimes use for clearing big ghost clusters. I was wondering if we might nick a few samples of each, Lockwood, just in case we run into any problems."

Lockwood's smile was wolflike. "You know, George, I think that's a very good idea."

It was a shame not to take the silver elevator. Its door was inscribed with the Fittes emblem: a noble unicorn, rampant, holding a lantern in its hoof. There was a tortoiseshell button on the wall, and a floor dial overhead, showing numbers from –4 to 7. Right now the arrow pointed to 7, the penthouse floor. That was where we *ought* to be going. But Lockwood was right: getting Kipps to safety was the most important thing.

We called up a bronze elevator. One arrived quietly and admitted us all in, though it was a squeeze. Lockwood pressed the button for the ground floor. We stood inside it, listening to the smooth hum. No one spoke. I adjusted my rapier. Even though it was the early hours, many Fittes agents would certainly be at work; we expected a confrontation before we were done.

There was a melodic *ting*, the humming stopped; the door opened onto the ground floor. Lockwood & Co. stepped out of the elevator into the Hall of Fallen Heroes. We had all removed our capes now, and were more or less as nature intended—swords at our belts; hands hanging loose; calm, implacable expressions on our faces. I had the ghost-jar under one arm. Kipps lay quiet on the trolley. The remains of Lockwood's coat had been laid over him as a blanket to keep him warm.

In the hall, flames burned on plinths to commemorate the many young agents who had died in action down the years. Urns of flowers and ancient rapiers sat beneath each shrine. Oil paintings of somber, serious-looking girls and boys lined the walls—all of them legendary, all of them celebrated, all long since dead and gone. They'd been cut down in their youth fighting the Problem; the same Problem that had in all probability been caused by the woman upstairs.

Our jackets swung, our boots tapped quietly on the marbled floor, the ghost in the jar grinned evilly as we strode in a line down the center of the room. The impressive effect was only slightly undermined by a squeaky wheel on Kipps's trolley. Even so, everyone we met stepped aside to let us through. Clerical workers stared from above their sheaves of typing; Fittes operatives gaped as we passed by. One old adult supervisor called out sharply to us; we paid him no heed and continued on our way.

At the end of the corridor was the Hall of Pillars—that grandest of all shrines, testament to the achievements of Marissa—where the nine famous ghosts hung imprisoned in their Relic Columns. At that hour it was dark—or almost so. The lights in the chandeliers had been turned down low, so that the ceiling frescos glinted in the shadows, bright but out of focus, like fragments of remembered dreams. In their pillars the ghosts moved soundlessly, spilling out twisting rainbows of other-light. The floor was stained with shifting blues and greens.

The hall was deserted. Beyond it was the foyer, and our exit to the street. We began to walk across it, boots tapping, wheel squeaking. In the nearest column I saw the translucent shape of Long Hugh Hennratty, the highwayman, grinning at us behind his billowing rags. And nearby, an array of other horrors: the swirling Dark Specter that hung above the tiny Frank Street coffin; the Gory Girl of Cumberland Place; the Morden Poltergeist; the Phantasm of the mad inventor, Gödel, forever searching for his missing arm.

We reached the center of the hall. As we did so, Lockwood slowed, then brought the trolley to a halt. He sniffed the air.

"Hello, Sir Rupert," he said.

A slight, slim figure stepped out from behind the Gory Girl's pillar, bringing with it a brash and overpowering whiff of aftershave. Sir Rupert Gale was bathed in the ghost's deep blue other-light. He clicked his fingers; a set of burly shadows pulled clear of the other pillars and stepped forward to block our way. Other men emerged from the darkness at the periphery of the room; they formed a ring around us. They wore the gray jackets of the Fittes Agency and were armed with cudgels and swords.

George, Holly, and I stood silently next to Lockwood. On the trolley, Kipps was a limp form.

"Well," Sir Rupert said, "it's Lockwood and his friends again! You *do* turn up in the most unexpected places." His voice was as urbane as ever, and his clothes were dapper, too; tonight he wore a gray-green jacket with black lapels, dark trousers, and a vibrant yellow tie. But the smile he gave was a gap-toothed grimace. There were bruises on his face, and a red weal from Lockwood's sword-cut on his forehead. When he moved his hand, I could see a strapping at his wrist where I'd struck him more than twenty-four hours previously. His eyes glittered with incivility.

"It's not unexpected to see *you* here, Sir Rupert," Lockwood said, smiling. "In fact, I've been actively looking forward to it. We have some unfinished business to attend to."

Sir Rupert Gale nodded slowly. "I thought you'd robbed me of the pleasure, stepping through that circle. It's good of you to give me a second crack at it." He gestured at the ring of men. "You'll see I'm not relying on stupid criminals this time."

There must have been at least twenty of them in the hall; they were all stocky and muscular, their shaven heads like small boulders on which rudimentary faces had been drawn. These were the thugs who'd killed Bunchurch, the ones who'd given George a beating. My teeth clenched; my hand stole close to my sword.

"Looks like you've got odds on your side of about five to one," Lockwood said. "Are you sure you don't need a few more?"

Sir Rupert laughed. "What a motley little company you are. Like a troupe of traveling players, tattered and battered and woebegone. Lockwood's lost his famous coat, Holly Munro's all covered in blood, and Cubbins here can barely stand. As for Carlyle cradling a hideous ghost in a jar, the least said about *that* the better. And who's that you've got lurking under there? It's not Quill Kipps? Oh, dear. Not dead already, I hope?"

I felt Holly and George shift slightly at my side. Lockwood didn't answer the question; he glanced around at the soaring roof, at the ghosts floating like pale fish in their prisons of glass. "You weren't very impressed with the location for our fight last time, Sir

Rupert," he said softly. "I hope the Hall of Pillars is a glamorous enough spot?"

Sir Rupert grinned. "I certainly have no complaints."

"Single combat again, then?"

"The thing *is*," Sir Rupert Gale said, "I'd like to, but that bloodthirsty young harpy, Miss Carlyle there, snagged me badly the other night." He raised his injured wrist. "I don't feel quite the ticket."

"I'm not on top form myself, either," Lockwood said. "All the same, I'd go easy on you."

The gap-toothed grin widened. "That's kind. Actually, I'm going to save us both the bother. Here's what the papers are going to say tomorrow. You were caught breaking into Fittes House. My team tried to stop you, but you resisted. A fight broke out. Fatalities ensued." The smile vanished; he clicked his fingers at his men. "Go ahead and kill them."

Raised swords shone in other-light; the men walked forward.

"Okay, Quill," Lockwood said.

The prone figure on the trolley lifted an arm; with a stiff swing, Kipps flung the coat aside, revealing the rows of weapons pressed beside him. We had a fine selection of egg-shaped flares and electrical guns, black and sleek and dully gleaming. George took up a gun, and flicked the safety catch. He sent out a zigzag blast of light that caught Sir Rupert Gale in the chest and sent him whirling through the air. Meanwhile, the rest of us had each seized a flare. We turned, took aim, and threw. We didn't aim for the men themselves, but for the columns behind them. Three flares exploded simultaneously. The results exceeded our expectations.

The silver-glass in the Relic Columns was famously thick, due to the notorious nature of the Visitors within; yet the egg-flares, which were designed to take out whole clusters of lesser ghosts, shattered them even so.

Great splinters of glass blew outward; shards capsized like toppling ice floes. After the first blinding flashes of magnesium fire, white smoke plumed sideways in saucer-shaped eruption clouds; and through this chaos of falling glass and spreading smoke, the liberated ghosts came swooping.

There: the sinewy form of Long Hugh Hennratty, stalking on its severed ankle bones. There: the Gory Girl, blindly crawling in a bloody nightdress. And there: the dreaded Morden Poltergeist itself. It had escaped its broken teapot. It had no discernible form, but had lifted the fragments of its pillar and was whirling them around in an upturned cone of broken glass. It caught up to the nearest of Sir Rupert's men and sent him screaming toward the rafters. The Specter of Long Hugh Hennratty advanced with a horrid sideways hopping motion, like a knight moving on a chessboard; it passed straight through the bodies of two adjacent men, stopping their hearts with its spectral cold, and would have jumped at me, too, had a blast from George's gun not made it leap away.

Lockwood had his head down; he was pushing Kipps's trolley forward with all his might, slaloming between the broken pillars, between the rushing ghosts and screaming men. "Make for the exit!" he shouted. "Keep on going! Don't get bottled in!"

We ran with him, trying to keep pace. Some of Sir Rupert's men had panicked and were fleeing for their lives; others still pursued us. I slashed at one with my rapier; he jumped aside and was engulfed by Long Hugh Hennratty's bony arms.

"Ah, yes," the skull's voice said—I still had the jar beneath my arm—"*a spot of proper carnage.* This *is what life is all about.*"

I didn't answer. My head was filled with the sound of people shouting; with the hoots and shrieking of the ghosts; the blasts and buffets of the bombs. Holly had broken another pillar. George, dancing like a mad thing, sent out burst after burst of electric charge.

"My God," I gasped as I ran. "The *noise* . . ."

"*These spirits are a bit showy,*" the skull said. "*All that hooting and cackling. Don't see me doing that. I ask you, where's the class?*"

The Morden Poltergeist whirled past, tearing chandeliers from the ceiling. It collided head-on with yet another pillar, cracking it like a breakfast egg. Now it blocked our path. Lockwood wrenched at the trolley; we swerved aside, continued on.

Out of the swirling shadows ahead of us, his face and body blackened, his hair spiked like the rind of some exotic fruit, Sir Rupert Gale came staggering. He held his sword outstretched.

"Stop!" he shouted. "Stop and fight!"

We slowed our headlong pace, came to a standstill. Not because we were going to fight him, but because we could see the thin blue glow of other-light expanding at his back; the pale face flowing ever closer. The Gory Girl of Cumberland Place was one of the slower and quieter of the spirits; she had made no noise in her approach, and she made no noise now as her slim, pale, bloodied arms stole around Sir Rupert's neck and drew him to her. Her jagged mouth opened in welcome; she was like a deep-sea fish swallowing her prey. As she hugged him close, blue veins of ice ran swiftly down his skin. Sir Rupert's limbs jerked and thrashed; he tried to speak, but could only make a gargling sound as he was drawn back into the dark.

"See?" the skull said plaintively. *"That's what I want to do. It's honest work. Why can't I have any fun?"*

"Come on." Lockwood began to move again. "We're almost at—" He gave a cry of warning. The pillar that the Morden Poltergeist had cracked was toppling. It fell toward us; I saw it coming as if in slow motion. I jumped one way; Lockwood and my friends went another. The pillar crashed down between us, shattering at my back. Blue other-light spilled out, like liquid floating in midair. I looked all around. I couldn't see the others through the swirling smoke. There was an explosion nearby. Ghosts screamed.

But from between the spars of the broken pillar soft streams of white were issuing. They flowed together into a squat and bulky form with gaping sockets instead of eyes. In one thick hand it held a serrated knife. The Clapham Butcher Boy swiveled its big round head and looked at me.

"Ooh, might be worth scampering, Lucy," the skull said. *"Remember—he's a fan of yours."*

I didn't need reminding. The ghost tittered. As it moved toward me, I'd already turned and was running in a panic across the chaos of the hall.

I darted this way and that, crunching through steaming glass, jumping across the ghost-touched bodies of the Fittes men, some of them already swollen and blue. Behind me drifted a soft white shape with a knife in its hand.

With all the smoke and eerie lights, it was impossible to see where I was going. I lost all sense of direction. I couldn't find my friends, I couldn't find the exit. I stumbled near a shattered pillar; on its far side, a faint green Specter, with the form of a wild-eyed man in chains, ducked into the floor like he was swimming in it, and bobbed up beside me, clawing with his hand. I slashed at him with my sword and leaped away—and suddenly saw an arch in front of me. Without pause, I ran through it, and down a corridor strewn with scattered papers. The place was empty; everyone had fled.

I drew to an abrupt halt. I knew where I was. Urns of swords and flowers sat beneath plinths on which were burning flames. The paintings of serious-eyed children watched me from the wall, and six elevator doors waited at the far end, five bronze, and one of them silver. I was not near the exit to the Strand. Instead, in my panic, I'd backtracked and retreated deeper into the building. I was in the Hall of Fallen Heroes again. Beside the elevators.

I looked at the corridor behind me. There was no sign of the Clapham Butcher Boy, but somewhere far off came the horrid sound of manic tittering. I stood in the hallway, regaining my breath, waiting for my intelligence to return.

"*So, you've gone the wrong way,*" the skull said. "*Nice one. Your pals will be out having tea and cream buns by now, but, frankly, you're toast. I make it at least seven major-league Type Two ghosts you've got to get past to reach the door.*" There was a distant explosion. "*Make that eight. That's another pillar gone.*"

I didn't say anything. Yes, Lockwood and the others *would* be out. I was sure of it. They'd get help for Kipps. Our luck would hold.

"*That Butcher Boy,*" the skull went on. "*He'll be lying in wait for certain. Feel like taking him on?*"

"No," I said. A sudden cold, hard certainty had filled me, a distillation of all my pent-up rage. "No, I'm not going to do that."

"Very wise. So are you going to sit down here and cry?"

"Oddly enough, I'm not going to do that either." I walked toward the silver elevator. "I've got better things to do."

Chapter 24

The elevator didn't take long to come. There was a faint, smooth hum as it descended from the penthouse floor. Distant mechanisms whirred; I watched the arrow flicking back across the dial above the door. A *ting*; the humming stopped. The door opened. It was a dark interior of gold filigree and inlaid tortoiseshell, with mirrored panels on the sides.

I stepped inside and turned to face the front. I adjusted the ghost-jar under one arm and pressed the button for the seventh floor.

The door closed; almost imperceptibly, the elevator began to rise.

"*Going up,*" the skull said. "*Next floor: cutlery, condiments, and underpants.*"

We stood staring at the door. There was a mirror there, too. Thanks to that and the soft warm light on the ceiling, I had a lovely, lingering view of just how tired I looked. My skin was puffy and sallow, my hair sticking out at impossible angles. My clothes were torn and dirty. I didn't care too much about any of this. A fire burned in my eyes.

It was a beautiful elevator, plush and very old; a private lift for an exclusive passenger. The air was heavy with a strong perfume that I recognized very well.

"*Marissa's scent,*" the skull remarked. "*We're getting close now.*" It hummed a jaunty tune, making extravagant faces at itself in the mirror.

I pulled back the side of my jacket and inspected the contents of my belt. My sword was there, and the hammer, and a couple of packets of iron filings, I had a silver net in one pouch, too. That was about it. I had no flares. There'd been no time to take a gun from the trolley, or one of the bombs. . . . It didn't matter. The sword would do.

"*So then,*" the skull said, as we passed the second floor, "*just fill us in, while we've got a moment. What's the plan when we meet Big M?*"

I didn't answer, just watched the dial.

"*Here's my theory,*" the ghost went on. "*You've got to take her by surprise, right? Well, nothing would be more surprising than you strip-ping naked now, daubing charcoal on your cheeks—I'm not specifying which ones—and rushing out of the elevator, whooping and leaping about like a mad thing. She'll be so startled, you'll be able to lop off her head with your sword before she gets out of her chair. Plus I'll have a good laugh. How about it?*"

"It's great," I said. "I'm tempted." The arrow pointed to the fourth floor.

The face regarded me. "*You do have a plan, I suppose?*"

"I'm going to improvise." It was strange, but in that moment I felt no fear, no doubt, and no regret. This was how it was meant to end. My friends were out of the building, I knew it with as much certainty as if I'd watched them leave with my own eyes. Lockwood was safe. I didn't doubt that he'd come back for me, but he had Kipps to tend to first, and by the time he'd done that, I'd have put an end to matters. Just me and Marissa: this was how it was always meant to be.

The elevator passed the fifth floor, then the sixth. . . . You could hear the mechanism slowing.

I looked down at my frost-burned boots, my skirt and torn leggings, my old jacket with the ghost's handprint on the side. I checked in the mirror again, smoothing down my hair a little. It was nice to look at myself, after everything. Nice to be reminded who I was. Lucy Carlyle.

Ting! The bell rang cheerfully to tell us we were there. The elevator stopped with scarcely a judder.

I drew my sword as the door eased open.

It would have suited the occasion if I'd immediately had a clear view of some kind of sinister throne room with a red carpet down the middle and bowing flunkies lined up on either side. In fact, all I got was a small vestibule, or waiting room, with a couple of chairs in it, and some nondescript modern art on the wall. Straight ahead, however, was a set of double doors. One was slightly open. A bright and cheerful light issued from within. Again, there was the heady scent of flowers. I tightened my grip on my rapier, pushed at the door, and went inside.

And then? No thrones. No flunkies. It was a chief executive's office—a very large rectangular space with a deep white carpet and low-backed sofas arranged against the walls. They looked angular, modern, and uncomfortably fashionable. Each had a glass coffee table beside it, scattered with books and magazines. There was plenty more modern art—paintings, and ugly sculptures on little stands—and a fair number of floor-to-ceiling wall mirrors that made the room seem even bigger than it was.

At the far end, a wide, deep window looked out over the Thames. It was night, and the river was a deep black band running between London's brightly jeweled banks. How beautiful the city looked from so high up, stretched out dark and glittering. Its ghost-lamps were pretty lights, twinkling like stars. All its imperfections were smoothed away. You couldn't see the people in it, either the living or the dead.

The business end of the room was up beside the window. A great oak desk sat there, piled high with books and papers; alongside it were bookshelves, a couple of safes, and one very big wooden cabinet, tall as a wardrobe, set against the wall. All of this I took in with one sweep of the eye, but I didn't pay attention to any of it.

I was looking at what waited for me behind the desk.

Two figures.

A dark-haired, smiling woman. And a ghost, floating at her shoulder.

Ms. Fittes was sitting at the desk in a black leather chair. She seemed at ease, no more put out by my sudden appearance than if I was an old friend she'd bumped into in the street. There was no sign of the hooded silver cape she'd worn on the Other Side; instead she had on a bottle-green knee-length dress and high-heeled shoes. One arm rested on the desktop, the other was draped casually across her lap. She would have been the image of a slick and elegant businesswoman were it not for the golden radiance that danced around her form, a radiance that stemmed from the thing hovering at her side.

Close-up, the spirit Ezekiel was no more clearly defined than when we'd seen it earlier that evening. It was a luminous figure with a crown of fire dancing above its head. It was very hard to look straight at it. If you did so out of the corner of your eye, you caught the suggestion of a man-sized form, slim and graceful and standing in midair. It made no sound, but I could feel the cold power that emanated from it. Long coils of light extended from its side and moved ceaselessly like squids' limbs around the woman in the chair.

I felt the ghost in the jar give a wriggle of unease. There was the barest whisper in my ear. *"Careful . . ."*

The woman in the chair raised an elegant hand. "Welcome, Lucy! Please come in. Don't stand skulking at the door."

She had a deep, melodious voice, calm and utterly self-assured. I walked forward slowly, my blackened boots scuffing on the carpet. On either side the mirrors reflected my ragged form, my drawn sword, my feral, vagrant air.

"Come over," Ms. Fittes said again. "There are seats for visitors." With a flick of the fingertips she indicated a canvas armchair near the desk. "Join me. I want to talk to you."

"That's good," I said. "Because I want to talk to *you*."

I didn't take the chair, but came to a halt a few feet away from the woman and the silent floating spirit. The cold that radiated from it was even stronger than its light. I didn't want to get too close.

Marissa Fittes watched me with her big black eyes. Her long dark hair was as lush and loose and impeccably aligned as ever. I had a sudden insight into how important her beauty was to her. The mirrors told their story. The windows opened out on London, but the whole penthouse reflected in on her.

"A sword?" she said suddenly. "I'm surprised at you, Lucy." Her eye lit upon the jar under my arm. "And—what's this bottled abomination? Some pet Lurker? A Pale Stench in a jar?"

The ghost-jar vibrated furiously under my arm. *"Hey!"* the skull cried. *"Don't give me that! You know who I am!"*

If the woman heard the skull's voice, she gave no sign of it. "You look so tired, my dear," she went on, smiling. "But, as always, your initiative astounds me. How did you get here? The elevator? What about security on the front doors?"

"Yes, I took the elevator," I said. "I'm not sure you've *got* any security anymore, to be honest. It's getting a little busy downstairs. But actually, I didn't come in through the front. I came up from the basement, you see."

Ms. Fittes hesitated a moment. Her eyes studied me. "Ah, I *do* see. Then you've made quite a journey. Sir Rupert assured me you'd never get across the Other Side. What a fool he is sometimes. I have to applaud you."

I smiled slightly. "You won't have to worry about Sir Rupert letting you down again. It's all over, Marissa. We know who and what you are."

I looked for a reaction to the name. Perhaps her eyes widened just a little. "Marissa?" She gave a lazy smile. "Why do you call me that?"

"Because we know you're not Penelope," I said. "We read your book—*Occult Theories*. Well, *George* read it, to be fair. Wading through the ravings of a lunatic isn't something the rest of us do too often. George isn't fussy. He'd read the memoir of a lavatory attendant if it were propped against his cornflakes. He told us about your theories of immortality, how the body might be rejuvenated by ectoplasm taken from spirits on the Other Side."

"Oh, he read that, did he?" the woman said. She tapped her fingers on her knee.

I nodded. "Your 'elixir of youth,' Marissa. We know you've made your body young again. We know you faked the life of Penelope Fittes to explain your reappearance. And we've seen the nets you use on the Other Side to get the plasm, the cylinders you store it in. . . . The only thing we haven't figured out is what you *do* with the plasm once you've got it. Do you drink it, breathe it in, rub it on your backside like an ointment? What?"

"Drink it," the woman said. "Or that's the theory."

"How unutterably foul." I raised my sword in the direction of the floating spirit. It was perfectly still, except for the golden rays that flickered gently at Marissa's back. Two dark gold eyes watched me from the center of its radiance. "George told us about your advisor, too," I said. "He told us about Ezekiel."

At this, the spirit stirred; the rays flexed and brightened. A strong breeze rippled out across the room. It lifted the edges of the papers on the desk, and riffled the corners of magazines on the far tables. A soft and velvet voice, somehow golden like the light, came from the shape. It said: *"Is this the girl?"*

The woman looked up at her companion; there was adoration in her face, but also wariness, even fear. "It is, Ezekiel."

"She is stubborn. Intractable."

"She has the gift."

"Maybe so. But how does she use it? See the kind of spirits she consorts with." A ray of light stabbed out and prodded the ghost-jar under my arm. *"This monstrosity, this coarse and loathsome thing . . ."*

The skull gave a cry. *"What? Come in here and say that! I'll wipe my feet on your ectoplasm! I'll tear you up and use you for toilet paper! Coarse? How dare you!"*

The woman was sitting upright in her chair. She looked pensive; she toyed with a bracelet of green stones hanging from one wrist. "She has the gift," she said again.

"Then make her the offer, but be quick. We have work to do downstairs."

I stepped forward. "I want no offer from you."

"Even so," Marissa Fittes said, "I'm going to give you one." She stood suddenly; she was taller than me, and very beautiful. In the luminous golden other-light, she looked like a fairy-tale queen. She was smiling now, and the aurora playing on her hair shone as bright as diamonds. "Lucy," she said, "we are very much alike, you and me."

"I don't think so."

"We both talk with spirits. We both seek out the mysteries of the dead. We have both walked on the Other Side and seen things forbidden to mortal eyes. Your Talent is as great as mine. We share it—and could share so much more." The smile broadened. "Eternal life, Lucy, can be yours, if you join yourself to me."

I noticed that though she had left her chair and walked toward me, away from her floating companion, she was still tied to its radiance. Golden rays clung about her like a wreath of chains. Suddenly I thought of Charley Budd. I said, "That's a nice offer, but I'm not sure I like the look of that glowing thing by your side."

The woman smiled; she played with a lock of her long dark hair. "You have your Type Three to guide you. I have mine. See? We are alike."

"Except that Lucy's got good taste," the skull put in. *"You don't remember, lady, but I talked to you years ago. I gave you my words of wisdom, had quite a civilized chat. Then what happens? I stay stewing in this jar, while you shack up with golden boy here. However you call it, that's just plain wrong."*

"Silence, Wisp!" The luminous spirit flared majestically. **"Do not interrupt Marissa when she's—"**

"Sorry, I do interrupt quite often, don't I? Oops, clumsy me! Just did it again."

There was a growl of irritation. **"If you weren't in that jar,"** the golden voice said, **"I'd grind your plasm into dust."**

"Yeah? And whose army?"

Marissa's eyes narrowed. She glanced down at the ghost-jar for the first time. "It so happens that I *do* remember you, vile spirit. I thought you evasive, cheeky, and lacking in intelligence."

The face in the jar frowned. *"Really? Sure that wasn't some other skull?"*

"No, she remembers you all right," I said.

"Charming."

"This obnoxious skull held no interest to me, Lucy," Marissa said. "Its many deficiencies aside, I already had my beloved Ezekiel. Since I found him as a little child, he has shown me wondrous things. He has guided me in all my works. He led me and Tom Rotwell to experiment with Sources; it was his insights that enabled us to first explore the Other Side."

She held up her arm on which the jade bracelet twinkled, and Ezekiel's golden rays moved to twine about her fingers playfully. Marissa laughed; there was wildness in the sound. Slowly, imperceptibly, I stepped a little nearer. I was gauging her distance from me, estimating the jump I'd need to make to strike her down. I wanted her close. Even so, she unnerved me. There was a darkness in the laughing eyes, as if something moved inside them, came separately to the surface to gaze at me. Now the golden aura on her hair looked like a crown, like the tiara worn by La Belle Dame Sans Merci.

She reminded me of La Belle Dame in other ways, too.

"Tom was slow and held me back," Marissa went on. "He could not listen to Ezekiel, could not understand the deeper truths. But *you* can, Lucy. You can. There has been no one else who could sit beside me with honor all these years."

"She does *gabble on, doesn't she, Lucy?"* the skull said. *"I reckon you'd be bored to tears if you started hanging out with her."*

"Yes," I said. "I would." With that I leaped forward, swung the rapier with all my strength at the woman's side. It didn't seem to go quite where I wanted. It slowed, slowed, came to a sickening halt a couple of feet from her neck. I tried to wrestle it nearer, but the air was gluey.

"Let us remove temptation from you," the woman said. "Ezekiel?"

The golden figure raised an arm. A buffet of air slammed me backward. I hit the side of the wooden cabinet standing by the wall; the force of it drove the breath from my lungs, sent me crashing to the carpet. I dropped the ghost-jar and the sword. Another buffet caught the rapier, sent it speeding across the floor.

Panting, cursing, I struggled to my feet. My whole body ached. The woman stood watching me.

"Why do you think you came here tonight, Lucy?" she said softly. "Why come up here on your own? And no"—there had been a snort of outrage from the floor—"I don't include that Lurker in the jar. Why come without your friends? Without your charming Lockwood, above all? It can't be because you *truly* think you'll destroy me. No, it's for a deeper reason. You're lonely, Lucy—you need companionship. You need someone who can understand and share your deep desires. Your friends are valuable, of course, as far as they go. I don't deny it. But they're not enough. They don't understand your fear of death. Indeed, they worsen it! You know full well that Lockwood's recklessness is practically suicidal—that his emotional emptiness will drive him to the grave. But how would it be, Lucy, if you had in your power ways to *save* his life—to keep him with you always? To keep him—and you—forever young, like me?"

I wiped a trace of blood from my lips; my body still trembled with the impact against the wood. At my back, the cabinet door had opened; it swung slightly ajar. And now the golden figure came drifting near, and the woman was stepping close, too. Her fragrance almost overpowered me.

"*We need to finish this,*" the spirit said, "*one way or another.*"

"Well, Lucy?" Marissa smiled. "You've heard my offer. What do you say?"

I looked for my rapier; no, too far away. There was the ghost-jar on the floor, with the skull upside down, rolling its eyes at me. I had no other weapons. What could I do? Perhaps the cabinet held something in it—guns, bombs, equipment for the Other Side . . . I could think of nothing else.

I said, "So you would give me the elixir of life? And Lockwood, too?"

The dark-haired woman shrugged. "You have no need of it yet, of course. Not for years. But I would share its secrets with you. You would live here. We would rule London."

"And the Orpheus Society? And the men and women who also cross to the Other Side?"

She shook her head. "They are fools, scrabblers in the dark. None of them know the full truth. *You* would know everything. Ezekiel would cradle you with his light. But what is your answer, Lucy?"

I drew myself up to my full height, every aching bit of my (almost) five feet six inches. I pushed white fronds of hair back from my face. "Marissa," I said, "I appreciate the offer. But even if you presented it to me gift-wrapped and accompanied by my body weight in jewels, it wouldn't be enough."

The woman's face darkened. Black lines like forks of lightning flickered through the spirit's golden light.

"*I told you,*" Ezekiel said. "*She's stubborn. So then . . .*"

"It wouldn't be enough," I said. "It wouldn't balance out the countless lives ruined by the Problem, the agents killed fighting against ghosts. And it wouldn't balance out the suffering you've inflicted on the spirits bottled up on the Other Side. No wonder so many are driven to return to this world instead! I've seen all this; I've seen my friends wounded, I've seen them almost dying! So thanks, Marissa, but no. There's no power on earth that would make me join you, and if it costs me my life, that's a penalty I'll willingly accept."

With that, I spun on my heels, and threw the cabinet doors open.

Guns? Swords? Weapons of any kind?

No.

But the cabinet wasn't empty, and what I saw there made me scream.

Chapter 25

It was a body.

Don't get me wrong. I've seen a *lot* of bodies, of all shapes and sizes, in all conditions. That's part of the job, and though it doesn't thrill me, it doesn't freak me out. And screaming? That's *definitely* not my thing. But this? It was shocking in part because it was so unexpected, in part because it was so horrible, and in part because it undermined everything I thought I knew.

The corpse was fixed upright on a sort of golden stand inside the cabinet. It was supported along its length by many golden rods and clamps that prevented sections of its black and shriveled flesh from falling to the floor. Even so, it was in a pretty shoddy condition, starting with the head. Some of this was gone—the left eye, for starters, and most of the cheek, jaw, and cranium on that side. Elsewhere, a black and rubbery rind of skin still maintained the vestiges of a face. There were sprouts of long black hair, and a bony neck like that of a plucked turkey. Below that, the torso was in a bad way, too, all dried and thin and twisted like one of those horrid roasted vegetable things Holly preferred to honest chips. The surface was as hard and black as cooled lava, and a couple of ribs poked through splits in the skin. The arms and legs were little more than bones encased in a loose and papery sheath. In places, screws had been driven through them to keep them in position. The thing was pierced, fixed, hung, and clamped. It was a parody of a body. The yellowed teeth grinned at me and the eye socket reflected no light.

None of *that* was what *really* threw me, though.

Here's what did. It was Marissa.

It was Marissa Fittes. Even though half the head was gone, I recognized her at once. The beaky nose; the jaw and forehead; the sweep of hair—it was the face from all the statues, books, and stamps. In fact it was roughly what I had expected to find in the crypt below the mausoleum, if everything had been natural and as it should be; if the dead had stayed in their proper places and the living in theirs.

"*Oh*," the skull said. The ghost's face was craning upward from where it lay in the jar beside my feet, trying to get a decent view. Its voice sounded as hesitant as I'd ever heard it. "*That's . . . unexpected.*"

"Are you surprised?" The woman behind me gave a husky little laugh. "Poor Lucy. You had everything so *nearly* right, as well. Turn around and look at me."

I twisted away from the horror in the cabinet, back to the two horrors standing with me in that smart and stylish penthouse room. The spirit, Ezekiel, had drifted closer; it no longer had quite such a golden radiance, but was a darker man-shaped form. Flashes of black laced the rays that rippled out and darted around the woman's body, shadowing the contours of her face. But she was smiling.

"I was very young, Lucy," she said, "when I wrote *Occult Theories*. Very young, like you. From dear Ezekiel's teachings, I had learned that the essence of the departed would help to sustain life. I thought that it would rejuvenate my body and keep it fair and youthful—and with this in mind, I began traveling to the Other Side. You have seen some of the techniques I use to gather the plasm that I need. I soon discovered that Ezekiel was right—by absorbing the essence I *did* replenish my own strength. And my spirit grew *powerful*." Her black eyes searched mine. "But there was a catch!"

"Of *course* there was," I said. "The catch being that what you were doing was both wrong and mad. What *is* this Ezekiel, anyway? What sort of ghost *is* it? Where did you pick it up?"

The woman raised her arm, tapped the jade bracelet on her wrist. "I found him, buried in the earth near an ancient grave. He is old, Lucy, and wiser than you'll ever know. He has seen kingdoms rise and fall. He has turned away from death. He rejects it. I reject it, too."

The golden shape drifted nearer to me. Its seeping cold blazed on my skin. "**Enough talk**," its deep voice said. "**This girl is not like us. She defies the mysteries. She wants death. She has said as much. We must give it to her.**"

"No," the woman said. "First I want her to understand. You see, Lucy, though my *spirit* grew stronger, my *body* was weakened by my visits to the Other Side, becoming prematurely aged. I began to need the help of others to venture across instead of me. My friends at the Orpheus Society were the first, and they have proved most reliable over many years. They are inspired by the same dreams as me, and carry out many of the experiments going on downstairs." Her smile thinned. "It is right that they do so. After all, the Problem funds their businesses and keeps them rich. But they are old and growing desperate. They seek immortality as I once did, trying to keep their bodies young. They do not understand that this is not the answer."

"So what is?" I said. The radiant spirit was so close now; I could feel its power thrumming against me, fixing me where I stood. Yet while the woman spoke, I kept my mind free of ghost-lock. My brain was racing, assessing my position, my options for attack and escape. "What *is* the answer?"

"It's going to be nasty," the skull said. *"Take it from me."*

Marissa leaned toward me. "Here's what I learned," she said. "A mortal body always fails you. A mortal body always lets you down. But if your spirit is sufficiently strong . . ." She touched my face with her ice-cold hand and stepped away. "There *are* other options."

And now a strange thing happened to her; it was like watching the face of a clay doll being stretched to the side by the motion of a giant thumb. Her nose, mouth, eyes, and cheekbones—*all* her features, were, for a second, smudged and distorted as something started pulling clear of them. Then they snapped back into position and a second face began to break free alongside the first. She had two faces—one solid, the other faint and see-through! At first they were almost entirely superimposed upon each other, then simply overlapping; finally the translucent, ghostly head emerged like a midnight insect from a chrysalis and hung independently beside the other. It was hard to say which was the more terrible: the malevolent glimmer of intelligence in the eyes of the spirit, or the sudden deadness in the eyes of the living.

The face of the woman known as Penelope Fittes hung slack and stupid, her breathing newly loud and ragged. And the face alongside? There *were* family resemblances, that much was true. The shape of the jaw and chin, the hairline on the forehead . . . Otherwise the spirit of Marissa Fittes had precisely the hooklike nose, the ravaged lines, and the haughtily imperious expression of the bust in the mausoleum or the engraving at the front of our *Fittes Manuals*. It was the same face as the one that was kept, decayed and ravaged, in the cabinet behind me.

"*Stone me,*" the skull said, from the jar on the floor. "*I didn't expect that.*"

I swore under my breath. Instinctively, as one does when faced by something repulsive and unnatural, I moved back a pace.

"*I always knew she was Marissa,*" the skull went on. "*But I just go by what's on the inside. I told you that, right? I call it as I see it. If I see Marissa's spirit, I assume the body's hers as well! I didn't realize she was* squatting *in someone else.*"

A faint blur beneath the spirit-head showed where its neck and shoulders disappeared inside Penelope Fittes's motionless body. Marissa's mouth moved; a voice came, faint and crackling, like something heard down a bad phone line. "Squatting?" it said. "It's a much closer, more perfect bond than that! See? I want to raise my hand"—Penelope's left arm rose, and gave us a cheery wave—"I do so. I want to move my feet"—the long legs made adjustments; the hand smoothed down the skirt—"I can. I inhabit dear Penelope just as snugly as one could wish. We are the same." The ghost head grinned at us. Alongside it, the solid head lolled sideways like an unloved doll's.

"So . . . so Penelope *was* a real person?" I said.

"Penelope was my granddaughter, yes."

"We thought you'd faked her life."

"Not at all."

I spoke harshly. "She was living, and you killed her."

The spirit-head clicked its tongue. "*Tsk, tsk.* I killed the *spirit*, by driving it out. The body is alive and flourishing, as you can very well see. It's been an extremely practical solution to my problem and should last me a good many more years. Now, excuse me a moment. I should put this back on."

With a horrid nuzzling, the spirit-head bunted up against the side of the living one and burrowed its way within. In an instant, it had disappeared. Penelope's head jerked and drooled. Intelligence snapped back into the eyes. The woman raised her hand and wiped her mouth.

"This is an atrocious thing," I said. "A wicked crime."

"Oh, come," Marissa said. "It *looks* odd, I grant you, but the benefits greatly outweigh the drawbacks. Besides, what alternative was there? My own body was worn out years ago—you see it in the cabinet behind you. Finally I lay near death, surviving only by pure will. The doctor who tended to me was a fool. He would have had me coffined up and buried! But my spirit raged for life. Instead of accepting death, it jumped across to a living vessel, my dear grand-daughter, Penelope, who at that time was still a girl. I had to wait a few years, while the body grew—and during that time I was forced to let my daughter, Margaret, run my company." The face twisted unpleasantly. "Margaret was weak in mind *and* body—she was not a good ambassador for my organization. Fortunately I was soon able to . . . remove her and retake control."

"**Marissa . . .**" the spirit said. The golden coils stirred in warning.

The woman nodded. "Ezekiel grows impatient. He wishes to finish you. What else is there to say? You can die with full understanding. I have told you all."

"*Not quite,*" the skull said. "*There's just one point, Lucy. If Marissa doesn't need her horrid old body anymore, why does she keep it in here?*"

That was something I'd been wondering, too. It gave me my final, desperate idea. The golden spirit was moving in to kill me. One of its coils of light, bent like a tentacle, flowed in my direction. I ducked away from it, and as I did so, reached out behind me into the cabinet. I caught hold of the stand that supported the twisted, blackened corpse and wrenched it free, pulling the whole thing outward. It toppled from the cabinet, fell across me, striking the floor hard. One of the legs fell off. Marissa gave a cry of pain and rage; she sprang down to clasp the body, and the golden coil of light jerked back to give her room.

Me? I picked up the ghost-jar and ran at full tilt toward the elevator.

I didn't get far.

Air exploded out across the penthouse suite. Sofas and coffee tables shifted, papers and magazines were blown skyward. The jar and I were sent tumbling head over heels across the carpet.

I wrenched myself up again. Looking over my shoulder, I saw that the body was already back inside the cabinet. Floating papers drifted to the floor. Two figures were coming toward me through them: a radiant spirit and a woman in a dark green dress.

The spirit waved a hand. The mirrors on the wall behind me cracked and shattered. The glass didn't fall. The fragments rotated outward. They shook like they were trying to pull themselves free. Great jagged shards broke clear and shot toward me like horizontal hail.

"Oh, not *this* again." I sprinted for cover. "I hate this Poltergeist stuff!"

Glass ripped the air around me. I threw myself over the top of the nearest sofa and fell to the floor behind it. Here I lay, pressed between it and the wall, as the rain of glass sliced into the cushions on the other side. The point of one especially long fragment jabbed right through the sofa back, just above my ear. The barrage ended. Shards dropped onto the carpet. I could hear Marissa's heels crunching through them.

The jar had spilled out of my hands and was lying horizontally next to me, the ghost's face gazing into mine. It would be a lie to say it looked any nicer than usual, though the grimace it wore was possibly an attempt at a smile.

"*You know this is the time, Lucy,*" it said.

I stared at it. "I can think of something."

"*You really can't. In thirty seconds you're going to die.*"

I bent low, squinted under the sofa: yep, there were Marissa's high-heeled shoes crossing the glass-strewn carpet with Ezekiel's radiance shimmering alongside. Little twists of ice formed on the carpet where the spirit passed. Gold tentacles were feeling their way toward where I hid. No respite.

"*The hammer's in your belt*," the skull said. "*Use it.*"

There was blood on my face, and just above my hip. So the glass *had* struck me. My side felt odd: cold and not my own. I grinned. "I was waiting for a real emergency."

"*Okay, fine, and while you're waiting, why not die here behind an ugly sofa, alongside all the dust balls and earwigs and coins people have lost. You want that?*"

"No." The first tentacles were probing under the sofa, radiant and bitter cold.

"*You want that old hag to win?*"

"No."

"*Do you trust me?*" the skull said.

I looked at it. I didn't see the hideous grimacing face. I thought of the sardonic spiky-haired youth standing on the Other Side.

"Yes," I said. "Sort of."

"*Then break the bloody glass.*"

I scrabbled at my belt, felt for the little hammer. My fingers were wet with blood, and the handle slipped through them. I caught hold and drew it out.

Already it was almost too late.

The sofa moved in front of me. Slowly at first, then with sudden violence, a psychic force swept it aside. I was left exposed, my back against the wall, with the ghost-jar in my lap and the hammer in my hand.

My enemies approached.

In some ways it was hard to know which of them was living and which was dead. They were very close together. Marissa Fittes's dark dress shimmered with other-light that extended from the figure at her side. Her face was ghastly with it. Her outline was wreathed in tendrils of gold light, making it curiously insubstantial. By contrast the ghost beside her, radiant and smiling, seemed almost solid, fizzing with energy.

"Poor Lucy," Marissa said.

And I suppose I *did* look pretty poor right then. I was lying in my own blood. I had my hair over my eyes. My clothes were torn and dirty. . . . You know the rest. I gazed up at them through narrowed eyes.

"Aren't you going to beg?" the ghost asked.

"She won't," Marissa said. "Let's get it done."

The shape drifted forward. I raised the jar, and had the satisfaction of seeing Ezekiel hesitate.

"You're not wary of *that* pathetic spirit?" Marissa said. "It's little more than a Phantasm."

"Something stronger than that. But it doesn't matter. He's trapped."

"No," I said. "Actually, he's not."

With that I raised the hammer, and struck it down against the jar with all my strength.

And the stupid thing bounced off. There was a slight chip in the glass, but otherwise all was as before.

The ghost in the jar had been braced as if for a mighty impact. It opened one eye and looked up at me. *"What are you doing? Don't tell me you can't break it."*

"Hold on." I struck the jar again. The hammer bounced away.

"Ohhh, you are so useless," the skull said.

With mounting panic, I tried again. This blow was even more ineffectual.

It gaped at me in disbelief. *"Hopeless! A toddler could tap this open!"*

"Don't criticize me!" I roared. "You're the one who suggested I use a stupid hammer!"

"I didn't think you'd be too feeble to lift it! Why didn't you say?"

"I've never broken a silver-glass jar before! How did I know how tough they were?"

"You might as well give it to that dead cockroach over there! He'd have more chance than you."

"Oh, why don't you just shut *up*?"

"This," Marissa said, "is priceless. But all good things must come to an end. Good-bye, Lucy. After you're dead, I'm going to seek out your companions, and watch Ezekiel suck the flesh from their bones. Think of that happening to your darling Anthony as you die."

"Or," a voice said, "we could save us all a lot of trouble, and finish this right here."

Marissa whirled around. The spirit rotated more slowly, its radiance flaring black with anger. I raised my head, but I didn't need to look to know what I would see. It was everything I'd hoped for, everything I'd feared.

The doors to the vestibule were open. Lockwood was standing there.

Chapter 26

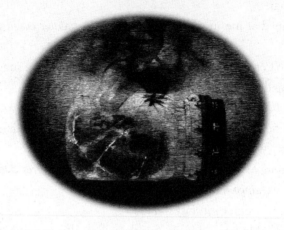

In so many ways, he didn't look like Lockwood. Not how he *liked* to be seen, so well-dressed and elegant in his long coat and slightly-too-tight suit. The coat was long gone, and the rest of his clothes were a wonder to behold, so ripped were they, so torn and peppered with ectoplasm burns. His shirt in particular had more holes in it than a string net bag; some of La Belle Dame's skimpier outfits probably had more fabric in them. One of his shoulders was gently steaming, and there were great clawed lacerations all the way down the sleeve on the other arm. His hair was gray with salt and magnesium; his bangs sagged over a cut eye. His face looked puffier, more swollen, more discolored, and more generally beat up than I'd ever seen it. In short, he was a mess. He didn't look like Lockwood at all.

And yet at the precise same time he was more *himself* in that instant than you could possibly believe. The way he held his rapier;

the casual stance he adopted as he stood between the doors; the slight smile playing at the corners of his mouth; the darkly flashing eyes that scanned the room, that took in its horrors and showed no fear. Above all, his twofold *lightness*—the way he radiated energy and brightness (so much stronger, so much purer than that coiling golden fog emanating from the floating spirit), and the way he seemed physically *lighter*, more buoyant, than everything around him. He'd always been less tied down by the weight of things than the rest of us, less restricted by life's drag. These qualities were his signature; they ran through him like a watermark in paper. And they did so now, more than ever, transcending the outward blemishes, those scrapes and rips and scratches, and the weakness of his body.

Just standing in that doorway, he was a living rebuff to Marissa. Forget her grotesque attempts at keeping young by body-hopping, by scurrying to the nearest, prettiest shell. *This* was how you did it. This was how your spirit stayed strong. This was how you looked death in the eye and defied it. Lockwood had fought his way up here to save me, past all the ghosts downstairs, and he had arrived at the perfect moment. I understood all that as I sat against the wall, bloodied and defenseless, and I loved him for it. My heart sang.

And yet I really didn't want him there.

"Hey, Lucy." As he met my gaze, his smile became a grin. "Having fun?"

"I'm having a lovely time."

"So I see." He came toward us across the carpet, walking carefully through the broken glass and scattered magazines. I saw that he was holding one of the snub-nosed electrical guns in his left hand. He had his eyes on Marissa and the floating ghost, and whether it was the gun or Lockwood himself that unnerved them, neither of them moved. "Do you need some company?" Lockwood asked me.

I smiled back at him. "Always."

A discreet retching sound came from the jar in my lap. "*You two make me feel ill,*" the skull said. "*Still, he's got timing. Got to give him that.*"

Timing. Yeah, Lockwood had it, and I didn't.

Because I hadn't gotten the job done.

Marissa had said I'd had a deeper motive for coming to the penthouse suite alone, that I'd wanted to join forces with her. Well, she was half right. There *had been* a deeper motive, and I only truly understood it now. I'd wanted to get things finished on my own; I'd wanted to do it with Lockwood left behind. Now he was here, and despite the joy and relief he brought me, the old fear sank back down onto my shoulders. It was the fear that fed off the predictions made by the fortune-telling machine at Tufnell's Theater; that clung to the memories of the empty grave waiting for him in the cemetery; that, above all, stemmed from my meeting with the ghost that wore his face, who had said that Lockwood would die for me.

So my heart sang, and my heart despaired, which was pretty much the usual combination for me whenever Lockwood was around. But he was here, and that was that. And I wasn't going to stay sitting with my backside on the carpet anymore. I forced myself to stand, blood welling from the glass cut in my side.

I wasn't the only one to decide to act. The spirit Ezekiel had become markedly less golden than before. The crown of fire and the coils of light that spun about its figure had darkened almost to blackness. Now the coils extended; they shot toward Lockwood, who raised the gun and fired. A horizontal lightning bolt cut straight through the spirit's body, cutting a jagged hole in the center of its chest. Ezekiel gave a horrid keening and bounded backward across the room, almost as far as the desk. The ropes or tentacles of light that connected it to Marissa were suddenly pulled thin. She gave a yelp of pain, and hurried after her companion, high heels slipping on shards of glass.

Lockwood walked over to me; he reached out, touched me with the fingers of his rapier hand. "You're hurt," he said.

"Not badly."

"That's what Kipps said, too."

"Kipps! Is he—?"

"We got him to an ambulance. I don't know, Luce . . . it's touch and go. He was still making grumpy comments as he went off, so perhaps he'll be okay." He looked along the room at the two retreating shapes. "So here they are. . . . Anything I need to know?"

"Couple of things. The ghost can shift stuff like a Poltergeist, and its Source is the bracelet on Marissa's arm. Her spirit is inside Penelope's body, possessing it, but she's got her old body shut in that cupboard, and I think she still needs it somehow. That's about all."

"Nice summary. You wait here." Lockwood grinned at me. "Don't get mad! I have to say it! I know full well you won't pay any notice."

I smiled back. "That's just the way it is, I'm afraid. Be careful of Ezekiel."

"I've got the gun. I'm a better shot with it than George. He almost blew Barnes's head off downstairs."

"Barnes? Barnes is here?"

"Yes, and Flo. Flo's the one who got him down here—I'll tell you about it later."

He moved away from me, firing the gun, making Marissa scream and dive behind an enormous potted plant. The electric bolt set the branches alight. Part of the carpet was smoldering. Near the desk, Ezekiel was busy knitting its plasm together. It raised a spirit-wind, sent it shooting outward. The blast was less powerful than the two it had directed at me earlier, but still strong. Lockwood somehow remained on his feet. He fired the gun again.

I could see my rapier lying halfway across the room. I made to get it—and then stopped. I looked down at the ghost-jar sitting on the floor. The face inside seemed thoroughly disgruntled with the proceedings.

"*Well, you won't be needing to get me out anymore,*" the skull said. "*Good old Lockwood. Came just in the nick of time. Looks like he's got everything nicely under control.*"

"Looks like it." I picked up the jar, carried it to the nearest coffee table.

"*Don't you stay hanging around with scum like me. You scurry on after him.*"

"I will in a minute." All the magazines had been blown off the table, but there was still a small stone sculpture there—a horrid pyramid of geometric pellets, like a pile of cubist horse droppings. I set the jar on the table, lying it on its side, and picked up the sculpture.

The ghost behind the glass had been pulling derisive faces: all at once it paused in doubt. "*What's that for? Are you going to lob it at Marissa?*"

I raised the sculpture above my head.

"*Being brained by some fossilized horse poo would be a pleasing way for her to—*" The skull fell silent. Its face was suddenly still.

I closed my eyes and brought the great weight down on the side of the jar with as much force as I could muster. There was a crack, a sharp odor, a hissing noise. I lifted the sculpture and struck the glass again—

"*Hey! Careful! You could smash a skull, going on like that.*" The voice came from close by. I was no longer alone. The spirit of a thin gray youth with spiky hair stood at my side. He was cloudy and translucent, but much clearer than when I'd seen him on the Other Side. When I looked down, I saw that one side of the jar had completely caved in. Pale green ichor was spilling from the cracks, floating up and outward like mist into the air. It trailed across to merge into the substance of the youth.

An old brown skull sat grinning up at me from the base of the broken jar.

I tossed the sculpture aside. "There. You're out."

The ghost was gazing at me. "*You actually did it. . . . You did it. Even though you didn't need to . . .*"

"Yes. Now, I'm a little busy. . . ." Lockwood had fired at Ezekiel again, but this time the glowing shape had dodged the strike, flexing its torso aside. It seemed to be recovering its power. Tentacles of blackness searched for Lockwood, who lopped them off with the tip of his sword. I couldn't see Marissa. I made for my rapier at a run.

"*You do know what you've done, Lucy?*" the skull called after me. "*There's nothing you can do to stop me now! I'm free! I could kill you—I could kill Lockwood fast as thinking. . . .*"

"You could!" I didn't look back. "That's up to you!"

I paid the skull no more attention, but scooped up my sword from where it lay.

Lockwood was swinging his rapier smoothly, slicing off the probing tentacles. I chopped at a couple, too. Black smoke was coming from the muzzle of the gun.

"Battery's almost out," he said. "I used it all up on the Butcher Boy downstairs. It would be nice to see the last of Ezekiel, Luce. Might be worth you getting the Source off Marissa, if you can."

I nodded grimly. "Not a problem."

I went in search of the woman, keeping clear of where the raging spirit thrashed and coiled. I found Marissa on her hands and knees, crawling along on the far side of the desk with her hair over her face. There must have been a drawer or some kind of a secret compartment back there, because when she stood up, she had a rapier in her hand.

Marissa Fittes kicked off her high heels and stepped toward me. That lovely face didn't look quite so good now; somehow its contours no longer quite aligned. The cheekbones seemed too high, the chin too protuberant—as if the old woman's spirit inside was almost showing through.

I moved in her direction, disregarding the pain in my side.

"Hey, Marissa," I said. "I've got a message for you. I forgot to tell you earlier. You know that old doctor of yours—the one you buried in your tomb instead of you? Neil Clarke, wasn't it? We met his ghost the other day. He was asking after you." I corrected myself. "Actually, he was asking *for* you. He badly wants to be reunited with you again."

For a second, the woman's expression became as static as one of the old masks we'd once had on our walls. Her hand twitched, making the green stones jangle at her wrist. Then she recovered. "Oh, dear, poor Neil. Is he *still* down there? And still angry? That *is* a shame."

"Maybe you'll see for yourself soon enough," I said.

Marissa scowled. "You're wounded," she said. "Look at all that blood. I think you're dying."

"Like you're an expert on that."

"You're bleeding to death."

"Oh, hardly." I lifted my sword, stiffly adopted the en garde stance, ready for battle. "Come on."

The woman raised her weapon, too. "It's not easy, Lucy, fighting with a wounded side. The muscles twist; they wrench and tear. I know that because I was a master with the rapier. I was the first to use one against ghosts. I invented the art. It was I who subdued the Mud Lane Phantom, I who—"

"Oh, shut up," I said. "That was fifty years ago and in another body. How long's it been since you actually raised a sword in anger, Marissa? I suspect you're a little rusty."

She brushed hair from her face. "Well," she said, "let's find out."

With that she darted forward; the rapier flashed down. I blocked it, twisted my blade in a Kuriashi turn—a complex series of feints and blows that came at her from either side. Gasping, she dodged and parried, kept my attack at bay.

And after that there was near silence in the penthouse, silence apart from clashing iron. On one side of the desk, the glowing spirit sent forth tentacles of plasm to snare Lockwood. On the other, Marissa threw herself at me. Lockwood and I retreated; we dug in, we held our ground. Just for a few moments we were side by side, him slicing at whirling tentacles, me parrying the woman's blows. Our reflections skipped along the fractured surface of the wall mirrors, swelling and shrinking, distorting on the jags of broken glass. There was no sound but the scuff and squeak and shuffle of our boots, the crack of glass, the tang of blades. In and out we went, twisting and spinning as if in synchronized flow. It must have been quite a spectacle.

And we *were* being watched. Once I caught sight of the skull's spirit looking at us from halfway across the room.

A while ago Lockwood had scarcely been able to walk, but you wouldn't have guessed that from his airy steps, the way he swung out of reach of the swiftest spectral blows. He moved with the utmost grace, with the same economy of effort as when practicing with Floating Joe and Esmeralda at home. I didn't have his fluency—I'd never had—but I matched the dark-haired woman blow for blow, and soon saw her expression begin to change. Confidence fell away, to be replaced by creeping doubt.

"Ezekiel," she cried suddenly, "help me!"

Lockwood's original shots had wounded the glowing shape, preventing it from unleashing its full strength. But the trouble with powerful ghosts—and Ezekiel *was* powerful, whatever manner of dark spirit it actually might have been—is that when they're inconvenienced, it's seldom for very long. And now, as if galvanized by Marissa's cry, it withdrew its tentacles into itself, mustered its energies, and raised its shining arms.

A blast of psychic force swept out across the room. Lockwood and I both staggered backward—but we weren't the focus of the assault. One of the sofas over by the wall was plucked from the ground. The spirit gestured; the sofa whirled forward with appalling speed, straight for where Lockwood and I were standing.

Straight for our heads. We couldn't react; we couldn't do anything. I closed my eyes.

And opened them.

I hadn't been struck dead. Nothing had happened. The sofa was hanging a few feet from me, quivering, shaking in midair.

Over by the desk, the spirit Ezekiel gestured again; the sofa twitched, jerked toward us just a little, then sprang back, pulled by a countering force. I turned and looked . . .

And saw the skull's ghost standing there.

The thin-faced youth wore a nonchalant, almost bored expression. He was inspecting the fingers of one hand, as if he'd noticed a trace of dirt beneath his nails. The other hand was, however, raised; it made a gentle pulling motion, and as it did so, the sofa jerked violently backward through the air, away from us, away from Ezekiel's control. The youth flicked his arm aside, and the sofa swung with it, spinning across the room to smash into the wall.

Ezekiel gave a cry of rage. *"Foul spirit! You dare defy me?"*

"What kind of a line is that?" the skull's ghost said. *"Honestly, can you imagine spending any time with him? I mean, where's the humor, where's the sarcasm? Where are the gratuitous butt jokes? Eternity with him would really drag."*

Ezekiel gestured again. A filing cabinet rose from behind the desk, came whipping toward us. The youth flapped a hand irreverently; the cabinet reversed its spin, shot back past Ezekiel's head, and crashed through the window.

The spirit was black with anger. It tried again. A storm of air raged around us—it was like the full fury of a Poltergeist—but met an answering wind from the skull that nullified it, canceled it out.

All through this, Marissa Fittes had been as transfixed as Lockwood and me. Now she recovered herself; with a snarl of rage, she stabbed at me with her rapier. The skull's ghost pointed a finger. A spirit-wind picked Marissa off her feet and sent her flying back to strike the side of the desk. She slumped across it, moaning.

"*Ooh,*" the skull said. "*Sore! I felt that.*"

"Lucy," Lockwood cried. "The Source!"

But I was already moving. I threw myself at Marissa's side, wrenched the rapier out of her feeble grasp and hurled it away. Then I ripped the bracelet of jade stones from her wrist. It was freezing cold; the feel of it almost made me cry out. I fumbled in my pouch for the silver net I knew was there.

The spirit Ezekiel gave a hideous yell. The nimbus of light around it died away. The radiant form shrank and hardened, became a dark and bestial shape with glowing eyes and a gaping mouth that sprang at me over the desk.

But I'd already pulled the net out of its pouch and wrapped it around the bracelet. The spirit seemed to disintegrate as it came, pieces falling off like twists of burning paper, until it was just the eyes that kept on rushing—and even these grew pale and faded into threads of smoke that were dispersed by fresh air coming through the broken window.

Ezekiel was gone.

"I don't know who he was," Lockwood said, "but he wasn't healthy company. That bracelet's one for the furnaces tomorrow,

Luce." Limping slightly, he walked over to the wall cabinet and flung the doors open, casting light on the horrible contorted body within. He shook his head in wonder. "And look what a state he's left Marissa in," he said. "In some way, her spirit's still bound to her body. Since she's refused to die, since she's in some sense still alive, this . . . this object must be still alive, too." He winced. "Doesn't bear thinking about, does it?"

He left the cabinet and came across to where I stood beside the thin, gray, cloudy apparition of the spiky haired youth. The skull's spirit was again affecting complete unconcern, pretending to be studying the cover of one of the fallen magazines.

Lockwood regarded the ghost. "Thanks," he said.

The skull's spirit said nothing. After a pause, Lockwood turned away and went over to Marissa, who was still lying across the desk.

I lingered by the ghost. "I want to thank you, too," I said.

The youth shrugged. *"Just a one-off,"* he said. *"Almost an accident, really. It's been so long since I stretched my energies. . . . I felt like exerting myself a little, that's all. If it also suited you, that was a coincidence."*

"Sure."

"It won't happen again."

"Of course not," I said. "I understand. So . . . what now?" I looked over to where the broken ghost-jar lay on the coffee table. "You're still tied to your skull, but I don't think you *have* to be. Like I told you, you could break the connection, head off to the Other Side." The ghost said nothing. "Or," I went on, clearing my throat awkwardly, "if you're not yet ready, you *could* stay with me a while longer."

The dark eyes regarded me. An eyebrow was slowly, sardonically, raised. *"What, just hang out with you? Become an associate member of Lockwood and Co.? Now that would be plain odd."*

"I guess." There wasn't much else to say. I turned away, walked over to the desk, where Lockwood was watching the dark-haired woman as she got painfully to her feet. Marissa's hair was disarranged, her lipstick smudged; her eyes were sunken in deep hollows. There was even a suggestion of blood about her lips. She looked as bad as I did on an average morning. It gave me a warm feeling, and it gave me an even warmer feeling to see Lockwood there, still in one piece. We'd actually done it. We'd gotten to the end.

He smiled at me. "I was just saying to Marissa that we might take an elevator ride downstairs. Barnes and his DEPRAC teams should be getting things under control by now. They'll be having a peep into the basements and making a few arrests as well, I expect. Holly and George were planning on giving them the tour. But it's high time that we joined them. If you're ready, Marissa, let's go."

The woman nodded slowly. She stood by the desk, head on one side, arms hanging loosely, like a broken doll's. "You know, Anthony, you're very like your parents," she said.

I frowned, stepped nearer. "Don't listen to her, Lockwood."

"You *look* rather like your father," Marissa said, "but it's your mother who gave you your impulsiveness and drive. I was there when they delivered their last lecture at the Orpheus Society. It was very good." She smiled at him. "Too good. That's why it was their last."

Just for a second, Lockwood didn't breathe. Then he laughed. "You can tell it all to Barnes," he said. "Come on."

He held out his arm to usher her forward. The woman moved, then suddenly lurched away from him, bent down at the desk. A catch was sprung, a compartment opened; she turned back to us, holding a small cylinder in her hand. There was something in the twisted contours of the body, in the way it hunched before us, in the snarling lines of the face and blazing eyes, that made it seem as if Marissa's shriveled spirit had exposed itself again.

"Do you really think I'd give myself up to you?" she spat. "To two stupid *children*? No. This is *my* house. My London. I built it all. I made it what it is. And if I'm not going to be here to enjoy it, I'll make certain that *you're* not either." She pressed the side of the cylinder. A small red light came on; there was a high-pitched beeping sound, a smell of oil and burning. "A cluster charge," Marissa said. "Can level a whole block. Twenty seconds. Say your good-byes. You're both coming with me."

With that she clamped the cylinder against her chest and ran toward me. I believe that in her final madness she would have clung to me, and ensured my doom. But now Lockwood moved, quickly as he always did, and grappled her from the side. He tried to wrest the cylinder from her, but she fought against him, biting, scratching, keeping him at bay.

He turned his head. "Lucy! Run! I'll hold her! *Run*—you can make it to the elevator!"

"No! Lockwood!"

"Go, Lucy! Do what you're told, for once!" His eyes met mine, dark and desperate. "Please! Save yourself for me."

"No . . ." I was frozen where I stood. "No, I can't. . . ."

And I couldn't. I couldn't leave him. What would I be running for? What would I be running toward? A world where the prophecies of evil ghosts came true, where dark predictions were fulfilled, where a third neat headstone sat atop a newly turned grave in a long-abandoned cemetery. Where all my fears were realized and all light gone.

A world without him. I couldn't run.

"No," I whispered. "I'll stay with you."

"Oh, for Pete's sake."

And then the ghost of the thin gray youth was standing beside Lockwood and Marissa. Unseen forces wrenched them apart. Marissa was flung away. The skull's spirit turned toward us. He gave me his old grin. *"Brace yourselves,"* he said.

He lifted his arms. The spirit-wind that struck Lockwood and me forced all the air from our lungs. It sent us off our feet and straight across the room.

As we flew back, the cylinder exploded. I saw the boiling plume of black and red expanding outward to engulf the penthouse. It cut right through the windows, sending molten glass spewing out across the Thames. It cut right through the ceiling, through the sofas, cabinet, and chairs. It cut right through the figure of the youth as he watched us go. It went with blinding speed. But we were still ahead of it, Lockwood and I. We were going so fast it could not catch us. We shot right through the open doors and into the vestibule, skidding across the floor, hitting the elevator door with a mighty *bang*.

Lockwood and I lay crumpled together as the fireball ballooned across the vestibule. I felt its heat upon my skin—then it drew back. Somewhere I could hear fire raging, and a mighty crash as the penthouse ceiling fell in. Black smoke swelled around us. It was hard to breathe. My mind drifted downward. My final sensation was relief that I could still feel Lockwood moving. My final thought was that I'd left the skull's ghost-jar lying on the table.

VI

The Beginning

Chapter 27

The blast that wrecked Marissa's apartments was large, but it was not the most destructive event that took place in Fittes House that night. Shortly before dawn, a series of controlled explosions cut through the Hall of Pillars and surrounding rooms on the ground floor. This was a deliberate act by a small emergency DEPRAC team, which had arrived some hours earlier, and had since been struggling to deal with the nine terrible ghosts rampaging through the building. Several investigating officers and a large number of Fittes staff had been killed or injured during attempts to corral the Gory Girl, the Morden Poltergeist, and the rest. At last the commanding officer, Inspector Montagu Barnes, gave the order to bring in heavy munitions. The lower floors were evacuated, and the charges set off. The explosions blew out part of the front wall, sending rubble spilling across the Strand. The famous glass doors, with their inscribed unicorn motifs, were utterly obliterated. One or two walls collapsed internally, as did part of the ceiling above the hall. All traces of the silver-glass pillars, their relics, and the ghosts they maintained were at once wiped out.

Fortunately, the explosions themselves claimed no extra casualties. Since they happened at five in the morning, the surrounding streets were mostly deserted. As the smoke cleared, the surviving DEPRAC forces and evacuated Fittes staff gathered in the Strand. Smoke hung thickly over central London, and a number of onlookers began to congregate in Trafalgar Square.

Inspector Barnes, whose raincoat had sustained significant ectoplasm damage in the battle, cast the tattered remnants aside and commandeered a leather biker's jacket from a bystander in the street. For the next few hours he was everywhere, summoning ambulances and medi-vans, bringing reinforcements from Scotland Yard, and rousing the wandering Fittes agents, who were mostly in a state of shock, to assist with crowd control. On the advice of George Cubbins and Holly Munro, who were temporarily assisting him, he also requisitioned two cafés across the street to provide a constant stream of food and drinks to all.

The smoke cleared; the heat in the building died down. Search-and-rescue teams went in. On the ground floor they discovered a number of white-coated scientists, wide-eyed and tremulous, who had appeared from the basement levels. The group was at once handed into DEPRAC custody. Four of Sir Rupert Gale's men, two suffering from ghost-touch, were also located alive; they were taken off to the hospital under armed guard.

At George and Holly's urgent behest, teams also immediately made for the seventh floor, from which black smoke could be seen pouring. The building's elevators were out of commission, so they took the stairs. Before they had reached the top of the first flight, however, they heard footsteps descending. It was Lockwood and me, coming slowly, arm in arm. Our clothes and faces were blackened with smoke. I had something small and round, wrapped in a piece of burned cloth, tucked beneath my arm.

By mid-morning, DEPRAC crews had cordoned off the end of the Strand, and the situation was under full control. A census of survivors was taken, and a tentative list of the dead or missing drawn up. Bodies began to be brought out of Fittes House. These included those of Penelope Fittes and Sir Rupert Gale. Another set of remains, located inside a cabinet amid the rubble of the seventh-floor penthouse, was carried out under a white sheet, placed in a DEPRAC van, and driven away at top speed.

The members of Lockwood & Co. watched this activity from a window table in the Silver Unicorn Café, directly opposite the disaster zone. The emergency services had already taken us under their wing; our cuts had been cleaned, dressed, and bandaged, and pep-shots of adrenaline administered to counteract our close exposure to ectoplasm. A hospital visit had been offered—and declined by all. I had been forced to protest particularly strongly to avoid this fate. The stab wound in my side was the most serious of our varied injuries, and an overnight stay was recommended. But I would not leave the others. In the end I was patched up, given a painkiller and a very reluctant temporary discharge, with strict instructions to report to a doctor the next day. Then I was allowed to go to the café with the rest of them.

There's no point in describing how we looked. We were just as bad as before, only now with added bandages and minor burns. The soles of Lockwood's shoes had partially melted in the explosion. Holly had the side of her face taped up—one of the blasts had burst an eardrum. George was still wrapped in one of the silver thermal blankets we'd been given by the emergency crews; it looked remarkably like a certain silver cape he'd worn recently, though none of us felt the need to mention it. As for me, my waist was so tightly wound with dressings I could barely move. We nursed our cups of tea, our toast—whatever the harried café proprietors had been able to bring us, for the place was packed. We stared out through the window condensation at the Strand.

"I don't like to say it," a voice said behind us, "but you all really need to spruce yourselves up a bit."

Flo Bones had materialized by our table. She looked precisely the same as she always did, down to the familiar stains on her puffer jacket and her mud-encrusted boots. Her straw hat was perched on her head at a jaunty angle, and she was spooning something hot and flavorsome from a Styrofoam dish into her mouth.

"Look at the state of you!" she said, shaking her head. "Soon I won't like to be seen in your company. Some of us have standards, you know."

"Flo!" Lockwood half rose from his chair and gave her a fleeting hug. "You look in excellent shape. I'm glad."

"Yeah, I'm just dandy. Enjoying a bit of pie and mash here, too."

George gave a start. "Pie and mash? Where'd you get that from?"

"Next door. You're in the wrong café. They do sticky toffee pudding there, and all."

George groaned into his mug of tea. "The best they've got here is fish-paste sandwiches! And it's too late to switch. All my muscles have seized up."

Lockwood grinned. "You were amazing last night, Flo," he said. "Barnes told me you were instrumental in getting him here. How did you persuade him to bring a team along to Fittes House?"

Flo's blue eyes stared off across the Strand. "It weren't easy—he's a stubborn old goat. Well, first off, yesterday, I took him down to your place in Portland Row. I showed him the state of it—you vanished, all hell broken loose, a spirit gate upstairs, and a couple of Winkman's men still systematically rifling through your stuff. That shook him. What the Winkman boys confessed to, when he got them back to Scotland Yard . . . well, that shook him even more. So he put a team together to have a quiet word with Rupert Gale. But he didn't exactly hurry, and by the time we got here, you was already in the middle of your little private war. After that, Barnes couldn't tiptoe about no more. He *had* to get involved." She made a scraping noise with her spoon. "Yep. That's the story. Nothing more to say."

"Hold on—Barnes also says you helped capture one of Gale's thugs, who tried to escape," Holly said eagerly. "Says he pulled a sword on you, but you disarmed him with six swipes of your slime-flange! That sounds incredible, Flo! I *so* wish I'd seen it!"

"I'm not sure I remember that bit." Flo retrieved the final trace of pie and mash with a finger, and tossed the dish onto the table. She glanced over at the café door, where Inspector Barnes had appeared. He was loudly giving orders to an officer behind him. "Looks like it's maybe time to go," she said. "DEPRAC officers and me don't normally see eye to eye. Special circumstances only. I'll see you later, maybe. Meantime—try to clean yourselves up!"

George pulled back the silver hood and adjusted his glasses. "Flo—when everything's settled down, couple of days or so, I was wondering if—"

She grinned at him, showing her bright white teeth. "Yeah, come and find me. I'll be under a bridge somewhere."

"I'll bring licorice," George said. But Flo had faded back into the crowd.

Barking a series of gruff apologies, Inspector Barnes pushed his way past the food lines to our table. He had one arm in a sling protruding from beneath his leather jacket.

"Hello, Mr. Barnes." Lockwood put on a fair attempt at his most gleaming smile. "Nice jacket," he added. "It really suits you."

The inspector regarded himself. "You know, I think it does. I just might keep it. So, you're being fed and watered, then. Anything else you need?"

"Pie and mash would go down nicely," George said. "Also some sticky toffee pudding . . . if you're offering."

"I'm not. And they're all out of that next door, too. One of my men just asked. What I really came to tell you is that we're almost done with the search-and-rescue operation over the road. I'll be wanting you to escort me down into the basement soon, show me what's what."

"Excuse me, Inspector," I said, "but is there any word on Kipps?"

Barnes rubbed at his mustache. "I believe he's been in surgery. The doctors are cautiously optimistic." He held up a hand as we all tried to speak. "And no, you can't visit him. You'd only cause disaster somehow. Cubbins would trip and impale him on his sword, or Lockwood here would grin him half to death. Just let him be. I need you all here, anyway." He frowned. "I want to see the basement before I begin my interrogation of those lab coats we found skulking down below."

"Most of the Fittes crowd will have had nothing to do with it," Lockwood said. "It's just a very small group of them—an inner core—who worked on the secret projects. But the same isn't true of the members of the Orpheus Society, and they're powerful people. What are you going to do about them?"

"I don't know yet!" The inspector glared at us. "I don't know! There are big decisions to be made, and much to be done." He sighed and rubbed his eyes. "The one good thing is that all those relics from the pillars have been destroyed. And I'm going to go one better. DEPRAC will ensure that any psychic object found inside that cursed building is immediately destroyed."

"Good idea, Mr. Barnes," I said. I glanced down under the table, at the roundish bundle of burned cloth resting between my feet.

"There's one more thing you might want to prioritize, Inspector," Lockwood said. He lowered his voice. "We talked about it earlier. Penelope's and Marissa's bodies . . ."

Barnes winced, and glanced anxiously across at the other café customers. "Not so loud! We don't want everyone overhearing this. . . ." He drew close, and spoke in an undertone. "What about them?"

"You'll want to dispose of . . . those *objects* pretty quickly," Lockwood went on. "Might I suggest they're taken to the Fittes mausoleum up the road? That's where Marissa *ought* to be, after all."

"There's someone down there who'll be *very* pleased to see her," Holly said. She took a fastidious sip of tea.

Barnes straightened; he had noticed one of his men signaling at the door. "We'll see what we can do. Well, I'll leave you for the present. There are legions of reporters clamoring for a statement. In the meantime, rest up, don't leave, and *don't talk to anybody here.*"

"At least the truth about the Problem will come out now," Lockwood said. He had been looking toward the square, where the crowds were continuing to grow.

Barnes patted him on the shoulder. "Ah, yes," he said. "About all that. You and I clearly need to have a little chat."

Our work at Fittes House lasted until after lunchtime; after that, further consultations at Scotland Yard took up the entire afternoon. The DEPRAC cars didn't drop us back at the end of Portland Row until after five. You could feel the onset of evening in the air, but the sky was still blue, and the rusted ghost-lamps were not yet buzzing into life. The momentous events in central London had yet to resonate here. Many of the houses still had their doors and windows open, and children were playing on the sidewalks and in their yards. The purple-blue splendor of the lavender bushes pressing against the railings almost gave the street the air of a formal garden. At gates and porches, beneath twinkling silvery defenses, neighbors discussed the events of the day. Old Arif, standing outside his general store, was tipping last night's lavender ash out of his street brazier, before readying another fire. His humming, the laughter of the children, and the voices of the adults merged and mingled on the ear.

We headed slowly, painfully, up the road.

The front of 35 Portland Row didn't look too bad. Aside from the magnesium stains on the path, the brightly colored DEPRAC tape wound messily across the gate, and the CONTAMINATED ZONE warning signs plastered on the old black door, you might almost have thought nothing had happened there.

Lockwood pulled the tape off the gate, crumpled it into a sticky ball, and cast it aside. He put his hand on the latch but didn't push it open.

We stood outside in the street looking up at the house.

Only one of the windows was obviously broken, but we could see the remains of boarding over the insides, and they all looked dark and hollow. There was salt and iron crusted on the path, too, presumably left by Barnes's team.

How many times in our careers had we stood like this outside a building rendered terrible by a haunting, where some violent incident or trauma had scarred it psychically down the years? How many times had we picked up our equipment bags and strolled purposefully in? We *never* delayed. Dawdling on the threshold wasn't our thing.

All through the aftermath in the Strand and Scotland Yard, we had maintained our composure and our energies. Now, suddenly, a great weariness descended on us. We stood frozen at the threshold of our own ravaged house.

It was Holly who drew herself up and pushed open the gate. "Come on," she said briskly, "let's get it over with."

Chapter 28

THE ULTIMATE BETRAYAL
Occult experiments in heart of London
Penelope Fittes involvement goes back years
Inside today: M. U. Barnes and A. J. Lockwood
finally speak out

Extraordinary developments continued yesterday in the Fittes House Scandal, a full week after explosions rocked central London, killing company head Penelope Fittes and many others, and leading to revelations that have turned the psychic defense industry upside down. With Fittes House itself still under quarantine, and many employees remaining under arrest, DEPRAC officials have been slow to provide details of either the hidden laboratories discovered beneath the building or of the secret raid that brought them to light. Now, in an exclusive interview with today's *Times of London,* two key players in the raid, Mr. Montagu Barnes of DEPRAC and Mr. Anthony Lockwood of the celebrated Lockwood & Co. agency, come forward to set the record straight.

"In the basement levels of Fittes House," Mr. Lockwood says, "we discovered evidence of unnatural occult experiments using forbidden psychic relics. Stockpiles of illegal explosives were also found, some of which were set off in the fighting that followed our arrival. We were attacked by fearsome ghosts— *and* by dangerous criminals, of whom Penelope Fittes was one."

After a hurried funeral service yesterday, Ms. Fittes's body was interred in the crypt beneath the Fittes mausoleum. Meanwhile, several of her associates at the Sunrise Corporation and other major companies have been arrested. DEPRAC emphasizes, however, that the public need not fear a breakdown in our national paranormal defenses. The Fittes and Rotwell agencies are being reconstituted as the United Psychic Response Agency, under the temporary control of Mr. Barnes. "Rest assured," he says, "that this scandal, shocking though it is, will not deter psychic investigation agencies, big and small, from continuing to serve you in our ongoing battle with the Problem."

According to Mr. Lockwood, the scale of the occult activity at Fittes House was enough to threaten everyone in London. "I know that DEPRAC is investigating the nature of these wicked experiments," he says. "There's no question, however, that

Penelope Fittes was orchestrating them, and had been for many years. It's a grievous betrayal of everything her grandmother stood for. Marissa Fittes will be turning in her grave."

Full Barnes and Lockwood Interviews: see pages 3–6

"Decline and Fall"—the Story of the Fittes Dynasty: see pages 7–11

Anthony Lockwood: "My Style": see fashion pullout, center pages

"What amazes me, Lockwood," I said, looking at him over the top of the newspaper, "is how much you manage to say in this interview, and how little. You and Barnes are as bad as each other now. I'm surprised you're not growing a little bottle-brush mustache."

Lockwood grinned at me from over his paint pot. He was standing by the window of our new spare bedroom, applying a top coat to the wall. A patch of sunlight bathed him, and since the paint was white, and he wore a new white shirt, and it was a particularly sunny morning, the effect was enough to make you shield your eyes. "I know what you mean, Luce," he said. "But you're being harsh. Most of it's accurate enough, in its way."

I folded the newspaper neatly (George would want it for our casebook) and went back to my own painting. "Oh, it's all *kind* of right," I said, "and yet somehow the truth manages to wriggle out of view. Penelope was bad! Technically true. But no mention of Marissa and how her wicked spirit ran the show. Unnatural experiments! True again. But nothing about the spirit gate in the basement, or journeys to the Other Side."

"That's the deal we made, Lucy," Lockwood said. "Barnes was

very persuasive. We know the reasons why. Hey, I think this last wall is almost done. How are you getting on outside, George?"

His voice echoed hollowly across the blank, bare walls of the spare room. The brand-new door swung open, and George looked in. His bruises were beginning to fade, but he still bore the marks of his beating, and—like all of us who had spent time beyond the spirit gate—he moved more slowly than usual. He wore the new pair of glasses he had bought that week, slightly smaller and less round than his previous pair. Even *I* had to admit they were almost stylish. Right now, however, their urbane effect was blunted by his enormous paint-spattered set of jeans. These were of remarkable and sinister bagginess, revealing untold acreages of George whenever he bent over or made sharp turns. He too held a brush; he was in the middle of under-coating the doorframe on the landing.

"I'm progressing well," he said, "though I could do with some breakfast. Oh, this is looking *great* in here. Very fresh, very modern, and not a single hellish portal to the land of the dead in sight. Now that's what *I* call a guest bedroom."

It was certainly a marked improvement on what had come before. Jessica's bedroom had been transformed. The day after the fateful events at Fittes House, Inspector Barnes had sent a DEPRAC clearance team to Portland Row. With some difficulty, they had dismantled the spirit gate and removed the Sources. They had also proposed to take out the ancient bed. After only a moment's hesitation, Lockwood had agreed. He had already noticed that the death-glow hanging over it was gone. The room was peaceful now, stripped bare of psychic tragedy. Jessica's presence no longer hung quite so heavily over either the house or Lockwood's heart. It was time to begin anew.

"I still think we maybe ought to do something about this stain," George said, pointing to the massive circular ectoplasm burn in the center of the floor. "All the eggshell white in the world won't distract people from something that size. Look, you can even see the marks of the chains."

"Got a nice cream carpet coming tomorrow," I said. "It'll all be gone. And a set of bedroom furniture on Friday. The room will be brand-new, and ready to be used again."

"Think Holly *will* want to move in?" George said. We could hear her calling us from the kitchen. "You asked her, Lockwood, I know."

Lockwood left his brush balanced on the paint can; we made for the door. "I don't think she will, actually. She says she likes having a separate place. Did you know she's got a roommate? A girl who works at DEPRAC. That was news to me."

We went downstairs slowly, feet clattering on the wooden steps. The carpet was gone here, too, and the walls were naked, stripped of ornament, marked with bullet holes and spear marks, blackened with magnesium burns. We would have to repaper them, start afresh. It was a big job, but that was okay. The windows were open, and there was a smell of toast and bacon floating upward through the house. It would all be done in time.

In the kitchen the toaster had just pinged, and eggs were frying in the pan. Holly was gathering cereal boxes from one of the new cupboards. It currently lacked a door, and she was simply reaching in and passing them back to Quill Kipps, who sat waiting at the kitchen table. His movements were slow and awkward—the stitches in his side prevented him from using his left arm—and he looked as thin and pale as a reheated corpse, but that last bit was nothing new. Basically he was in good shape. He was the only one of us who didn't have new white flecks in his hair, courtesy of the Other Side. Right now he was frowning at our crisp new Thinking Cloth, which winked out at us behind the spread of breakfast things.

"Holly says I have to christen the new cloth," he said. "Write or draw something on it. Seems a weird ritual."

"Got to do it if you want to join us for breakfast," I said. "That's a rule."

"Just do a rude cartoon," George said. "That always works for me, I find."

Lockwood nodded. "Yes, and it always ruins my appetite."

"Speaking of which—" Holly went over to the toaster. "Lucy, could you *please* move that horrid, disgusting skull away from the center of the table? I don't want to touch it. We're eating now."

"Sorry, Hol."

"I don't know why you insist on having it with us for each meal. It's a lovely sunny day, and it's not going to rematerialize here."

"I suppose it isn't. But you never know. Where are you going to perch, George?"

"Here, next to Quill."

Kipps eyed George's jeans cautiously. "Just try not to bend over too much when you sit down."

I took the laden toast plate from Holly, and went to my chair. Lockwood had already taken his position at the head of the table. He began pouring us all tea.

"Let's see," George said, settling himself with satisfaction. "Tea, toast, eggs, jam, and chocolate spread, various sugary cereals . . . Looks like a traditional Lockwood and Co. breakfast. Wait! What's *that*?"

Holly nodded grimly. "It's that horrid charcoaled skull Lucy insists on carrying around with her. I wouldn't object so much if it was actually in a jar or something."

"I don't mean the skull. I'm talking about those bowls of sunflower seeds and funny healthy nut things. Eeesh, they're not even salted. Where'd we get these?"

"The storeroom," I said. "Holly's got a stash down there."

George gave Holly a reproving look. "You creep down to the basement to secretly eat nuts and seeds? It's not the good you're doing to your body that disappoints me; more the underhandedness of it all. Don't we have any cake?"

"Not for breakfast, we don't," Lockwood said. "Eat up."

George did, and he was right: it *was* a proper Lockwood & Co. breakfast, and it felt good, even if our surroundings weren't as normal. The kitchen had been one of the worst-affected portions of the house, with its doors and windows shattered, most of its furniture destroyed, and bloodstains and scorch marks on the linoleum floor. So we'd stripped the linoleum and removed the broken cupboards. The windows had been replaced. A new back door, unpainted, awaited our attention. Our first priorities had been a replacement table and a Thinking Cloth. With these in place, it was possible to function again. The house would be all right. Like us, it was taking time to heal.

And it *was* a beautiful morning to be healing in. Outside, in the garden, the tree was dark and heavy with apples. The rings of burned grass below the steps and outside the basement door were almost lost in the general greenness. Soon I would pick the apples— I would make time for that this year—and reseed the lawns. We would repaint the windows and repair our basement office. We would build new straw dummies and hang them in the rapier room. We would restock our shelves with books and curios. New artifacts would be found to replace the ones torn from the walls, and new furniture would be bought. We had received a generous stipend from Inspector Barnes for just such a purpose. Above all, we would decide how Lockwood & Co. should begin again.

It was a time of beginnings, and a time of endings.

"How *is* our friend today, Luce?" George asked suddenly. I'd moved the skull away from the center of the table, but it was still sitting by my plate. It was very charred and blackened, and there was a large crack running up from one socket almost to its crown. I could see why Holly objected to its presence, but I didn't care.

"Silent."

"No change, then?"

No, there hadn't been any change. This was the way it had been since the day of the explosion, since I'd pulled it from the mangled remains of the jar amid the steaming debris of the seventh floor. I'd wrapped it up and taken it home, and kept it with me ever since, just in case. But nothing had happened. Whenever I put my fingers on it, I got no psychic charge. The bone was dry and cold.

"Nope, he's still quiet," I said.

Lockwood glanced at the others. "Well, that *was* a pretty big explosion, Luce," he said. "Like the ones DEPRAC let off in the Hall of Pillars. All *those* ghosts are gone, too."

"I know. But that's because their Sources were completely destroyed. Here's his Source," I said. "I saved it. That explosion wouldn't destroy his *spirit*, would it?"

"I don't know. Maybe."

"It wouldn't. I'm sure it wouldn't." I thought of the fireball swallowing up the ghost.

"It might disrupt his connection with the skull," Kipps said.

"No. That doesn't make sense. I guess it's true he won't come back in daylight. He's not protected from the sun by the silver-glass now that he's out of the jar. But at nighttime . . . he *should* come back."

That's what I kept telling myself, but I didn't actually believe my theory. It had been a week now and he hadn't returned.

"Could be he's just . . . gone, Luce," Holly said. She smiled at me. "You freed him from the jar. He helped you in return. Maybe that has encouraged him to do what he *should* have done a century ago—which is move on."

She was probably right. We ate our breakfast. After a while Kipps put down his fork. "Talking of Sources and moving on," he said, "there's something that's been bothering me. I know they buried Penelope's body in the mausoleum, in a special silver casket and all that, but what about Marissa's *real* remains? From what you and Lucy said, Lockwood, her spirit was still linked to it in some way. If the nice body died, wouldn't she just pop back in *there*? And if it's hanging around in some DEPRAC mortuary . . ."

Lockwood smiled. "Don't worry. It isn't. This is something I've been meaning to tell you. When they opened up the crypt yesterday, Barnes and his team took the opportunity of tidying up Marissa's old body, too. You remember how shrunken it was, Luce? They were able to tuck it away in her original coffin, *alongside* the bones of our old pal, the doctor. They'll be nice and snug in there together. I rather think his ghost will be quite pleased." Lockwood paused; he took another piece of toast. "If Marissa's spirit *is* stuck there, I'm not sure she'll enjoy the arrangement quite as much."

The sun shone in on us; we finished our meal, and sat back happily in our chairs.

"Okay," Lockwood said. "There's one bit of important business to attend to today. Yesterday Barnes gave me those official DEPRAC papers, which we all need to sign. You know, they're the ones where we promise not to make public statements about what we saw at Fittes House, about the Other Side—all the secret stuff, basically."

"I don't like having to sign that," I said.

"I know you don't, Luce. None of us are particularly comfortable about it. But we know why we have to. If people knew that the Problem was probably caused by the first psychic detection agents, if they discovered that the heads of many top companies were complicit in what Marissa was doing, there'd be anarchy. Society would fall apart. And to what end? It *still* wouldn't have solved the Problem."

I shook my head. "It's about being honest. DEPRAC needs to come clean."

"First they've got to fix things. Don't forget that Barnes has to keep his side of the bargain with us, too. He's agreed that the spirit gate at Fittes House will not be destroyed. From now on, DEPRAC will work to clear up the mess left by Marissa. That means removing whatever . . . obstructions have been placed on the Other Side."

"The silver fences," Holly said.

"The fences, yes, and whatever else they've been doing to disrupt the onward passage of the dead. The trouble is, we don't yet really understand how their operation worked, or how far they went to gather the spirits' essences. We don't even know whether there are any *other* gates. It seems probable, as the Problem's spread so far across the country."

"Our friends at the Orpheus Society might help," George said, "and the scientists from Fittes House, if DEPRAC applies a bit of pressure."

"I'm sure they will. Even so, it's going to take a long time to unravel this, and there's no telling whether it'll fix the Problem quickly, or at all."

"Meanwhile," I said, "the Visitors will keep on coming."

"I should just mention," Lockwood said, "that Barnes *did* ask me whether we might help out a bit with DEPRAC's clearance program. We're uniquely experienced, he said; they could use our skills. We could give them a lot of advice about how the Other Side—"

"I'm not going back," George interrupted. "No way."

Holly nodded. "Once was enough. Once was *more* than enough."

"Personally speaking," Kipps said, "Dark London's a bit like George's jeans. I feel as if I've already seen too much."

"That's exactly what I told Barnes," Lockwood said. "Except for the bit about the jeans. You're all quite right. We've done our bit.

We'll stick to simple ghosts from now on, and not think about the Other Side or its secrets anymore."

There was a general murmur of approval.

"Of course, you know what *my* theory is?" George said, after a short pause. "Dark London's just an interim stage. You linger awhile, then move on. Those black gates . . ."

"Gates? I saw them as doors," Kipps said.

"Black pools," Lockwood said. "Hanging vertically. All shimmery, but not wet."

"So more like curtains, then?"

"I suppose."

"Getting back to my theory," George went on, "I think the spirit passes through those door things—however you want to call them—and reaches yet another London, but this one's shining with light. . . ."

"Where's your evidence for that?" I asked.

"Haven't got any. Just feel it."

"That's not like you."

George shrugged. "Sometimes research only goes so far."

"You'll have to write a book about it," Lockwood said. "If you do it quick, and publish it when the Problem's fixed, lots of people will buy it and we can make some money."

"Not that we're going to be paupers," Holly said. "We've got hundreds of calls waiting for us to respond. Some *really* juicy cases. With Fittes and Rotwell in such bad odor, we're the most popular agency in London right now. We should take advantage, maybe even hire a new assistant. They could have your little attic, Lucy, and you could move down to the nice new bedroom. . . ."

I grinned at her. "No, that's fine, Hol. I'm very happy upstairs." I stretched back into a patch of sun. "So what are these juicy cases we've got pending?"

"Oh, Luce, you'll *love* them. There's a Screaming Spirit in a vestry; a gabbling voice coming from a well, and a haunted yew tree that utters guttural remarks. Also a cowled Wraith in a shopping center in Staines—my correspondent wasn't sure if it was a nun or a kid in a hoodie—a bleeding boulder in a quarry, a Raw-bones on a barge . . ."

She went on telling me. Lockwood listened, too; from time to time he looked at me across the table. George stole a pen and drew a dubious cartoon that made Kipps choke on his toast. I drank some tea and sat peaceably in our kitchen in the morning sunlight. Beside my plate, a cracked, burned skull stared out at nothing.

I hadn't lied to Holly. I *was* happy with my little attic bedroom. This room alone had been overlooked by our enemies after our flight through the gate, and was just the same as it had always been. I often went there, in the evenings of those first few days, to rest and think a little under the low-slung eaves.

That evening was no different. The windowsill was bathed in the last warm dregs of sunshine. You could see rings in the dust where the ghost-jar used to sit. I set the blackened skull on the sill in its traditional place. Its simple presence satisfied me. If he wanted to return, he would. If not—well, that was good, too.

I stood at the window, and looked down into Portland Row.

The sky was gray and pink, and the sun was shining on the

houses on the opposite side, making them glittery with life. White curtains shone, and the ghost-wards in their windows sparkled. Children were playing in the street below.

There was a knock at the door. I turned and answered, and Lockwood looked in. He had his new long coat on, as if ready to go out, and was clutching a sheaf of papers to his chest.

"Hi, Lucy. Sorry to disturb you."

"Not a problem. Come on in."

We smiled at each other across the little room. In the days since Fittes House we hadn't been alone together much. To begin with, we'd been exhausted and emotionally washed up. It had been a busy week, too, what with trying to fix up the house and negotiating with Barnes. Like the rest of the team, neither of us had wanted to do anything much other than eat and sleep and enjoy the simple mechanics of being alive.

But now he was here. He took a few steps toward me and then stopped. The warmth of his presence filled the space between us. "Sorry to disturb you," he said again. "It's just there's something I wanted to give you, and there's too much going on downstairs. You know, George painting away like a man possessed; Kipps and Holly trying to fix those cupboard doors . . ."

I breathed out sharply. "Yeah, okay. I can see what you're holding. That wretched DEPRAC statement. All right, I'll sign it, but not now. Chuck it down somewhere."

He hesitated. "I'll just put it on the bed, shall I?"

"Yeah."

I turned away and looked out of the window at the iron railings and sparkling ghost-wards. A small kid with a plastic rapier ran down the other side of the street, chasing two of his friends. Lockwood came to stand beside me. He put his hand on the sill, next to mine.

"The Problem's still here," I said, after a pause. "Another half an hour, everyone will be hiding away indoors."

"Maybe things *will* start to improve," Lockwood said, "now that those idiots are no longer messing around on the Other Side. I mean—it *should* help, shouldn't it? More spirits will be free to move on to their proper place, and not come back here."

I just nodded. Truth was, neither of us knew.

Lockwood opened his mouth to say something, then shut it again. For a moment, we didn't speak. He was very close to me. Our hands stayed on the windowsill like they were glued there. All at once he stepped back. "In the meantime," he said, "there are ghosts to foil and lives to save. But right now it's a lovely evening, and I'm going for a stroll. That was the other thing I wanted, to see if you'd come with me." He adjusted his collar. "It's the first outing for my new coat. What do you think of it?"

"It'll need a few claw marks to really make it look like yours, but other than that, it's nice."

"You don't think I ought to get a macho leather jacket, like Barnes?"

"No."

"Okay, well, if you *do* want to come with me, Luce, I'll be in the hall." He went to the door, paused, and grinned back at me. "And don't forget to sign the statement!" With that, he was pattering down the stairs.

As always, I found myself smiling after him. As always, the room felt a little darker after he left. Yes, I *was* going for that stroll. I started over toward the bed to get my jacket. As I did so, I thought I heard a little noise behind me. I turned and—just for an instant—saw a faint and greenish light showing on the windowsill.

I blinked and stared at it, heart racing.

It had probably just been a last reflection of the waning light. My little attic was filled with the dusk of early evening. On the sill, the skull was a squat shadow. Its cracked sockets were black and dull. I could hear George whistling as he painted the door on the landing below.

Probably nothing . . .

Then again, it wasn't yet dark.

For a few seconds I stared across at the quiet windowsill, a smile slowly widening on my face. Then I turned away, and went to get my jacket off the bed.

Lockwood had put the DEPRAC documents beside my jacket. The papers formed a neat rectangle on the darkness of the counterpane, gleaming white in the fading light, but also softly sparkling.

Sparkling . . . ?

I bent close, frowning. It was only then that I saw the beautiful golden necklace curled on the papers, with the sapphire glinting at its heart. Lockwood had taken it out of the old crushed box that his mother had kept it in. Even in the dusk, the gem was glorious, undying and undimmed. It was as if all the light and love it had gathered in the past was shining out on me.

I stood gazing at it for a long time.

Slowly, carefully, I picked up the necklace and hung it around my neck. Then I put on my jacket and ran for the stairs.

Glossary

* indicates a Type One ghost
** indicates a Type Two ghost

Agency, Psychic Investigation—A business specializing in the containment and destruction of **ghosts**. There are more than a dozen agencies in London alone. The largest two (the Fittes Agency and the Rotwell Agency) have hundreds of employees; the smallest (Lockwood & Co.) has four. Most agencies are run by adult supervisors, but all rely heavily on children with strong psychic **Talent**.

Apparition—The shape formed by a **ghost** during a **manifestation**. Apparitions usually mimic the shape of the dead person, but animals and objects are also seen. Some can be quite unusual. The **Specter** in the recent Limehouse Docks case manifested as a greenly glowing king cobra, while the infamous Bell Street Horror took the guise of a patchwork doll.

Aura—The radiance surrounding many **apparitions**. Most auras are fairly faint, and are seen best out of the corner of the eye. Strong, bright auras are known as **other-light**. A few **ghosts**, such as **Dark Specters**, radiate black auras that are darker than the night around them.

Bone Man*—Name given to a particular variety of **Type One ghost**, probably a sub-type of **Shade**. Bone Men are hairless, emaciated forms, with skin clinging to their skulls and rib cages. They glow with a bright, pale **other-light**. Though superficially similar to some **Wraiths**, they are always passive and generally somewhat dismal.

Chain net—A net made of finely spun **silver** chains; a versatile variety of **Seal**.

Chill—The sharp drop in temperature that occurs when a **ghost** is near. One of the four usual indicators of an imminent **manifestation**, the others being **malaise**, **miasma**, and **creeping fear**. Chill may extend over a wide area, or be concentrated in specific cold spots.

Cluster—A group of **ghosts** occupying a small area.

Creeping fear—A sense of inexplicable dread often experienced in the buildup to a **manifestation**. Often accompanied by **chill**, **miasma**, and **malaise**.

Curfew—In response to the **Problem**, the British Government enforces nightly curfews in many inhabited areas. During curfew, which begins shortly after dusk and finishes at dawn, ordinary people are encouraged to remain indoors, safe behind their home **defenses**. In many towns, the beginning and end of the night's curfew are marked by the sounding of a warning bell.

Dark Specter**—A frightening variety of **Type Two ghost** that manifests as a moving patch of darkness. Sometimes the **apparition** at the center of the darkness is dimly visible; at other times the black cloud is fluid and formless, perhaps shrinking to the size of a pulsing heart, or expanding at speed to engulf a room.

Death-glow—An energy trace left at the exact spot where a death took place. The more violent the death, the brighter the glow. Strong glows may persist for many years.

Defenses against ghosts—The three principal defenses, in order of effectiveness, are **silver**, **iron**, and **salt**. **Lavender** also affords some protection, as does bright light and running **water**.

DEPRAC—The Department of Psychic Research and Control. A government organization devoted to tackling the **Problem**. DEPRAC investigates the nature of **ghosts**, seeks to destroy the most dangerous ones, and monitors the activities of the many competing **agencies**.

Ectoplasm—A strange, variable substance from which **ghosts** are formed. In its concentrated state, ectoplasm is very harmful to the living.

Fetch**—A rare and unnerving class of **ghost** that appears in the shape of another person, usually someone known to the onlooker. Fetches are seldom aggressive, but the fear and disorientation they evoke is so strong that most experts classify them as **Type Two** spirits, to be treated with extreme caution.

Fittes furnaces—The popular name for the Greater London Metropolitan Furnaces for the Disposal of Psychic Artifacts, in Clerkenwell, where dangerous psychic **Sources** are destroyed by fire.

Fittes Manual—A famous book of instruction for ghost-hunters written by Marissa Fittes, the founder of Britain's first psychic investigation **agency**.

Ghost—The spirit of a dead person. Ghosts have existed throughout history, but—for unclear reasons—are now increasingly common. There are many varieties; broadly speaking, however, they can be organized into three main groups (*See* **Type One, Type Two, Type Three**). Ghosts always linger near a **Source**, which is often the place of their death. They are at their strongest after dark, and most particularly between the hours of midnight and two a.m. Most are unaware of or uninterested in the living. A few are actively hostile.

Ghost-bomb—A weapon consisting of a **ghost** trapped in a **silver-glass** prison. When the glass breaks, the spirit emerges to spread fear and **ghost-touch** among the living.

Ghost-cult—A group of people who, for a variety of reasons, share an unhealthy interest in the returning dead.

Ghost-fog—A thin greenish-white mist, occasionally produced during a **manifestation**. Possibly formed of **ectoplasm**, it is cold and unpleasant, but not itself dangerous to the touch.

Ghost-jar—A **silver-glass** receptacle used to constrain an active **Source**.

Ghost-lamp—An electrically powered streetlight that sends out beams of strong white light to discourage **ghosts**. Most ghost-lamps have shutters fixed over their glass lenses; these snap on and off at intervals throughout the night.

Ghost-lock—A dangerous power displayed by **Type Two ghosts**, possibly an extension of **malaise**. Victims are sapped of their willpower, and overcome by a feeling of terrible despair. Their muscles seem as heavy as lead, and they can no longer think or move freely. In most cases they end up transfixed, waiting helplessly as the hungry ghost glides closer and closer. . . . *See also* **psychic enchainment**.

Ghost-touch—The effect of bodily contact with an **apparition**, and the most deadly power of an aggressive **ghost**. Beginning with a sensation of sharp, overwhelming cold, ghost-touch swiftly spreads an icy numbness around the body. One after another, vital organs fail; soon the body turns bluish and starts to swell. Without swift medical intervention, often in the form of adrenaline injections to stimulate the heart, ghost-touch is usually fatal.

Glamour—The ability of some ghosts to *appear* beautiful and good, even if the reality is markedly different. It often takes great effort of will for an onlooker to see past this illusion.

Glimmer*—The faintest perceptible **Type One ghost**. Glimmers manifest only as flecks of **other-light** flitting through the air. They can be touched or walked through without harm.

Greek Fire—Another name for **magnesium flares**. Early weapons of this kind were apparently used against **ghosts** during the days of the Eastern Roman Empire, a thousand years ago.

Haunting—*See* **Manifestation**.

Ichor—**Ectoplasm** in its thickest, most concentrated form. It burns many materials, and is safely constrained only by **silver-glass**.

Iron—An ancient and important protection against **ghosts** of all kinds. Ordinary people fortify their homes with iron decorations, and carry it on their persons in the form of **wards**. Agents carry iron **rapiers** and chains, and so rely on it for both attack and defense.

Lavender—The strong sweet smell of this plant is thought to discourage evil spirits. As a result, many people wear dried sprigs of lavender, or burn it to release the pungent smoke. Agents sometimes carry vials of lavender water or small explosive lavender grenades to use against weak **Type Ones**.

Limbless**—A swollen, misshapen variety of **Type Two ghost**, with a generally human head and torso, but lacking recognizable arms and legs.

With **Wraiths** and **Raw-bones,** one of the least pleasing **apparitions.** Often accompanied by strong sensations of **miasma** and **creeping fear.**

Listening—One of the three main categories of psychic **Talent. Sensitives** with this ability are able to hear the voices of the dead, echoes of past events, and other unnatural sounds associated with **manifestations.**

Lurker*—A variety of **Type One ghost** that hangs back in the shadows, rarely moving, never approaching the living, but spreading strong feelings of anxiety and **creeping fear.**

Magnesium flare—A metal canister with a breakable glass seal, containing magnesium, iron, salt, gunpowder and an igniting device. An important **agency** weapon against aggressive **ghosts.**

Malaise—A feeling of despondent lethargy often experienced when a **ghost** is approaching. In extreme cases this can deepen into dangerous **ghost-lock.**

Manifestation—A ghostly occurrence. May involve all kinds of supernatural phenomena, including sounds, smells, odd sensations, moving objects, drops in temperature, and the glimpse of **apparitions.**

Miasma—An unpleasant atmosphere, often including disagreeable tastes and smells, experienced in the run-up to a **manifestation.** Regularly accompanied by **creeping fear, malaise,** and **chill.**

Night watch—Groups of children, usually working for large companies and local government councils, who guard factories, offices, and public areas after dark. Though not allowed to use **rapiers,** night-watch children have long **iron**-tipped spears to keep **apparitions** at bay.

Operative—Another name for a psychic investigation agent.

Other-light—An eerie, unnatural light radiating from some **apparitions.**

Pale Stench*—A **Type One ghost** that spreads a dreadful miasma, a smell of noxious decay. Best confronted by burning sticks of **lavender.**

Phantasm**—Any **Type Two ghost** that maintains an airy, delicate, and see-through form. A Phantasm may be almost invisible, aside from its faint outline and a few wispy details of its face and features. Despite its insubstantial appearance, it is no less aggressive than the more solid-seeming **Specter**, and all the more dangerous for being harder to see.

Phantom—Another general name for a **ghost**.

Plasm—*See* **Ectoplasm**.

Poltergeist**—A powerful and destructive class of **Type Two ghost**. Poltergeists release strong bursts of supernatural energy that can lift even heavy objects into the air. They do not form **apparitions**.

Problem, the—The epidemic of hauntings currently affecting Britain.

Psychic enchainment—While most **Type Two ghosts** sap a victim's willpower using **ghost-lock**, some are able to ensnare onlookers by making a psychic connection with them. Typically, the victim will become fascinated with the **apparition** and seek to follow it at all costs, even if this costs them their life. Such ghosts usually appear charming or seductive or empathetic: they do this using the weapon of **glamour**.

Rapier—The official weapon of all psychic investigation agents. The tips of the **iron** blades are sometimes coated with **silver**.

Raw-bones**—A rare and unpleasant kind of **ghost**, which manifests as a bloody, skinless corpse with goggling eyes and grinning teeth. Not popular with agents. Many authorities regard it as a variety of **Wraith**.

Relic-man/relic-woman—Someone who locates **Sources** and other psychic artifacts and sells them on the black market.

Revenant**—A fortunately rare variety of **Type Two ghost** in which the **apparition** can temporarily animate its own corpse and cause it to break free of its grave. Though Revenants generate powerful **ghost-lock** and strong waves of **creeping fear**, they are easy to deal with because their body *is* their **Source**, thus giving an agent plenty of opportunity to encase them in **silver**. Also, if the corpse is old, it usually falls to pieces before doing too much damage.

Salt—A commonly used **defense** against **Type One ghosts**. Less effective than **iron** and **silver**, salt is cheaper than both, and used in many household deterrents.

Salt-bomb—A small plastic throwing-globe filled with **salt**. Shatters on impact, spreading salt in all directions. Used by agents to drive back weaker **ghosts**. Less effective against stronger entities.

Salt-gun—A device that projects a fine spray of salty water across a wide area. A useful weapon against **Type One ghosts**. Increasingly employed by larger **agencies**.

Screaming Spirit**—A feared **Type Two ghost**, which may or may not display any kind of visual **apparition**. Screaming Spirits emit terrifying psychic shrieks, the sound of which is sometimes enough to paralyze the listener with fright, and so bring on **ghost-lock**.

Seal—An object, usually of **silver** or **iron**, designed to enclose or cover a **Source**, and prevent the escape of its **ghost**.

Sensitive, a—Someone who is born with unusually good psychic **Talent**. Most Sensitives join **agencies** or the **night watch**; others provide psychic services without actually confronting **Visitors**.

Shade*—The standard **Type One ghost**, and possibly the most common kind of **Visitor**. Shades may appear quite solid, in the manner of **Specters**, or be insubstantial and wispy, like **Phantasms**; however, they entirely lack the dangerous intelligence of either. Shades seem unaware of the presence of the living, and are usually bound into a fixed pattern of behavior. They project feelings of grief and loss, but seldom display anger or any stronger emotion. They almost always appear in human form.

Sight—The psychic ability to see **apparitions** and other ghostly phenomena, such as **death-glows**. One of the three main varieties of psychic **Talent**.

Silver—An important and potent defense against **ghosts**. Worn by many people as **wards** in the form of jewelry. Agents use it to coat their **rapiers**, and as a crucial component of their **Seals**.

Silver-glass—A special "ghost-proof" glass used to encase **Sources**.

Snuff-light—A type of small candle used by psychic investigation **agencies** to indicate a supernatural presence. They flicker, tremble, and finally snuff out if a **ghost** draws near.

Solitary**—An unusual **Type Two ghost**, often encountered in remote and perilous places, generally outdoors. Visually it often wears the guise of a slender child, seen at a distance across a ravine or lake. It never draws close to the living, but radiates an extreme form of **ghost-lock** that may overwhelm anyone nearby. Victims of Solitaries often hurl themselves over cliffs or into deep water in an effort to end it all.

Source—The object or place through which a **ghost** enters the world.

Specter**—The most commonly encountered **Type Two ghost**. A Specter always forms a clear, detailed **apparition**, which may in some cases seem almost solid. It is usually an accurate visual echo of the deceased as they were when alive or newly dead. Specters are less nebulous than **Phantasms** and less hideous than **Wraiths**, but equally varied in behavior. Many are neutral or benign in their dealings with the living—perhaps returning to reveal a secret, or make right an ancient wrong. Some, however, are actively hostile, and hungry for human contact. These ghosts should be avoided at all costs.

Stone Knocker*—A desperately uninteresting **Type One ghost**, which does precious little apart from tap.

Talent—The ability to see, hear, or otherwise detect **ghosts**. Many children, though not all, are born with a degree of psychic Talent. This skill tends to fade toward adulthood, though it still lingers in some grown-ups. Children with better-than-average Talent join the **night watch**. Exceptionally gifted children usually join the **agencies**. The three main categories of Talent are **Sight**, **Listening**, and **Touch**.

Touch—The ability to detect psychic echoes from objects that have been closely associated with a death or **haunting**. Such echoes take the form of visual images, sounds, and other sense impressions. One of the three main varieties of **Talent**.

Type One—The weakest, most common, and least dangerous grade of **ghost**. Type Ones are scarcely aware of their surroundings, and often locked into a single, repetitious pattern of behavior. Commonly encountered examples include: **Shades** and **Lurkers**. *See also*: **Bone Man**, **Glimmer**, **Pale Stench**, **Stone Knocker**, and **Wisp**.

Type Two—The most dangerous commonly occurring grade of **ghost**. Type Twos are stronger than **Type Ones**, and possess some kind of residual intelligence. They are aware of the living, and may attempt to do them harm. The most common Type Twos, in order, are: **Specters**, **Phantasms**, and **Wraiths**. *See also*: **Dark Specter, Fetch, Limbless, Poltergeist, Raw-bones, Revenant, Screaming Spirit**, and **Solitary**.

Type Three—A very rare grade of **ghost**, first reported by Marissa Fittes, and the subject of much controversy ever since. Allegedly able to communicate fully with the living.

Vanishing point—The exact spot where a **ghost** dematerializes at the end of a **manifestation**. Often an excellent clue to the location of the **Source**.

Visitor—A **ghost**.

Ward—An object, usually of **iron** or **silver**, used to keep **ghosts** away. Small wards may be worn as jewelry on the person; larger ones, hung up around the house, are often equally decorative.

Water, running—It was observed in ancient times that **ghosts** dislike crossing running water. In modern Britain this knowledge is sometimes used against them. In central London a net of artificial channels, or runnels, protects the main shopping district. On a smaller scale, some homeowners build open channels outside their front doors and divert the rainwater along them.

Wisp*—Weak and generally unthreatening, a Wisp is a **Type One ghost** that manifests as a pale and flickering flame. Some scholars speculate that all ghosts, given time, degenerate into Wisps, then **Glimmers**, before finally vanishing altogether.

Wraith**—A dangerous **Type Two ghost**. Wraiths are similar to **Specters** in strength and patterns of behavior, but are far more horrible to look at. Their **apparitions** show the deceased in his or her dead state: gaunt and shrunken, horribly thin, sometimes rotten and wormy. Wraiths often appear as skeletons. They radiate a powerful **ghost-lock**. *See also* **Raw-bones**.

Not ready to say good-bye to
Lockwood, Lucy, and George? Enjoy
"The Dagger in the Desk," a

Lockwood
&Co.

short story.

Chapter 1

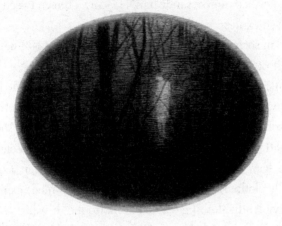

It was a winter's morning, the day after the messy conclusion to the Case of the Floating Fingers, and Lockwood, George, and I had assembled in the kitchen for a very late breakfast. Rapiers, chains, and salt-bombs lay scattered on the table. George's jacket, peppered with ectoplasm burns, hung steaming on a chair. A severed hand, securely contained in a silver-glass case, sat by the cornflakes, ready for disposal later. This sort of thing is normal in our house, and it didn't spoil our appetite. We were just helping ourselves to another round of tea and toast when there was a clanging on the bell outside.

"Could be a client," Lockwood said. "Go see who it is, Lucy."

I frowned. "Why me?"

"I'm still in my pajamas and George's face is covered in jam."

They were decent points; I couldn't argue with them. I answered the door. On the step stood a small, roundish man with a pink face and a disheveled mop of sandy hair. He wore a brown tweed suit and a wild-eyed expression of deep horror.

"I—I'm sorry to disturb you, miss," he said, "but I—I believe I've seen a ghost."

I smiled cheerily. "Then that's our business, sir. Come in."

If anything, the man's unease grew worse once I'd settled him on the sofa with a biscuit and a cup of tea. His fingers shook, his teeth chattered, his eyes darted side to side as if he expected something to leap from the wall and devour him. When Lockwood (now fully clothed) and George (partially de-jammed) came in, he jumped violently, sloshing tea down the front of his shirt.

Lockwood shook his hand. "I'm Anthony Lockwood. These are my associates, George Cubbins and Lucy Carlyle. How can we help you today?"

"My name," the pink-faced man said, "is Samuel Whitaker, and I am the headmaster of St. Simeon's Academy for Talented Youngsters, a well-known school in Hammersmith. It is an old school, but much modernized over the years. Only last month, indeed, we opened a new library, and it was then"—he swallowed audibly—"that the *incidents* began.

"It was the children who noticed the change first," Mr. Whitaker went on. "Pupils in class 2A. They complained of an unpleasant odor in the air. Of course, 2A is just along from the boys' toilets, so I thought nothing of it. But they also spoke of a spreading chill, a feeling of inexplicable dread—and of hearing a faint clinking sound."

"What kind of clinking?" George asked. "Chains?"

"I don't know. I am an adult. I heard nothing."

"When do these phenomena occur?"

"Always late afternoon, as the light starts fading. Anyway, yesterday things got worse. I was teaching in class 2A. Just as the pupils were packing up, complaining again of the cold and the troubling smell, something was thrown into the classroom. It smashed straight through the glass of the door, whizzed through the air, and plunged deep into the side of my desk. A knife, Mr. Lockwood! A long, thin knife with an antique handle! When I got over my shock, I ran outside and looked up and down the corridor. Just for a moment, I fancied I saw—out of the corner of my eye—a shadow standing by the library door: a hunched and disfigured shape. I turned my head—and the presence was gone. Yet I had the impression that something was watching me, something filled with terrible wickedness and spite . . ." Mr. Whitaker shuddered. "That was enough for me! I have closed the school and come to you in the hope that you will help."

"We will certainly do our best," Lockwood said. "One question: Where is the knife?"

The headmaster blinked. "It was deeply embedded in the desk and I could not pull it free. I left it when we evacuated the classroom. It will still be there."

Lockwood clicked his tongue. "I hope so . . . Well, we will find out tonight. Is class 2A in one of the original sections of the school?"

"Yes, it is a hundred years old. You can tell from the wood paneling on the wall."

"Is it close to the new library?"

"Not far. Just along the corridor."

"Thank you, Mr. Whitaker," Lockwood said. "That's fine. We'll be at St. Simeon's an hour before dusk. You will leave the door open, I hope?"

"Certainly . . ." The little man hesitated. "But I trust you won't want me to—"

Lockwood grinned. "Don't worry, we'll look around on our own." He stood and held out his hand. "Well, good-bye. We'll report to you first thing tomorrow."

"So what do we think?" I said as we watched our client totter down the path and hurry up the road. "A Poltergeist?"

Lockwood shook his head. "Poltergeists chuck things around, but they don't take bodily form, do they? And Whitaker saw a shadow."

George had taken off his glasses and was polishing them dubiously. "I don't like it," he muttered. "I don't like it at all. This is a ghost strong enough to throw sharp objects around before it's even dark! We're going to have to be careful."

"Oh, you worry too much, George," Lockwood said. "It'll all be fine." He stretched his arms and yawned. "Now, who wants another piece of toast?"

The day grew late. We worked in our basement office, sorting through our equipment. Ghosts hate iron and silver, and they don't much like salt, either, so most of our equipment involves combinations of these. I tested the links on our protective iron chains. George refilled our canisters of salt and iron filings. Lockwood handed us each an explosive magnesium flare. We checked our work belts, and did a final bit of sword practice in the rapier room. After that, we wolfed down some sandwiches, shouldered our bags, and set off for Hammersmith. It was a squally, gloomy afternoon, and the wind blew leaves and litter across the road in little gusts. The ghost-lamps were already on.

St. Simeon's Academy for Talented Youngsters turned out to be a rambling set of unattractive buildings situated not far from the highway overpass. The main schoolhouse, stained dark from years of London smoke, was a mess of steep roofs, gothic turrets, and narrow windows that glinted blackly as we approached. Newer, equally ugly wings in glass and concrete stretched on either side.

George considered it gloomily. "That place is simply *packed* with ghosts," he said. "I can just tell."

"Nothing we can't handle," Lockwood said. "Right, here's the door."

A single light burned in the front porch, and the door creaked open to the touch. Lockwood stepped in first; I followed. George came along behind.

We looked around.

We were in a tiled foyer, with kids' art on the walls and a receptionist's desk along one wall. The air had that familiar tang of floor polish, socks, and stale dinners that most schools share. Ahead of us a long paneled corridor stretched away, punctuated by heavy doors. The shadows were lengthening now; the light was almost gone. The end of the corridor could not be seen.

We stood there, using our individual Talents. Lockwood and George looked for ghostly traces. I listened for spectral sounds.

All was very quiet. Nothing could be heard. Or *almost* nothing, because just for a moment I thought I caught a faint, metallic rattling. . . .

Gone. It wasn't anywhere close. Not yet.

"All right," Lockwood said. "Let's push on. We'll go straight to class 2A."

George held up his hand. "Wait a sec, Lockwood. First rule of investigation: always establish a safe base before going deep into a haunted building. We should rig up a strong iron circle here, so we can retreat inside it if anything goes wrong."

Lockwood frowned. "No point putting iron down here. We're miles from the ghost. It's a waste of a chain."

George glared at him from behind his little spectacles. "Dozens of agents get killed every year because they don't bother with the correct precautions! It won't take a minute, and it's better to be safe than sorry."

"Well, *I* think we need to go straight to the heart of things and hunt the enemy out," Lockwood said. "What do you think, Lucy?"

"I'm just wondering whether we should pay a visit to this new library," I said. "According to Whitaker, the hauntings only began when it was built. Maybe the construction work disturbed something—perhaps *that's* where we'll find the ghost."

Lockwood nodded slowly. "That's not a bad point, Luce," he said. "We'll take a peek in the library on the way to the classroom, do some readings there. Speaking of which—what's the temperature now?"

George, who'd been grumbling under his breath because we'd ignored his advice, unclipped his belt thermometer and checked the luminous display. "Sixty degrees."

"Okay. Keep watch on it. Let me know if it starts changing."

A sudden, unexpected fall in temperature is one sure sign of upcoming supernatural activity. Sometimes it's a hint that saves your life. In the case of the Bay House Horror, I saw the temp plunge ten degrees when I walked inside that attic bathroom. It gave me just enough time to draw my sword before the Wraith stepped through the tiles.

But sixty degrees seemed safe enough. Adjusting our bags, keeping our hands close to our belts, we set off up the corridor.

It was clearly an original part of the school, with oak paneling covering the lower half of the plastered walls. Ranks of notice-boards and photographs rose almost to the ceiling. There were sports teams, prize winners, and whole-school photos, with rows of pupils and teachers staring at the camera. It was too dark to make out the details. To keep our senses sharp, we mostly kept our flash-lights off—flicking them on occasionally to check the signs outside each door.

"Class 1A, 1B . . ." Lockwood murmured. "1C . . . the science lab. Where *is* this library, anyway?"

A sound echoed in the darkness—a deep, harsh creaking, instantly cut off.

I stopped short. "Was that your stomach, George?"

He looked at me blankly. "Was what my stomach? I didn't hear anything."

"Nor me," Lockwood said. "What did you get, Lucy?"

That's my Talent, you see. I hear things other people don't. "A horrid, wrenching creak. Sort of like a rusted door hinge, or a coffin lid opening."

"What?" George said. "And you thought that was me?"

"Your belly makes weird sounds when you're hungry."

He paused. "Fair enough. I suppose it does."

"Where was this noise?" Lockwood asked.

"Somewhere up ahead, maybe. I don't know."

"Good. So we're going in the right direction."

We continued steadily, our boots ringing faintly on the wooden floor, and soon came to the end of the main corridor. Side passages branched out left and right. Ahead of us was a prominent glazed door, somehow more modern than the ones we'd passed. There was an engraved wooden sign on the wall. Lockwood shone his flashlight on it.

"'Ernest Potts Memorial Library,'" he read. "Here we are, then."

As he spoke, a cool breeze flowed over us, a stirring of the air. We swung our flashlights wildly up and down the passages, but saw nothing.

"Temperature's down," George said. "Fifty-two degrees now."

"Rapiers at the ready," Lockwood said. He opened the door.

Nothing jumped out at us, which is always nice. The library was large and airy, with pleasant, trendy shelves of light-colored pine. It smelled new. Rows of neatly ordered books covered the walls. Tall windows looked out over a small, drab playing field. There was a half moon in the sky over London, lighting the room with a feeble light.

Without words George opened his bag, took out a length of iron chain, and began laying out a protective circle in the center of the floor. Lockwood didn't protest. He looked and I listened for danger. We didn't get anything.

A small plinth sat on the wall between the central windows. On it was a marble bust of a stern, well-fed Victorian-looking man sporting an enormous pair of muttonchop whiskers. I went to take a look.

"'Ernest Potts,'" I said, reading the plaque below it. "'Headmaster, 1925–1957.' He looks a dreadful old grump."

"What sideburns!" Lockwood said, marveling. "You could stuff a cushion with all that hair. I wonder if—"

"Hold it!" I said. "I hear something."

Silence in the library. We listened. We stood dead still.

Out in the corridor, beyond the half-closed door, there came a soft, intermittent chinking sound. Not far off, and coming closer. And with it now: the sound of footsteps, limping footsteps—a firm step, then a drawn-out *drag*, as if a lame leg was being laboriously swung along the floor. . . .

"Got it," Lockwood whispered suddenly. "I hear it, too. Get inside the chains."

We stepped inside the circle.

"Temperature's dropping," George muttered. "Forty-five degrees . . . Now six . . ."

We took our rapiers from our belts.

Closer, closer came the horrid dragging footsteps. Closer came the clinking sound.

"Keys," I breathed. "It sounds like keys."

"Forty-one degrees," George said calmly. His breath was pluming in the air.

We stood and faced the door.

The footsteps stopped. Thin threads of ghost-fog came trickling round the side of the door. Cold blistered my skin.

Something struck the door on the outside, making the wood reverberate. It struck the wood again.

"Lockwood," I hissed. "What do we do?"

"We sit tight," Lockwood said. "It's loud, it's scary, but it's not actually attacking us directly. If it comes in the room, that's a different matter. Wait and see."

Even as he spoke, a third colossal bang resounded on the door. Flakes of plaster fell from the ceiling, and the floor shuddered. George and I flinched back inside the circle. We raised our rapiers, tensed our muscles, waited—

Waited . . .

Nothing came through.

Silence fell outside the door. A pressure lifted from the room. The little trails of ghost-fog dwindled and were gone.

We each exhaled long and loudly. I hadn't realized I'd been holding my breath.

"Temp's back to fifty degrees," George reported.

Lockwood nodded. "It's over. For now." He stepped from the circle, strode to the door, and flung it open. We emerged into the darkened corridor, shining our flashlights all around. Straight ahead, and to left and right, the passages stretched away. All was still.

"Nothing," George said.

"Not *quite*," Lockwood said soberly. "Look at this." He angled his flashlight's beam at the wall beside the door, shining it on the wooden plate, the one that said "Ernest Potts Memorial Library." The sign didn't look quite as smart as it had before: two great, deep gashes had been scored diagonally across the wood, carving through the words. A knife might have done it. Or claws. Or long, sharp fingernails. There were lots of possibilities, basically, and none of them too pleasant.

"Is it just me," I said, "or is something not very happy about this nice new library?"

George was squinting at the sign through his thick, round glasses. "Either that or it doesn't like this Ernest Potts geezer. Look at the way his name's sliced up."

I nodded. "Maybe it took exception to his ridiculous facial hair. I know I did."

"Whatever the reason," Lockwood said, "I don't feel that the library is quite at the center of the haunting. Our readings weren't strong enough inside. The Source must be somewhere else."

Oh, did I mention Sources before? Here's the thing about ghosts, you see. They don't just float about wherever they like. All of them are tied to a specific thing or place—the spot where they died, something important to them in life, or (most often) their bodily remains. We call this tethering point the Source, and *that's* what agents look for. Find it and destroy it, or seal it up with silver—and that's the end of the haunting. Then you can all go home for tea.

"We'd better check out that classroom now," Lockwood was saying. "Take a look at this mysterious knife, which— Yes, George? What is it?"

George was jiggling about urgently. Either he suddenly had to use the restroom, or he'd had an idea. Or both. Sometimes the two *did* go together. Whichever, it was best not to ignore him.

"I might hang out in the library, if that's all right," he said. "I want to see if there's a book about the school's history, or some old school magazines or something. I'd like to discover a bit more about old headmaster Potts if I can. You never know, it might come in useful."

This is George's forte—he finds stuff out. Lockwood nodded. "Sure you'll be okay on your own?"

"Of course. You don't need to hold my hand. I can lug anything I find inside the chains and read them in there. I'll be absolutely safe. See you in a bit."

George went back into the library. Lockwood and I set off down the left-hand passage. We were once again in an old portion of the school, with walls of paneling and plaster. A number of doors opened on our left, and we checked them briefly as we went. The first was a storeroom, filled with mops, vacuum cleaners, and stacks of toilet paper. The temperature was chilly here: scarcely forty-five degrees. The next was little more than a walk-in storage closet, containing paper, pens, and other stationery. It, too, was very cold. The third, the boys' toilets, was stinky, but much warmer—almost twelve degrees. The fourth—

The fourth was an open door. We didn't need to read its sign to know it was the one we sought. Its window panel had been smashed; bright shards of glass glinted in our flashlight beams and crunched beneath our boots as we entered the room.

Everywhere was evidence of the pupils' rapid departure the day before: books and pencil cases littering the table, bags and coats lying crumpled on the floor. At the front of the class, the teacher's chair lay upended. And close by, jutting from the side of the desk that faced the door, we found the object that had so terrified Mr. Whitaker.

It was a long, thin-bladed knife. The hilt was wound with leather strips, very old and frayed. Fragments of gray cobwebs hung from it, too, swaying slightly in small movements of the air.

"That's not an ordinary knife," I said. "That's a dagger."

"You know what it looks like to me?" Lockwood said slowly. "An old military weapon. If I had to guess, I'd say First World War issue, the kind all soldiers carried."

"Well, where's it come from?"

"Answer that, and we find our ghost." Lockwood straightened. "Listen, Lucy—I'm going to double-check farther down the corridor. I'm pretty sure there'll be nothing to find; I think the Source is between here and the library. I'll be back in a minute, but while I'm gone, just start some readings in the classroom, would you?"

"Sure."

He slipped out the door and was gone into the dark. I scarcely noticed him go. I was too busy staring at the dagger in the desk. One of my Talents, you see, is that of Touch. Sometimes, if I hold an object that has some kind of psychic charge, I feel or hear things associated with its past. Not every time. It doesn't always work. And if the psychic charge is too strong, it can be uncomfortable or even dangerous for me. But the insights *are* often useful.

I stared at the dagger and wondered if I should risk it. . . .

Of *course* I should! I was an agent. Taking horrible risks was part of the job description. We might as well have put it on our business cards.

I reached down and placed my fingers on the hilt.

At first there was nothing: nothing but the cool roughness of the leather strips that had been wrapped tightly round the metal. Nothing but the icky-sticky wispiness of the cobwebs trailing against my skin. I closed my eyes, tried to empty out my mind.

And all at once sensations came.

I took a sharp breath in. They weren't nice sensations, and they filled me with a swirling tide of bitterness and fury. There was pain and dull resentment there, and envy, too. But most of all there was *greed*—a hard, tight avarice that lusted after valuable things. Fleeting images came and went: I saw laughing children, school passages and classrooms (old-fashioned, but recognizably the same as the ones we now explored), and (dimly) soldiers struggling in a muddy field. But by far the strongest picture was that of an open box or chest filled with coins, and it brought with it a feeling of dark glee.

I nearly took my hand away then, but suddenly, rising from the past, I saw a face I recognized—a beefy face with enormous side-whiskers. It gazed at me fiercely and seemed to speak. And now I was awash with fear and hate, and I was fleeing through the corridors, trying to get away, trying to reach my secret place. . . . A door slammed. . . . I was alone and safe! Safe for the moment! And, best of all, I still had my precious—

"*Lucy!*"

My eyes snapped open. The voice broke through my trance. I snatched my hand away from the knife and, turning, peered through the open classroom door and down the passage. I did so almost blindly. It's always hard when you've used the Talent. Your head's all woozy, and your senses don't quite work. Like waking from a dream, it takes you a few moments to come around. Plus it was very dark.

"*Lucy . . .*"

Halfway back toward the library, I saw a figure standing, tall and thin. It beckoned to me quickly.

"Lockwood?" I felt in my belt for my flashlight. "Is that you?"

The shape beckoned once more; slipped out of sight toward one of the storerooms. By the time I'd stabbed my flashlight on, it was gone.

"Lockwood?" I called again.

No answer. But I'd heard the urgency in the voice, seen the eager beckoning. I hurried out of the classroom and down along the corridor. It was very cold out there.

"*Lucy . . .*"

No mistake this time. The voice came from behind the door to the storage closet. I reached out to turn the handle . . .

A cough sounded right behind me.

I whirled round, shone my flashlight up. Lockwood stood there—calm, unflustered, one eyebrow elegantly raised.

"Luce. What are you doing? I thought I told you to stay in the classroom."

I blinked at him foolishly. "Er . . . yes, you did. But didn't you just call me?"

He looked at me.

"Didn't you just beckon me to come?"

"I did neither. I've just been exploring further down the corridor like I said I was going to. As predicted, I found nothing. Because it's *here* that the action is. As you've just proved. What did you see?"

I shuddered, looked toward the cupboard door. "I don't know. But whatever it was, it wanted me to join it in there."

Lockwood's eyes narrowed. "Well, perhaps we can oblige it shortly. But only when we're properly armed. Learn anything in the classroom?"

I took a deep breath. It's always hard to express what you get through psychic sensations. But I didn't even have a chance to try this time, because at that moment a loud, shrill, and unmistakably George-like scream resounded down the corridor from the library. It echoed off the walls and faded.

Lockwood and I stared at each other, wide-eyed.

"Oh, you know what George is like," Lockwood said. "He's probably dropped an encyclopedia on his toe."

Even so, he was already running.

Well, it wasn't a *single* encyclopedia that was the problem, as we discovered when we burst into the library. To aid his reading George had evidently taken a lantern from his bag and set it burning inside the iron circle, and by its flickering light we saw a startling scene. Almost all the books that had been so neatly arranged around the shelves had been ripped out and hurled across the room. They lay scattered every which way, spines up, spines down, pages ruffling and twitching. The only spot free of them was the space inside the iron chains, and it was there that George was crouching, white-faced, hands crossed protectively over his head.

"I know you're an avid reader, George," Lockwood remarked, "but this is a bit messy even for y—"

"Watch out!" George's cry came too late. Even as he spoke a heavy, hard-backed book struck Lockwood in the side of the head, sending him toppling to the floor. And now hosts of others were rising into the air, carried by a random, unseen force. They whizzed this way and that, thumping into walls, bouncing off the windows. I dived to the side: one shot straight past me and crashed against a shelf. All across the room, books were shifting, shelves rattling, chair and table legs scraping as they moved across the floor. On the plinth beside the windows, the marble bust of Ernest Potts was shaking violently, as if it was about to burst. I bent beside Lockwood, who lay on his side, half-dazed.

"I think I know who it is!" George called. "He hates Potts, that's why he's come back and—" He ducked as a book spun viciously past his nose.

I looked desperately around the room. The violence of the attack was escalating. More and more objects were beginning to move.

First things first. I needed to get Lockwood to the circle. I grabbed him by the arms and began to pull him across the room. It wasn't easy; he's bigger than me and was carrying a lot of equipment, and the whirling books that struck me made things worse. George jumped over the chains and sprang to help me. He bent to Lockwood. As he did so there was a disturbance in the air behind him. Glimmering threads of other-light appeared. They grew and melded, fusing into a tall, thin shape that reached for George.

I let go of Lockwood's hand, tore my rapier from my belt, and swung it over George's head. The iron blade cut straight through the glowing form. The figure vanished. The rushing air went still. All across the library, books dropped, crashing to the ground.

A moment later we'd gotten Lockwood inside the chains and were sprawled there, gasping. Lockwood was sitting up now, with a bad bruise on his temple. He still looked a trifle dazed.

"So you think you know the identity of our ghost, George?" I said, once I could speak.

"Yeah," George said. "I reckon. I found it in a history of the school. His name was Harold Roach, and he was caretaker here almost a hundred years ago. He'd been badly wounded in the First World War, one arm shot off, and injured in the leg as well. So he was an unlucky guy, but it sounds like he was already a nasty piece of work. He used to stalk round the school terrorizing the pupils. Apparently he always carried an old army knife, and he'd wave it at any kid who crossed him, threatening to cut off their ears."

"Ah, the great British education system," Lockwood said. "Made us what we are."

"There was also speculation that he used to steal from the school funds," George went on, "though nothing was ever proved. Anyway, it all changed when this Ernest Potts became headmaster." He jerked his thumb toward the bust beside the window. "He wasn't having any truck with Caretaker Roach. Seems he confronted him— more or less accused him of nicking the cash. Roach denied it, but when Potts threatened to bring in the police, the man promptly slipped away and vanished. He was never found. Everyone assumed he'd scarpered with the money."

"Or else," Lockwood said softly, "he's still here." There was a brief silence.

"That all fits in with what I sensed, too," I said. I told them about my experiences with the dagger and, briefly, the figure I'd seen in the corridor. "I think he hid somewhere in the school—the place where he was stashing the money he stole. Maybe he *did* plan to slip away with it, but for some reason was prevented from doing so. As for *where* he is, I think we know the answer to that, too."

"There are two storerooms, George," Lockwood said. "One's full-size; the other's little more than a cupboard: it doesn't go far back at all. Lucy saw the ghost there. We think there's plenty of space behind it for a hidden room."

George nodded. "That's it, then. That's where Harold Roach will be." He reached wearily for his bag. "So let's get on with it, shall we—before his ghost comes back."

Soon afterward we had assembled in the passage, ready for the final part of the investigation. We'd checked our kit. We had our rapiers, salt-bombs, and canisters of iron. We had our chains. We had our explosive magnesium flares that really shouldn't be used in confined spaces on account of setting fire to things. We had our bags of silver seals to use on the Source when we found it. Yep, we were all sorted, raring to go. Aside, that is, from Lockwood's continued grogginess, and my sense of overwhelming fear whenever I looked at those storeroom doors. I remembered that little wheedling voice, calling me in.

George hitched up his belt, which had sagged slightly under his tummy. "Right," he said. "You're clearly not up to this, Lockwood, and Lucy's understandably edgy after what happened to her out here. So how about I go in first?"

I looked at him askance. "Really? Sure you're okay with that?" George isn't usually the one who leads the way.

He chuckled. "Trust me."

"Nice and quiet, then, George," Lockwood said.

George raised his rapier. He pulled at the left-hand door—the one to the larger storeroom. It swung slowly open. He aimed his flashlight inside. His circle of light passed over vacuum cleaners, paper towels, tins of paint . . . everything exactly as before. George stepped into the room. Lockwood and I followed. We were calm, silent and professional, moving with panther-like stealth.

"There," George whispered. "Nothing to worry about so far." He swung his flashlight to the side, gave a yell like a howler monkey, and leaped back two clear feet, colliding with Lockwood and me. We all careered back into a shelf. There was an almighty crash and splintering as the shelf snapped and we toppled to the ground. Paint pots and toilet paper rolls bounded and trundled out across the floor.

We struggled to our feet. Three frantic flashlights spun light around the room.

"Oh," George said. "It's all right. Relax, everyone. It was just a mop."

"What?" Lockwood and I both stared at him.

"I thought it was a very thin ghost. But it's only a mop. Look! It's got the floppy bit at the top. I ask you: Who does that? Who stores a mop upside down?"

"George—" I began.

"Wait!" Lockwood was staring at the wall. "Look at the paneling! It's floor to ceiling here! Everywhere else in the school it only goes halfway up. Behind this wall is the store-cupboard, which we know only goes back a few feet. So these panels would be the perfect place for a hidden door."

George frowned. "We've got crowbars. Let's smash our way in."

"Finding the lever or switch would be easier." Lockwood placed his hands on the paneling and instantly jerked them away. "Ow—it's cold!"

Even as he said this, we noticed we could see our breath-plumes again. That's never a good sign. Nor, to be honest, is the sound of dragging footsteps or the rattling of keys, both of which I could suddenly hear again, not very far away.

"He's back," I whispered. "I can hear him coming."

Lockwood was running his fingers along the edges of the paneling. "Didn't take him long," he said. "Okay. George, give me a hand searching the wall. Lucy, do me a favor, and just have a quick look out in the corridor, would you?"

I peeped into the passage. In the direction of the library, all was dark. In the direction of the classroom, a pale haze of otherlight had gathered in the center of the passage. In its heart I saw a tall, thin figure, limping in our direction. The apparition was faint, but getting stronger, and I could already see the ragged clothes, the dragging leg, the loosely hanging arm. . . . Also the cold metallic shimmer of a dagger, held outstretched in bony fingers.

I ducked back into the storeroom, where Lockwood and George were tapping at the panels. "Bad news," I said hoarsely.

Lockwood didn't look up. "How long have we got?"

"I'd say about thirty seconds."

"Okay." Lockwood pressed a discolored portion of panel speculatively. Nothing happened. "Lucy," he said, "George and I are going to need a little longer than that. Two minutes, maximum three. Think you can delay our friend Harold for that long?"

I turned back to the door. "I'll see what I can do."

Out in the corridor, the ragged, limping figure had drawn much closer; it had passed the restrooms and was level with the other storeroom. Harsh cold radiated from its glow, and the malevolence of its purpose struck me like a solid thing. My head felt suddenly woozy, my limbs listless, heavy as concrete. The thud and drag of each maimed footfall beat like a drum against my ears. I could see the glittering of the knife.

All of which meant it was high time I did something. I flicked my coat aside, plucked a salt-bomb from my belt, and threw it hard and fast, so that it burst on the floor just below the glowing form. The brittle plastic snapped; salt spattered out across the passage, flaring bright green as it hit the ectoplasm. The apparition flexed, distorting like an image seen in water, and blinked out—only to reappear instantly, some distance farther away.

I ducked back into the storeroom. "How's it going?"

Lockwood and George were crouched beside the wall, their attention focused on one particular panel, no different from the rest. "Found it," Lockwood said. "Little clasp hidden at the base. Think it opens inward, but it's hellish stiff. Sixty seconds."

"Right."

I took a magnesium flare from my belt, hefted it in my hand, and went back out into the passage. As I did so, something flashed past me, close enough to waft my bangs across my face. I looked— and saw the dagger, still vibrating, buried hilt-deep in the plaster of the wall. And now the pale, thin figure was rushing up the corridor, legs trailing, rags flapping, single arm reached out to clasp me.

Well, it had annoyed me now. I lobbed the flare.

A blast of magnesium fire, peppered with filaments of burning salt and iron, is white enough and bright enough to momentarily blind the living, as well as do considerable damage to the dead. So I screwed up my eyes and waited for the initial surge of heat to fade. And when I looked again, pockets of white flames were licking up across the passage floor, and the walls were pebble-dashed with smoldering pin-sized burns. The ghost itself had vanished.

I dived back into the storeroom, where Lockwood and George seemed in an almost identical position to before. "How's it going now?"

"George has blisters, and I've gotten my hand stuck."

"I was thinking about the door."

"It's jammed. Either rusted, or something heavy on the other side."

"Help give it a shove, can you?" George gasped. "Three of us might do the trick."

I looked behind me. The silvery light was fading; already the fires were dying down. "I used a flare," I said. "It's flummoxed him, but he'll be back any moment. He's strong."

"I know," Lockwood said, "but we've got to get this open. Your weight might make the difference, Luce."

"Exactly what are you saying?" But I arranged myself alongside them and took the strain. I could see the hidden door now, a faint dark outline in the wood. Lockwood's fingers were prying at one edge; George was heaving at its base. When I pushed, I felt the panel move.

"That's it," Lockwood breathed. "We're almost there . . ."

Air stirred. I looked to the side. A figure stood beside us in the dark. It had long white hair, and naked, grinning teeth.

I screamed and gave a final desperate shove. The wall moved: the panel swung open. Lockwood, George, and I fell forward through the hole.

Whatever we landed on was both soft and brittle. Dry things snapped beneath us; I heard the sliding chink of coins. Momentum carried me farthest; I did a brisk head-over-heels and ended in a sitting position, with my boots wedged against the opposite wall. I jumped to my feet, whipped out my flashlight, and switched it on.

We were in a tiny, windowless room, made smaller by the piled chests and boxes ranged along one wall. Some were closed; others, lidless, were filled to overflowing with a strange medley of objects, candelabras, vases, even paintings. Everything was swathed with layers of dusty cobwebs. No surprises there. Spiders *love* Sources; they can't get enough of them.

Speaking of the Source, it was right beneath us. We'd landed on it. Lockwood and George were hastily rolling clear. Directly in front of the secret panel, a body lay facedown upon the floor. It was pretty cobwebby, but you could see the old-style jacket, the flannel trousers, the rotting leather shoes. Here and there were glimpses of yellowed bone. The head was hidden beneath a heavy wooden chest, the lid of which had broken open, and by a mass of greenish coins that had poured forth from it, half swallowing the skull. A certain amount of white hair still poked through, but the face was mercifully concealed.

None of us said anything. George was pulling his bag from his back, Lockwood tearing it open, looking for the silver. I kept my eyes trained on the secret door, on the dark corners of the room. I could feel the presence close at hand. But nothing stirred now. Maybe I'd sapped the thing's strength out in the corridor, or maybe it finally accepted what we were here to do. Who knew with ghosts? It was impossible to say.

Lockwood took a silver net from the bag, unfolded it to its full size, and laid it over the body. At once I felt a lifting of the spirits, a change in the atmosphere in the secret room. I listened, tense and ready. No . . . it was okay. The presence was truly gone.

We stood in silence in the secret room.

"Look at all the stuff he pinched," Lockwood said at last. "Quite the little collector, wasn't he?"

"That shelf broke," I said. "Look there. Just above the door. He was hiding in here, maybe getting ready to sneak off after dark. He had his chest of stolen money sitting on the shelf. Then it fell down and brained him. Cracked his skull or broke his neck. That's how it happened."

"Just deserts, I suppose," Lockwood said. "He shouldn't have nicked so much. Well, it's over now."

George stepped over the corpse and began rummaging in his bag. "Great. So, who fancies a celebratory bun? I've got some iced ones here."

Lockwood hesitated. "Er, possibly in a minute. When we're somewhere else." He smiled. "Well done, everybody. Especially you, Luce. You did really well tonight. Made the right decisions at every turn."

I grinned back, flushing a little, as I sometimes do when Lockwood trains his smile on me. "Oh, that's okay," I said. "It wasn't just me, really. This job's all about teamwork, isn't it? I couldn't have done it on my own." I gazed down at the pile of coins and at the boxes lined against the walls. "Think this stuff'll be worth anything now?"

"Expect so," Lockwood said. "Mr. Whitaker can probably afford more refurbishments to the school."

George picked up his bag. "He might start with the boys' restrooms. I can smell them from here. So, is that it, then? Are we done?"

Lockwood nodded. "Yes . . . Yes, I think we are."

And with that we left the room behind us and went to have a bun.

A Gallery of Ghosts

CHANGER

Unlike most ghosts, which always maintain the same appearance, the Changer can alter its shape and behavior. Animal guises are common, and far weirder shapes are not unknown. This unpredictability makes a Changer very hard to destroy.

COLD MAIDEN

The traditional floaty female ghost, usually featuring long hair, longer dresses, and plenty of weeping and hand-wringing. Generally racked by ancient grief or guilt, Cold Maidens are too self-absorbed to be much of a problem for agents.

DARK SPECTER

A mercifully rare Type Two apparition, revealed as an undulating cloud of blackness. Hangs in the air, swelling and shrinking, while sending out tendrils to snare the onlooker. Also leaves behind appalling ecto-plasm stains on wallpaper and soft furnishings.

PHANTASM

A formidable Type Two spirit, ethereal, translucent, and hungry for contact with the living. Phantasms are hard to spot—even for those with psychic Sight—and are best observed out of the corners of one's eyes.

POLTERGEIST

This Type Two spirit produces no visible apparition, but moves material objects using telekinetic power. Weak Poltergeists ruffle curtains and knock books off tables; strong ones can wreak havoc across whole buildings.

SHADE

The most common variety of Type One ghost, a Shade is weak, faint, and unresponsive to the living. It keeps to itself, endlessly replaying a single moment from long ago. Easy to subdue using salt and iron.

SPECTER

The solid-seeming Specter is the most common of Type Two ghost. At a casual glance, it may be hard to distinguish from a living person; closer analysis will reveal its old-fashioned clothes, unnaturally bright eyes, and undead pallor.

WRAITH

Not the variety of ghost you'd want to meet on a dark night. Voracious, malevolent, and cloaked in the shape either of a skeleton or a rotting corpse, a Wraith can overpower its victims through power of terror alone.